S0-ASG-318

Raves for the *Foreigner* series:

"Cherryh's gift for conjuring believable alien cultures is in full force here, and her characters ... are brought to life with a sure and convincing hand."
— *Publishers Weekly*

"A seriously probing, thoughtful, intelligent piece of work, with more insight in half a dozen pages than most authors manage in half a hundred." — *Kirkus*

"Close-grained and carefully constructed ... a book that will stick in the mind for a lot longer than the usual adventure romp." — *Locus*

"A large new Cherryh novel is always welcome ... a return to the anthropological science fiction in which she has made such a name is a double pleasure ... superlatively drawn aliens and characterization."
— *Chicago Sun-Times*

"As always, Cherryh alternates complex political maneuvering with pell-mell action sequences in an intensely character-driven SF novel sure to appeal to the many fans of this series." — *Publishers Weekly*

"Her lucid storytelling conveys enough backstory to guide newcomers without boring longtime series followers. The characters are well drawn, and Cherryh's depiction of both human and alien cultures is riveting."
— *Library Journal*

".... transforms the book into an absorbing combination of anthropological SF and 'The Ransom of Red Chief.' Faithful Foreigner saga followers, in particular, will have a ball." — *Booklist*

Logan Hocking County
District Library
230 East Main Street
Logan, Ohio 43138

DAW Titles by C.J. CHERRYH

THE FOREIGNER UNIVERSE

FOREIGNER	PRECURSOR
INVADER	DEFENDER
INHERITOR	EXPLORER
DESTROYER	CONSPIRATOR
PRETENDER	DECEIVER
DELIVERER	BETRAYER

INTRUDER
PROTECTOR
PEACEMAKER

THE ALLIANCE-UNION UNIVERSE
REGENESIS
DOWNBELOW STATION
THE DEEP BEYOND Omnibus:
Serpent's Reach | Cuckoo's Egg
ALLIANCE SPACE Omnibus:
Merchanter's Luck | 40,000 in Gehenna
AT THE EDGE OF SPACE Omnibus:
Brothers of Earth | Hunter of Worlds
THE FADED SUN Omnibus:
Kesrith | Shon'jir | Kutath

<u>THE CHANUR NOVELS</u>
THE CHANUR SAGA Omnibus:
The Pride Of Chanur | Chanur's Venture | The Kif Strike Back
CHANUR'S ENDGAME Omnibus:
Chanur's Homecoming | Chanur's Legacy

<u>THE MORGAINE CYCLE</u>
THE MORGAINE SAGA Omnibus:
Gate of Ivrel | Well of Shiuan | Fires of Azeroth
EXILE'S GATE

OTHER WORKS:
THE DREAMING TREE Omnibus:
The Tree of Swords and Jewels | The Dreamstone
ALTERNATE REALITIES Omnibus:
Port Eternity | Wave Without a Shore | Voyager in Night
THE COLLECTED SHORT FICTION OF C.J. CHERRYH

C. J. CHERRYH

PROTECTOR

DAW BOOKS, INC.
DONALD A. WOLLHEIM, FOUNDER
375 Hudson Street, New York, NY 10014

ELIZABETH R. WOLLHEIM
SHEILA E. GILBERT
PUBLISHERS
www.dawbooks.com

Copyright © 2013 by C.J. Cherryh

All rights reserved.

Cover art by Todd Lockwood.

Cover designed by G-Force Design.

DAW Books Collectors No. 1619.

DAW Books are distributed by Penguin Group (USA).
Book designed by Stanley S. Drate/Folio Graphics Co., Inc.

All characters and events in this book are fictitious.
All resemblance to persons living or dead is coincidental.

If you purchase this book without a cover you should be aware that this book
may have been stolen property and reported as "unsold and destroyed" to the
publisher. In such case neither the author nor the publisher has received any
payment for this "stripped book."

The scanning, uploading and distribution of this book via the Internet or any
other means without the permission of the publisher is illegal, and punishable by
law. Please purchase only authorized electronic editions, and do not participate
in or encourage the electronic piracy of copyrighted materials. Your support of
the author's rights is appreciated.

First Mass Market Printing, April 2014
1   2   3   4   5   6   7   8   9

DAW TRADEMARK REGISTERED
U.S. PAT. AND TM. OFF. AND FOREIGN COUNTRIES
—MARCA REGISTRADA
HECHO EN U.S.A.

PRINTED IN THE U.S.A.

To Jane and Lynn—above and beyond.

1

Lace was back in fashion this spring—starched and delicate at once, layers of it flowing from cuffs and neck. It was a damned bother at a formal dinner, but there it was: the Lord of the Heavens had to be in fashion, and a state dinner in the court of Tabini-aiji meant a new coat, no question about that. So Bren Cameron arrived at Tabini-aiji's door, accompanied by his four black-clad bodyguards, in a mode quietly equal to any of the lords present.

This new coat was a subdued beige-and-gold brocade, able, in this sparkling crowd, to fade into the background, and Bren Cameron—paidhi-aiji to that same Tabini-aiji, the ruler of the aishidi'tat, the Western Association of the atevi—liked it that way.

Paidhi-aiji. Official human-language translator—at least as he'd signed up for the job years ago. Back then he'd been the interface between the human enclave, restricted by treaty to the island of Mospheira, across the straits—and the atevi, native to the planet, who ruled the rest of the world.

Things had changed since then. Humans were in space, now. So were atevi.

And the paidhi's office? The paidhi-aiji had become both diplomat and courier—become, in fact, paidhi in the sense in which atevi had always interpreted the office, long before the word *human* entered their vocabulary. *Translator* had ceased to be much of his job at all, since humans and atevi interfaced daily on the space station, *with* free access to the once-forbidden dictionary. Mospheira now worried far more about the space station orbiting overhead than they did the vast continent immediately across the water from them.

There had been a profound psychological shift in the attitudes on both sides of the strait. The earthly power that had threatened Mospheira in the past had ceased, at least in Mospheiran minds, to threaten them in any direct sense. The current worry of the human population on earth was the power of the human population in space versus their own insular ways and aims, most of which involved their comforts, their economy, and their sense of self-government.

Atevi were a presence onworld and off, had always been there, would always be there ... and would always be different from them. Politically ambitious Mospheirans had little to gain these days by pointing out that obvious fact. Much more to the point, the meager trade that had gone back and forth between Mospheira and the continent for two hundred years had suddenly become a large and important commerce, linked to space in a triangular relationship. *Business* was now *interested* in what happened on the continent—deeply interested.

But Mospheiran businessmen knew they had no control over it. They could only watch the ebb and flow of the market and adjust accordingly. Production once based on the direct advice of the paidhi must now flux according to a true supply and demand market.

The island government was also on its own these days. They no longer controlled the paidhi-aiji—who remained conspicuously human, in any gathering here on the continent, but who had all but ceased to represent Mospheiran interests. Translate at need, yes. Advise, yes. But circumstances ... and ultimately his own inclinations ... had made him an intrinsic part of the atevi world.

He'd gained property on the atevi side of the straits. A title. A seat in the legislature, too, if he wanted to press the point. He didn't. He had more power, in terms of influence with the most powerful people in the atevi world, than that seat could ever wield . . . something he found it wisest not to advertise: those to whom it mattered—knew.

His *official* niche in the court, a unique position, with Tabini's—and Tabini's grandmother's—backing, was still that of paidhi-aiji, but in gatherings such as this, he preferred to style himself lord, not of the ill-defined Heavens, but of Najida peninsula, a quaint little rural section of Sarini Province, out on the western coast, not all that far from the island on which he'd been born. Lord of Najida gave him social cachet in terms ordinary atevi more easily understood, not too high nor ancient a title, but a respectable title over a little peninsula whose ruling family had died out, a title granted for services rendered the aiji, and to all of the aishidi'tat.

Accordingly, he chose to wear beige, a no-color, amid the colorful rivalry of atevi clan heraldry, and he persistently tied his queue *not* with the starry black ribbon of the Province of the Heavens or even the more approachable blue of Najida, but with the paidhi's neutral white . . . *I am not part of regional matters. My standing is through the aiji.*

It was a language every atevi understood without a moment's conscious thought.

"Nandi," his senior bodyguard said, by way of parting as they reached the door. The four tall atevi who were as close to him as family—closer, in point of fact—were not given a place in the gathering of lords and ladies milling about beyond the foyer, not this evening. The only bodyguards allowed in the gathering tonight (and indeed a veritable wall of black Assassins' Guild uniforms guarded that door) were the aiji's security. There was, for one thing, limited space—and for another—

For another, all security anywhere belonged to the Assassins' Guild, and the fact that the only armed guards present were the aiji's own bodyguard freed the *rest* of the members of that secretive Guild to disappear the same way Bren's did, down that inner corridor toward the deeper recesses of the aiji's apartment—and into a meeting far more important and more critical than the state dinner going on in the front rooms.

It was a state dinner being held in honor of one Lord Geigi, Bren's sometime neighbor on the coast and current house guest, here in the Bujavid. Bren entered the packed room alone: Geigi had been invited here early, and was doubtless still with the aiji, back in the private part of the apartment.

Lord Geigi, provincial lord of Sarini, having helped straighten out a significant mess in that province, was headed back to his preferred post in the heavens, that of stationmaster on the atevi side of operations. Sarini was quiet, even improved in security, and the prospect of peace and trade and profits sparkled in Geigi's wake. It was a happy occasion, this departure, a triumph, and the lords and their consorts—and the paidhi-aiji—had assembled to wish Lord Geigi a good flight and a safe trip back to the station.

Unfortunately, where power and profit bloomed, power brokers had a way of getting into the game. That was precisely why the not-so-clandestine Guild meeting in the back rooms was so critical, and why, while the lords and ladies were smiling and sipping drinks and offering politenesses to each other, most were likely wondering how *much* their own bodyguards were going to be told about the recent events and current situation in the south and the west coast, and how far they themselves, consequently, would be drawn into the loop . . . or deliberately excluded from it.

His own bodyguard would definitely be in the loop. The aiji's bodyguard, most of whom were on duty out here, ironically would *not* be. And that uncomfortable situation—

Was politics. Pure and simple. Or rather neither pure *nor* simple. And that exclusion was one additional matter that might well be a topic in that meeting, at least among the most senior bodyguards.

"Nand' paidhi." As he passed into the crowd, a servant offered a selection of drinks on a silver tray. Bren took the white wine, a safe choice for a human, and walked among the tall black-skinned lords and ladies, with a nod here, a word there. He was comparatively comfortable tonight, despite the stiff new coat and stiffer lace, since—in present company, and with his own residence just next door in the ornate halls of the Bujavid—he could go without the damned bulletproof vest that had been mandatory since the Marid affair . . . but he had to navigate, as did everyone, on his own.

Of course for him it was slightly more challenging a feat than for most of the others assembled here. He was a tall human, but that was still a head and shoulders shorter than the average atevi. It meant looking up to talk to anyone he met, and it meant looking between shoulders to spot someone he was looking for. It meant being able to turn up at someone's elbow relatively unnoticed, but it also meant watching out for people taking a step backward in crowded conditions. Dark-skinned and golden-eyed, wearing generally bright colors, they all towered above a fair-haired, light-skinned, quietly dressed human, who walked in a canyon of taller bodies.

His aishid would normally weave him comfortably through such a crowd. But he managed. He smiled, he talked, he kept his eyes open, and noted who was talking to whom . . . so far as he could see, until, finally, he did spot two others who did not tower. One was the aiji's son Cajeiri—who at eight was already as tall as the paidhi-aiji—and who was holding a stemware glass of, one trusted, plain fruit juice. The other, the ancient lady with him and only a little taller, was the aiji-dowager herself, Ilisidi.

Notably absent was Ilisidi's chief bodyguard, Cenedi. If there had been any exception to the rule of no-attendance tonight, it would have been Ilisidi, because of her size and her age. But then Cenedi was likely the main source of information backstairs. Along with Banichi and Algini—of Bren's own bodyguard.

"Nand' Bren!" Cajeiri waved at him, and several lords looked and spotted him, while the aiji-dowager gave her great-grandson a sharp word and resettled that cane of hers with a thump Cajeiri would feel even if he couldn't hear it in the general festivity.

And indeed, Cajeiri immediately resumed official propriety. He'd grown so mature in so many ways, had Cajeiri, though his enthusiasm still overwhelmed him from time to time.

And there, the tall old man in green and white, was Lord Tatiseigi—right beside the dowager, depend on it. He was Cajeiri's great-grand uncle, or however many greats one had to work into it: atevi were extremely loose about such niceties, even in the same sentence, so he was uncle as often as he was great-uncle. Lord Tatiseigi was Atageini clan—a member of the family on Cajeiri's mother's side—*and* a sometime lover of the aiji-dowager, grandmother to Cajeiri's father.

Cajeiri's little exclamation had turned Tatiseigi's attention in Bren's direction—no problem there—but it had also let a lord he had *not* particularly wanted to have corner him on a particular issue—notably his vote on the cell phone issue—draw dead aim on him.

A light bell rang. The dining hall doorway opened on salvation in the form of Lord Geigi. The attention of the lord in question turned immediately away from Bren in favor of Lord Geigi, who embodied a far rarer opportunity.

Geigi, rotund sun around which half a dozen such lesser lords immediately orbited, reached past them all to snag the new proxy lord of Maschi clan—and so of all Sarini Province—a proxy Geigi himself had appointed during this visit. He headed for Bren with the new man in tow—and his little planetary cluster following in his wake.

The new lord of the Maschi, a lean, elderly fellow, was a little countrified and old-fashioned in dress—which by veriest chance was halfway *in* fashion, in the latest trend. The man seemed very overawed by the attention, and engagingly delighted to see Bren, whom at least he recognized in the crowd—how could he not, even had they not met before.

Haidiri was this new lord's name.

"Felicitations, nandi," Bren said.

"I have told nand' Haidiri," Geigi said, "that if he has any difficulties, any worries, he should contact your office directly, nand' Bren."

"Indeed, without hesitation, do so," Bren said. "I *am* your neighbor, after all, at least when you visit Kaji-minda. Since this will be your first sitting in the legislature, the marshal of the legislature should be in contact with you, and if he is not, let me know, nandi. Do not hesitate in the least." He discovered two lords in sight: Haijdin and Maidin, strong supporters of the aiji, on the liberal side of the legislature. "Let me introduce you, nandi, to two gentlemen you very much need to meet. Lord Geigi, your indulgence."

"Go, go," Geigi said. "I shall pay my respects to the dowager before we are called to dinner."

In point of fact, Lord Haidiri was definitely going to need the paidhi's help—and the aiji-dowager's, and the help of the two gentlemen ahead, and likely the aiji's help, too, if Tabini could be persuaded. Important issues directly affecting Haidiri's clan, Sarini Province, and the peace of the region were centermost in the current session of the legislature, and this country gentleman had many of the keys to the situation in his district. One was certain Haidiri was well aware of those keys—Geigi would not have appointed him otherwise. But having the keys and having the associations to best utilize that knowledge were two different matters.

Bren made the introductions. There was a round of bows. And there was, by opportunity, as a third man strolled into range, another name to add to the new lord's resources, Paturandi—a scholarly, middle-aged man, unhappily as long-winded as his notorious predecessor, Brominandi, but a goodhearted fellow who had suffered socially from his predecessor's reputation. Paturandi was happy to make any new acquaintance who would engage him socially—and as lord of a small southern district he definitely had a regional interest in this new lord in Targai estate.

"Such a great pleasure, nandiin," Paturandi said, and

went on to join Haijdin and Maidin in asking about trade negotiations with the newly-opening Marid, right at Targai's doorstep.

Those introductions were a thorough success.

Bren wended his way back to Geigi, to effect a rescue of the situation should Geigi and Tatiseigi have crossed glances . . . those two gentlemen being long-time rivals for the dowager's attentions. Tatiseigi was a jealous sort, and a conservative, which Geigi, a Rational Determinist who denied the validity of numerology, certainly was not.

But at that very opportune moment the servants re-opened the dining room doors and the major domo invited them all in for the seating.

There followed the usual sorting out by place markers at the long table. The highest lords were relatively sure of their seats—alert, of course, for any untoward significance in the positioning they might discover in those markers. The lowest at the table, conversely, had to do a little searching.

Bren found his own place with no more than a glance at the card and white ribbon. His seat was very close to the head of the table, with the honoree, Lord Geigi on his left, closer to Tabini-aiji's seat. Lord Geigi and Lord Tatiseigi were *very* diplomatically seated across from each other, at *exactly* the same level . . . particularly well done on the part of the major domo. Young Cajeiri was sandwiched between Lord Tatiseigi, his mother's uncle on his left and his as-yet-to-arrive mother on the right. That seated the boy across the table from his great-grandmother, Ilisidi being seated on Lord Geigi's left . . .

More significantly, Ilisidi's seat would be directly opposite her granddaughter-in-law, Lady Damiri. *That* was a scary balancing act. The two were famously *not* getting along at the moment . . . not that they ever had, but it had become bitter.

Tabini was the only chess piece capable of blocking those two—and that was exactly where his seat was—between them. Bren was relieved to find Lord Haijdin on his own right, a pleasant positioning, with Maidin almost opposite, next to Tatiseigi. Haidiri's important but new status kept him midway down the table, next to, one was glad to see, a set of affable and reasonable people. The lord who had had Bren in his sights was safely down among the lower seats.

Bren slipped into his chair, white-lacquered ironwood, massive, ancient, and so heavy that a human, momentarily unattended by servants and bodyguard, had rather slip sideways into it than wrestle it further in any direction. The linen-covered table sparkled end to end with crystal and silver. Candles contributed a warmer glow as servants dimmed the room lights. Flowers of fortunate number, color, and type were arranged in banks not quite high enough to pose a wall to a human guest, or to Ilisidi or Cajeiri.

And with guests in their places, the whole gracious machinery of the aiji's personal dining hall clicked into operation, drinks being renewed, the servants ascertaining special needs of the diners—and assuring the paidhi-aiji quietly that there were certain dishes to avoid, but that those were few. By ironclad tradition, there could only be light, pleasant talk in this room, no business done, no serious matters discussed, except the routine warning to the paidhi about alkaloids in the sauce.

Chatter resumed briefly. Then Tabini-aiji arrived with Damiri at his side, and everyone had to rise—excepting the aiji-dowager, who simply nodded. The aiji was conservatively resplendent in the black and red of the Ragi atevi. Damiri arrived in, yes, *white and green* this evening. She was pregnant—imminently due, in fact—and she had been through personal hell in recent days: her father, head of Ajuri clan, had recently quitted the capital in scandal, which might well have justified a less cheerful expression. But instead she appeared smiling, relaxed and gracious beside her somber husband, and—for the first time in years—wearing her uncle Tatiseigi's colors.

That was a statement. One wondered if she had chosen to do it—or if she had been ordered to do it, a question undoubtedly on the minds of every guest present.

Everyone settled again. Polite chatter resumed at the lower seats. The upper ones, where lords were in the know about the intimate politics, remained in stunned silence, at a public shift of the consort's allegiance that no one had quite expected.

Damiri's color choice had definitely surprised and pleased Lord Tatiseigi. The old conservative had already been in a good mood this evening, rejoicing in his rising importance in court—and in the imminent departure of his chief rival, Lord Geigi.

And now Damiri, mother of the eight-year-old heir, and of a baby soon to be born, was wearing her uncle's white and green. Granted she had not been likely to appear in her Ajuri father's colors this evening, but she had not taken the neutral option, either. She was sending a clear signal, taking sides, and Ajuri clan, when they heard of it, would not be happy, no.

Bren had a sip of wine and smiled politely at Lord Tatiseigi—and at Lord Haijdin, who remarked, in a moderate degree of innocence, "Well. One is very pleased to see that."

The servants meanwhile moved about like an attacking squadron, pouring liquids, arranging napkins. Geigi carried on a conversation directly with Tabini-aiji, while Ilisidi sipped her wine and watched a major shift in allegiances play out.

A move to her advantage? Ilisidi could work with the situation.

And meanwhile Tabini—who had spent his *own* youth in the aiji-dowager's household—was not letting his wife's shockwave take its own course down the table.

"We wish to honor our old ally Geigi of Kajiminda tonight," Tabini said, and his rising brought a quick hush to the dining room. "We shall regret his departure for his post of duty in the heavens, but despite the efforts of our enemies, he is leaving his affairs here in good order. Sarini Province is again at peace. He has amply provided for administration of his clan, in the appointment of Lord Haidiri, whom we welcome to our table for the first time tonight."

"Aiji-ma," Haidiri murmured, half-rising, with a deep bow of his head to Tabini, and to Lord Geigi as he settled awkwardly back into his chair.

"Should Sarini Province or Maschi clan ever need our intervention," Tabini said, "we shall of course respond to such a request; but we have great confidence in you, Lord Haidiri, to manage the district."

That covered the recent shooting match in as diplomatic a fashion as one could bring to bear. Assassins' Guild enforcement teams were all over the region Haidiri would govern, mopping up pockets of their own splinter group, pockets established in the failed administration of Haidiri's predecessor, Geigi's young scoundrel of a nephew, Baiji.

Baiji had been forcibly wedded, bedded, and was bound for well-deserved obscurity in the relatively rural districts of the East, deep in Ilisidi's domain. Baiji would quickly produce an heir, if he wanted to continue a reasonably comfortable lifestyle; and that heir would be brought up by the mother alone, a girl with familial ties to Ilisidi. Only if Geigi approved would the offspring become the new Maschi lord, succeeding Haidiri.

Baiji, fool that he was, had been targeted by the Marid, the five southern states, who wanted—badly—to take control of the west coast, and who had hoped to bring the sprawling, sparsely populated Sarini Province under Marid control. Baiji had dealt with fire and gotten burned—badly—when the Marid plans had failed—badly. The Marid had lost leadership of their own plot a year ago, when Tabini, out for two years as the result of a coup, retook his capital. The usurper, Murini, had fled to the Marid, unwelcomely so. Murini had died—which removed him from the scene.

Seeking a power base in the destabilized south, the group that had supported Murini had made their own try at the Marid, creating the mess which the Assassins' Guild was currently mopping up. The Marid had gotten a new overlord in the process, Machigi, one of the five lords of the Marid, who had managed to keep three of the five districts under his control, and who had *not* let Murini's people displace him.

Machigi was now back in his capital of Tanaja, presumably keeping the agreement of alliance that he had just signed with the aiji-dowager. Geigi's west coast estate at Kajiminda, freed of threat from the Marid, thanks to that alliance, was given to the servants to keep in good order until there *should* be a young Maschi heir resident ... and Geigi's essential belongings were standing in crates in Bren's front hallway, ready to be freighted out to the spaceport tomorrow morning.

So, as Tabini said, all Geigi's onworld affairs were wrapped up, nailed down, and triumphantly settled. The world was in better shape than it had been, with an actual prospect of peace and development in the southern states for the first time in centuries.

"We have notified the rail office," Tabini added as a postscript, "so the red car will be at your disposal tomorrow morning, nandi."

"One is very honored," Geigi murmured with a bow of his head.

That arrangement made things easier. The red car was the aiji's own transport, not only the personal rail car, but the baggage car that went with it, and the engine that pulled it—occasionally complicated with freight attachments on long treks, for economy's sake, but rarely allowing passenger cars, for security reasons. The aiji's train ran rigidly on time, since it had universal priority on the tracks, and Bren had schemed to escort Geigi out to the spaceport personally, hoping to use that car, knowing he was pushing matters of personal privilege just a bit.

"Well, well-deserved, nandi," Tabini said. And with that, Tabini gave a little signal to the serving staff lined up in the corridor to the kitchen, and appetizers began to flow out, along with spectacular soup tureens and meticulous arrangements of small sausages.

"We shall indeed miss you, nandi," Lady Damiri said graciously, over the soft clatter of service. "We regret we have had so little personal chance to enjoy your company this visit."

"A mutual regret, nandi," Geigi said.

Ilisidi ladled out spicy black soup, an amazing quantity for a diminutive lady. "We hope for a very safe flight for you, Geigi-ji, and do note that we are sending up some preserves of that sort you like. Do not let some rascal make off with that box or misplace it."

There was not a flicker of a glance between the two ladies.

"One is very grateful," Geigi murmured.

"How is your office aloft holding out?" Bren asked, into that half-breath of silence, forcing a complete change of topics. "Have they coped with your absence, nandi?"

"One has heard of no crises up there," Geigi said, "but one always suspects one's staff of reserving all the worrisome news."

"Well, they will surely be arranging a party for your arrival there," Ilisidi said. "I tell you, there has been a significant dearth of parties in Shejidan lately. We are sorely disappointed this season."

Never mind the last festivity she had attended had erupted in inter-clan warfare and cost Damiri her relationship with her father.

Tatiseigi said, immediately, "One would very gladly oblige with a dinner invitation, if the dowager would find pleasure in so modest a table as mine."

Cajeiri shot a questioning look at his father and mother—*not* first at his great-grandmother. The boy was learning: the boy indeed had a party of his own to offer—a desperately longed-for party. Bren knew it. And the boy clearly wanted to say something gracious to his great-grandmother. Then wisely didn't.

"We shall indeed be pleased," Ilisidi said in the meanwhile. "Gallantly offered, nandi."

Cajeiri's lips had gone to a thin line, clamped shut, hard, on the matter of his own impending birthday, that postponed and still very fragile arrangement. Bren well knew the politics of that situation: Damiri did not look with favor on the guest list—which involved human youngsters, and the space station, and the ship where her son had spent two very formative years of his life, in his great-grandmother's hands.

Bren said, flinging himself into the breach, a conversation pitched only to the upper table: "Even *I* shall oblige you, aiji-ma. I have never dared offer a social event. But I have my staff back now. And one has been extremely honored with a small dining room—" A modest nod toward Tabini and Damiri, referencing the recent remodeling of this end of the floor, "—and one is consequently willing to risk one's reputation with an invitation."

"Well you should be willing, nandi!" Tatiseigi exclaimed, "since you have stolen my cook! And a very fine cook he is! You should be *amply* prepared!"

It might be a slightly barbed joke. One could absolutely take it for one—if lordly Tatiseigi had ever in his life joked with the paidhi-aiji.

"One is about to be extremely bold," Bren said, "and offer the lord of the Atageini an invitation to the same dinner, in honor of your generosity, which one can never forget."

"Ha!" Tatiseigi said. And one *still* had no idea whether he was joking.

"Please do consider it, nandi."

"We shall look at our calendar."

That was no answer. But he had not expected ready agreement.

"Lord Geigi," Tabini said, covering the moment. "Lord Haidiri of the Pasithi Maschi. —Lord Geigi, would you care to make a more formal introduction of this gentleman to all the company?"

"Delightedly," Geigi said, and rescued them into far safer topics: the formal presentation of his proxy to the lower end of the table.

On that topic, and in meeting a completely innocent bystander with no history and an uncertain party affiliation, the company could safely enjoy their soup.

Ilisidi said, slyly, under the whisper of compliments to Haidiri, "One believes Lord Tatiseigi would be delighted to accept your invitation, nand' paidhi, given a more certain date. And *we* shall be quite flexible."

Cajeiri, who ordinarily would be beside himself with desire for an invitation, was still being extraordinarily quiet this evening. The boy read what was going on, with the back halls of his residence swarming with Guild in a not-quite-secret meeting, and his mother and father and great-grandmother and Uncle Tatiseigi all sitting within earshot of each other.

The newcomer lords lower down the guest list had no guidebook to the goings-on at the upper end of the table. It was not public knowledge that Damiri was only just speaking to Ilisidi. It was not officially admitted that Tabini was currently asking himself what his grandmother was up to, making a peace between her own clan and his former enemy, Machigi of the Taisigin Marid.

And it was not yet public knowledge that Cajeiri was trying to arrange a birthday party with young human guests coming down from the space station, who were very inconvenient associates of his, and *not* approved by his mother.

What everyone at table *did* know was that not only had Damiri's father just been banned from court, her servants and her bodyguard had been sent packing that same stormy evening. Everyone could see the shift to Atageini colors and the sudden importance of Lord Tatiseigi in the family, and they would be looking for clues about new alignments. Bet on it: Damiri's choice of colors would be national headlines the moment any attendee got within range of the news services.

Meanwhile the paidhi-aiji, who'd negotiated the Marid agreement *and* hosted Geigi as a guest in his apartment, *and* gotten Tatiseigi's support for Ilisidi's Marid venture—just wanted to have his soup in peace and not have Ilisidi launch another issue with Damiri.

Truth was, he felt very uncomfortable in this gathering, without the company of his bodyguard. They more than protected his life, more than steered him through crowded rooms—they signaled him. They read connections and body language of people around him far more accurately than any human could, even one with years of experience . . . and where he was now needed deep reading.

Damned mess. Yes. It was. And an ongoing mess. The Guild in the back halls would be doing their own assessments of the security situation in the Bujavid, talking about the dismissal of the Ajuri lord and the disaffection of the Northern Association; and about the security crisis in the aiji's household, the fact that the aiji had ignored recommendations from the Guild and chosen his own bodyguard—all young men without adequate Guild rank—to replace those lost in the coup.

It had been a highly controversial decision on Tabini's part, but since those bodyguards appointed through normal Guild channels following his return to power had immediately tried to assassinate him ... it was not exactly an unreasonable one.

As for those backroom discussions, some would hear all of it, and others would hear part. The seniormost would, within their Guild, pass information where they chose, selecting some households to brief, and excluding others. Hence a certain amount of the tension in the gathering of lords. *Something* was going on, regarding power, and who held it; and who was in favor; and who was not. Who came out of those meetings knowing what might well change the political landscape.

Geigi's aishid would be at the top of the need to know list. When Geigi went back to space tomorrow, his bodyguards would leave the earth completely up to speed on matters they needed to discuss with the station security structure. While the shuttle was en route, likely the bodyguard would be putting Geigi current with whatever went on tonight—and providing a high-level assessment of Tabini's situation. Geigi, once back on the space station, had his finger on weaponry that most of the current gathering didn't even imagine existed. When Tabini had nearly gone down to defeat in Murini's takeover, Geigi had made moves to reconstitute the government on the mainland, and had scared hell out of the rebels, dropping robotic communication relay stations on their land—preparatory to sending those mobile stations into action. Those stations were still out there. Still armed. Still dangerous.

That was how powerful Geigi had become. And Geigi

was still the counterbalance to the administration. Geigi didn't *want* power, but he had it. His own house was down to the questionable genes of a single fool of an embezzling nephew, and Geigi was happier in space than he was on his estate, even with his orchards.

Everyone who knew the situation—was very grateful for Geigi's presence in the heavens. *Nobody* could easily stage another coup, with Tabini on high alert for treachery and Geigi's finger on the button up on the station. If they a second time contemplated dislodging Tabini from power—they knew now that Geigi was a threat, and capable of unifying the aiji's supporters no matter what happened to other communications networks.

What else Geigi and the station might be capable of, no ateva knew, and Bren hoped they'd never have reason to find out.

The last of the dissidents who'd staked their lives on Murini's coup were fighting with their backs to the wall, trying to carve out a territory where they could do things their way. They'd enjoyed a temporary safe haven in the Marid—until they'd gotten greedy and taken on Machigi *and* Lord Geigi.

Now they had lost that security. They had lost a pitched battle. They had lost a clandestine operation.

Unfortunately they still had their underground ... and they still had a sting.

Even after the business in the Marid, a few fools who'd thought they'd scented weakness in Tabini had pushed to get influence. The most outstanding fool had been Damiri's father, Komaji, lord of Ajuri.

The man had gotten into power on the death of his brother, and lost all common sense—as witness his public tantrum in the halls of the Bujavid. Komaji had let his rivalry with Tatiseigi blind him, perhaps because Tatiseigi had been included in an honor and he had not, but even that wasn't clear. He had thrown a tantrum, tried to force his way into Tabini's home, had terrified the staff, and sent Cajeiri into hiding. It had been extremely embarrassing for Damiri, who at that point had a clear choice: leave her marriage—or leave her father's clan.

The world had suspected, when she had not departed with her staff, and tonight, with that shocking arrival in the dining room, she had laid any lingering doubts firmly to rest.

The second course arrived, and then the third, with the traditional pause for applause for the aiji's truly excellent personal cook. The old man, reasonably new to the aiji's service, bowed happily, accepted the praise, and then had his staff bring out the next, the fourth course, a set of imaginatively arranged dishes which filled the ample table to overflowing.

Bren took the vegetables he knew, and did *not* trust the seasonal tubers, last of the winter root crop, traditional to use up before the first breaking of the vinebuds.

The traditional recipe, alas, rich in alkaloids atevi thought wonderful, would have a human dead in short order.

"You are missing the traditional dish, paidhi," Tatiseigi chided him.

"Alas, one must leave it to your enjoyment, nandi. One is very strongly advised against it."

"Oh, surely, just a sample . . ." Tatiseigi said, not because Tatiseigi wanted him dead, Bren hoped—such an ungracious way to get out of a dinner invitation. The old man's relaxed, somewhat wine-assisted complacency indicated he was in an unprecedentedly happy mood this evening. It was, Bren decided, actually rather touching, that solicitude about the dish, as if Tatiseigi was certain the paidhi-aiji had become atevi enough now to survive the diet.

2

Brandy always followed a formal dinner. With brandy, business talk, banned at the dinner table, could be conducted in an alcohol-fueled but somewhat torpid contentment. It was a social hour in which there was much leeway and little offense taken.

In the case of the aiji's dinners, there were always more guests for brandy than would possibly fit at the aiji's private dinner table—guests who did not fit for reasons of rank; or who did not fit for reasons of politics; or for a number of other considerations including the frequency with which they had lately been invited.

People kept track of these matters. Tabini's master of kabiu more than arranged flowers, he arranged people. And he would keep *everyone* properly happy, even those not invited at all to the evening's festivities, with small gifts, elaborate invitations, and special recognitions that substituted for invitations, keeping all the contacts polished, as it were.

So it was out to the large reception hall for brandy, more people, and light refreshment. There was still enough food on the buffet tables for a reasonable meal, had one not had supper yet—and it was shoulder-to-shoulder in places. There were Names in the room. That these were all well-wishers of the administration was a comforting notion, considering the political variety of the gathering, and considering the tradition-breaking legislation about to arise in the session. It augured well for everything they were trying to get settled.

Ilisidi was definitely a focus of attention in this room. Her personal understanding with Machigi, the new over-lord of the five clans of the Marid, as he was shaping up to be, was certainly at issue. Machigi himself might have gone home to take care of business, but he had set up a new trade office down the hill from the Bujavid, and Ili-sidi was doing business for that office wherever she walked, setting up meetings, extolling the virtues of the southern porcelains. She was simultaneously courting votes for the admission of the two west coast tribal peo-ples to the legislature—a matter which was *not* near and dear to her new ally Machigi, but which was definitely connected to her recent dealings with him—and an issue most certainly connected to Lord Geigi, whose Kaji-minda staff came from the local Edi people. She talked to this lord and that, the redoubtable cane grounded for a prolonged time, occasionally thumping the antique carpet in emphasis.

Bren judged himself not remotely as effective with the conservative set as Ilisidi, who, as the most powerful lord of the traditional East, had immense influence among western conservatives. Tatiseigi led that faction, and attended the dowager in her tour of the room. Bren just watched, taking mental notes as to who had a pleas-ant expression, and who looked less happy.

"Bren-nandi!" someone said, behind him. He turned, recognizing the voice with pleasure: the young lord of Dur, Reijiri, son and often proxy of the sitting lord, was the bravest, staunchest, and most reckless of his own al-lies. Reijiri was not in his usual flight-casuals this eve-ning, but wore a very plain formal dress in this company of glittering elite.

"Jiri-nandi," Bren said, with a quick bow. "So good to see you. Is your father here with you?"

"I tried to persuade him to fly." The elder lord's reluc-tance toward his son's bright yellow, open-cockpit plane was a standing joke in present company. "But you know how that is. At least I shall have his apartment in order when he gets here."

"Will you sit this session," Bren asked, "or will he take the seat himself?"

"My father has declared he will," young Dur said. "Which is good for the bills. He carries far more weight than I do."

"His support is very welcome," Bren almost had time to say. Cajeiri arrived with:

"*Nandi!* One is very glad to see you!"

Reijiri, he meant. Reijiri was one of Cajeiri's favorite people in the whole world.

"Young gentleman," Reijiri said with a bow. "Delighted. One wondered if you would be in attendance this evening."

"Oh, one is obliged to be here," Cajeiri said. He had yet another fruit drink in hand—a charge of sugar, instead of the sedation steadily progressing in the company. "One is so *bored* already with being shut in! Did you come with your plane? Might you possibly, possibly persuade my father to let me go up over the city, just once? Seeing the city from the air would be *very* educational!"

"Alas, though I do have my plane here, young gentleman, I fear your father would never consent to that, under current circumstances."

"I am a prisoner in the Bujavid, nandi! I am bored!"

"Are you indeed, young gentleman?" Ilisidi had come up uncommonly silently. "Come, come, a pleasant face, Great-grandson. Smile. And good evening, nand' Reijiri. We are so glad to see you." She laid a hand on Cajeiri's shoulder, turning him to face the sparser center of the room. "We wish to introduce our great-grandson to his second cousins."

"Cousins?" Cajeiri asked, wide-eyed.

The dreadful cane, only slightly elevated in the press, pointed across the room. A contingent of strangers, two of them younger folk—a girl and a boy, accompanying a father, as seemed—held a corner. They all were Eastern in their dress.

"Calrunaidi clan," Ilisidi said, which explained everything, even to Cajeiri, and certainly to Bren. He wondered for an instant was one of the two younger folk Maie-daja, who was now married to Geigi's nephew.

But no, the girl looked much too young ... very early teens, closer to Cajeiri's age.

"We shall introduce you, shall we not?" the dowager said. "Take your leave of Lord Reijiri and nand' Bren, young gentleman."

The Calrunaidi had *not* been at the dinner. That was a piece of delicate footwork, Bren thought. They had not been invited to mix in western politics, but it was mandatory that these people receive careful attention now.

"Nandiin," Cajeiri said obediently, with a glance at Reijiri. "One has to go."

"Young gentleman," Reijiri said solemnly, and bowed, amused.

"Just a few days short of fortunate nine," Bren said, regarding Cajeiri's age, and watched Ilisidi maneuver the boy into a meeting.

"Quite a youngster," Reijiri said.

"He is that." Bren had an eye on Damiri-daja, too, who was, yes, entirely aware that her son had been drawn by the dowager into a meeting with relatives of the dowager's association. Damiri had a smile on her face, but it was thin.

And one did not want to be caught noticing that fact.

"So," Bren said cheerfully, glancing at Dur, "one wishes you might join us on the train tomorrow, when we deliver Lord Geigi to the spaceport. Might we hope for it?"

"Alas, nand' paidhi, one would far, far rather, but I have to meet my father at the train station in the city and get him safely to the hotel. He will come in tired and out of sorts, one would never say, confused, and I have all the requisite papers and authorizations and keys. He will never let the major domo have them, and he is bound to be overtired."

"Indeed." One less piece in motion tomorrow morning was likely to the good, though he and Geigi would have enjoyed the company. "Ah, but I shall be giving dinner parties this season. A formal card will come when I have a date established; but please, both you and your father, do save room for me on your schedule, sometime before the session ends. I should much enjoy it. And I should be happy to have a quiet evening with you both."

"I shall answer for my father, in greatest confidence. Consider such an invitation accepted."

"Excellent." It was very certain, given the situation with the Ajuri, to the east of Dur, and to the north of Tatiseigi, that those two had an urgent need to establish contact. If he could succeed in managing Tatiseigi at dinner once, with the dowager in attendance, he might try twice, with Dur. He dared not promise anything—but he hoped. "Well, well, I had best go do my job tonight, should I not?"

"Nand' paidhi."

A courteous bow, on either side. He and Reijiri broke apart to wander. He targeted a convenient pair of committee heads he had to deal with. He needed those votes on the tribal bill. And he had them reasonably happy on his change of vote on the cell phone bill.

"Paidhi-aiji."

Tatiseigi wanted his attention.

Tatiseigi with half a brandy in hand, and several glasses of wine taken at dinner. Overindulgence was *not* the old man's habit, but he was in a rare mood, tonight.

"One notes," Tatiseigi said, "that you are conspiring with the west coast again."

A joke, a slightly barbed one, but he was sure it was a joke this time. "Arranging guests for yet another dinner, nandi. Dare one hope you will actually consider my invitation? I am quite serious. I would be very honored. And getting together with Dur—I had you in mind in inviting them—if your first trial of my hospitality with the dowager persuades you."

"Two opportunities to savor Bindanda's dishes," Tatiseigi said, and dropped his voice to a confidential tone. "I shall be hosting a festivity of my own soon, be it known, to which you are reciprocally invited. One assumes you will be free on the twenty-third. Perhaps we shall include Dur. He *is* bordering Ajuri's association, a provisional member. One considers you may have that fact in mind."

The gesture amazed him. "One is very highly honored by your consideration, nandi. Might one ask what occasion the twenty-third marks?"

"One might indeed. You have inspired me, paidhi. I have had a grand notion. I shall be bringing certain of my own collection in by rail." Porcelains, the old man meant. "You need to talk to the subcommittee on imports, in the dowager's cause, and you will have my support in the effort. She has explained her plans to me, and this new Marid trade initiative is a very bold move on her part. A very bold move, paidhi. And I shall support it. My exhibit will put porcelains in public view which have not been seen outside Atageini territory in two hundred years. It will mark the connection of this profound art with the southern Marid trade. I have no few pieces of that origin."

God. Amazing. The old man was a shrewd campaigner, and he was a passionate collector of an item the south had produced from ancient times. The paidhi-aiji had, trying for something relatively non-controversial, proposed the south's famous porcelains as an opening trade item in the new agreement with the Marid. And in vague hope of at least appeasing Tatiseigi, he had gifted the old man with, as he increasingly suspected, a very special piece. "One would be profoundly grateful for your support, nandi."

"I have also told the aiji my views. We should follow up on our advantage in the south. We also shall open trade talks. We shall bolster the dowager's agreement with this young lord—Machigi—*and* we must assure he reciprocates in his acceptance of *all* guilds from outside his province." *Aha*, Bren thought, pricking up his ears a bit—the old man lived for agendas, and *nothing* regarding the guilds and their ancient prerogatives was entirely disconnected from the conservative platform. "That *was* certainly a part of your discussion with the aiji."

"It was certainly part of our discussions," Bren said.

"And remains so." Things had gone a little surreal. Ilisidi had surely been talking to the old man, and now a new twist had become an issue. The Marid's acceptance of the northern-based guilds' authority within its bounds — yes, that had been on the table in the agreement. It was in there, in the fine print. But the conservatives seemed to have gotten it into their heads to run farther on that matter than discussions with Machigi had yet gone. The Assassins' Guild was down in that district in major force — mopping up the renegade elements of their own Guild who had supported Murini. There had been a little talk of the Transportation Guild getting involved in improving rail service to the south.

The *conservatives,* however, suddenly envisioned the whole Shejidan-centered Guild system going into place in the Marid, in every district, never mind the Marid's long tradition of locals-only in the only two guilds they had historically accepted — the Assassins and Transportation. *That* was not going to be a totally smooth road — though he was working on that matter with similar hope, particularly for the Scholars and the Physicians.

"I shall be offering these items of my collection," Tatiseigi added, "for public viewing in the museum downstairs. And we shall catch the public imagination. The *television* service may be advised."

Tatiseigi proposed television coverage? The famed Atageini porcelains on television? Tatiseigi had had three atevi-scale glasses of wine at dinner and at least, from the snifter in his hand, three-quarters of a brandy. Bren had had one of the former, and decided that going slow on what he currently had in his hand was a very good idea.

"One has become sensible," Tatiseigi continued, "to what truly rare items one has in that collection. The honor of the Atageini is to possess them — and to offer the experience of them to the people of the aishidi'tat, who will not have seen the like, ever in their lifetimes or their parents' lifetimes."

"A generous gesture. A very generous gesture." It was, indeed worth a bow, while the less worthy thought was cycling through one's brain—that the rush of publicity and the sudden availability of southern porcelains for the collector's market was going to mean something to certain individuals, too. Collections of scope and antiquity would become more valuable, in status as well as monetarily.

And in Tatiseigi's blue-blooded circles, status was as negotiable as currency.

More so, if you had long been considered old-fashioned, out-of-date, and a little eccentric, were politically ambitious to the hilt, and had just had the aiji's consort turning up in clan colors. Tatiseigi had never scored such an evening.

And if the other guilds could be gotten into the Marid without reference to the historical, Marid-born-members-only policy, the backers of that agreement would have political capital to put any financial gain to shame.

Was that it? Was the old man making a move for influence in the new shape of the aishidi'tat?

"One is certain such a gesture will be well received across the aishidi'tat, nandi."

"Well, well, all due to the aiji-dowager's wise notions. —Ah," Tatiseigi said, spying someone of immediate interest across the room. "I shall speak to you about this, paidhi-aiji. Be assured I shall. But remember the date!"

Tatiseigi was off, at fair speed for an old man, and the alcohol was curiously not that much in evidence.

Bren drew a slow and careful breath, and was relieved to note that their little conversation had not appeared to draw undue interest. Only a few steps away, Tabini was deeply involved with Geigi, and across the room, Cajeiri was still talking to his young female cousin from the East, as Ilisidi carried on a lengthy conversation with the Calrunaidi lord.

He hadn't been able to intervene in *that* situation, which was not Ilisidi's nicest move, damn the circumstances. Damiri was on a permanent hair trigger regarding the dowager's influence over her son, and, making matters worse, there was a very political cast on that meeting of

second cousins. Calrunaidi was the clan of the bride of
Geigi's miscreant nephew. That meant ties to Lord Geigi
on the one hand, and ties to Ilisidi on the other. Cajeiri
was good and he was perceptive, but an eight-year-old was
not up to negotiating the tricky grounds between his
mother and his great-grandmother . . . and the boy could
not refuse either's orders.

Oh, damned right Damiri was keeping an eye on her
son, at the moment, watching with whom he formed
associations—particularly female associations; and at
the moment she did not have a happy look.

Bren shifted objectives, and went to be introduced to
the Calrunaidi guests, which gave him a chance to bend
aside and say, quickly and quietly into Cajeiri's young
ear—"Your *mother,* young gentleman. Go attend her.
Quietly. Now."

It was not a case of warning the average eight-year-
old. Cajeiri was a veteran of literal fire-fights *and* palace
intrigue.

Did the boy blurt out, I don't care? Or ask, sullenly,
What does *she* want?

No. The boy did none of those things. Cajeiri said in a
low voice, with a deep bow, "Please excuse me, nandi. I
have just received a request from my mother."

Bren did not even glance at Ilisidi as Cajeiri left. Ilisidi knew exactly what he had done and he knew she
knew he knew, and suspected there had been no message
from Damiri whatsoever. Ilisidi might well make her displeasure known in some minor way, over the next several days. Bren paid that prospect no heed, smiled and
bowed in all courtesy to the lord of Calrunaidi. "One is
very pleased to make your acquaintance, nandi. The aiji-
dowager speaks very highly of you."

"Delighted, nand' paidhi."

Conversation then rapidly went from, "Will you be in
the city long?" all the way to "If you find yourself in need
on the East Coast, nand' paidhi, consider my house open
to you."

So it was not a bad meeting at all . . . give or take Ilisidi's grip on his arm as he left the conversation, and a whispered, "Paidhi, *do not meddle.*"

"Forgive me, aiji-ma." He was not in the least penitent.

Her firm grip headed him in Damiri's general direction. As good as walking into a war zone.

"One advises against a meeting with the consort tonight, aiji-ma."

"Nonsense. This is my granddaughter-in-law. What could possibly be amiss?"

The hell! he thought. If his bodyguard were present even the aiji-dowager would not take advantage as she was doing. But he dared not object as Ilisidi steered them straight into hostile waters. Cajeiri was in conversation with his mother, receiving some instruction when they arrived. Cajeiri shot them a very dismayed look.

"Granddaughter-in-law," Ilisidi said smoothly. "The festivity is a complete success. We heartily compliment you."

There was scant warmth in Damiri's eyes when she said, "My husband's staff deserves all the compliments for the evening, of course. You may recall my own staff is no longer in the city."

Ilisidi stood, both hands on her cane. "Yet you are the hostess," she said, and with a thump of the cane. "And you have been admirable. —Let us say something long unsaid, Granddaughter-in-law, which we should have said long ago. We *applaud* your choice to remain with my grandson. We *support* you in doing so. And we *entirely* understand your reasoning."

"Nand' dowager, it is a *clan* matter."

"So was your marriage," Ilisidi said sharply, thank God in a low tone of voice. "Age grants us some perspective on these things, and since our chances for conversation have been limited in recent days, Granddaughter-in-law, bear with us: we are moderately private in this noisy crowd. I freely admit, I counseled my grandson against taking an Ajuri consort. I knew the peace between Ajuri and Atageini would be temporary . . ."

God, Bren thought. There was *no* way to stop the aiji-dowager once the aiji-dowager had decided to say something. At least the buzz in the room had not quieted: no one had appeared to notice the exchange.

"We were keenly *aware* of your opposition, nand' dowager."

Ilisidi tipped her head back a little, giving Damiri, who was much the taller, a somewhat oblique look. "I was opposed to the union and strongly opposed to the formal marriage. Granddaughter-in-law, I am *rarely* wrong. But you have astonished me. You have grown far beyond what subtlety Ajuri could ever have taught you. You have *qualities* I attribute to your Atageini blood. My grandson chose very well, and I freely admit it."

"Do you?" Damiri's glance was steel-hard. "Your approval is some years late in coming."

"Whether or not we can ever be allies is questionable. But one would *prefer* alliance."

There was still the general buzz and motion of a crowded room about them. Their voices had remained low. Bren stood there with his heart racing, he, the diplomat, frozen in dismay, and not seeing a damned thing he could do to divert the train wreck. Tabini was the only recourse, and Tabini was not looking this way.

"Alliance?" Damiri said stiffly. "Alliance with you, nandi, is dangerous for an Ajuri. What do *you* want that I can give? —Because I am well assured this is *not* an act of generosity."

"Peace," Ilisidi said firmly. "Peace in my grandson's household and my great-grandson's life. Peace in which my great-grandson can *enjoy* having a sister."

"You have never called on me," Damiri said. "Ever. Only on your grandson."

"*You* have never invited me," Ilisidi said sharply.

"I *am* inviting you," Damiri retorted in the exact same tone. "*Tomorrow,* morning tea."

"Perfectly acceptable," Ilisidi snapped. The dowager, in fact, had *never* accepted invitations from those of inferior rank or junior years. Tonight she had solicited such invitations at dinner, and now as good as asked for another, far harder come by. The tones involved, hers and Damiri's, were steel on steel.

But that was the way of these two; and the lords of the aishidi'tat, when they made war or peace, did so for policy and in consideration of clan loyalties. A second try at harmony, in changed circumstances, *could* well work. Bren just held his breath and courted invisibility.

"Our division is well-known," Ilisidi said. "Come, leave the young gentleman to the paidhi's very competent care and walk about with me. Let us lay these rumors of division and amaze your guests, who think they know us so well."

"Ha," Damiri said, and off they went, a tall, young, and extremely pregnant woman side by side with a diminutive grandmother with a cane. They walked slowly, Atageini green and white and Ragi black and red, moving through the crowd, pausing to speak to this and that person.

Bren cast a look at Tabini, who had stopped talking to Geigi and gazed at a Situation that was bound to have its final act sooner or later in private—likely with both women in his sitting room.

Bren drew a deep breath then, and exchanged a look with Cajeiri. "Well, young gentleman?"

"Do you think they really are making peace, nand' Bren?"

"They are both very smart," Bren said. The show out there was the focus of Tabini's attention, and Calrunaidi's; and Tatiseigi's, and Geigi's. It was an Event. It was going to make the news, no question, like Damiri's wearing Atageini colors—two pieces of news that would probably overshadow Geigi's return to the station.

That part would suit Geigi. A blowup between the dowager and the consort would not.

"My great-grandmother wants something," Cajeiri said.

"One is very certain she does," Bren said uncomfortably. "One only hopes they both want the same thing."

"I am on my own right now," Cajeiri said, stolid-faced as any adult, then volunteered. "Not just for the party.

My bodyguard is away at the Guild for days and days. Antaro and Jegari are getting certified."

"For weapons, nandi?"

A nod. "I have two servants, now, all my own. And my tutor. I wish I could come stay with you, nandi. I am so bored. And the place is very quiet at night."

"When will your aishid be back?"

"A day or so, they said." A pause. "My father is too busy and my mother is very uncomfortable. And I *hope* I am going to get my party. Please see to it, nandi."

"One wishes one could help, young gentleman. One very much wishes it. Why are they advancing your bodyguard's certification? Do you know?"

"My father did it. Antaro and Jegari know about guns, of course." A shrug. "They have hunted since they were little, in Taiben. But Lucasi and Veijico say they have to have a certificate to have guns in public places. And to use Guild equipment."

"That is so," Bren said. "So no one is staying in your suite with you?"

"Just Boji."

Boji was small, black, and furry, and lived in a large cage in the boy's room.

It was unfamiliar solitude for a young boy, particularly a boy who, in his life, had traveled on a starship, dealt with aliens, been kidnapped by his father's enemies, nearly run down at sea, and habitually went armed with a slingshot—which was probably in his pocket even here. The empty rooms must be particularly unnerving for a boy who, in the last year and in part *because* of his tendency to collect adventures, had acquired an aishid of his own, four bodyguards dedicated to keeping him safe in every moment of his life.

"And how is Boji?"

"Very well, nandi! I am training him to be without his cage sometimes."

"Excellent." The women had made half the circuit of the room. And unfortunately, he could not afford to be a babysitter at the expense of the Marid treaty. He spied, finally, a committee head he urgently needed to talk to.

"One has to speak to this gentleman a moment. Will you be well for a moment, young sir? Will you stand right here?"

Cajeiri gave a two-shouldered shrug, a little grin and a wink. "Oh, with no trouble, nandi. There are no kidnappers here. And if they come back arguing, I shall have to go with my mother."

Of course the scamp would find his own way. He had been doing that all his life. And Cajeiri absolutely had the priorities straight. Bren went off to intercept the head of Transport, and the head of the Commerce Committee walked up to join the conversation.

The talk became intense, and substantive, and encouragingly productive.

When he looked for the boy again, he found no sign of him. He did see that the aiji-dowager and Damiri had gone their separate ways, busy about the fringes of the room, and that conversation, which had hushed progressively as the two went about the room, had resumed.

Tabini-aiji, however, looked his direction, gave a little nod, and that was an immediate command appearance.

He went. And bowed. "One is currently looking for your son, aiji-ma, and one is just a little concerned."

"His servants took him to bed a moment ago," Tabini said. "He is quite safe."

"One is relieved." He let go a breath. "One should not have left him. Even here."

"Oh, he has been on his own all evening. And he could not have gotten out the door unremarked," Tabini added with a little wry humor. "My whole staff has their instructions. My son has entirely understood the current difficulty, and he has stayed very well within bounds." A sharpening of focus, and a frown. "My grandmother. Did she plan that?"

That the aiji had to ask *him* what Ilisidi was thinking . . .

"One does not believe so, no, aiji-ma. One believes she was quite taken by surprise, reacting to your honored wife's choice of colors this evening."

"It was Damiri's choice," Tabini said somberly. "Her father has left her none. But these are not easy days in the household."

"One well understands, aiji-ma."

"Have you heard anything in the room?"

"Nothing regarding that matter, aiji-ma."

"Come aside a moment."

"Aiji-ma." He followed Tabini to the far side of the room, through the door and into the deserted dining hall, tracked, at a slight remove, by Tabini's bodyguards.

Servants, working at polishing the table, withdrew quickly. Two of Tabini's bodyguards went across the room and shut those doors. The other two, from outside, shut the dining room doors. The likelihood of eavesdroppers on the aiji's conversation outside this room had been very scant: nobody crowded in on Tabini without a clear signal to do so. But clearly there was something else, something that could not risk report. And they were in as much privacy as could be had.

"They have put a public patch on the matter," Tabini said quietly. "But be aware Damiri is entirely uneasy, and unreconciled. She does not trust my grandmother, and I worry for my son's impression of the situation. You talked to him. Was he upset by it?"

"Not discernibly, aiji-ma."

"Were you warned?"

"Aiji-ma, I had no forewarning."

"She planned it," Tabini said, with utter conviction.

"Aiji-ma, one would tend to agree she had intended some discussion on the Ajuri matter—which I think it may have been. But she had not planned it tonight. Not that I know."

"Damiri has said—" Tabini drew a careful breath and let it go. "You well know, paidhi, that Damiri has lost one child to my grandmother, and she has requested me to promise not to put this next one in my grandmother's hands for any reason of security. She has bluntly said, this very evening, and I quote, 'I am forced to choose my uncle. I have your grandmother on one side and her lovers on the other. They control my son and now they are the only relatives I have. I shall *never* concede my daughter to them.'"

"Aiji-ma." What could one say? Damiri had lost her son's man'chi through no fault of hers. The separation had broken the bond, when Tabini had sent Cajeiri away to space for protection. He had bonded to his great-grandmother. Intensely so. And he felt deeply sorry for Damiri.

But *not* sorry enough to take her side over Tabini's, and not sorry enough to regret his own part in bringing up Cajeiri. The boy was alive. And he might not be, if he had stayed with his parents through the coup. If they had had a child in tow, they might themselves not have survived the constant moving and the hiding in wilderness conditions.

And, damn it all, if Damiri had never slipped into her father's orbit last year, however briefly, and if Damiri had been less openly antagonistic toward Ilisidi once Ilisidi brought the boy back—

"Damiri declares," Tabini said, with a muscle standing out in his jaw, "that she still has man'chi to Ajuri clan. But that she has no man'chi now to her father. She says *she* will take the lordship of Ajuri herself, before she settles to be Tatiseigi's tributary."

My God. "Can she muster support to do that, aiji-ma?"

"Possibly. I think it has one motive. She views it would set her on a more equal footing with my grandmother."

Clan lord or not—it was not likely lordship of Ajuri was going to set anybody equal to Ilisidi. But he didn't say that.

"Will you back her in that, aiji-ma?"

The muscle jumped. Twice. "Ajuri *swallows* virtue. That her father killed his brother-of-a-different-mother to get the lordship, one is all but certain. How the late lord himself got the lordship was also tainted. My wife wants to be lord of Ajuri—in her father's place—and no, it is not a good idea, and *not* something I support, or will even tolerate, while she brings up my daughter—even if, in every other way, it would solve the threat Ajuri poses."

Tabini folded his arms, leaned back against the massive dining table. "I have a problem, paidhi. She is too proud to be Tatiseigi's niece, in Atageini clan, even were he to make her his heir—which might happen, and which I would accept. She feels no kinship with them. Would she consent to become Ragi?" That was Tabini's clan; and Ilisidi's clan only by marriage and the bond of a son born in it. "I have invited her to take those colors. She is, I think, struggling with that idea. She cannot seem to attach." *Attach* in the clan sense. In the atevi emotional sense. In the husband-and-wife sense. A human had no idea, except to say that Damiri was not at home among Ragi, didn't feel it, couldn't get her mind into her husband's clan—

—And that said something disturbing about the tension in that marriage.

"A human cannot offer advice here."

"I do not court advice, paidhi. I know exactly where I am, and where she is. But your bodyguard outranks all but my grandmother's, and *they* are back there right now discussing how to manage a situation *I* have created."

A slight hesitation on that unusually personal *I*.

"Your bodyguard, aiji-ma?" Bren guessed.

"My bodyguard—and my wife. Ajuri poses a more serious threat than one might think: I have been directly briefed, and *my* bodyguard has *not*. That is only *one* of our problems. Then there is this: if my wife does *not* recognize the increasingly grim situation with Ajuri, and is naive in her thinking, then she is too stupid to be my wife. If she *does* know it, and is attempting to involve herself in this clan's longstanding politics, it can lead to much worse places—danger to her, naturally—danger to the aishidi'tat itself from her associations within that clan, and temptations to actions which are—what is the human expression? On the *slippery slope*?"

"One understands."

"I do not believe she would harm her own son to set her daughter in his place. And she knows our son is too stubborn to change his man'chi. But she has possession of another Ragi child, the one she is carrying. And this is what I have told my grandmother's bodyguard, and indirectly, yours. *You* need to know. My *grandmother* may well know. In fact I am sure she knows. This approach of my grandmother this evening was *not* in ignorance of the situation. Hence its troubling timing."

"I understand." Not *one understands,* the formal, rote answer that equaled *yes, sir.* But *I* understand. *I* am hearing and agreeing. And he did understand. Far too much to be comfortable at all. "I am at *your* orders, aiji-ma. They take precedence over hers ... though I shall try, by your leave, to find a course where both work."

"You have that skill. Use it. About certain things, your aishid will brief you. Know there may be a time my son may resort to you on his own. Do not refuse him. Put him immediately within your security perimeter."

"I shall, without fail, aiji-ma."

"There may be a time *I* send him," Tabini said further. "That will signal a far more serious situation."

"Aiji-ma. We will defend him with all our resources."

"I have no doubt of it," Tabini said, "and that is all I can say until events prove the outcome." He himself opened the door into the reception hall. They quietly reentered, past the two bodyguards. Numerous eyes turned their way, and Bren took his cue from Tabini and smiled, as if it was some light, pleasant business.

Far from it.

Tabini moved off to speak to another partisan.

Deep breath. Keep smiling.

He presented courtesies to a lord of the mountain districts, and to the Chairman of Finance.

Thank God the boy had gone to bed. The atmosphere had gone dangerous, and he was, God help him, *not* as good as some at keeping worry off his face.

And he was not surprised when, a few minutes on, one focus of that worry—Ilisidi—walked up and stopped beside him.

"Well?" she asked, expecting at least no outright prevarications.

"Your grandson is concerned, aiji-ma," he answered her. The evening was, one was sure, needing to wind down soon. There was drink enough that voices were getting a little loud. "But the situation is of long standing."

"There is every reason my granddaughter-in-law should make peace with us," Ilisidi said. "We did not speak of the baby. Nor of the young gentleman."

The dowager, Tabini had said, likely knew what the issue was—probably more than he did, and maybe more than Tabini did, seeing the dowager's guard was more plugged in to the security surrounding the aiji than were the aiji's own bodyguards. And they all knew why there had to be some settling of the issues. Ajuri was hoping to drive a wedge into that marriage. And to cloud the issue of the clan of the impending child—by getting Damiri to give birth under an Ajuri roof.

"We did express hope we might improve relations," Ilisidi said smoothly, softly. "We are about to retire for the evening, however. We understand the young gentleman has already gone to bed."

"So I am told, aiji-ma."

"They have taken his young guards in for training," Ilisidi said. "All at once. He is alone in his suite. We are not pleased with that situation."

"One believes they are raising the level of his security, aiji-ma. And certainly your grandson has taken measures to remove Ajuri access to him."

"Except his mother," Ilisidi said bluntly. "In the meanwhile he is alone, and his mother will take no servants from Tatiseigi, none from me, none from Sarini Province, and none from the Taibeni."

"Dur, possibly?"

Ilisidi lifted a brow. "Suggest it, if you find the time and can manage the access. My granddaughter-in-law's feuds have eliminated half the continent. More than half, if one counts the Marid."

"Dur would be a *good* choice. In a position, geographically, to checkmate Ajuri. And Cajeiri has ties to Dur. One of the mountain clans, associates of her son's bodyguards, would be another choice."

"She is a difficult woman," Ilisidi said. "But at least

never a fool." Ilisidi resettled her cane on the floor, under both hands. "We shall meet tomorrow for tea. We shall discuss what cannot be discussed on the floor. We shall see." She walked off, then, and with uncharacteristic warmth, greeted the lord from Talidi, and conversed with him.

3

The evening was going to go on as long as it took for the Guild meeting in the back rooms to wind up, at very least—Bren was sure that meeting *was* why the evening had spun out as long as it had. It was worrisome, to say the least, as the hour grew very late indeed.

He was not sure whether what Tabini had told him even played the most major part of what was at issue in the Guild's meeting—there was the whole business down in the Marid, for one major unknown. In breaking down the Guild splinter organization, people had to be set in place to keep order. Others had to be removed. Discoveries of all sorts were being made down there, connections being brought to light.

He knew at least he had to stay until the last; and the dowager was clearly going to stay on. She had others of her young men, as she called them, that she could call on ... but was the aiji-dowager going to go to bed tonight until she had found out what had gone on in the back rooms?

Not likely.

In very fact, the first few guests were taking their leave—a little the worse for drink, and probably incapable of being interviewed by the news services lurking in the downstairs of the Bujavid. Their departure meant their bodyguards would be leaving as well. Not bodyguards of the level, however, that might be participating in the deepest briefings. These were lords of small districts, and a few committee members, such as might have a Guild-trained servant in attendance, but no actual uniformed Guild bodyguard: minor players, these, in what had gone on this evening.

In this slight ebb of guests from the hall, amid farewells and well-wishes, Ilisidi found an opportunity to stand near Damiri again, and the two women talked without looking at each other, each with smiles to match departing guests' courtesies.

Hell, no, Damiri was not leaving the hall, either, to be the object of discussion once she had left. She stayed on.

Geigi strayed over to Bren quite casually, stood beside him and said, "Is there any emergency afoot, Bren-ji?"

"No emergency," Bren said, gazing out over the room, and keeping his voice very low. "Simply the situation in the household. Nothing that will trouble you on the station. One is certain you will be briefed on the matter in the back halls. So will I."

"One understands," Geigi said. "One prefers to hear it en route, for security's sake. Such things too easily escape the bag. Advise me if I can be of use tonight. Meanwhile, I see the head of Transport. I do need to speak to him before I leave."

So it went. It was the better part of an hour, with minor lords and department officials trickling away, and the major ones becoming more and more significant in the room, before the first of the senior Guild showed up at the door of the reception hall to gather up their own.

The trickle of departure became a flood. Maidin left. Haidiri had gone some time ago. Paturandi departed. Bren took up a position near Damiri, testing the atmosphere, then walked close to her, bowed, and said, under his breath:

"I shall be leaving soon, daja-ma. My assistance, for what it is worth, is always available to you as to your husband, with greatest good will."

"Everyone in this hall has attempted to place servants on my staff," Damiri said somewhat sharply. "Are you the sole exception, paidhi-aiji? Or will you disappoint me?"

"I have no such proposal, daja-ma. I only offer—"

"Information?" Damiri asked. "Dare one suppose you will tell me what the dowager said? Or what my husband said?"

"Both were gratified by your choices tonight, daja-ma. Your husband is no fool. Nor is the aiji-dowager. Nor, may one say, is your son."

"You are not my confidant, paidhi-aiji. Do not presume!"

"I shall not, daja-ma, but neither shall I ask a confidence and then break it. I serve your husband primarily; and the dowager at times, yes. But your interest is my concern, because your happiness affects your husband and your son. If I can ever be of service, I say, I will serve your interests as man'chi allows."

"A sentiment humans notoriously lack!"

"We have compensatory sentiments. I offer them. Bluntly, I have wondered myself whether the dowager would seek to influence your daughter yet to be, and I have been concerned. The answer is, bluntly, *no*. She will not."

That had gotten a sharp, mistrustful look. "She has said so?"

"She has said everything that makes me believe it."

"Then you do *not* know, and yet you present it as truth!"

"I would certainly wager my credibility on it. She is not your enemy, nor wishes to be. She finds no profit and a great deal of disadvantage."

"She is a—!"

"And you likewise have an agenda regarding the dowager. Forgive me, daja-ma, but I am not a fool. Here is the dowager's position. It is specifically in her interest and in the interest of your husband that you and she not be enemies. For her to interfere in your custody of your daughter would assure that you would be. The situation that brought Cajeiri to her will not be repeated. The Guild action in the south is assuring that. So have no doubts. Nothing is being discussed that will separate you from your child."

Damiri shot him a look that, were it a weapon, would have gone straight through him. Question. Doubt. Apprehension. The mask atevi wore over emotion was quite, quite gone. *Are you threatening me?* she might have asked. Or: *What did my husband say to you?* Those seemed to be the thoughts behind that look.

"You say that, with inside knowledge?"

"With no hesitation, daja-ma. The dowager is not your enemy, nor in any wise wishes to be. If she could make alliance with you, it would well serve her—and you. *And* your husband and your son."

The look was only marginally less intense. "You have taken a great deal on yourself, paidhi!"

"In concern for the house I serve, daja-ma. Yes. I am concerned. Deeply so. I have no wish to see any harm to this household—including you, daja-ma, *and* your daughter."

A long, long stare followed that. He did not look away. He was aware Geigi had come close. And that Tabini had.

"One asks," he said quietly, "the favor of your patience, daja-ma, with a person who, however handicapped in understanding, wishes you to continue as consort. You have been an asset to your husband. You were with him through difficult times. You have fought for your position at risk of your life. And one would guess that there were times in those two years when you could have taken refuge in Ajuri, which was surviving Murini's regime untouched and remote. You stayed with your husband. And were a great asset to him."

Her eyes moved, flashed fire. "Do not flatter me."

"I do not. Your husband values you. And approves your choice of colors."

"Do not dare!"

"You asked me what he said. That was part of it."

She drew a deep breath. "My *son* respects you."

"One is honored by that, daja-ma."

"He has too great an attraction to humans."

"I know that has been the case. I agree."

"Yet you support him in calling down these foreigners to associate with him."

"The forbidden becomes a stronger attraction. If you asked my opinion, daja-ma, which you have not, I would say there is an equal chance that reacquaintance may dim that attraction. They will find him changed. He will find them changed. And then he will understand."

She continued to frown. At last she said, "You will observe that interchange, paidhi. You will have an opinion. But I doubt it will favor separation."

"I have yet to form my opinion, daja-ma. My thought now is that they will have become strangers—who may reassociate; or not. His man'chi to his great-grandmother—which you deplore, I know—is an absolute guarantee that he *is* atevi. And the human children will have to deal with that, at a depth he understands far better than they do. He understands man'chi. I assure you—they do not. You will not lose him. He belongs to this earth."

She was disturbed. It was something positive that she momentarily let it show, a shared intimacy, gone in a flash. "You say so."

"I know so, daja-ma. He cannot get from them the affirmation that is so abundantly available to him on this earth."

"*You* live among us. *You* claim you deal in man'chi."

That was ever so slightly—painful. "I am an association of one," Bren said quietly, and dropped his own impassivity. "My house is scattered, daja-ma. My deepest feelings have no point of congruency with those I most regard. I have learned over the years, what I can expect, and what I cannot. The human children, immature as yet, do not remotely understand what your son is: but your son has had long exposure to *me,* and to my brother and his lady, and he has a certain understanding of what we are. His associates from the ship will likely be troubled at what they find, and if they can patch together a way of working together it will stand them all in good stead. But your son has set roots in the earth, now. He is a little afraid of complexities between his elders that he does not understand—but he is inclined toward you as he is toward his father. Do not turn him aside, daja-ma, and he will not turn elsewhere. His connection with you is important."

Damiri's lips were a thin line. Then relaxed, a serene mask. "How can you know *anything?"*

"There is, for humans and for you, *curiosity* toward the foreign. And then there is *instinct.* Satisfying one—satisfies the mind. Satisfying the other—goes much deeper."

Nostrils flared. Intake of breath. A sharp flash of dark gold eyes. "When will *you* be satisfied, paidhi?"

"When I finish my job, daja-ma. When I see no more wars. No more dying."

"Then you are in for a long, long wait, paidhi."

"I know that," he said.

"What do you get from it?"

He shrugged slightly. "Satisfaction of my instincts, daja-ma. Deep satisfaction."

"You find it enough."

"It is enough, daja-ma, that I have moments of satisfaction. I think that is all anyone gets."

A brief silence. A stare. Then: "Keep my *son* safe, paidhi."

"I am determined on that, daja-ma."

Tabini had moved closer. Bren saw him. And Tabini moved again, this time to intervene, all casualness, all smoothness and ease.

"Your aishid and Geigi's are waiting, nand' paidhi. Dami-daja, we should let the paidhi-aiji get his distinguished guest home. Lord Geigi has a flight tomorrow and a long train ride to get there. Nand' Bren, we hope there will be *some* sleep for you both tonight. We have kept you so late."

"We shall manage, aiji-ma." Bren speared Geigi with a glance and flung another toward the door, a signal. He bowed to Tabini, and to Damiri, and had to pass Ilisidi on his way—not without a sharp glance in return. He bowed. And he got a look back that made his skin prickle.

Well, he had tried. For good or for ill, he had stepped into that sticky relationship and tried to patch the wounds. It was family business, now. It was as much as he could do, and he was glad the boy was abed. One hoped he was sound asleep, because the dowager was still there and showing no sign of leaving.

He gathered up his aishid, Banichi and Jago, Tano and Algini, in the foyer. Geigi collected Haiji and his company, and they were very quickly out the door, escaped into the coolth and lower emotional pressure of the hall, a startling, ear-numbing silence around their presence.

"*Brave* paidhi," Geigi said.

"It had to be said," Bren said as they walked together. It was only a short distance to Bren's own front door—that being the first apartment after the aiji's.

One still heard silence behind them as Tabini's doors shut. And the dowager, Cenedi, and *her* bodyguard definitively had not yet left Tabini's apartment.

He was not sure he wanted to know what might happen back there, but he had done as much as he could, and perhaps more than he should. Black Guild uniforms were securely about them both, now, the presence of those nearest and most faithful, in every emotional sense. And he didn't know whether he *was* going to sleep tonight, playing that business over and over and trying to think of what he should have said, and whether he should have said less.

"Return becomes a relief, Bren-ji," Geigi said. "In my steel world up there, in the atevi sector, I am free. The Guilds cooperate, and our little community is so reasonable."

"May it remain that simple," Bren said. They reached their own door, and Banichi or Jago had already passed a signal. It opened just as they got there, and Narani and Jeladi met them to take coats and ease their way into the safe quiet of a house at rest.

Interior lights were dimmed. There was not a sound of revelry to be heard, and the air smelled only of the flowers in the hallway. The aiji's had not been the only party going on. His domestic staff and Geigi's had held their own farewell celebration; but in the discreet way information flowed in a well-put-together staff, he had absolute faith they would have begun to set things in order once they knew the party in the aiji's residence was ebbing down. He was sure that nothing now was out of order, and that he would find all the preparations for Geigi's trip were on schedule.

He thanked Narani and Jeladi, who had stayed awake and dressed to let them in, and he dismissed Geigi and his bodyguard to two servants who turned up quietly in the inner hall—Geigi's valets appeared; and his own valets, Supani and Koharu, had not gone to bed yet either.

"Koharu, if you will attend my aishid," he said. His bodyguard was perfectly capable of seeing to their own persons, and usually did so, but they had a short turn-around before them, with breakfast scheduled for day-break, and that train trip to make to the spaceport. Anything that would aid his bodyguard to get a little more sleep tonight was to the good, and Koharu went off in that direction.

Geigi, however, had not gone to his room. Geigi quietly dismissed his own bodyguard, with his servants, and cast him a significant look.

"A moment, nadi-ji," Bren said to Supani and Supani bowed and stood aside.

Geigi said quietly, "A moment of conversation, Bren-ji."

"My office," Bren said, and weary as he was, came quite, quite awake. It was nothing casual that brought a request to talk at this hour. He was sure of that.

He led the way into his small office and shut the door when they were inside. "Is it a one-pot problem, Geigi-ji? Or would you wish another brandy?"

"Tea would not help my sleep and the other would hasten it too much, Bren-ji. What I have to say is fairly brief. But you should hear it."

"Indeed." He gestured Geigi to a sturdy chair, and took its mate, at the side of the office. "I am listening."

"The children. The young gentleman's guests. And

station politics," Geigi said. "I have attempted twice to explain to the aiji. I have postponed saying anything to trouble you, in the notion that I would have the chance to speak to the aiji tonight. I did so. He has promised the young gentleman his festivity. You should know I argued against it."

"*Against* it," Bren said. Geigi was the one who had conveyed the children's messages, who had acted as intermediary in setting up the forthcoming encounter.

"The children the young gentleman knew on the ship," Geigi said, "are, you recall, from Reunion." Geigi cast a look at the side table, where a brandy service did reside. "I think I will have that brandy, if you will. But none of the staff to serve it, Bren-ji."

"No need to trouble them," Bren said, and got up and poured a small dose apiece, not that they either one had much capacity left.

Geigi took a sip, shut his eyes—composing his thoughts. Bren waited, not expecting good news.

The station's politics—and mention of Reunion in connection with Cajeiri's birthday guests—was not a well-omened beginning.

There resided an infelicitous *four* distinct populations currently on the space station. There were the ones atevi called the ship-humans, who had lived their whole lives aboard *Phoenix*. The ship had been absent from the world for centuries, and on its return had opened up the mothballed station and made contact with the planet.

The human enclave, centuries settled on the isle of Mospheira, were descendants of colonists who had come down from the space station, some to get freedom from the station authority, and the rest because the ship had left them and the station had lost so much population it could no longer sustain its operations. With the ship's return, humans from Mospheira had reoccupied the station. That was the *second* population aboard.

But humans had not come up to the station alone. Atevi had come with them, the *third* population, thanks to Tabini-aiji's insistence on an atevi space program— and the fact that most of the necessary resources to build a shuttle operation were on the continent, and not on Mospheira. In return for materials and items the ship-humans sorely wanted from the world, which the vast continent could supply, Tabini had demanded an atevi share of the station, the building of an atevi starship and the training of atevi crew . . . in short, a piece of every-thing going—an instant leap from an earthbound civili-zation that believed shuttles would puncture the atmospheric envelope and let all the air escape—to awareness of the whole solar system and the galaxy be-yond it. Starflight. Operation translight.

It had all come as a shock to traditional beliefs on the continent—and a shock to human perceptions of their situation as an earthly island expecting invasion from the mainland. The aftershocks were still rumbling through the world. But the agreement had worked for everyone—until the ship-humans finally decided to contact the col-onists *they* had left at their former base of operations, at Reunion Station, light years removed from Alpha Sta-tion and the world of the atevi.

Another species had taken exception to the human presence in that remote location. Removal of that colony had become a necessity.

And collecting every human from Reunion Station and transporting them here had brought a fourth popu-lation onto the space station, five thousand technologi-cally sophisticated humans they'd naively assumed were going to fit right in.

But the Reunion-humans had run their last station as they liked and thought they should run this one. In point of fact, their ancestors had governed the first space sta-tion, and were the very ones the Mospheiran humans had fled the station to escape.

Mospheirans, ship-humans, and atevi all united in ob-jection to the Reunioners' assumption they were the in-coming elite. Together, the three populations outvoted the Reunioners—who were not happy, not in meeting the Mospheirans' ancestral antagonism toward them, not in the ship-humans, who voted *with* the Mospheirans, most of all not in the number of non-humans in residence and in authority. Expansion of the station to accommodate the larger population would have been logical—but they were not, politically, happy, and they could not agree on how many hours should constitute a day, let alone how the station resources and manpower should be directed.

To mediate the problem, the Mospheirans had suggested resurrecting the Maudit Project, first proposed centuries ago, when the ship had arrived at a too-attractive, inhabited planet and the ship-folk had begun to lose control of the colonists, who wanted to land. The ship-captains of that day had wanted to pull their whole operation off to the next planet out from the local sun, where planet-dwelling was not so attractive a lure, where there would be no talk of colonists abandoning the station and landing on the planet, outside the authority of the captains and the crew.

Park *Phoenix* at Maudit, they'd said in those days. Build a station, mine the asteroids and moons which were not so far distant from Maudit—and stay entirely space-based, above an uninhabited planet nobody in their right minds would want to choose as a residence.

Their colonist population had wanted none of it. They'd deserted the station in droves as relations between the station administration and colonists deteriorated—the colonists absolutely dead set *against* pulling off to Maudit, the ship's captains and crew dead set on doing it. So they'd finally drawn *Phoenix* off with a complement of high administration and willing colonists—with the stated objective of finding a better world at another star.

In point of fact, they'd seen no chance of winning under current circumstances, and had set out, in the typical Long View of their spacefaring kind, to win the argument and give their ship the base they wanted by producing a new batch of colonists who'd support their ship at another base, far away, at a planeted system—so they said. Their real objective had been to get far from the temptation of the atevi world and build a civilization in space.

Now, centuries later, back on the original station, with the rescued Reunioners, the ship-captains had a problem. They'd not anticipated the antagonism between colonists. Neither Mospheira nor Tabini would let them land the Reunioners and be rid of them *that* way—

So, during the last eventful year, the captains had fallen in with the Maudit plan again—give the Reunioners a whole station of their own at Maudit. And gain all the mineral resources Maudit offered. Gain the wider spread of human population. It was a quiet suggestion. It had taken off on the wings of Mospheiran agreement.

The Reunioners, Geigi had reported, had also leapt on that idea. It seemed to be win-win. The Mospheirans were for it . . . as the fastest way to see the last of most of the Reunioners.

There was just that troublesome issue of who was going to be in charge of the Maudit colony. Depend on it—*that* question had immediately surfaced. There was no getting away from the fact that the Reunioners expected to be in charge of whatever they built new; and the Mospheirans were bent on seeing they were in charge of nothing.

True, Cajeiri's young associates were Reunioner children—but one might have assumed the *children* were innocent of plots.

"So," Geigi said eventually, on his one sip of the brandy and a long pause for thought. "You have had as much experience of the Reunion-humans as I have. And with far more understanding. One has not wanted to poison the situation by bringing politics into the matter. But—"

"The Reunion humans are a difficult lot," Bren said. "I was on the ship with them."

And Tabini hadn't been. The whole Mospheiran-Reunion question was a human question. Tabini, at the moment, was not taking on additional problems. Tabini had come back from two years of hiding and dodging assassination attempts and had a great deal on his mind that didn't at any point involve understanding the Reunioners.

His son, with whom he had a difficult relationship, *wanted* the Reunioner children for a two-week visit. Cajeiri had been promised it—last year. Cajeiri had looked forward to it, clinging to his ship-speak and his memory of the only children he had ever played with in his adult-surrounded life.

No, Tabini had had no expectation the *children* were going to cause a problem, since the paidhi-aiji hadn't been convinced there was a problem. Tabini wanted to keep a promise to his son and win his son back—the same as Damiri wanted, only more so. *Cajeiri* was Tabini's heir. Next in line to be aiji.

And on that boy's man'chi, his sense of loyalty to his father and his kind, the future of the world depended.

"What problem do you see in this visit happening, Geigi-ji? Inform me. And you need not be politic at this hour. Have I been wrong?"

That Tabini didn't understand was possibly his fault. But it might be one of those damnable instances of inter-cultural reticence. Which is worse—to have the boy re-new acquaintances with children of a troublesome population—or to have him always *wanting* it, into his adult life?

"There are nuances of behavior in this which trouble me," Geigi said, "the more since I began to help this contact along. The parents at first strongly opposed this association, and that seemed natural, given the general mistrust of the Reunion-humans toward us and the slow poisoning of the relationships on the station. I had met with the captains some time ago, to try to explain the situation on Earth, but then one parent began to ask why the children's letters went unanswered, and the captains *and* the children's parents seemed to lean in favor of a meeting. This led me to bring the letters down. This is where one belatedly asks human advice."

"Tell me what you observe."

"This. You know about the Maudit issue."

"Yes."

"The Reunion humans have, for most of the year, been unanimous in favor of going to Maudit. Now they have developed a splinter group that opposes the idea—the ship-aijiin believe them to be a labor group that has fallen out with Reunion leaders. This group, about five hundred of the five thousand, want to become citizens of the station here, assuming the Maudit expedition does eventually launch. They claim they will sustain themselves in the trades. This does not please us, of course, since we have our own industry, and a niche for them limits us. The ship-aijiin, for their part, do not trust their political motives and do not trust the faction that wants to leave, either. Mospheiran humans are asking atevi to join them in a call for a referendum on allowing any Reunioners to remain on the station, and to vote *against* the Reunion humans being allowed to stay. This was going on when I left."

That was a nasty chain of developments. But—

"Do you think the children's parents are trying to avoid being sent out to Maudit? That they hope a connection of this sort could prevent their being removed?"

"There is, as always, the subtext," Geigi said. "Remember, Bren-ji, half a year ago, there had attempted to be a vote about the use of *Phoenix* as a transport for Maudit, to get the operation underway immediately. The Mospheiran humans wanted it—they wanted to be rid of the Reunion humans as soon as possible. We were with them at the start. But the ship-humans denied that any station vote could bind their ship to do anything at all. A station vote would challenge their authority, on a matter of principle and their law. We then abstained from that vote, as an uncivilized suggestion, if the ship-aijiin were standing on privilege of their territory. The vote, you recall, failed."

A very small sip of brandy. Geigi had talked a great deal tonight. His voice grew hoarse.

"And that meant the Maudit venture was foreseeably delayed. Then came the counter-proposal: to have shuttlecraft built specifically for Maudit, largely robotized, to deliver cargo and colonists in stages and continue to serve as freighters, followed by the usual infighting: the Mospheiran humans demand Mospheiran piloted craft all under the control of the Alpha station; the Reunion humans want piloted craft controlled by Reunion humans, based at Maudit. The ship-humans are now standing with the Mospheiran humans and have abandoned the robotic option. I have tended to the idea we should vote with the ship-humans and the Mospheirans. But now I think this whole Maudit matter should be reconsidered. These two populations hate each other. I am beginning to think it will lead to trouble nobody will benefit from."

He had heard about the business. Mospheiran news had reported it. He had had his reports from Geigi. In the Mospheiran press, the Maudit colony had begun to look very much like a dead issue. He had brought it up with Geigi. But when they had talked about it, it had not been in the context of the children's visit, and something had interrupted the conversation: he could not recall what, at the moment—the assassination attempt in Sarini Province had jarred his attention sharply elsewhere.

"One strongly agrees," Bren said. "Neither side will keep agreements, Geigi-ji, so long as one group thinks they should rule the other. Maudit will not settle it. It would make it worse."

"The crisis will come on the station, then," Geigi said, "and one dislikes to see it. Station-humans are politicking very hard with the ship-humans, to secure a lasting association between them, being space-born humans. I can use their words, but what I am asking, Bren-ji, is whether my interpretation is accurate. We *and* the Mospheirans can out-vote the Reunion-humans. But one asks—will Mospheira then break from us at some future date? Are we placing ourselves in the midst of a human quarrel in which human loyalty will dictate some turn we do not foresee?"

There was nothing Bren could say, no reassurance he could give, and Geigi nodded. "It is some human signal I have missed, then."

"It is not."

"Which brings us to this business of the children."

"How so, Geigi-ji?"

"The Reunion-humans who do not want to go to Maudit, the ones who want to stay, use this word *assimilation*."

"To become in-clan," Bren said. "To become one with the Mospheirans. This is what we initially hoped would happen. But the way politics has so readily sprung up, no, not so easily. This is a power struggle. These people have seen a very frightening situation out in space, alone. Fear of being abandoned. Fear and distrust of their leaders— remember that their leaders *take* power by having a coalition of supporters. Distrust of the leaders is very possible. There will be a rival set of leaders attempting to gain followers. They will turn to the ship-humans, once they see the Mospheirans will not give them positions of authority. Maudit is an issue—but one they will politicize and argue for years. I suspect the Maudit issue is already dead, though some will not admit it. And as I see it, Mospheirans and ship-humans would be very wise to stay united with atevi."

"This insanity equals Marid politics."

"It is not that different. Except that among these humans there are no clans. There will be a committee in charge, and you will see a great deal more milling about than atevi will do. Let me guess now. The children's parents are in this number who want *assimilation*."

"Yes. Precisely. Three of them seem not so enthusiastic about their children being guests here, and one of those three, oldest of the boys, named Bjorn, aged thirteen, is now in an advanced training program—he is very bright, and has real prospects. His mother is very reluctant to see him give that up, since he might risk dismissal, should he accept the young gentleman's invitation. The questions of the parents of the other two boys were reportedly about safety and supervision, which seems a natural thing. In the case of the girl Irene, however—I have this from the ship-humans—her mother has been fearful and suspicious of atevi. She was embarrassed by Irene's meetings with the young gentleman on the ship, and was strongly against any association. I have been warned of this. Yet at a certain point she personally brought a set of letters which she said *she* had withheld, and was very polite, if highly nervous. One is suspicious that these letters are of recent composition. They lack the historical references of the others. And yes, we have read them."

"One would not fault that at all, Geigi-ji."

"There are indications, my sources say, that this woman has been approached by others of exactly the sort you forewarn . . . but it would not be a turn of man'chi driving this change of mind, would it? What, then, can so profoundly change this mother's opinion? She is a woman without administrative skills. She has been public in her detestation of atevi. Now she approaches my office bowing after our fashion and begging to have her daughter go."

"She is not likely leading anything," Bren said bluntly. "But may have someone urging her to be part of this. One cannot fault your observation in the least, Geigi-ji. The three reluctant ones ask proper questions. Irene-nadi's mother believes her child will be in the hands of those she hates. Yet what she can gain from sending her must matter more. That is my opinion."

Geigi drew in a breath. "All this came up just as I was leaving and trying to gather information on the situation on the coast. I brought the letters. I have apprehensions I attempted to convey to the aiji. But I am feeling I am caught between whatever these Reunioners are up to and my aiji's determination to keep a promise to his son. I attempted to explain the situation to Tabini. He asked me only if I saw any danger to the young gentleman at the hands of any of these children, and I pointed out that they might attempt to gain favors and influence. He said that that goes on daily and that is fully within the young gentleman's understanding. I argued the situation further tonight, attempting to explain that these are not Mospheiran children, and that their parents may attempt to use the connection to political advantage. He said I should discuss the matter with you, and that we should take measures, but that he cannot now go back on his promise. Excuses can still be found to stop this meeting or at least delay it until some of these issues are settled. I can prevent their coming. I shall take it on my head, if necessary."

"It would greatly distress the young gentleman," Bren said, "and I have every confidence our young gentleman himself is no fool where it comes to people trying to get their way. If one of his associates presses him too far, I have every confidence they will rapidly meet his great-grandmother's teaching face to face. The changes in him and the changes in them in the last year will, I think, more confuse the human children than they will him. I have thought about this. I am most concerned that there have *been* no other children in his vicinity—unless one counts two of his bodyguards—and he has never forgotten what he considers the happiest time in his life. If we attempt to stop him meeting with them—we create a frustrated desire that may have the worst result, *particularly* if these children develop political notions."

Geigi nodded. "So. In the aiji's view, he expects the meeting will go badly and that disappointment will cure all desire in the young gentleman. But in my view, Irene-nadi's disappointment will not blunt the ambitions of Irene-nadi's *mother.*"

"One other thing could happen, Geigi-ji. One or more of these children *might* become a useful ally for the young gentleman, in his own day."

"One would wish that," Geigi said. "For the young gentleman's sake. Or if not—he does have you to set it in perspective." He finished the little left in the glass and set it down. "I have grown quite happy in my human associates, Bren-ji. In a sense—one could wish the young gentleman as felicitous an acquaintance as we both have. But I do fear the opposite is more likely the case. Note— the boy Gene, too, is a rebellious sort, already acquainted with station security. But then—one could say that of the young gentleman himself. At least—whoever supervises them should be forewarned of that."

That somewhat amused him. "We keep a watch on the young gentleman. So we shall at least give them the chance, Geigi-ji. We shall. The young gentleman will deal with it. I think his expectations actually *are* tempered with practicality. Remember who taught him."

"Well, well, you greatly reassure me." Geigi rose, and Bren did. And then Geigi did something very odd. He put out his hand and smiled. "I have learned your custom, you see."

Bren laughed and took it, warmly, and even clapped Geigi on the arm. "You are unique, Geigi-ji. You are a most treasured associate. What would I do without you?"

"Well, we are neither of us destined for a peaceful life, Bren-ji. But we take what we can, baji-naji. I have so enjoyed your hospitality."

"Good night, Geigi-ji. I shall miss you."

"Good night, my host," Geigi said, and exited the office, into the hall.

Supani was still waiting. But not waiting alone. Banichi was there, and walked with Bren and Supani, into Bren's bedroom.

That was unusual. "Is something afoot?" he asked Banichi, quietly, while Supani took his coat.

"Important business," Banichi said. "But not urgent, at this hour. Rest assured everything is on schedule. Security is arranged, the car is under watch tonight, and we shall have no delays in the morning." Then he said, to Supani, "The paidhi will wear the vest tomorrow, Pani-ji. And on every outing until I say otherwise."

"Yes," Supani said without missing a beat.

The vest was only good sense, Bren thought. He was not surprised at that requirement, given recent history.

"Jago will be here," Banichi said, and that Jago would arrive in his bedroom was nothing unusual: they had been lovers for years. But that Banichi said it—Banichi meant something unusual was going on.

"Yes," he muttered. He suddenly felt the whole strain of the past several hours. He wished he had more energy, to dive fresh into whatever the Guild had done, or was doing, and he wanted desperately to know, but he was running right now on a very low ebb.

"It can wait," Banichi said.

The hell it could. Tension that he had dismissed in his conversation with Geigi had entered the room with his bodyguard. He smelled it, he felt it in the air. Supani, a servant of whom not even his bodyguard had doubts, helped him off with his shirt, and Supani asked in a very low voice, "Will you still want the bath in the servants' hall, nandi?"

"Yes," he said. Geigi, his guest, a man of great girth, facing a long flight, absolutely needed the master bath. The little shower in the back passages was all he needed. He stripped down, flung on his bathrobe, and headed out, with Banichi, whose route to his bodyguards' rooms, next to the servant quarters, lay in the same direction.

"Truly it can wait?" he asked Banichi, in the dim hallway outside the servants' bath.

"It was an interesting meeting," Banichi said quietly. "Not surprisingly, the matter involves Ajuri."

God. It was very possible he'd stepped squarely into the middle of that situation, intervening with Damiri tonight.

"One hopes not to have caused a problem tonight, Nichi-ji. The dowager made a gesture of peace toward Damiri. One attempted to intervene on the side of reconciliation, for good or for ill. One has no idea of the outcome. Tabini-aiji suggested, in private, that Damiri may try to take Ajuri as lord and he would oppose it."

"An assessment he has also given us," Banichi said. "The consort taking Ajuri would sever her from the Atageini, even if she then makes peace with them. There are things we do not believe either the dowager or the aiji yet know, Bren-ji."

"About Damiri?"

"About Ajuri," Banichi said, which widened the range of possible ills by at least a factor of two, and assured he was not going to get a restful sleep tonight. "Jago will tell you. Be extremely careful where you discuss any of this."

"Get some rest," he said to Banichi.

"Things did not go that badly," Banichi said to him in parting. He was sure it was for his comfort.

"One hopes not," he said. "I have learned things from Geigi I should mention, too."

"Your bodyguard knows," Banichi said, and Bren blinked. Of course there was monitoring. He hadn't expected it to go on that late, with Geigi. But it was a relief to him that they *had* heard. Reconstructing it all, tired as he was, was beyond him.

"Good," he said.

"We shall just have a cheerful trip tomorrow," Banichi said, "and discuss the weather throughout. Leave Geigi's briefing to Geigi's bodyguard once they launch. None of it affects him. Have your bath, Bren-ji. And rest."

Bath. It was a shower. He no more than scrubbed and rinsed, threw his bathrobe on, and was on his way out the door when Jago came into the servant bath, in her robe.

"Jago-ji."

Jago folded her arms and shut the door. "We can talk," she said. "Narani and Jeladi have been extremely careful."

Not all Guild went in uniform. Narani, that elderly, kindly gentleman, was an example. Bindanda, the cook, was another.

And if Jago said the area was secure and Narani had kept it that way, it was secure.

"One asks," he said. "One does not even frame a specific question, for fear of misdirecting the answer. Tell me what I need to know, Jago-ji."

"First, dealing with any aspect of it can wait until we have seen Lord Geigi into orbit."

"He is not involved," he said. He would bet his life on Geigi's integrity. He had made that bet. Repeatedly.

"He is involved as an ally. But if we told him everything we know, we might not get him off the ground. We have briefed his aishid: they will brief him."

"One understands." He did. Perfectly. "And the aiji?"

Jago drew a deep breath. "By the Guild Charter, we *can* inform the aiji directly of whatever touches his security and the security of the aishidi'tat, and what he then chooses to tell his bodyguard is not regulated—which has been our route for this and other matters."

Since the last Guild-chosen bodyguard had attempted to kill him, Tabini had hand-picked four young distant relatives within the Guild. He had done it over conservative objections, bitter regional objections, and very heated Guild objections; and the Guild now had constantly to maneuver around that stone in the information flow at the very highest levels. It *would* not grant the aiji's bodyguards a higher ranking or higher clearance until they certified higher. And that temporarily left the aiji-dowager and, ironically, the paidhi-aiji, with the highest ranking bodyguards on earth and above it . . . and the aiji guarded by young men who had to get their information from next door.

"We have several immediate problems," Jago said, "and your need to know, Bren-ji, has also come up against Guild regulations. So we, and Cenedi and his team—we have observed several things regarding which we are routinely going to violate Guild regulations. You need to know these matters. First is something the aiji can deal with—the Ajuri feud with the Atageini. Lady Damiri's father, Lord Komaji, is back in Ajuri, telling his version of what happened, and why he was dismissed, and why Lady Damiri's staff was dismissed. His lies involve your influence, and the desire of the aiji-dowager to subvert her great-grandson. His version states that Damiri-daja is being held prisoner and abused, and that Tabini intends to take her daughter from her."

"One is not surprised he would lie," Bren said.

"The troubling matter is that these lies have a purpose and a clear deadline, beyond which they will start to unravel."

"The birth of the baby. News coverage."

"We have concerns. Lord Komaji's bodyguard is not that highly ranked: he has somewhat the aiji's problem. But four other, higher-ranked teams have moved into Ajuri and we cannot get at their records even to find out the names involved. We have access that should be able to do so. But that access does not turn up these particular records."

"Shadow Guild?" That splinter group lurking within

the Assassins' Guild. The driving power behind so much of what had gone wrong in recent years.

"We have that concern. We know that that organization was not all located in the Marid. And we know some that are dead. But we have not accounted for others. That is one matter. Lord Ajuri with his own aishid poses no great threat. We are no longer sure that it is *just* his aishid protecting him, or even that he is the one giving the orders in Ajuri district. Second, Lord Tatiseigi has persistently offered Damiri staff from his estate. We advise against this and have advised Tabini-aiji to that effect. We have also advised Lord Tatiseigi's household to keep him from going home until further notice."

That, for a tired brain, required two thoughts to parse. Then he did. Damiri had been born at Tirnamardi, Lord Tatiseigi's estate, in Atageini territory. "Damiri's father was in that house," he said.

"He was resident there for a year and a half," Jago said.

Servants moved into other houses as lords married: they formed associations, left, or stayed on as their lord moved home, at the end of a contract relationship, or in its breakup. They were a lingering and troublesome legacy of any ill-fated marriage between clans.

"You think Tirnamardi is infiltrated," he said. "A servant who came in with Komaji."

"An assassination attempt against Lord Tatiseigi from within is not our chief worry, given Komaji's rank at the time, the disposition of Guild-trained servants usually not running to violence. However the leaks on that staff we have generally attributed to the Kadagidi relationship with that house—may not all flow in the direction of the Kadagidi. Or not *only* in that direction."

Kadagidi. The usurper Murini's clan. Neighbors and one-time associates of the Atageini, a relationship which had, over time, gone very, very bad.

There went all inclination to sleep. *How,* he wanted to ask, but Jago had already warned him she could not say.

The Kadagidi were not in attendance at the current legislative session, and would not be, by their announced intention: *We are taking a year of contemplation and assessment . . .*

Like hell. They would not be in attendance because they had not yet been permitted to show their faces in court. They were Murini's clan. The usurper had been *their* clan lord, though not a popular one. Aseida, the new lord of the Kadagidi, had bodyguards who claimed to have been attached to Aseida from childhood, but . . .

But . . . there was some question on that point. It was an ongoing investigation. Algini had revealed, in one of his rare, need-to-know briefings, that Aseida, lord of the Kadagidi, was nothing but a figurehead. Algini believed the true force within the Kadagidi was one Haikuti, seniormost of Aseida's aishid. Haikuti was a man Algini didn't trust. Tano had said Haikuti should be taken out, but that that would simply scatter the problem.

And, he'd said, Haikuti might not be acting on his own. That he might have a superior hidden deep within the Guild.

Now nameless senior teams had been moved into Ajuri, to call the shots for another noticeably underpowered lord.

Someone able to position units in the field. He had this image of some senior administrator up in Guild Headquarters, quietly moving the right people about like pieces on a chessboard, somebody the honest Guild would never suspect . . . shuddery thought.

When they'd come back from space, there'd been an immediate house-cleaning in the Assassins' Guild, retired members coming back to take their old offices and Murini's supporters leaving town in haste.

They might have missed one, however, someone in a position to affect records, cover tracks, and protect others who should have been caught.

"Are you saying Kadagidi is tied to the Ajuri, Jago-ji?"

"We know at least that a leak in Tirnamardi ran to both the Kadagidi *and* Ajuri—regarding one matter: the specific names of the servants offered to Damiri-daja. One," Jago added with a grim laugh, "was misspelled the same way in both instances."

He had for several months been a little worried about Ajuri—a minor clan, head of a minor association. Minor in every way but one: being Damiri's paternal clan.

Tabini had married Damiri because of her *Atageini* connections. Atageini clan, Tatiseigi's, was a solid, and important, key in the ancient Padi Valley Association.

And Atageini had supported Tabini in his return—at the risk of its entire existence.

Only then, once the tide had started to turn, had Ajuri shown up and joined Tabini's cause, which was being fought on Tatiseigi's land. They'd arrived late: they'd tagged onto Tabini's triumphant return to Shejidan—and once safe in Shejidan others of the family had come in, all anxious to cluster around Cajeiri and Damiri and her father. Her aunt, her cousins . . . all had arrived full of solicitation and professed support.

Next time they blinked—the Ajuri lord was dead and Damiri's father was lord and still hovering around the aiji's household, laying claim to his grandson, wanting special privileges and trying to push both Tatiseigi and Ilisidi out of the family picture.

He'd pushed, until one incident in which Tabini had lost patience, thrown the man out on his ear, and tossed Damiri's Ajuri bodyguards and servants directly after him . . . one of them a nurse from Damiri's childhood.

"What of Damiri-daja?" He really didn't want to ask that question. But he had to.

"Carrying a viable heir," Jago said, completely off the track of Damiri's personal man'chi. "And if the aiji *and* his firstborn son were dead, Damiri-daja would *still* be carrying the heir, and Komaji would be the heir's grandfather. Damiri would likely become aiji-regent."

It was a warm room, the bath. But the heavy air held a chill. He felt all the fatigue of the day and rued that extra half brandy. He needed his brain. And tried to assimilate what Jago was saying.

"One is quite appalled, Jago-ji," he murmured, while the human side of his brain just said, *damn!* "She talked, Tabini said, about taking the lordship of Ajuri from her father. Tabini opposes it. We are not talking about

Komaji's forced retirement in that case. Are we? We are talking about assassinating her father. Is that talk from her a smokescreen?"

"We are concerned," Jago said. "We want Geigi back in the heavens, where the aiji's enemies have to fear him, and where his authority cannot be threatened. We have tried earlier this year to improve Lord Tatiseigi's security, and he would have none of it, then—but now we have the cooperation of his aishid. They are not young men, not agile, not familiar with modern equipment, and we have told them enough to have them very worried. We are moving in two young teams from Malguri, under the guise of an investigation of the neighbors—not entirely untrue. Their principal duty will be protection of Tatiseigi's household, and instruction of his bodyguard in certain equipment they have not used before. This is entirely outside Guild approval, understand: we have not consulted anyone. The dowager is calling it a courtesy. A loan. And Cenedi has not mentioned it in Guild Council." Jago stood away from the wall, square on her feet. "Two of Cenedi's men are going down to the station tonight to go over the red train thoroughly, and we will be sure the transportation is safe and secure. So do not worry about tomorrow."

"Do you think this situation with Ajuri is going to blow up, or simmer away for a season? We have Cajeiri's guests coming down. That seems certain now. We shall have a fairly controversial, politically sensitive handful of children on holiday. This will be a magnet for Ajuri interest, among others."

"And the news services will be very occupied with it."

"Geigi says he could still prevent this visit."

"Best," Jago said, "that it proceed—barring something we have not foreseen. It will let us move about, too, and shift assets without questions raised."

He was appalled. And his brain was overloaded. "Jago-ji. We cannot use these children for a decoy."

"We shall not," Jago said. "*Our* man'chi is to you, and to Tabini-aiji. We simply ask you let us do as we see necessary for your protection. The young gentleman and his guests—assuming you will be involved with them, which is likely—will give us an opportunity to move in additional security, at various places on the map, assigning them as if they were temporary, without anyone asking too closely into why. We shall be ready to deal with any adverse situations on the peripheries, and once we have sent these visitors back to the space station—we shall simply fail to remove some of our precautions. We *will* be in a better position, and Ajuri may reconsider its adventurous moves."

That made sense. The balance was what had gotten grossly disrupted. Getting the various sub-associations to settle into a sense of security—or at least a conviction that they would be fools to make a move to upset the peace—was a restoration of the status quo. The whole last year had been full of threats and adjustments—aftershocks from the coup and Tabini's return to power—and that was nothing to the disruptions of the previous two years under Murini.

Getting the balance back—settling the aishdi'tat at peace—that would let them deal with the problems Geigi had talked about in the heavens, which were no small matter in themselves.

Deal with them *before* the aliens that had caused the Reunioners to be withdrawn in the first place showed up for a visit and for a look at this place where two species managed to get along . . .

They had *promised* the kyo that was the case, and they had to demonstrate it. The kyo did not share a human *or* an atevi mindset, and agreement with the kyo, *peace* with the kyo, rode on things here being as advertised.

"Meanwhile," Jago said, "well that we all get some sleep, Bren-ji. Tomorrow we shall start to solve these things."

Solve things. He liked that notion.

Saying so didn't make them safer, or make the situation more secure. God, there were so many angles on what was going on, he didn't know what to take hold of, or what to look at askance.

He and Jago had their own methods of distraction, when they had a problem that, as Jago said, made a very poor pillow.

And they were going to need all of them, to get any sleep tonight.

4

Morning brought Cajeiri his two servants, Eisi and Lieidi, stirring about in the suite. And Cajeiri's head hurt.

That could be the brandy. It was supposed to be really good brandy. It had not tasted that good. Like a cross between medicine and really rotten fruit.

But he had only had half a glass of it. There had been a lot of glasses sitting about, and he had had to go entertain himself while his mother and great-grandmother went about the room chatting as if they were closest allies. He had seen adults, when they had to deal with something upsetting, have a whole glass at once. It was supposed to make them feel better about their problems, at least for the moment.

So he had stolen a mostly-full glass and gone off behind a group of guests to drink it.

If he had drunk a whole glass last night, he was sure his head might explode.

"Are you well, young gentleman?" Eisi asked, standing by his bed.

With one's servants one could be entirely honest, and had a right to expect loyalty.

"You are not to tell my parents," he said, with his arm over his eyes, "but I drank a little brandy from a glass someone left and I am not feeling well this morning. One does not think it was poisoned." That was always a worry, in a large company, but these were his father's closest allies, and somebody had already drunk half of it and not died, or there would have been a commotion. "I only had half a glass."

"You should not be having brandy at all, young lord," Eisi said. "Not for a number of years."

"One knows that," he said. "But how long before this goes away?" An excruciating thought came to him. "Please do not tell my mother."

"Your mother, nandi, is having tea in the sitting room with your great-grandmother."

That. Gods. It was not good. "*Please* do not let either of them know I am sick."

"We can bring you something that will help," Eisi said.

"Please do not draw questions!"

"I shall be extremely quiet about it, nandi."

Eisi went away for a while. Cajeiri heard the opening and closing of the distant door, hoped that Eisi would not get stopped and questioned, whatever he was doing. A long, miserable time later, he heard someone come back into the suite.

Footsteps. Eisi turned up by his bedside with a small glass of fruit juice. "Drink this. It will help."

His stomach was far from certain it could even hold on to what it had. Or that it should. His head was sure it was a bad idea to move. But Eisi had risked everything getting him this remedy. He got up on one elbow.

"It is salty," Eisi forewarned him. "But it will help. Drink it all."

No punishment ever tasted good, and he was sure this was punishment. Salted fruit juice was awful, but not as awful as it sounded, and he actually had no trouble drinking the whole glass.

Then he let his head down to the pillow to be miserable again.

"Feed Boji, nadi-ji," he asked Eisi. "I shall lie here a while."

"About half an hour," Eisi said, "and you should feel significantly better, young gentleman."

"I hope so," he said, and Eisi left and shut the bedroom door, leaving him in the dark, in his misery.

His aishid, who ordinarily lived with him, in those rooms just outside his door, would tell him he had been an idiot to drink it ... especially Lucasi and Veijico. Better yet, they would have told him that last night, *before* he did it. They would have told him the consequences. They were older, and probably knew about things like drinking. *And* they were qualified to carry guns, which was what Antaro and Jegari were trying to become. He so hoped Antaro and Jegari would not become all proper and forget how to laugh.

But they had to—get qualified to carry guns, that was; not forget how to laugh. They were over at Guild Headquarters, taking tests to get an emergency qualification, not just to carry weapons, but a lot more that most Guild didn't learn 'til they were much, *much,* older, because they were *his* aishid, and being the aiji's son put *him* in more danger than most bodyguards had to deal with. He understood the necessity, miserable as it was, and worrisome as it was to have anybody but him telling Antaro and Jegari what to do.

Before he'd gotten *his* aishid, he had had borrowed older Guild protecting him. High-ranking Guild—and *they* had not been able to prevent things happening. They could not even prevent *him* doing things he shouldn't ... like drinking that brandy last night.

But the four he had now ... they were good. They understood him and when *they* advised against doing something it was for good reasons, not just arbitrary adult reasons. Antaro and Jegari were only a little older than he was, but they had grown up hunting in the forests in Taiben, so they'd learned to shoot and hit a target and walk very softly a long time ago.

It was just handling weapons in public places, Lucasi and Veijico said, that took special training ... and they could pass. He was sure they could. And they would be back soon. *Very* soon.

But not soon enough. He sighed and wondered how

long it had been since he'd had Eisi's medicine, and how long before his head stopped hurting.

Veijico and Lucasi were older, but not *that* old. They were real Guild, though, and his father had assigned them to him, when he had been in the middle of the trouble over in Najida. They were good. They had had a reputation in the Guild for being too independent, too stubborn, and too reckless. He had overheard that from his great-grandmother and Cenedi. They had had problems. They had gotten in a lot of trouble, over on the coast.

But Banichi and Cenedi had gotten hold of them and they had reformed. They had been downright arrogant, and thought themselves too good to be assigned to guard a boy. But they had changed their minds, after everything, and they had sworn man'chi to him and meant it. He so wished he had had them to stop him last night. They might have done reckless things, themselves, but he was very sure they would have stopped him from drinking the brandy.

And he was so glad they were not here to see him this morning, even if he did wish they were all here now.

Last night—when he had had that very bad notion to try the brandy—because it was supposed to make one calm and happy—

Last night had been gruesome. Most of it, anyway. Mother and Great-grandmother had made peace. Officially. But not really. They had put on a show for politics and they were having tea this morning, and he was glad they could at least agree to do that. But it did not mean they were going to get along, and that his mother was going to forget she was upset.

He wished they really could get together, but Mother and Great-grandmother, his mani, were just too different. And worst of all, their quarrel mostly was about him, and things he just could not change. Mother was jealous of Great-grandmother. His parents had sent him off to Great-grandmother right before the troubles started in Shejidan, and there was no fixing it now. He had been with his Great-grandmother, up in the space station, and then on the starship, and he had been with her all the way, when they had met the kyo and gotten the Reunioners off their station and all—it had taken them two whole years, most of it just traveling, but he'd been learning all the time from Great-grandmother, and he couldn't help it if, sometimes, he turned to her first.

But his parents had had a terrible time, while he and mani had been in space. Murini of the Kadagidi had gotten together a conspiracy and shot up his parents' apartment and killed innocent people there, and in Taiben, where his parents really were; and his parents had had to get away into the woods and the mountains and move from place to place with people hunting them. That was what his father and mother had been through.

And when he and Great-grandmother had gotten back, the whole world was in a mess, and Greatgrandmother and nand' Bren had gone down anyway—they had gotten to Uncle Tatiseigi and started an uprising against Murini. And his father and mother had come in, and they had gone to Shejidan, with the people cheering them all the way. It had felt very good, then.

Except his mother was very jealous of Greatgrandmother, because he had come back older and smarter, and knowing how to do things, and she had not taught him. Great-grandmother had. Great-grandmother was powerful. Great-grandmother did whatever she wanted. And people cheered for Great-grandmother, and for Father—but maybe not so much for his mother, and he did not know what to do to patch things. He knew what he knew. He knew that what Great-grandmother had taught him was the proper way.

It probably had not helped that he and his father and his mother had had to live all together in Greatgrandmother's apartment with Great-grandmother's guard and Great-grandmother's staff until they could take all Murini's things out of their proper apartment and rebuild and repaint it, top to bottom, for security reasons.

It had not helped, too, that Grandfather showed up, and Aunt Geidaro, who had once been married to, of all people, Murini's cousin—who had had nothing to do

with the coup, since he was dead; but still, Father had
sent *her* home. Maybe Mother had not favored that. And
then there was Grandfather —

Grandfather had pitched a fit, when they finally got
into their own apartment. He had shown up at the door
when it was just *him* at home — with the servants and his
aishid — and Grandfather had wanted in, *really* wanted
in, and Cajeiri had locked himself into his room — *that*
had been scary. Grandfather had acted crazy. And he had
not wanted Grandfather in the house.

Father had had his own fit when he got home, and
banished Grandfather from the capital and banished all
Mother's staff, every one of them, from her bodyguard
to the maid who had been her nurse when she was a
baby — that last had been the one he would have stuck at,
himself, but he understood. It was the people closest to
you the longest who could be really efficient spies, and
could turn and kill you and everybody if you were wrong
about their man'chi. She had become a security risk, and
so she had to go, and that was probably the person his
mother missed the most. That was the person who had
been with his mother when *he* was born, but who would
not be there for this new baby. His mother was upset
about that.

His father said his mother would be less excitable
once the baby came. He hoped so. His mother wanted
him when he was absent and wanted rid of him when he
was there; and that was the way things were, three and
four times a day.

It had been the worst when all of them together were
trying to live in mani's apartment, and when mani's rules
were what the staff followed.

He had so hoped his mother would calm down when
they got their own apartment back.

But mani was right. Mani always said: that there was
no way to change somebody else's mind, that *that person*
had to change, and that they had to *want* to change, and
the older they were, the less chance they were ever *going*
to change, so there was no good expecting it to happen
some morning for no particular reason.

That sort of summed the numbers up. No matter which order you added numbers, they always added the same. Mani said that, too: if you ever thought you would get a different answer from the same numbers—you were wrong, that was all.

So he doubted mani and Mother were really making peace, not in the party last night and not in the sitting room over tea.

He heard the sitting room door open and close again as he was lying there. He heard footsteps go from the hall to the foyer. And he heard the outer door open and shut.

Then, farther away, he heard his mother's door shut. Hard.

He heaved a deep, deep sigh, with his stomach still upset.

Lord Geigi was going away to space again. He was sad about that. He was going to miss Geigi. Geigi was fun. And Geigi had brought his letters from the station. *All* his letters from his associates on the ship. And Geigi had spoken up for him and his father had agreed to have his associates come down for his birthday. He would be grateful for that for all his life.

He just had to be really, really good for the next number of days, and not make his mother mad, and he would get his birthday—if nobody started a war and if nobody found out about the brandy he was so stupid as to have drunk last night.

He would have his guests, all his associates from the ship, that he had not seen in a whole year, his eighth, which was not a lucky number, and not a lucky year. One did not celebrate it, mani had said.

But this year, his ninth, was supposed to be *very* fortunate, because it was three threes of years.

Oh, he wanted that year to start, because a lot of bad things really had happened in his eighth, his infelicitous year, which was two sets of two sets of twos, and just awful. He was still scared his mother was going to try to stop his party happening—his mother did not favor nand' Bren, or any human. His mother blamed nand'

Bren's advice for his having been sent to mani in the first place, and she was appalled at human influences on him. That was what she called it: *appalled*. She had said he was going to grow up abnormal. That he should not *have* human associates,

But she had said that months ago, when she and his father were fighting. And his father had said that if they had not had nand' Bren and Jase-paidhi and Yolanda-paidhi, up on the station, the whole world would have been in trouble.

And his mother had shouted back that if they had not had them advising them, Murini never could have had his coup and they would not have been living in the woods in the winter.

His father had had the last word. His father had said what was the truth: that the heavens were wider than the Earth and that if they had not had nand' Bren and the rest advising them, they would have been sitting on the Earth with the space station totally in the hands of the worst sort of humans . . . who had had their own coup going, except for nand' Bren and Jase-paidhi.

His father was right about that. But things had just gotten quiet again. The walls in mani's apartment were just thick enough to prevent one hearing the end of arguments, and he had no idea what his mother had said then. She at least had never called him abnormal again.

Sometimes during that *beyond* infelicitous eighth year he had just *had* to do *something* to get his mind off the problems. He *had* gotten in trouble a few times, but he had not *stolen* the train to go to Najida.

He had just gotten on it.

He *had* stolen the boat, though.

Well, he had *borrowed* it.

Or it had run off with him. But nand' Bren had made that right, and paid the fisherman. He was sorry about that. He was glad nand' Bren had fixed it.

But he had been on exceptionally good behavior since he had gotten back from the coast. He had come to realize that he was very close to his birthday.

And he had his letters, now. And his father's promise.

He was *reformed*, now. He really was. He was going to be nine and do better. And he would get smarter. . . .

He was so *stupid* to have stolen that brandy last night.

Now he was at the mercy of Eisi and Lieidi, who had a sort of man'chi to him, but they were not entirely his, the way his bodyguards were.

He *hoped* would not tell his parents.

He hoped, hoped, hoped nobody took his birthday away.

5

The train was in open country now, the city left behind. Bren had been over this route so often he knew every turn of the track, every bump and swerve of the red-curtained car.

He was a little anxious in the outing—he was always a little anxious about well-publicized moves in this last year. He and Geigi were both high-value targets, and the business Jago had handed him last night . . .

That was more than a little worrisome, but it was one not apt to become acute overnight. Their enemies had taken a hammering down in the Marid, they were still being hunted out of holes down there, and it would take them time to reorganize and replot. They *might* even reform, depending on how the local man'chi sorted out.

Dealing with atevi was not dealing with humans. The sense of attachment, man'chi, that one could call loyalty, but which was so much more fundamental to the atevi instinct—was the emotion that held clans and associations together. Man'chi was as intense as human love and just as subject to twists and turns, but man'chi was a network of attachments, not a simple one-on-one. Sometimes, when the configuration of alliances changed, people changed. One could always hope a reconfiguration of possibilities and objectives could allow some who had been enemies to reinvent themselves—and have it stick.

It did happen. It was why atevi had feuds, but didn't often nurse grudges, and had *no* trouble shifting politics when situations changed.

The problems Geigi had handed him out on the peninsula ... problems involving Geigi's estate ... those he could certainly deal with. He had a good major domo at Najida, Ramaso, who had connections to the tribal people of the area, and he trusted he had established a very good relationship in that district, with his handling of recent events. Geigi, sitting across from him on the red velvet seat, sipping a little fruit-flavored tea, was heading back to space—from a world much better than the world he had landed on—and Geigi remained their ally in the sky, a powerful deterrent to complete idiocy on Earth. That situation too, and the knowledge certain people had earned Geigi's wrath, might reconfigure a few alliances.

There was morning tea and there were breakfast sandwiches, courtesy of the staff—a few of whom might not have been to bed at all last night. The staff party in the apartment had broken up to get Lord Geigi's last personal baggage and their breakfast down to the train in a secure condition—and not *just* Lord Geigi's own belongings, but baggage and breakfast for Lord Geigi's bodyguard, his several accompanying servants, *and* four more new staffers chosen from among the Edi people. That little group had arrived from the peninsula last night.

So their company numbered him and his four bodyguards; Geigi and Geigi's bodyguard, another set of five, and twelve of Geigi's staff. They were, uncharacteristically for Bren's train trips, a full and excitedly noisy car this morning, with most of them and all of the baggage heading into orbit in a few hours. The new staffers from the Edi people were facing their first flight of any kind, having come in last night by train—and they were moderately terrified, being reassured by everyone that it would be a grand experience.

It might be—for everyone but portly Geigi, who did not take to cramped shuttle seating and the necessary ground-waits in the spaceport lounge, and who dreaded the climb to orbit only as a prolonged misery.

They were down to tea, now, absolutely stuffed, in Bren's case. Satisfying Lord Geigi's appetite took a bit more, but even Geigi swore he could not down another sandwich or pickled egg, and swearing that he was always spacesick in free fall.

It did not prevent him taking another sip of tea and a little sweet cake.

"This has been quite a trip, Bren-ji. And outside of the difficulties and the gunfire, a very profitable trip. My estate saved, my nephew married—and lastingly out of my view. Which is, one hesitates not at all to admit, a very good thing."

Bren laughed. "Favor us more often, and without the gunfire, please. You will *have* to come down to see the new wing on Najida. Not to mention seeing the Edi estate built. It would be very politic for you to visit next year, Geigi-ji."

"Sly fellow. I shall try. No, very well, I *swear* I shall get down to the planet at least once a year hereafter, even if my estate is *not* missing its portico."

"Next time we may do that fishing trip. Bring Jase down with you." Jase Graham, *Captain* Jason Graham these days. Their best plans for that long-promised trip had run up against a series of disasters. "You should simply kidnap him. Stow him in baggage."

"One fears that will be the only way we may have him," Geigi laughed. "But we at least shall try. Kindly keep the world peaceable for a while and I shall do my very best."

"I shall most earnestly try, Geigi-ji."

"And most imminently, I shall go ahead and send Cajeiri's associates. I have slept on it, and I agree with you: the boy *should* have this business resolved, however it turns out, poor lad. Now *you* frown."

"Worry that we are doing the right thing, Geigi-ji."

And more worry—which he had learned last night, *after* his conversation with Geigi—that the Ajuri situation still had volatile potential. Not on the scale of the west coast mess which had brought Geigi down to the planet, and not likely immediate. There was that.

"Damiri-daja is opposed to the visit," Geigi said. "I greatly admired your approaching her after the party. I was aghast. But well done, Bren-ji. Very well done. I must say that before I go."

"You heard *all* that."

"I have excellent ears."

God. Atevi hearing. It was *so* hard to judge. "One hopes no one *else* did."

"Had Damiri-daja wished otherwise, she would have stopped it. Still . . . well done."

"One is still worried about Ajuri's reaction, Geigi-ji. They may have envisioned the aiji's displeasure being short-lived. The rebuff from Damiri will sting."

"Well, well, most clearly—the boy will have little to do with Ajuri, hereafter, in any form, so long as his grandfather is acting the fool. I have heard it from him: he wishes not to deal with the man. Protect him from Tatiseigi's sillier notions, too, where possible. Man'chi to his father is his safest course, and I sense it *is* developing in a perfectly natural way. A future aiji is bound to develop stubborn notions at a certain stage of life. That is the nature of aijiin, always the independence, the search for associations which just do not come to them in any normal way. And this boy—is his great-grandmother's child. In a sense—so is Tabini-aiji. They are in that sense brothers, more than father and son. The boy is already making appearances at his great-grandmother's side. *As* Tabini-aiji also did, in his youth, I well recall. Tabini-aiji sees the boy as growing up exactly as he did, and he finds both pride and reassurance in the occasional misbehaviors and risk-taking—another matter which Damiri-daja resents, if one may speak the absolute truth of the matter. Tabini-aiji will *not* side with his wife if she pushes the issue of the boy's attachment to the dowager. Look to Ajuri not to leave this situation alone. The gesture Damiri-daja made, in her choice of gowns—that will indeed hit hard. I swallowed half my glass in sheer amazement."

"One hopes she can make peace with her uncle Tatiseigi. As one is surprised to see *you* have done."

"Ah, that old scoundrel." Geigi gave a gentle laugh, rocking back, hands on knees. "Tatiseigi and I have at last found common ground on this visit: idiot nephews, and porcelain-collecting. I have promised him the loan of certain rare books from my library, and made him a gift of a very special regional ceramic his collection lacks. We have, in fact, become steady correspondents. Fools, both of us, where it comes to glazes and clays."

"We have become each other's dinner guests," Bren said, and they both laughed, because Tatiseigi at the paidhi's table was the least likely thing in the world.

The salted fruit juice helped, actually. Cajeiri made it to his feet and into his bathrobe, intending to go have the bath he had missed last evening. He went out into the sitting room of his little suite and Boji immediately jumped to the door of his cage, clinging to the grill, glad to see him. Boji let out a head-splitting shriek, little feet and hands shaking the door in great hope of being taken out of his cage.

"Hush," he said. Boji was not to make noise and bother the household, and it hardly helped his head. Silence was one condition of having Boji, and if he was going to leave the suite to have his bath down the hall, he could *not* give Boji the impression he was going to get out of the cage for a while and then put him immediately back in. That would guarantee shrieks and bad behavior.

It was a large cage, as big as the couch and as tall as he was, an antique brass cage. Its bars were filigree work of vines and flowers. It was specially made for Boji's kind, who, collared and leashed, retrieved eggs for their owners.

But Boji, in the city, had no way to hunt and there were no trees to climb. He was fed all the eggs he could want. His black fur was sleek and brushed and he was getting a little plump. What he lacked most was exercise. Cajeiri gave it to him when he could; but this morning

Boji just got a second egg, delivered through the little feeding gate, and was quite happily appeased, at least momentarily.

His room was very different from the rest of his father's apartment. It had white walls—everything did, and he could not change that. But he had covered the walls where he could. There was Boji's cage, and the brass vase taller than even Lucasi. There were animal carvings on all the furniture, and tapestry pictures of outdoors, mountains and fields and fortresses and such; and most of all there were plants, plants hanging from hooks all over, in every place where they could get light from fixtures in this windowless, closed-in suite. They were special lights. They shone like the sun. Housekeeping had provided them to help his plants.

His mother called it a jungle. He was sure it was not a compliment, though if anyone else had said it, he was sure he would like it. He had never been able to show his rooms to his great-grandmother, but he thought she would approve his choices. It *felt* like his great-grandmother's sort of room.

And this morning he was not so sure he really wanted his bath until he absolutely had to. He wanted to let his headache go away. He wanted no one to say anything unpleasant to him, and most of all he wanted no one to ask him why he was walking around with his face all squinched up as if he had a headache, which he certainly did. And the condition of his head and his stomach was not something he wanted gossiped about on staff. It was bad enough Eisi and Lieidi had to know he had misbehaved and drunk something from leftover glasses. He was really quite ashamed of himself. Or it was the effect of the headache and upset stomach.

Geigi and nand' Bren must be on the train at this hour, well on their way to the spaceport. He so wished he could have gone with them, to say good-bye to Lord Geigi, and just to be outside the Bujavid and out of the city entirely for a few hours. The spaceport, too, would be something to see—he had been there once in his life, but he only just remembered it as big white buildings and a long strip of concrete. When he and Great-grandmother and nand' Bren had landed back on the planet, they had landed at an airport over on the island of Mospheira, where only humans lived—*that* had been something to see.

And from Mospheira, at Port Jackson, they had crossed the straits on Bren's brother Toby's boat, and then stowed away in a rail car, and ridden mecheiti—so many ways they had traveled to get back to Shejidan. He had done all these things most people never had and before that he had had the run of the starship, and known secret passages and places nobody in the Bujavid could imagine. He had floated in air. He had seen water hang in globes you could chase.

Now he was limited to a suite of rooms in a nest of potted plants, with poor Boji in a cage.

It was because of his grandfather that he had no idea when he was going to be allowed out. And if these were the conditions he had while his guests were here, it was going to be embarrassing.

Let us see the ocean, they would say. And he would have to say no.

Let us see mecheiti, they would say. And he would have to say they could not.

He would be embarrassed to have them know how strictly he was locked in, now. He could tell them about the adventures he had had, but he could not show them any. They might think he was lying, and he could not prove anything.

And being locked in was likely the way things would be, and he would have to make the best of it and just hope his mother was polite and did not call any of *them* abnormal.

They had been through a lot. But they had settled matters on the west coast. They had had a big signing where Lord Machigi of the Taisigin Marid made an alliance with Great-grandmother. Everything had been going so well.

And then his grandfather, from just embarrassing and annoying, had gone crazy, for all he could understand,

and thrown a fit because he was excluded from Great-grandmother's party, and he had come upstairs and scared the staff. His parents' marriage had almost collapsed that same night, because of Grandfather. Beyond that, he had a strong notion there were things going on with Grandfather that, being a boy, he was not supposed to know.

If Grandfather had gotten in—what would he have done?

The scene his grandfather had made had not made his father approve of his grandfather, which he now did not, at all.

It certainly had not made *him* approve of his grandfather, either.

And it probably had made his mother mad, too, though she would not admit it.

Would his own grandfather have tried to kill him, to force his father to take his unborn sister for his heir?

That was a smarter move in some ways, but stupid, too, because there was no guarantee his father would not teach his sister just who was responsible for shooting her brother, and he could not think that shooting him would persuade his sister to trust Grandfather much, either . . . granted his sister was no fool.

And while he and his mother were at odds, he did not believe that his mother would ever forgive anybody who shot him.

So doing away with him could not have been the reason Grandfather had made the scene at the door, either. And he had thrown a very indecorous tantrum in Great-grandmother's reception and gotten himself thrown out in full view of everybody.

He kept thinking about it and thinking about it. He had nightmares about his grandfather turning up by his bed. He could only imagine what his mother felt about the situation.

He had met people with perfectly understandable reasons for shooting him, like meeting him in a basement hallway when they were searching the house, trying to kill anybody they found—that was sensible. He had had nightmares about that. But to have Grandfather replace that man in his nightmares—

That was scarier, somehow.

There was a little suspicion, by what he figured out by hanging around doors, about Grandfather's brother, the Ajuri lord, dying conveniently, which had made Grandfather the Ajuri clan lord. Grandfather's brother had not been that old, or sick. He had just died.

And his father had said Grandfather was insane.

And he was not at all sure it was a joke.

That was when his father had decided it was time to make his whole bodyguard official, and arm them, and get them all the proper Guild equipment.

Was Grandfather the reason for that? Or only *one* reason?

He was going to be really mad if Grandfather made trouble while his guests were here.

Or if his mother and his father had a fight when his guests were here.

Was his father even right to go on trusting his mother?

Or was his mother still living here only because his father did not want the baby born in Ajuri? He certainly did not want a baby who was half Ragi brought up Ajuri, by Grandfather, either. That could be a lot of trouble in the future. So he was sure his father was not going to let his mother leave here until the baby was born.

It was a mess, was what it was. Mani said reckless alliances could scatter man'chi into very bad places. Jago had said it too: relationships always create gaps in your defense.

He went to his little office, which he used for his homework, but it was not homework he had in mind. There was a huge wall map, which was one of his most special and prized possessions. He had stuck pins in it, pins for people he was sure he had for associates.

Two days ago, after his mother and his father had had another argument, he had gotten mad and taken out the pins for Ajuri clan. Now after thinking about it, he replaced them with bright yellow ones.

Yellow for danger. Yellow for enemies. They were a

little clan, but they were dead center of the territory of the Northern Association: he knew how to look at a map. All the clans of the Northern Association were little clans, but together, they were something more—the whole upper section of the aishidi'tat, for one important thing, everything above the Padi Valley Association and stretching clear to the coast up by Dur.

And he had to turn those once-family pins yellow, a whole little knot of yellow pins for cousins and aunts and uncles, and his stupid, *stupid* grandfather.

He had been so smug about all the connections he had had, and now his beautiful map had that nasty yellow spot of trouble on it, trouble that might still be as hot an issue when he was aiji in his father's place, since he could not imagine how he was going to turn his grandfather sane or make his reputation better in the south. Father had said he wanted no Ajuri servants serving *him* tea, and that was just about the way he felt. Forever.

The new baby, that Mother said would be a sister, would have been heir in *his* place, if *he* had not come back from space nearly a year ago, surprising everybody.

Maybe Grandfather had not been happy to find out that the real heir was back, and that he had turned into *Great-grandmother's* student. Maybe when Grandfather had found out Mother was going to have a baby, and that Father was on his way to taking back the capital, *that* was when Grandfather had gotten ideas about getting close to the new baby. Even before he was lord of Ajuri he had started planning. And who was in Grandfather's way?

He was.

That was a scary thought. It was what had upset him so much last night, when Great-grandmother, who was very, very smart about politics, had taken hold of his mother and gotten her to listen for the whole course around that big room—Great-grandmother had had that very grim look she wore when she was giving orders, and Mother had listened, and he had seen all sorts of motives going on, powerful motives. Motives that could get people killed.

Maybe his mother stayed with his father because she

really had man'chi to his father, and because that man'chi mattered more to her than any other, anywhere.

Maybe it was because she liked being important and being the aiji-consort and having parties and pretty clothes. It had to be better than being home in Ajuri in a little house and not in charge of anything at all. That was a reason, but his mother had a lot more on her mind than parties and nice furniture. She was smart. And if she had had moments lately when she was not very reasonable, he had no doubt she was thinking hard whether to stay or go or what to do about him, and Great-grandmother, and the new baby, and Grandfather.

It was all what nand' Bren called a damned mess. He was not supposed to use that language, but *damned mess* did describe it. And he just had to tread very, very carefully, not only to get his birthday party the way he was promised, and try to keep all the pins on that map—but to be sure he did not *cause* his mother to leave his father.

Once his sister was born—well, his mother would probably be more comfortable, and she would have a lot to do. He had to set his mind in advance that his mother was going to be treating his sister as her favorite, and she was probably going to start pushing to get his sister special honors, and make his sister important, and powerful. He saw that coming. His mother never would be on his side, because he was Great-grandmother's, and his mother would try to make his sister take *her* side about everything, so long as she lived, by giving her absolutely everything she wanted.

He looked up at his map, wondering what he could do about Grandfather.

Fortunately, just to the west of the Northern Association, there was Dur, head of the North *Coastal* Association, and young Dur was *his* ally, and there was no way Dur was ever going to swing over to his crazy grandfather.

And the Gan people would be with Dur, because Dur was backing them for membership in the aishidi'tat; and that meant they would be on *his* side, because the Edi were on his side, too, backed by nand' Bren, and the Gan sided with the Edi. And if Najida and Kajiminda and the Edi were his allies, and the new proxy lord of Sarini went along as Lord Geigi would want him to, that meant the whole South Coastal Association was his. Not even to mention Lord Geigi himself, who ran half the space station, and Jase-aiji, who was one of the ship-captains.

So if Grandfather thought the Northern Association would be all behind Ajuri, the way he was acting, he was going to get a nasty surprise. *Dur* had some influence, too.

And *he* had. He took a look at his map, took up two red pins, and stuck them over at the other end of the continent, across the Divide and just beyond Great-grandmother's estate at Malguri, Calrunaidi. The Calrunaidi girl, his cousin, had been nice. Her father was well disposed. They both were allied to Great-grandmother, and now Calrunaidi was allied to Lord Geigi because of his nephew.

So he had just had a few pins go yellow.

He put new red ones in, at the other end of the world.

One lost a few. And gained others. He knew how this game worked.

Even if he *was* still just infelicitous eight.

6

The oldest engine in regular service pulled up to the platform and small office, puffing steam — luck of the draw, last night, when it had been sequestered and prepared for its run, but it was fast, and it often pulled this particular set of cars.

There was not much to see at the train station, beyond the simplest of sidings, a line of blue-green trees, and, if one knew what one was looking at, a long runway that stretched out of sight behind the little transport office. The main buildings, a little outpost of the space program, were far in the distance.

A large, sleek bus was waiting, and a conveyor truck stood at the platform, ready to whisk people and baggage through a hidden gate to the spaceport itself, which operated in high security, behind fences and sensor-systems. It happened to be the oldest shuttle in the fleet that was waiting for Geigi, too, over that gentle roll of the land, but it was oldest only by months: that was how hard they had pushed, in the earliest days of the space program. It had been two weeks on the ground undergoing the sort of servicing the ground facility did best. And within hours, it would be winging its way across the ocean on a long ascent, up to where the blue of atmosphere gave way to the black of space.

The station's modern world started here, with that bus, the conveyor truck. From this point on, Geigi would be too busy with procedures to be socially engaged. So it was prearranged that the paidhi-aiji was to go no farther than the doorway of the train car and that Geigi would immediately board the bus, no lingering about outside, and little to see, in this vast flat grassland.

"Well, well," Geigi said, heaving himself to his feet, "one can only thank you, Bren-ji, for all you have done, from a very difficult beginning."

"For you, Geigi-ji, my neighbor, an honor. Come back soon."

"Nandi." They bowed properly to each other, and moved toward the door, and their parting. Geigi's staff was already shifting personal luggage out very efficiently, gently tossing things down, and Tano and Algini went outside to supervise the baggage car's more extensive offloading. Baggage from that car entered the hands of Transportation Guild and Assassins' Guild waiting outside, agents who worked the port.

From here, everything Geigi brought had a series of procedures and inspections to go through, not so much for mischief—although it was always a concern—as to discover those small thoughtless items like pressurized bottles which might need special containment or outright exclusion.

"I shall visit," Geigi promised him in leaving. "I shall assuredly visit next year. And I shall give your regards to your on-station staff."

"I owe a visit up there, before long," Bren said, thinking of that place, those faithful people. "But as yet I have no date I can plan on. They know the circumstance. Assure them they are in my thoughts. And take care. Take very great care of yourself, Geigi-ji. Good fortune."

"Baji-naji. Let fortune favor us both, nandi, and new ventures delight us."

With which Geigi stepped off the train to the platform and Bren went back to his seat at the rear of the car, beyond the galley, with all the baggage suddenly gone, all the car emptied of noise and laughter. He felt a little at loose ends for the moment, a little *between,* and not knowing how to pick up his routine life—but with a huge sigh for a complex business handled.

Came finally a definitive thump. The baggage door had shut, in the next car. Tano and Algini came back aboard, and their own door shut with a louder thump. Banichi stood by that door, talking to someone absent, likely port security, or the driver of the bus. Jago walked back to the rear of the car where Bren sat, and leaned back against the galley counter.

The train slowly began to roll again.

"Sit down, nadi-ji," Bren said to her, and in a voice to carry over the sound of the train: "Everyone sit down. We are on our own again. Rest. Take refreshment. You have certainly deserved it. This has been a long several weeks."

Jago sat down. The rest of his aishid came back down the aisle, collected soft drinks from under the counter, uncapped bottles, and sank down on the bench seats nearest—Banichi handed Jago a bottle, and got his own before he settled with a sigh.

His four, his irreplaceable four. It was a relief, as the train gathered speed, to be at last in their company, solo, and to be going home with no crisis ahead of them.

"Our package made it aboard," he said. It was a question.

"It did, Bren-ji," Tano said.

"Excellent." He was a little smug about that item. He had slipped a sizeable and very well-padded case into Geigi's luggage, one that, under instruction to Geigi's servants and bodyguard, would not come to Geigi's attention until Geigi got all the way back to the station. It involved a budding relationship with a really fine porcelain maker in Tanaja, one Copada, whose card he had included with the piece. The artist had expressed the piece up to Shejidan two days ago. Geigi's own collection was all at Kajiminda, less a few pieces sold off by his fool of a nephew. But one fine piece would now grace Geigi's station apartment.

They settled for the trip.

But then Algini drew papers from inside his jacket and gave them to him without a word, very flimsy stuff, very closely written.

Jago had said a report would be forthcoming—about the content of the meeting in Tabini's back rooms. Bren turned on a reading light and paid that report his full attention, while his aishid had their refreshment and waited, all watching him, he was quite aware.

It said, for a header:

Because of the sensitive situation within the aiji's household and the fact that his aishid is involved, please consider this car insecure for the purposes of this report: we should not discuss these things aloud.

Then: *There is reason to consider normally acceptable persons potentially compromised, not by their intention, but by their secondary associations.*

Certain individuals, including Tabini-aiji, Lord Dur and his son, Lord Haidiri, Lord Calrunaidi, Baiji late of Kajiminda, and Lord Tatiseigi are all under special protection of Guild known to us, and assigned by the aiji's seal, at the request of the dowager's guard, without Guild approval.

Security for Cajeiri is being upgraded as far as immediately practical. The two young Taibeni are being licensed to carry sidearms and to use signaling and tracking systems. Their licenses were being held up, two tests ordered retaken. The aiji himself has ordered them home without the tests, with the equipment. The Guild Council reluctantly issued the licenses without the tests retaken. We do not find this hesitation justified. These young people have seen more action than most licensed Guild of their age.

What went on inside the Guild was information usually restricted. Tightly restricted, as a matter of policy.

Security for you, for the aiji-dowager, and for Tatiseigi and the new lord of the Maschi is being tightened, and we are going over the latter two with particular care. We suspect there may be moves to infiltrate, possibly to get information, possibly to do physical harm.

The following matter was generally discussed between us, the dowager's aishid, the aiji's, Lord Geigi's, and very frankly with Lord Tatiseigi's guard, who have been cautioned not to speak of the matter even among themselves.

Lord Tatiseigi's aishid reports that Tatiseigi is revising his own position toward several clans due to the fall from favor of the Ajuri. Tatiseigi's long feud with Taibeni clan has become detrimental to his security, and he is repositioning himself—cautiously so, because many of his conservative allies have strongly opposed the aiji's close relationship with the Taibeni and his choosing low-ranking Taibeni bodyguards for himself and his son. This is a delicate matter and Tabini-aiji is asking the lord of Taiben to accept Tatiseigi's offer without comment or reservation.

We all concur that Lord Ajuri's breach with the aiji forces Tatiseigi himself to move closer to the aiji's position regarding the composition of the aiji's bodyguard. Tatiseigi is therefore committing to the aiji, and leaving safe political territory, his massive influence among the conservatives. Tatiseigi requires support in this, and conspicuous political successes and high favors are being given him in order to maintain his political importance. His physical safety at this time is critical.

That explained certain things. Definitely. Tatiseigi was taking a position that was going to upset the conservatives. And strong signals were going out that the conservatives might get significant concessions from Tabini if they backed off their fuss about Tabini's relationship with the liberal-leaning Taibeni clan. *Ajuri* had been a conservative clan, once close to Tatiseigi, then distanced, and now completely beyond the pale. The Kadagidi had been a conservative clan. But *it* had backed Murini, and Murini's excesses had alienated the whole aishidi'tat. The conservatives were not in good shape, since Tabini's return.

Then *he'd* backed off his support for cell phone technology, and upset the Liberals.

And Tabini had urged Tatiseigi, geographically sandwiched between the Ajuri and the Kadagidi, to reach out to his other neighbors, the Taibeni—who were unshakably loyal to Tabini. Welcome to the family, Great-uncle. Ignore our dealings on the tribal bill. We're backing off on the cell phone bill. We've broken the association between the Marid and the Kadagidi, and gotten our own agreement with the Marid. With us, you don't have to worry about your neighbors.

Damiri—showing up in her uncle's colors.

He drew a deep breath. And kept reading.

The old alliance of Tatiseigi's Padi Valley Association with Ajuri's Northern Association is now broken, at the same time that the Marid under Machigi is reconciling with the aiji, through a private agreement with the dowager . . . in effect trading the north for the south and the West Coast. If Machigi does not keep his agreements, or if political opposition from the Conservatives defeats the Edi bill and frustrates the West Coast, the Western Association will face a worrisome and dangerous situation, with disaffection in the Northern Association, led by Ajuri, and in whatever results in the Marid and Sarini Province should Machigi's agreement with the dowager fall apart. Therefore passage of the tribal bill is critical and advancement of the trade agreement between the dowager and Machigi is critical.

We have noted that Tabini-aiji, when attack came on him at Taiben and Shejidan, did not first resort to Ajuri or to Atageini, though Damiri-daja was with him, and related to both. He believed that his going to either for help would make them a target—and neither is noted for strength in arms.

When we all, the heir, and the aiji-dowager returned from space, it was the aiji-dowager's natural choice, through geographical position, to resort first to her husband's associates, the Taibeni, then to her own longtime associate Lord Tatiseigi. This gave Tabini-aiji no choice in where he must first make an appearance. His return to power began on Lord Tatiseigi's land, and by virtue of that, Lord Tatiseigi became the aiji's first and foremost supporter in his return to power, joined by the Taibeni, and rapidly by many smaller central and coastal clans who had had their district authorities suppressed and replaced by outsiders in favor with Murini. The popular movement gathered force.

At that point the Ajuri lord arrived, and began to promote the Ajuri connection to Damiri-daja.

The Ajuri lord died under questionable circumstances. Lady Damiri's father Komaji took the lordship of Ajuri. Komaji had an excellent chance to have mended his personal feud with Tatiseigi, and chose instead to exercise it. Simultaneously he pressed his relationship with Lady Damiri and spoke detrimentally about human influence on the heir, and about the dowager's teaching, while he was in the dowager's care. His presumption on his relationship with Damiri-daja culminated the night of the dowager's agreement with Machigi in an attempt to gain access to the aiji's apartment, which greatly alarmed the heir's young bodyguards.

He is now barred from the Bujavid and the capital, though he has not been forbidden communication. He has set himself in an untenable situation. We do not credit him with good judgment, and the heir's insistence on bringing human associates down for his ninth and fortunate birthday celebration is likely to light a fuse, where Komaji's resentment is concerned. If anything were to happen to the heir, Damiri's second child, soon to be born, will become the heir instead—without the dowager's influence, and without human influence.

In general principle, conservatives would greatly prefer this. Komaji would be that child's grandfather, and his jealousy of Lord Tatiseigi suggests several moves that would work to his extreme advantage: assassinating the heir, and/or Tatiseigi—provided the event could be sufficiently distanced from Komaji.

We have suspicions regarding the death of the former lord of Ajuri. We wonder what other clans might have wanted the silence of the grave over their dealings in the Murini era. We have directly asked Tabini why he avoided Ajuri during his exile, and he confirmed he had his own suspicions of that clan, but did not voice them to Damiri. We suspect the former Ajuri lord's own bodyguard conducted that assassination, and subsequently removed records of Ajuri dealings during those years—records that might have proved theft and assassination—even within the clan and the subclans. Komaji is regarded within his own clan as a man who allows emotion to guide his actions. He is not respected, but he is feared. His relatives may not tolerate him much longer, but we cannot rely on that situation to protect the heir.

We have strongly suggested to Tabini that a Filing would assist us.

Return this note now. We shall destroy it.

Bren handed it over. Algini touched it with a pocket candle-lighter and it went up in a puff of flame, leaving only a fluff of gray ash that fell apart.

"I understand," he said.

Tabini didn't want Damiri to take over Ajuri. He didn't want her to have any part of it.

Why? Because, Tabini had said, Ajuri *swallows* virtue.

And he had said that Damiri couldn't settle on a clan. Even when she was wearing Tatiseigi's colors, and bearing a Ragi child.

Problem, Bren thought.

Problem, of a sort a human was very ill-equipped to feel his way through. Damiri was not a follower, but a leader—of a strong disposition to wield power. That disposition had made her valuable to Tabini. She had a quick mind, an ally who understood him to the core; but in the way of atevi leaders—it made an unruly sort of relationship, a unison of purpose very, very difficult to keep.

Interpret Damiri's actions as emotion-fueled and self-destructive?

He didn't think so. Not even considering her condition. She might have shaky moments, but that brain was working on something. And she had a father she was not that close to, who was nowhere near Damiri's level, not in intelligence and not in leadership qualities.

No. Damiri was no fool. She would do *exactly* what she considered in her own interest. Tabini would do *exactly* what he considered in his—which included, above all else, the survival of the one association that kept the atevi world peaceful and prosperous: the aishidi'tat.

The dowager's ambitions were much the same. The

dowager had helped *create* the aishidi'tat. She had created the last aiji; she had created Tabini; *and* she had taught Cajeiri.

What did Damiri fight for? What was *her* driving interest?

It was disturbing that she opposed the dowager ... and that he had no real answer for that question.

7

Cajeiri, at his homework, because he had nothing else
to do, heard the front door open, out in the foyer
beyond the hall. That was an ordinary thing. Servants
came and went all the time.

Then he heard a familiar young voice out there, and
another, and with that, he was out of his chair, out the
door of his own suite and down the short hall as fast as
he could run.

"Nadiin-ji!" he exclaimed. Indeed, in the foyer he saw
not just two, but all *four* of his bodyguards.

In uniform. All of them. Antaro and Jegari, had traded
the greens and browns of their clan, and went black-
uniformed, black-ribboned, and armed. They carried pistols in holster, just like the other half of the team, Veijico
and Lucasi; and just like any Guild anywhere.

Now—they were *real* bodyguards.

"Nandi," Jegari said with a proper little bow, while
Seidi, the major domo, stood in the background.

"Are you to stay here now?" he asked, hoping that
was the case. And: "You look tired."

"They are not entirely through the first level," Lucasi
said—Lucasi and Veijico, also brother and sister, like
Antaro and Jegari, were years older; but it was Antaro
and Jegari who ranked seniors, having been his since he
came back to the world, even if they were only apprentices. "There are tests yet to pass, nandi, but we are all
back to stay. The rest we can do in stages. From here

on—they are no longer apprentices, and we shall race each other up the levels."

"We shall be sending in the written course work," Veijico added. "We have a special dispensation, both to test outside the Guild headquarters, and for us to administer the tests. Your father ordered that. We shall be spending time in the Bujavid gym, in hours when you have your father's aishid on premises, and on the firing range, the same. But otherwise we are intended to stay on premises, nandi. So we shall not leave you again."

"Well, one is very glad!" Cajeiri said. "Come in, come in!"

He was used to Veijico and Lucasi having guns. There was a special locker in each of their two rooms, where those and other equipment stayed. But he was not used to Antaro and Jegari's new appearance. He was used to them in ordinary clothing, like him, or lounging about in a variety of tee-shirts and casuals when they were entirely alone in the evening. Seeing them as somebody he had to obey instead of ordering—that was a little different thing, though he could not think of anyone better for him. They both seemed to have grown overnight, to have gotten bigger, and taller, and actually dangerous-looking. Like many Taibeni, they had a look, a little sharpness of face, that made a frown quite convincing.

Now everybody had to realize they had authority. That was the point of it all.

Now when they told somebody to move aside, they had better move and not argue.

It also meant Lucasi and Veijico had real partners to back them up in case of trouble, and the four of them all together meant he had a real aishid, who would be with him all his life, more permanent than any marriage. How important that was, he had come to understand in the way Great-grandmother's aishid and nand' Bren's aishid operated—and how his father's aishid was desperately trying to operate, except they were all young.

Trust? He had always had that for Antaro and Jegari, from the day they had met. Lucasi and Veijico were much newer in the house, and they had made a bad start, when they had thought they were above belonging to a child. But after they had acted out and gotten people hurt, and after Great-grandmother's and nand' Bren's bodyguards had had their say, Lucasi and Veijico had come back with a deeply changed attitude and begged to stay.

And he'd known, then, that they meant it. Just ... known, somehow, at the bottom of his stomach. From that time on, trust had happened, which was very important. Best of all, they were *really* good, and they knew interesting things, and they were perfectly accepting of Antaro and Jegari now, saying that they were no fools, that their skills had been very high to start with, and that after a few years, being five years older or younger would not be that much, anyway.

"We have yet to get our briefing from your father's guard," Veijico said.

"Go," he said, "And then tell me what you find out, nadiin-ji! No one ever tells me anything. There was a party last night, and a big Guild meeting about something. I think my grandfather is making trouble, and I want to know. It is *important* that I know. I have things also to tell you!"

They had set down their baggage by the door of his suite. It was black leather bags, the same sort that all Guild carried and not for anyone else to touch. "We shall take this to our rooms," Antaro said, and they did.

Then they went out again, on their grown-up business.

He was too excited now to go back to his homework — not knowing quite what to do with himself until they got back, and hoping more than anything that their having passed the tests might let him go places again — like to the library to pick out his own books, and maybe to visit mani and nand' Bren.

His birthday was coming; his guests were going to come; and now that his entire bodyguard had qualified to carry weapons, at least no one could turn up at the last moment saying he did not have professional guards.

"When we all come back," Veijico had said to him privately, the day they had gone to the Guild, *"when we*

come back, Jeri-ji, we will be a whole aishid. We will be a weapon in your hands—a real one. You will have to be very careful what you ask us to do, because we will do what you ask us to."

That was the scariest thing anybody had ever said to him—scarier even than anything mani had said. He thought of that, standing alone in his sitting room, with heavy weapons probably in those bags. He could tell them to kill somebody.

And they would.

And maybe get shot doing it.

Maybe die.

Boji chittered at him from his cage, diverting him into the real moment. Boji rattled the cage door, and reached fingers through the convolute metal flowers of the cage.

He felt a lot like Boji. Locked in. Kept.

And all of a sudden he felt that he was getting a lot more cautious than he had used to be. A lot smarter. A lot more aware what could happen in the world. He was not sure he liked the changes the year was making in him. He was not sure he liked it at all.

I could not steal away downstairs today and catch the train, could I? I did that when it was just Jegari and Antaro and me—we three could do that.

But now Lucasi and Veijico would get in trouble. Now everyone is Guild, and we cannot go back, can we? We cannot sneak out and catch the train, we cannot even sneak down to the library—not because I would get in trouble, but because they *would get in trouble.*

And they would do it, if I asked.

But I cannot ask them. Can I?

Damn it.

He was caught. He did not want to grow up. Not yet. He wanted to be a boy. He wanted to slip away the way they had on the starship, and go places where he could still play games.

But there were no places like that on this floor. And any *other* floor of the Bujavid was not safe.

The world had gotten serious and stayed that way. His guests were going to say, "Come on, Jeri, let's go . . ."

And he'd have to say no, it probably wasn't safe . . .

Because his stupid grandfather had made things worse just when they could have really gotten better.

Maybe, he thought, *I can think of something.*

And: *I can still get my way. I just have to be smarter about it.*

My associates are coming down here. I have to be good until then. I have to follow all the rules and do my homework and be so good even my mother will be happy.

And once my guests get here, then there has to be something to show them when they come. They have never seen the ocean. They have never seen trees and grass. They have never seen a sunrise. I had to describe it all for them.

I have to show them everything. I have to show them the best things, so we have something to talk about, and they will want to come back.

I would like them to come back. I would like them to be here when I grow up. I would like to have people like nand' Bren, who have no clan, and owe nothing to anybody else. Just to me.

8

Morning brought mail and a last cup of tea to follow the paidhi-aiji's solitary breakfast. The apartment was very quiet now—not that Geigi had ever made a lot of noise as a houseguest, but the sense of lordly presence in the place was gone.

So was Geigi's company at breakfast, the distraction of his cheerful conversation on completely idle but interesting topics. That part had been pleasant.

The shuttle was well on its way, safely clear of the atmosphere. Geigi was headed home, and the complex affairs and troubles of the space station had become just a little less intimately connected to the problems of the continent.

That was, over all, a good thing.

So was the quiet, in which he could, at last, think without interruption. They were not necessarily pleasant thoughts, regarding the problem of the Ajuri, and the imminent legislative session with its necessary committee meetings, and committee politics. And there was going to be a question of what he was going to do with guests whose parents had an agenda—

But those were questions he could sidestep. The *parents* weren't coming. Wouldn't be allowed to come. Just deal with the children as children, don't let anyone get hurt, and translate for them—Cajeiri's ship-speak had to be a little rusty after a year—and he was sure he'd be drawn in for all the tours and the festivities, to be *sure* the guests had a good time.

Of all jobs he had ahead of him—that one might actually have some real enjoyment in it.

Give or take a boy who'd already been arrested by station security.

But that was, he said to himself, possibly Cajeiri's influence.

He could handle it. Absolutely.

And Geigi by now, thank goodness, understood their earthbound worries, *and* the security issues his bodyguard would have explained by now. The paidhi-aiji's security could protect the kids; the parents were Geigi's problem.

He had his own share of loose ends to tie up.

The tribal bill. The cell phone bill. He had to arrange meetings, formal and informal, talk to the right people, have his arguments in order, and get done what had to be done before the next shuttle landed and brought him kids who might, on first seeing a flat horizon, heave up their breakfasts.

The cell phone bill was certain to raise eyebrows. Explaining *why* he'd pulled his support from it, and would in fact *veto* it—technically, Tabini still granted him that ability, where it regarded human tech—that was going to be the problem with that one. He didn't want to dust off the veto power. He *really* didn't. He wanted the atevi to vote it down.

The tribal bill was far from a sure thing, and potentially could blow up. Problems regarding the status of the tribal peoples had hung fire since the War of the Landing, which had displaced the Edi and Gan peoples from the island of Mospheira, and settled them in two separate coastal areas. They—quite reasonably, in his opinion—wanted full membership in the aishidi'tat, and even with the favorable report of the two Associations nearest the tribal lands, they still had some old prejudices to deal with. The most bitterly opposed, the Marid, was going to vote *for* the measure: *Ilisidi* had accomplished that miracle. The southwest coast, Geigi's district, was going to vote for it; the northern Coastal Association, where the Gan lived, had Dur's backing, and *that* vote was assured.

He just had to budge, principally, the six very small hill clans who sat between Shejidan and the Marid, who had made their living partly from agriculture and hunting, partly from trading, and who, as much as they felt that being ancestrally native to the mainland made them superior to the tribal peoples, believed that the new trade agreement between Ilisidi and the Marid was going to kill off *their* trade with the Marid, and therefore they wanted the tribal bill to fail—so as to make Ilisidi's trade agreement fall through.

He had an answer for that one, if he could get them to stop shouting and listen. The Marid was going to develop an economy that would flow uphill to them. And the same benefits would be available to them, if they would stop spending all their resources on the Assassins' Guild and allow the Scholars' Guild to operate in their districts—which could be said of the Marid as well. Too many of the atevi clans were still mired in their rural past and needed the world perspective that came with education. *That* part, however, he very much doubted he was going to mention in this session. Several new rail stations, with a favor given their local products *by* Sarini Province, however, might be an inducement.

Bribery? Bet on it. It was a time-honored tradition.

Meanwhile . . .

Meanwhile the mail arrived, brought in by Narani. Jeladi, arriving through the door Narani held open, brought him tea, and both silently vanished.

Lord Machigi's was the most conspicuous message cylinder. Machigi, in his capital at Tanaja, declared he was writing simultaneously to him, the aiji-dowager—and to the Physicians' Guild, who had asked access to all districts of the Marid, in another of those many-sided deals.

Machigi pointedly reminded them that he could not give any other guild the access and assurances they wanted until the *Assassins' Guild* had gotten the lords of Senji and Dojisigi to come under his authority. Since those clans had wanted to assassinate *him*, Machigi understandably and reasonably wanted that to happen. Soon.

He wrote: *One entirely understands this reasonable position. The paidhi's office will explain the urgency to the parties in question.*

That was going to have to be his answer to a lot of queries for the next while. The Assassins' Guild was mopping up its own splinter group in the two districts, and trying to figure out who was a loyal and proper member of their own guild and who was one of Murini's leftovers—that took some investigation, or there was the possibility of a lethal injustice, the sort of thing that could set back the operation and dry up sources of information. It was not easy to untangle the division that had been building in the Guild for, apparently, decades, before it found expression in an overt move for power. It was particularly not easy since the Assassins' Guild kept every family secret in the aishidi'tat in its workings, and the rule of secrecy, reticence, clan loyalties, and personal honor were all involved. They *were* the legal system, the lawyers *and* the judges, the spies, the keepers of personal and state secrets, and they were experts at covering and uncovering tracks.

That was one worry.

Then there was, in a cylinder from the director of his clerical office an advisement that the tribal peoples bill had been diverted to the Committee on Finance.

Finance? Damn!

That was a conservative committee. He knew Tatiseigi hadn't done it. *Surely* Tatiseigi hadn't engineered it.

That meant the aiji-dowager urgently had some meetings to organize and some favors to call in. There was nothing, frustratingly nothing, a human could do to aid the bill in that particular committee. Humans were not popular among the conservatives, where the tribal peoples found hardly more welcome, and that meant the aiji-dowager and Tatiseigi had that situation entirely in their hands. They had to get it recommended *out* of that committee, or it stalled and died.

And the trade agreement with Machigi would likely die with it.

The second letter was a well-timed letter from young Dur regarding plans to integrate the barter-economy of the Gan state with Dur—and by extension, with the rest of the country—via setting up, not a bank, which the Gan would not trust, but an exchange, where both barter and use of coinage could go on side by side. This brilliant plan would be under the auspices of the Treasurers' Guild . . . assuming the tribal bill passed. The theory was that, while goods were comforting in an exchange, the convenience of currency would win out.

Not coincidental, that timing. Well done, Reijiri, Bren thought. That item would be extremely useful, in the dowager's hands, especially now: the Committee on Finance supported the Treasurers' Guild.

It occurred to him, too, that Lady Siodi, of the Marid Trade Office, might have some useful suggestions on that problem. The Marid had its own difficulties trading with three local currencies, plus barter, and conducting commerce with the rest of the aishidi'tat.

Time being of the essence, he penned a small note to that effect, rolled both letters together, slipped them into one of his white message cylinders and took it directly to Narani to be couriered to the dowager wherever she was at the moment.

Satisfied that he'd done all he could on that front, he returned to his office and three letters from companies seeking a recommendation to Mospheira. He still handled trade cases, mostly by routing them to the appropriate office on the island. He attached notes for his clerical office, and turned to the final cylinder, one in a style he knew well: Ramaso, his major domo at Najida.

Ramaso reported on the construction on the estate, on the road improvement, and on the arrangements for a village wedding he had promised to occur at the estate if they could get the new dining room, hall and sitting room in order fast enough. And the news was good, very good indeed. The work would be completed on time. The wedding was going to happen. That lent cheerfulness to the day.

Ramaso reported as well on the order for wine and food, for his approval.

Granted. It made him particularly happy to keep that promise.

And finally Ramaso wrote that the framework for the new wing was not only up, the paneling was being shaped and carved in situ, and stonemasons were at work.

Excellent news. All of it.

He answered Ramaso, and in the same train of thought, thinking of his last visit to Najida and a particularly painful, several-day cross-country trek in court-dress footwear, he dashed off an order to a shop on Mospheira. He imported his boots, by preference, from an old-fashioned bootmaker up by Mount Adams. He requested another three pairs of boots, one for indoors, one for court . . . and *one* of them the stoutest hiking boots possible. *With* a metal shank.

After that, he was at leisure to draft routine letters to several of the guilds, official letters to certain legislators regarding personal meetings. . . .

He was actually glad to be back to the routine of his office, even with the tension over the vital tribal bill.

Statistics and statistics. Stacks of financial reports — those were not his favorites . . .

But there were far worse ways to spend an afternoon, and lately, he had seen all too many of them.

9

Life was very much better now, in Cajeiri's estimation. He had his aishid for company and conversation, and the imminent prospect of his guests and his party.

Training for his aishid in the gym or on the firing range was daily, it turned out, and the place was very quiet when they were gone. But in the evenings, on their little private dining table, Veijico and Lucasi were doing a lot of interesting instruction with the equipment they had brought in.

It was supposed to be just Antaro and Jegari. Cajeiri was not really supposed to hear the lessons, they said, because some of it was classified and it was Guild regulations—the Guild was being very strict about regulations, since the Troubles. But he still heard a lot that was going on, and he already knew how the locators worked, and about wires, and explosives, which he had learned mostly from Banichi, aboard the ship.

Finally they said he *was*, after all, his father's heir, and the aiji *could* override the lesser rules, so they said it was probably all right for him to hear, so long as he did not talk about it with anyone but them.

Electricity became a very fascinating subject—he understood now a lot of things it could do besides turn on lights.

His tutor was willing to tell him a lot about electricity, things which were *not* classified, but he began to see how those theories might relate to things that *were* classified.

He had had Banichi and the exploding car in mind, when he had first asked his tutor about circuits.

He really learned about explosives, now, and how Banichi had known how much to use. And he came to realize that explosives were very good if you had a big target, or room enough, but that electricity was more subtle. That was Great-grandmother's word: subtle.

And most subtle of all were the wires, which could do terrible damage and which atevi were not supposed to have, but they did. They were illegal for anybody but Guild, and that only under very special circumstances and with Guild approval.

He'd known about wires before, but now he *knew* about them. He was excited about that.

Lucasi was kneeling on the floor in the bedroom doorway, showing him, with a real wire that was not powered up, how to detect such a trap, telling him where they were most often used, and why—when a knock came at the door.

Cajeiri ignored it, trusting Antaro to see to whoever it was.

She brought back a letter, to the table where they were working, and it was not a regular letter, but one in a plain steel cylinder with just the Messengers' Guild crest stamped in it, and dented and scuffed as this sort of cylinder often was. It was so odd for him to get such a letter that Antaro insisted on opening it herself, just to be sure.

It was machine-printed, because it had come down from orbit, from Lord Geigi himself.

"To me?" he asked, but he could see it was. A letter directly to him—and saying that his associates from the station were all coming on the next shuttle. Bjorn could not come, but Irene could. And that was the tightest group of them, Gene, Artur, Irene, and him, even if they were an infelicitous number, they had Bjorn sometimes, for a fortunate fifth.

The shuttle was coming *early*.

Electricity could wait. He had to tell his father immediately, even if he was sure it was not the only letter from

Geigi that would have come to the door. If he *had* received any information his father had not, he had to be prompt in reporting it, and just—proper. He had to be absolutely proper. Proper about everything. And not offend anybody. It was really happening.

His birthday was still days away, and they were coming early and they would have two weeks or however long it took them to service the shuttle before they could go back up to space.

It was happening, it was happening, it was happening.

He put on a better coat, to show respect, and he took himself and his aishid straight to his father's office door.

"Honored Father," he said, when he was let in. "I have a letter from Lord Geigi, addressed to me. He says my guests are coming! And the shuttle is coming early."

His father had a serious, even frowning expression. He realized he had interrupted his father at work, reading his own mail. Maybe coming quite so fast was not such a good idea after all.

Or maybe there was something really the matter.

"We are aware," his father said, in a flat tone, and he thought it wise just to bow and back out of the room.

"Excuse me, honored Father."

"The legislature is in session. The tribal bill, nefariously diverted into a conservative-dominated committee, has run into opposition, and your great-grandmother is now asking me to get a letter from the six highland clans giving their support. These six clans cannot agree with each other. How shall I persuade them?" His father pushed back from the desk with an annoyed expression on his face. "Against these other problems, do you truly have a concern, son of mine?"

"Honored Father, only to inform you."

"Properly so."

"One would wish—"

"You are about to ask me for permission to go out to the spaceport."

"One would hope—"

"You will be lodged in your great-grandmother's care

during that visit. What she does I am sure will be out of my hands, so you will have to arrange that with her."

"One is grateful, honored Father." It was good news. It was wonderful news.

His father's expression grew less angry. Slowly.

"You have given no thought, yet," his father said, "as to where to lodge your early guests before and after. Do you propose to put them into the guest quarters here? Or in your small suite? I do not think that would be the best idea."

"Honored Father." He bowed. No, he had not thought about where he was going to put them. He had been trying to think how he could take them to interesting things, or any of those matters. "One thought some things would be planned by staff."

"My staff is busy. Staff in general is greatly reduced, your mother is having nerves, and a set of foreign children crowded into the guest quarters and trooping through the sitting room will not improve her mood. How will cook accommodate them? How will staff inquire about their needs? One assumes they are no more tolerant of sauces than is nand' Bren."

"Perhaps—" He cast about desperately for an answer. "Perhaps nand' Bren will help. He has a guest room. His cook understands about humans."

His father hooked one arm about the side of his chair. "A reasonable suggestion. Undoubtedly nand' Bren will have to assist. So will your great-grandmother be fully capable of handling details. Do not distress yourself, son of mine. I have thought about these things. And the logistics of the festivity itself. One only wondered whether you had in fact devoted any thought at all to the practical matters in this visit. Jase-aiji grew quite ill when he simply looked out over a flat surface. He had all manner of difficulty with dizziness."

He had not thought about that. He could look like a fool. He was very anxious not to misstep and make his father think he was a fool.

"If I can write to them, I can warn them, honored Father."

"Your great-grandmother will be in communication with nand' Bren, son of mine. I am sure he will foresee a great many of the difficulties. Go enjoy the day."

"Honored Father." He bowed and started for the door.

And then he had a thought, how everything including himself was being turned over to the people his mother most objected to. He stopped and looked back, catching his father regarding him with a particularly thoughtful look. He bowed. Asked very cautiously: "What does Mother think about my going to Great-grandmother?"

His father let go a deep breath. "She will not be happy. But she would be far less happy at the attendance of three human children at close quarters. The baby is troubling her a great deal."

"Is she all right?"

"She seems to be. In all honesty, son of mine, I do fear she is not going to be at her most gracious."

Mother was his father's deepest problem. He knew things had not gotten better. And he had the feeling that his father was taking fire for him on the matter of his guests. He did not know how to say that in words.

"Shall I go tell her about them coming early, honored Father? And about me going to Great-grandmother?" he asked. "I think she should know it before the servants happen to mention it."

His father thought about it a moment with that look he used deciding serious, serious things. Then he nodded. "Go, son of mine. If you have learned anything of nand' Bren's art, use it."

"Yes," he said respectfully, and bowed, and left, back out into the hallway, where his aishid waited.

"I am to see my mother, nadiin-ji," he said, feeling all the while he was not going to have any good reception, and walked down the hall as far as his mother's door.

His mother did not like surprises. And he knew for certain that his great-grandmother having his birthday was the kind of thing that would have his mother and his father shouting at each other, the sort of thing that just tied his stomach in knots and scared the servants into whispers.

But he had said it: it would be far worse if his mother was surprised by a servant talking about plans she had no idea about. He gave a tug at his shirt cuffs and at the lace at his collar, took a deep breath and had Antaro knock before he tried the door—it was unlocked—and just went on in.

His mother's suite, with that beautiful row of windows, and white lace curtains, and the crib where the baby would sleep, seemed an unhappy, lonely place at the moment.

It was one of Cook's staff who came out to see who had come into in the nursery. That woman, and two of the girls who ordinarily washed the dishes and did sewing, were the only staff his mother had at the moment. His mother was not happy about it, and by their habitual faces, neither were the girls.

"Young gentleman," the woman said.

"Please tell my mother I am here," he said in as matter-of-fact a tone as he could manage, and waited to be let into his mother's sitting room.

The door opened wide to admit him. His mother, wearing a pretty white lace gown, was sitting, reading by the light of a flower-shaped lamp. She folded the book, and looked at him, expressionless as if he were some servant on business.

He bowed. "One wished to tell you without delay, honored Mother. The shuttle schedule is changed. My associates are coming down early, three of them. One is not certain how much early, but very soon."

"Indeed."

"One knows you are not happy to have my guests here. Father says I am to go to Great-grandmother and let her and nand' Bren take care of things and not be a bother to you." The last part was his invention, which he thought was a good thing to say.

"Sit down," his mother said, with no hint of expression, and he found a seat on her footstool, and sat quietly. "Are you pleased with this arrangement, son of mine?"

"Yes, honored Mother." He sat on the very edge of the footstool. Mother was not as good as Great-grandmother about leading one into traps, but one had to be very wary. Great-grandmother just thumped his ear when she was angry. But his mother went on being mad for hours. Days. He really had rather Great-grandmother.

"You think your great-grandmother will be more patient than I am?"

That was a trap. "I think Great-grandmother is not having headaches."

"One supposes the paidhi will be involved."

"One thinks, yes."

His mother frowned. "Could you ever even *talk* to these people, son of mine? How do you speak to them?"

She had never asked him that. He did not want to admit he was fairly good at ship-speak, though he supposed she was going to find out. "We use signs. They know a little Ragi. I know a little ship-speak."

"You know it was illegal for them even to speak to you not so many years ago. It was illegal for them to know Ragi at all. And very illegal to speak it."

He was amazed. "Why?"

She laughed, shortly and not very happily. And he had no idea why. "You *are* still young. Ask nand' Bren someday. He can tell you."

"I am almost felicitous nine. And I shall be much smarter and not get into trouble this next year."

"Do you promise?" She reached out and he steadied himself, not to flinch. He had a stray wisp of hair that never grew long enough to go back. She smoothed it back even if it did no good. "I hope your sister's hair grows to an even length."

"I put a little goo on it."

A laugh. Actually a laugh. "I know you do. I am glad you have two servants now."

He wanted to say, One is very sorry about yours, but he did not want to get his mother off onto that topic. A little silence hung in the air, uncomfortably so.

"So," she said. "Your great-grandmother will house these foreign children. That should be interesting, amid her antiques. And *her* staff will plan the events."

He saw where this was going. Right then. The piece of hair had fallen down again. He felt it. And his mother reached a second time and put it in order.

"What did you do on your last felicitous year, son of mine? How did you celebrate, aboard the ship?"

"I do not remember that I did at all," he said, and that was the truth. "Time on the ship gets confused."

"Your great-grandmother forgot your birthday?"

"Sometimes the ship does strange things. And you lose days. Day is only when the clock says, anyway."

"So you have had no festivity since your fifth. Do you remember that one?"

"No, honored Mother."

"We had a very nice party. Flowers. Toys. Very many toys."

He shook his head. He had a good memory, but sometimes he thought his life had begun with the ship. The memories from years before it were patchy, tied to places he had never been. They told him about his riding a mecheita across wet concrete at Uncle Tatiseigi's place. And he almost could remember that. At least he had pictures in his head about it, but he could not remember much about the house the way it had been then—only the house when they had all been there, with shells falling on the meadow around it. Most of his memories were like that. They were things that had happened, but he had no recollection of where and nothing to pin them to. It seemed they had been on the train once. He remembered the train. He remembered woods that might have been Taiben on a different trip than when he had met Antaro and Jegari. But he had no idea.

"What would you like for your birthday?" his mother asked him. "Is there any gift you would like?"

He was beyond toys, really. Most of what he liked were books. And he wished he could get the human archive back. *There* were his memories, of horses, and dinosaurs, and humans, all of which would appall his mother.

So he thought of something that would not come in a box. But he did want it. "I want you and Father to be there."

"Son of mine." His mother sat looking at him, and did not finish that.

"I wish you and Great-grandmother would not fight."

"Try wishing that of *her*."

He knew nothing to say, to that, because mani was mani and that would never change.

"Well," his mother said, "you shall have your party here, in the Bujavid. In our sitting room. Your great-grandmother may come. I shall invite her. And the paidhi-aiji. Are there others?"

"My tutor."

"Not the Calrunaidi girl."

"My cousin. She would not know anyone. Everybody will mostly be adults. And she could not talk to my guests. And besides, I really do not know her."

She nodded, not disapproving that information. "Well. A very modest request."

"I have everything I need. I have my aishid. I have a good tutor. I have my own rooms. I have Boji."

"That reprehensible creature. Will you take *him* to visit your great-grandmother?"

"May I?" He was really worried about Boji if he had to leave him. Eisi was a little afraid of him, since he had gotten his finger nipped. "And I know Great-grandmother has servants, but might I take Eisi and Lieidi with me?"

His mother smiled that secret smile she had when something amused her. "Son of mine, this is your household. You may deal with it as you wish. I see I have nothing to do. I leave everything up to your great-grandmother."

That was down a track he wished she would not take. And there were, regarding her and his grandmother, things he wanted to know.

"What did you talk about?" he asked. "When you walked with Great-grandmother at the party, *what* did you talk about?"

His mother's face went suddenly very serious. "Things," she said. "Things that truly are not that interesting."

"*I* would be interested, honored Mother."

"Ask her. And when you do ask her, perhaps you will do me a favor."

"What favor, honored Mother?"

"She offered me staff. And a bodyguard. If you will do me the particular favor, son of mine, tell her a skilled hairdresser who has also had a child would gain my deep gratitude at this point."

"A hairdresser, honored Mother."

"Truly," she said. "Such a gift might win my gratitude. Shall I tell you my logic? It is very simple. The secrets of your father's household are no secret from your great-grandmother. This is *not* the case with other clans who have offered. So tell her yes, I have thought about it. I shall *accept* such assistance, not the bodyguard, not the wardrobe mistress. I wish to see how a small instance runs, and where man'chi may truly lie."

"I shall ask her, then, honored Mother. I shall be glad to ask her."

"I shall be relieved," his mother said in a low voice, "beyond telling. But if this hairdresser bears tales to your great-uncle, understand, she will regret it—I want *no* such connections. I am trusting your great-grandmother in this one thing." She made another tweak at the straying lock. It was hopeless. It was loose again in the next instant. "Even your hair is stubborn. Go. Be good. Look forward to your guests."

He felt good. Truly happy. He had never in his memory had so good a conversation with his mother. But his great-grandmother's teaching immediately nudged at him to be a little suspicious.

There was *one* place to go with such a confusing situation: man'chi was a clear guide on that matter. When he took his leave of his mother, he gathered his aishid and went back to his *father's* office, interrupting his father's work one more time.

He bowed slightly and said, quietly, "Honored Father, Mother has asked me to ask Great-grandmother for a hairdresser."

"Gods less fortunate!" His father shoved his chair back from his desk and looked at him, up and down.

"One feared there might be a problem with that, honored Father."

"Who first suggested this?"

"I think Great-grandmother might have offered. When they were at the party."

His father had no expression at all for several heartbeats. Then he lifted an eyebrow and said, *"Women."*

"Shall I ask mani, honored Father?"

"Oh, do. Better *my* grandmother than *her* uncle." His father kept looking at him, or through him. He stood still. It was never a good idea to interrupt his father's thinking.

"It is *not*," his father said, "a bad idea. —And you did not suggest it."

"No, honored Father."

His father waved a dismissal. "Go. Send a message to your great-grandmother. You are not to leave the apartment until she sends for you. She is occupied with the legislation. But she will read your letter."

He had not at all expected to be able to go in person. They were still under the security alert, about Grandfather. "Yes," he said, bowed again, went out to the hall and took his aishid back to his own sitting room.

"What happened?" Jegari asked.

I think my mother is sniping at my father, was what he thought. She knew his father did *not* want Great-grandmother entangled in his affairs. He had fought that all his life.

But Father himself had had a lot of trouble getting staff. The aishid and staff his father had grown up with had died in the coup. The ones he had gotten next had tried to kill him. He had picked distant relatives that he knew he could trust, and now there were a lot of lords *and* the Guild upset about it.

Mani's bodyguards . . . nobody fussed about.

So maybe it was a good thing. Maybe his mother was being very practical. His mother had looked sad and different, now. Her hair very plain, her nails unpolished. Maybe his mother simply did not feel like dressing up, with headaches and all. But her servants had used to do her hair, and press the lace, and the two girls from the kitchen probably could not be trusted with the iron and the lace.

So . . . he had better write a letter and have one of his aishid take it before his mother changed her mind.

He was very careful about it. He had no wish to have everything collapse into another argument from mani's side. He wrote:

To mani, honored Great-grandmother, from Cajeiri, your Great-grandson. My mother has no staff. She has asked me to write to you asking for help which you offered at the party. She does not feel well now. She particularly wants a hairdresser. She wants a woman who has had a child.

He took a new piece of paper and changed the words: instead of *wants,* which was rude, he wrote, *she particularly wishes to have,* and *she also wishes to have.*

He wrote, after that: *I have told my father too and he thinks it is a good idea.*

That was hedging the truth a little. But it made a good ending and it might make Great-grandmother curious enough to go along with it.

If Great-grandmother could *get* a good hairdresser. She might have to fly somebody in from Malguri.

It will make me happy if you can make my mother happy. Please do it.

And then he remembered the whole other business, astonished that it could all have slipped from his mind.

Mani, my guests are coming early, and my father says I shall go to you as soon as you send for me, and you will be in charge of everything we do just as soon as you send for me. My mother wishes the party to be here, in our apartment—but all the days before and after, until my guests go home on the shuttle, I shall be staying with you, or with nand' Bren if I am inconvenient. I am very happy. I am very much looking forward to this. I shall pack right away.

He revised it in a third copy, just because he had been careless in his penmanship. He wanted it perfect.

Then he dashed off a letter to nand' Bren, who did not care about his penmanship.

He put the one to mani in his best message cylinder, and sent that one with Lucasi. He put the other in his second-best, and sent it with Veijico.

Then he sat down in his own little sitting room, on the edge of his chair, all happiness, and looked at Antaro and Jegari, who still amazed him, they looked so official and grown-up.

"We are going to stay with Great-grandmother," he said. "We have to pack. We have to take Boji with us, but Eisi and Lieidi are going with us, too." He drew a deep, shuddery breath, and let it go. "I think, I think, nadiin-ji, that my birthday is really about to happen."

10

The Committee on Finance was meeting, and the committee room doors were shut. The paidhi, down the hall in the legislative lounge, was on his second pot of strong tea, while his aishid kept contact with the dowager's—who were in touch with Tatiseigi's bodyguard, Tatiseigi being a very important force behind those closed doors, and doing a great deal of talking, on that committee.

Reports came in slowly, by runners who stood at the front of the room and reported succinctly on the progress of the bill. The bill was being read. Again.

He had two of his secretarial staff doing exactly the same thing, from the gallery of the large meeting room, observing not only the progress of the bill, but who was talking to whom that might be significant. The two cycled back to him in turns, bringing him notes, occasionally a whispered word—not the only such runners communicating with individuals in the lounge.

There were motions to table. Again.

Damn, Bren thought. And there was not a thing he could do. The aiji might intervene, as the alleged author of the bill, but even Tabini didn't have the clout with Finance that the dowager did . . . and she had enemies in that room, too.

And the fact that he, the paidhi had written much of the bill—was *not* something its supporters were advertising to anybody in that conservative-dominated meeting

room. One had to wonder if that fact might yet get out
and sway votes.

The bill didn't need any more problems. It was a sensitive matter, the inclusion of the tribal peoples as equals
in the aishidi'tat. It meant dismantling the tribes' special
status, giving them a voice in the Bujavid, and releasing,
for many of the clans, an ancient prejudice, at least, that
held the tribes as foreign to the mainland.

On the other side of the scales, tribal peoples would
agree to abandon their independence and their separate
languages for official use—the only exception being
their own ceremonial and festival observances. It *also*
entailed something the conservatives wanted: an agreement to accept operations of all guilds within the former
tribal lands, and, by separate agreement with the tribes,
they would not insist on tribal peoples serving only their
own clan—they would adopt, in essence, the same rule
the Ragi clans followed, which would put Edi and Gan
in service in households all across the aishidi'tat. Tatiseigi and the dowager weren't making any noise about
that matter, yet, just letting that separate little bomb skit-
ter through unnoticed.

In effect, if it passed, there would be a fairly rapid
blending of the tribal peoples into the mainstream of the
aishidi'tat. The centuries-old practice of allowing special,
nearly rule-free local branches of some guilds to exist in
the Marid, and in sections of the East, was going to be
used one last time, to get the tribal peoples within the
Guild system—after which the tribes themselves—and
the Marid, and the East, would all remove that provision.
He didn't personally like it: that practice had provided
the shelter that had let the Shadow Guild get organized,
and he wanted it gone.

All in all, it was a very delicate push and pull going on
in that chamber, which had started out as a death-trap
for the critical bill. The paidhi waited, listened to the official reports, always ready to step in if for some unguessable reason someone wanted to ask him any question
that he actually wanted to answer.

But so far, and thank God, no, no one asked. So the

legislative lounge, safely removed from the committee rooms, was as close as he had to come to the battleground.

Race, religion, language, finance, and a history of double-crosses and broken promises were all involved. So was the long-simmering issue of the Marid's ambition to take Sarini Province, and the resentment of the tribal peoples about being settled where they had been settled in the first place, after Mospheira had been ceded to humans—another reason he did not want to be called into that chamber as a district lord.

The next report, delivered by the marshal to the whole lounge, said that motions to table had been denied. Again.

Thank God.

Then—periodic reports by his runners—Tatiseigi again got up to speak, arguing for the necessity of the bill and attaching the approval of his own local Padi Valley Association, the heart of the Ragi district.

The Morisoni lord, of the second largest northern clan, objected and cited the disapproval of the Northern Association, including Ajuri, who was not present, and the disapproval of the Kadagidi, who were also not present, a major clan of the Padi Valley. There were, that lord added, unvoiced objections, and had the gall to suggest the Taibeni lord was absent from the floor because, due to personal links to the aiji's clan, he would not speak *against* the bill.

The Morisoni lord did not call Tatiseigi a liar. But it was damned close. And one could imagine Lord Tatiseigi was taking notes, in that inscrutable way of his, and meant to have another say.

But Dur got up at that point, the *elder* Lord Dur, bringing with his oral statement the written approval of the Coastal Association.

Then Tatiseigi (the runner arrived fairly bubbling with satisfaction) arose to object to the prior statement, and produced a proxy signed by his former enemy the Taibeni lord, *authorizing* a vote in favor of the bill. Bren almost wished he had been in the room for *that* piece of theater.

So much for the Morisoni claim as to where the Taibeni stood.

The dowager *and* Tatiseigi spoke, backing the bill, interests at opposite ends of the continent. Geigi's shy proxy, Lord Haidiri, then got up and offered his own handful of West Coast proxies backing the bill, for Sarini Province, the South Coastal Association, and Najida, which, of course, was Bren.

Hard upon that moment, the dowager produced a document from Lord Machigi, backing the bill in the name of the entire Marid. There was no one to speak for the two embattled northern sections of the Marid.

A motion was then made by the Northern Association, in the person of a western range lord, Ajuri being absent, to *add* the objection of the missing two northern clans of the Marid.

Tatiseigi objected, saying it was indecent to use the votes of two regions currently under occupation by the Assassins' Guild because of subversive activity and attacks on Sarini Province.

Tatiseigi called for a vote. And was observed to be talking in the aisle to three of the opposition.

The motion to add the votes was denied. By two votes.

God, it was a war in there.

Then the opposition tried again to table the bill, which would have killed it.

Lord Tatiseigi, rising, immediately called for a vote on the bill.

Bren called for another cup of tea and wished it were a brandy. He ordinarily did not vote. He *was* voting on this occasion, while sitting in the legislative lounge, not because he was a member of Finance, but because he was a lord in the most affected districts. He had given his proxy to Haidiri, Geigi's proxy, who had a vote in this business for the same reason, and he had privately urged those in the Liberal caucus, who followed the paidhi-aiji and Lord Geigi, to back the bill with everything they had—with the few members they had on that committee. With the dowager, *and* the dowager's ally, Lord Machigi— and Lord Tatiseigi, the head of the Conservative Caucus, voting *with* the Taibeni, another district that usually did not appear in the legislature—the proponents of the tribal bill forced a vote. The vote *for* voting on the bill—passed.

Bren did mental math, trying to predict which of the conservatives would stand with the committee head, opposed to the bill, and which might follow Tatiseigi.

The vote was delayed, with a call for a quorum of regions. Certain of the legislators had showed up in the lounge, conferred at extreme leisure, then went back to the floor as the vote progressed, restoring the required quorum.

God. Four of the oldest clans were in the For column, plus all those associations geographically affected by the bill, plus the two largest sub associations on the continent—what more could honest folk want?

But the math, with the smaller regions, in this hostile committee, was still dicey. There was yet another try, this one on the Against side, at tabling the bill for later debate and possible revision, saying it was being rammed through at indecorous speed.

That failed.

Then an amendment was proposed—good God!—from their own ranks: Separti Township's representative, coming back from a break, wanted a prohibition against the Edi enlarging the port on the Kajiminda Peninsula. It was a not-too-veiled suggestion the Edi, with a larger port, would continue their attacks on Marid shipping, but it came from Separti, whose shipping would be affected by competition, and it came after a break.

Someone had cornered that man. If Geigi were here, he'd back the Separti representative into a convenient corner, exuding dominant man'chi, and make him understand the value of sticking with one's district in a crisis.

Haidiri was only Geigi's proxy. He was new to this business, and timid. He should be the one to pull his subordinate district into line, with whatever deals or force he had, and by all reports from the runners, he was asking the marshal what he could do to object.

The amendment, however, failed. Tatiseigi's sometime

ally to the east, beyond the Kadagidi, slipped to Tatisei-gi's side during the recess. With the dowager, *and* Lord Machigi's proxy—and, belatedly, Separti, who came back to their side—the proponents of the tribal bill mustered a yea vote to prevent any more amendments.

Opposed to the bill were the third-largest association and some of their more remote associates. If the bill could get to the legislative floor—it should have the numbers. But the more obstinate conservatives owned this committee, where the bill was still stuck without a recommendation to pass it.

And now the vice-head of Finance, a rival of Tatisei-gi's, got up to speak.

And speak.

Jago came in and dropped into the vacant leather chair across the little table. He *expected* news from the committee room.

It wasn't.

"The young gentleman," she began, "has just written the dowager, requesting she supply staff for his mother. And stating that he and his guests will be *the dowager's* guests, excepting for the actual birthday festivity itself."

He was concentrating so hard on the committee matter it took several heartbeats for the words even to make sense.

And another several for the implications to snap together into a structure.

Are you serious? The question occurred to him, at least. But Jago, on duty, was *always* serious.

"Have *you* arranged this?" he asked. Plural. Meaning any of his bodyguard.

"The request," Jago said, "came in the boy's own hand, from him. He states that his mother made the suggestion and his father has approved."

His *mother* requested staff of Ilisidi. He'd have sworn there was no way in hell Damiri would want that clan attending her.

And Tabini had agreed. When there was no way in hell Tabini had wanted his *grandmother* getting information from inside his household.

"What," he asked Jago, with his mind suddenly jittering between the committee situation, the aiji's admittedly dicey security situation — and that remarkable set of interactions at the reception, *"what* precisely is going on, Jago-ji? Do *you* have any idea?"

Someone walked past. Jago leaned forward, nearly forehead to forehead and whispered, to avoid being overheard in this cavernous and treacherous room. "Cenedi received the message, couriered by Lucasi. He had Casimi bring the letter to us, rather than transmit anything. Cenedi wishes to know if *you* had mediated this move, Bren-ji."

"No," he whispered back. "Not officially nor privately. I am as surprised as anyone."

"Indeed. Banichi suggests Damiri-daja may actually be the prime force behind this request. Considering her appearance at the reception, she will *politic* with Lord Tatiseigi and send him signals. But she will not request staff of him."

The green and white dress. When Jago put it in the context of holding out promises to Tatiseigi, but not taking staff from him, it made a certain sense. Tabini himself was not going to go to his grandmother begging favors: he had rather be roasted over a slow fire. But what had Damiri said at the reception? *Everyone in this hall has attempted to place servants on my staff . . .*

Evidently Damiri had added two and two and come up with a way in which she could avoid being tributary to her uncle — namely allying herself with the one person on earth whom Tatiseigi deferred to without reservation or embarrassment: the aiji-dowager. Accepting *any* other offer would offend Tatiseigi, who was a connection Damiri had to preserve. The dowager, seeing the situation, had apparently offered her an alternative. And now he had a *far* better idea what Ilisidi had said to Damiri that night.

Hell, *yes*, it was a good move. It positioned Damiri not as an Atageini hanger-on, dependent on her uncle, nor as Tabini's almost-divorced consort; nor yet as Lord Komaji's alienated and, through most of her life, *unwanted* Atageini daughter —

The marriage with Damiri had been a match of sexual attraction, in Tabini's case, with more attention to her Padi Valley connections than to an undistinguished father in a fairly minor northern clan.

But if Damiri suddenly became a close ally of the aiji-dowager, the one force on earth who held her own toe to toe with Tabini himself . . . it was damned certain Damiri saw something to gain.

If Damiri *had* mentally and emotionally gotten past the alienation of her son—and started thinking in a practical way of her own future, and of her soon-to-be-born daughter's future—

Damn. He had been watching one hand while the *other* had been moving. It was not an unknown situation in the aiji's court, but he rarely these days found himself so blindsided.

"Interesting," he said. In the legislative sitting room, with an attendant now moving within earshot, replacing a pot of tea, it was all he could say. "Jago-ji, keep me informed."

So Tabini was going to send Cajeiri and his foreign guests to his great-grandmother's very conservative, very traditional house—the mediaeval stronghold of Malguri.

His whimsical revenge on his grandmother—for his having to accept Malguri servants in his house?

No. Affairs of state might occasionally have petty motives, but there was deeper purpose when it regarded security. Tabini's household, with a crisis between Tabini and his consort, was *not* the best place for a collection of clueless and provocative human children.

He had expected to be the one called in to assist with the event. He had expected to house the heir's young guests, as the person who could actually *talk* to them and educate them in protocols before they made any really serious mistakes. No doubt he would still serve in that capacity—though the dowager *and* Cenedi and others of her staff actually understood ship-speak, a fact she was never going to advertise.

Tabini played excellent chess. One should never forget that fact. So did Damiri.

And so did the aiji-dowager.

God, he could almost see the pathways of it. But some of these winding trails had *two* layers. At least two.

Jago left him, and he was sure she would be back. The sitting room attendant had provided a fresh pot of tea, poured a cup and took the cooling pot away. Tea was an unending resource, once one had ordered a pot.

News came, finally, not with Jago's return, but with the gentleman with a long pole and a hook, who, in the traditional manner, reached up on the wall to the framed agenda board, and slid bill number 2823 over to the right, into the slot for the hasdrawad.

The tribal bill had just passed committee, by a vote of 43 to 41.

Bren let out a long, slow breath.

Passed. Now the legislature would debate the tribal bill, presumably would pass it—and the paidhi did not officially want to hear the reasoning behind some of the yes votes it would draw: the expectation that both tribal peoples would be swallowed up in large regional associations where they would be junior, small, and never, ever have any political force.

That expectation didn't take into account that little bomb in the package, the business with the guilds.

And given the character of the Grandmother of the Edi, and Her of the Gan, he had every confidence the tribal peoples would not fade into quiet compliance. He only hoped the Grandmothers would appoint two of the quieter voices actually to sit in the legislature. He could not imagine *them* in that committee room.

So with all the potential troubles yet to come—the bill had now gotten to the floor, and it, thank God, had the votes to pass.

He felt like celebrating. He considered giving the whole staff the next day off and just sleeping in.

Then the representative of the Messengers' Guild brought over the official bowl for the sitting room, and in it was one black cylinder with a red seal.

Word from Tabini.

He absently poured himself yet one more cup of tea

for reinforcement and cracked the seal with a thumbnail, expecting something about the bill—or the security arrangements.

It said, beyond the usual salutations:

Remember our conversation. This is that moment. My son is going to my grandmother, who will host his guests and handle all events up to the festivity.

Following a heated discussion in which my wife concluded the world does not contain a hairdresser who can pass both security considerations and her requirements, my wife has applied to my grandmother for staff and my grandmother has just agreed. I am sure you will not need to tell your bodyguard, but should it have escaped notice, confirm it for them.

It must have been a message passed to the committee room. With all *that* going on. God.

The tribal bill, I am assured, will clear committee today. The cell phone bill will be tabled as we have requested, to be brought up in some future session. The resolution in favor of the Marid agreement will likely pass.

My wife is having recurrent dreams that there are strangers in the house. I am not superstitious, but she has wanted the kabiu of the house adjusted, and she does not sleep well. She takes alarm at bumps in the night and our son's parid'ja will occasionally cry out in the daytime, which does not improve her feeling of danger. Therefore I am sending the animal with my son and his guests, while my wife and I resolve our difficulties regarding staff and security, which will likely involve more than a hairdresser.

I leave it to my grandmother and to you as to where to entertain these children. My son will celebrate his birthday here in Shejidan, where both his parents can properly congratulate him. He may at that time avail himself of the museum and the natural history exhibit as well as the services of the Bujavid staff, provided that we shall have been able to arrange adequate security.

Careful thought persuades me that my wife's decision, which we wish understood, is entirely her own, has moved the household expediently toward the best source of auxiliary security available.

The new arrangement will entail a hairdresser, and added security, and we are confident this is the best solution.

This letter is not for the official archive of our correspondence. We request you burn it and preserve no word of it.

You may of course rely on the red car and all official assistance in dealing with the visitors.

In caring for my son, care also for your own safety and my grandmother's. These are unsettled times. But when have they not been?

Deep, deep breath. He read it again to be sure of the nuance. And put the letter back into the cylinder and the cylinder into his most secure pocket, to have it dealt with by his aishid.

His problem. Tabini was giving *him* the children. He had to refocus.

He gathered up his work, had the attendant notify whoever of his bodyguard was at the door at the moment, and walked out.

Banichi smoothly intercepted him.

"The shuttle has launched from the station, Bren-ji," Banichi said, before he could say anything. "It is on its way."

He waited until they got upstairs, into the foyer of their own apartment, and only Narani was witness. Narani took his coat, and his case of papers.

And offered the message bowl, in which there was one cylinder he well knew.

Cajeiri.

"I shall read this," he said, "in my office. Banichi-ji, nadiin-ji, if you will be there."

"Yes," Banichi said.

They walked back to the office. Bren gave them Tabini's letter, with its cylinder, then sat down in his work chair, opened Cajeiri's cylinder, unrolled the little paper and flattened it under a heavy glass designed for that purpose.

It said, *To Nand' Bren, from Cajeiri,*

I am very happy. I am coming to visit you and mani as soon as you send for me. I am supposed to be in mani's apartment, but she is busy in meetings. Will you come get me until she can?

PS. I have to take Boji with me. He eats eggs. About four a day.

He looked at his aishid. "The boy is still at home. He wants to come here now. His father's standing order is that whenever he wishes to come here, I should not delay him. Banichi, Jago—go get him. Quietly. One does not know what the situation is over there."

"Yes," Banichi said.

Tano and Algini stayed, and Banichi and Jago shut the door behind them.

"Likely we shall be housing the human children until the birthday festivity," he said, "and Cajeiri will have Boji with him—one hopes, *with* his cage. We may be somewhat disrupted, but we will manage. Please advise Cenedi of whatever of the situation he might not have heard. About Boji, among other things."

"Yes," Algini said. And added, "We shall arrange for the red car, for the spaceport, when the shuttle is ready to land. Either we or the dowager will need to pick up the children."

"Do that, Gini-ji." He let go a slow breath, thinking of that conversation he had had with Tabini, about problems in the household, and about his own subsequent conversation with Damiri. The dowager *had* had tea with Damiri, the morning after—but as to the outcome between those two, his aishid had not been able to tell him. So either Cenedi didn't know what the two women had said to each other—or wouldn't say, even to them. "As to what may be happening next door, with Tabini-aiji and Lady Damiri, one has no idea. One hopes for a good outcome."

"We are surprised the boy is sent out on such short notice," Tano said. "Shall we contact the aiji's guard and ask the reason?"

"Discreetly," he said.

"You will wear the vest, Bren-ji," Algini said. "Lord

Geigi has moved a shuttle off-schedule to provide a shortened time frame—for any plans Ajuri might make."

"He has said so?" He was astonished. Shuttles delayed at times, on technical issues. They rarely rushed a launch to be early.

"On our advice, Bren-ji. We requested he move the schedule. He said he would attempt it. He has put *Paisien* up in the flight order, ahead of *Shai-shan*. There are no passengers listed on the manifest for *Paisien*. There are four listed for *Shai-shan*. The manifests will stay as they are, so *both* lie."

Five days early.

Early. To throw off any plans Ajuri had laid, and disrupt any mischief.

"One understands," he said. "We have the legislation as settled as we can manage. We are assured it will pass. We can go wherever we need go."

If Tabini could somehow find the time alone with Damiri to sort out the problems within his household, all to the good. It might be the best timing—at least to have Cajeiri elsewhere.

In the meanwhile, given the boy suddenly on *his* hands, and the dowager rearranging her plans, there were things to do.

It started with phoning his own clerical office, commending the runners who had served him today, and asking the director to come meet with him in his apartment.

Tea with the worthy gentleman, who had served him under some very dicey circumstances, including during the coup.

He would instruct the man to lay down a preliminary official schedule that looked—at least until they were out at the spaceport picking up Cajeiri's guests—as if the paidhi-aiji were doing business as usual.

It was a minimal sort of ruse, one they could adjust by the hour, and it might end up being one of several such schedules he let leak, but he thought it prudent.

He also had to arrange with Lord Dur, quietly, to have that very respectable gentleman attend the Tribal Peoples bill on its course through the legislature, and advise his office of events.

Then he notified Bindanda that the young gentleman was dining with them, that the dowager might be. And that they needed a supply of eggs.

He had only time to draft the first half of his message to Dur before he heard Narani open the front door.

That would be Banichi and Jago, with the young gentleman in hand. There might or there might not be baggage. If there was not, if the young gentleman were quitting his residence in a Situation, his staff might have to go next door a little later and collect it from Tabini's staff.

Well, it sounded, out there, that there was something more arriving than the usual luggage cart, something that rolled and rattled in an odd way. He guessed what *that* might be, even before he heard a sudden bloodcurdling shriek in his foyer.

Doors opened and closed and staff stirred from every recess of the servants' halls, startled out of whatever they were doing.

He left his letter unfinished, capped the inkwell, and blew out the waxjack before he rose and opened his office door.

There in his foyer was the boy and a very large antique cage.

"Nand' Bren, we are here!" Cajeiri said. "And Boji." There was an earsplitting shriek. "We are sorry about Boji. He is excited."

Tano and Algini came from the security station. The sitting room door opened, the young kitchen girls peering past the junior cook, who had arrived with one of the kitchen knives in hand.

There were, with Cajeiri, with their baggage, but still partly outside the doors, the young gentleman's bodyguard and two servants in Ragi livery.

"These two young men are—" Bren asked.

"My servants, nandi." Another bow, more nicely delivered. "We are all here! We are so glad! *One is grate-ful!*"

"Well, well, your great-grandmother will decide where you will stay this evening, and in what state." He almost added, And who will house Boji and the servants, but he feared he already knew that answer. "She has been all day in a meeting, and one does expect she will be getting out of it about now, but you may at least settle long enough for tea and cakes, shall you not? Ladi-ji, if you will move the cage into the guest room for now." The latter to Jeladi. He feared for the antique carpet runner, and feared an escape with the door still open, but the sitting room was a far worse choice, considering the vases.

Meanwhile baggage was inbound, Narani and Jeladi, Cajeiri's servants, and his young bodyguard all handing it in, more and more of it piling up in the foyer. "Welcome," he said to all and sundry, and to Narani: "Tea for myself and the young gentleman. Advise the dowager's bodyguard and say that the dowager would be welcome for a modest and informal supper here, should she wish."

Narani gave a little bow, and all those things would happen in short order. Bren showed the young gentleman into the sitting room, and they sat and had tea and cakes, quite spoiling any potential dinner, but Cajeiri was in a high good mood, chattering on about the party he hoped to have and asking questions about the shuttle and could he, could he, could he go to the spaceport to meet his young associates?

"That rests with your great-grandmother, young gentleman," Bren said. "You will have to ask her. And do be somewhat prepared for her to forbid it: we have some security concerns, and you know such situations can change on very short notice."

"But is there a *chance,* nandi?"

"There is a chance, but one cannot promise: we get our advice from our bodyguards. And one has no idea what their landing schedule is, nor are they likely to decide it yet—as with all these things, they will watch the weather."

"Is it going to be good weather? I hope it will be good weather."

In point of fact he had absolutely no idea what the weather was outside. It could be pouring a monsoon over the city, and he had been so locked in his work, in an apartment without windows, and offices without windows, that he had not the least notion what was going on in the natural world.

"I shall inquire," he said. But Cajeiri's question to his own bodyguard brought the answer that, indeed, it had just been raining, but the weather was due to clear tomorrow.

"I hope they may hurry," Cajeiri said.

"They will be down in good weather, likely morning after next, young gentleman."

"Might we go to Najida and go on your boat, nand' Bren?"

"Only your great-grandmother and your parents can say that, young gentleman." He could not fault the boy for being excited and full of ideas. But negotiating with a Marid warlord was no more strain than dealing with Cajeiri—who had his hopes all up and a justified fear that everything could fall apart on some adult whim. He would not promise things not in his hands. He could not appear to promise anything, and the boy had more changes of direction than Malguri's upland roads.

"When do you think they will actually land?" the boy asked. "At what hour?"

"All depending on the weather, young gentleman. You know these things. You took the same flight."

"I was not entirely paying attention," Cajeiri said, looking down, then up, sharply. "And I was upset about my birthday, nandi."

It *had* been that time of year, when all hell had broken loose.

"And anyway," Cajeiri said, "we were going to land over on Mospheira, not in the aishidi'tat."

"It is very little difference," Bren said, "when you are moving that fast. You would only be a few minutes off."

"Can we see them land? Can we be there to watch?"

"Ask your great-grandmother such things, young

gentleman." He had *so* many things he had to do, letters he had to write, arrangements to make before things started moving—but he was not about to leave the young gentleman unattended and in a state of high excitement.

He was very relieved when Jago came in to say they had been in touch with Cenedi, that they had informed the dowager as requested, and that the dowager was arriving to take charge of her grandson—and his baggage—at any moment.

"Well," Bren began, but just then came a knock at the door, and it opened. That, he was sure, would be Ilisidi herself, or at very least, Cenedi.

Rescue.

"I am sure we will take care of Boji for you," Bren said to his young guest. "I have ordered sufficient eggs."

"He likes them raw, nandi."

"One is not surprised to hear it."

"You just give them to him. But sometimes we boil one. For a joke. He will eat it. But it confuses him."

"We shall never have eggs left over from breakfast, then." He rose, thinking he would have to meet Ilisidi, and *offer* to keep Boji.

The door opened. Jeladi ducked in, shut the door at his back and bowed. "Nandi. Lord *Tatiseigi* is in the foyer, nandi."

He tried not to register utter dismay. One thing was certain: he could not sit in lordly splendor in his sitting room and ask Tatiseigi be brought in like some visiting client. He bowed to his young guest, and went to the door as Jeladi opened it.

Indeed, Lord Tatiseigi, with his full bodyguard, stood in the foyer, awaiting the courtesy of his appearance.

"Nandi," Bren said, "you are very welcome here. Do accept the hospitality of the sitting room. The aiji-dowager or her bodyguard will be here at any moment to pick up the young gentleman. I took your arrival for hers. Would you care for tea?"

"Things are running in a very slipshod way, nandi. This spaceship is proceeding ahead of plans and we hear only by our bodyguard's advisement that the young gentleman has been turned out and sent here—with no warning, nandi, with no notice at all. We hope that there is some *planning* involved in this!"

He was not about to explain Geigi's meddling with the shuttle launch schedule. Tatiseigi liked all events well-planned, on firm schedules. He simply said, "Once the young gentleman knew the shuttle was coming, he was very anxious to be underway, nandi, and you and the dowager have been so very involved in the committee meeting ..."

"Which is over," Tatiseigi said somewhat more mildly.

"One heard it had gone well, with all gratitude to your efforts, indeed. I listened from the tea room, discreetly. I was available to get the message, and I was able to be here to meet the young gentleman. And to take custody of the young gentleman's parid'ja, which needs to be housed, temporarily." He was absolute sure Tatiseigi would not want *that* duty.

"Uncle," Cajeiri said from the doorway.

"My boy," Tatiseigi said. "We trust you have not been a burden to the paidhi."

"No, Great-uncle! Nand' Bren has been explaining the shuttle schedule. And he says we might go to Najida!"

"I said," Bren said quietly and quickly—a visit to Najida surely *not* being Tatiseigi's fondest wish—"that all such questions would be the dowager's to decide."

"Well!" Tatiseigi said. "How would you like to go to Tirnamardi instead, young gentleman, and ride mecheiti?"

Tatiseigi's estate? With human guests? Three—possibly four—very *young* human guests?

He thought of his conversation with Jago, in the servants' bath.

And that with Geigi, in his office.

But Cajeiri didn't waste a second.

"To *Tirnamardi,* Great-uncle?"

"We have made arrangements with your great-grandmother, considering this madness with the shuttle schedule and the inconvenience of having these guests in residence in the Bujavid. We have *ample* room."

And Kadagidi clan next door. And a feud with Ajuri, not that far to the north.

"*Yes!*" the young rascal cried. "Oh, *yes!*"

"Well, well," Tatiseigi said. "You shall, then!" He turned a glance toward Bren. "These young people do not speak Ragi, do they?"

"It is not likely they do, beyond a few words, nandi."

"Well, then, nand' paidhi, so the aiji-dowager said, and you will surely attend," Tatiseigi said. And added, whimsically, "I do trust your aishid will *not* blow up another of my bedrooms!"

"Assuredly not, nandi!"

Oh, the man was in a good mood. But he could not be taking possession of Cajeiri and taking him off to his apartment, however short the walk—he had promised Tabini to take the boy into *his* keeping, and that was what was authorized. Tano and Algini had an unobstructed view, where they were standing, and he passed an emergency hand-signal that non-Guild were not supposed to use.

"The aiji-dowager is on her way, nandi," Tano said immediately.

"Indeed," Bren said. "Lord Tatiseigi, will you like a pot of tea, and to wait for the dowager?"

"We have had tea enough at the legislative reception," Tatiseigi said, not budging, "but so, well, we shall wait. Will you need to send for riding clothes, nephew?"

"No, Great-uncle. I have everything with me."

"Who has seen to your wardrobe, young man? Has your father's staff?"

"I have *servants,* now, Great-uncle! I have my *own* staff."

"With you?"

"Indeed, Great-uncle, I have two servants and my bodyguard."

"Well, well," Tatiseigi said. "Servants, indeed! Have you a warm coat? Formal clothing as well?"

"One had thought we might go to Najida, Great-uncle, or Malguri, so I have everything in my baggage."

"Exemplary foresight," Tatiseigi said. "Exemplary! Well. Well." They were standing with enough Guild in attendance for a small war, with Tatiseigi's bodyguards outside and Cajeiri's four and Banichi and Jago now in the foyer, and Tatiseigi in the doorway itself so that Narani had not been able to close it.

But they were about to acquire a fourth set of bodyguards. Bren heard the sounds of another approach to the door, men's footsteps, and the light tap of Ilisidi's cane on the stone flooring of the hall.

He was not the only one hearing it. "Mani is coming," Cajeiri said, and indeed, Tatiseigi's bodyguard moved out of the way in advance of that oncoming presence.

Tap. Tap. Tap. At her own pace, Ilisidi appeared in the doorway.

"Well," she said, resting hands on her cane. "Well, Great-grandson. Tati-ji. Nand' paidhi. Are we holding a meeting in the hallway?"

"Mani, Great-uncle has said we shall go to Tirnamardi!"

"That we shall," she said, both hands on her cane, with Cenedi and her guard behind her. "We shall go to the spaceport, gather up your young guests, and take them to enjoy a healthful sojourn in the country. Nand' paidhi, we trust you can clear your schedule to go with us."

Her idea. Or Cenedi's. He recalled, again, that conversation in the bath. The business about positioning forces.

"I am in process of doing that right now, aiji-ma."

"Well, well, we shall have a day or two to see the bill passed. You are packed, nand' paidhi?"

"I shall be, aiji-ma."

"Tati-ji?"

"My staff will assure it," Tatiseigi said.

"Well, we all three will be busy. Lord Tatiseigi and I will speak for the bill in the tashrid tomorrow. We expect the paidhi-aiji will have a statement to read into the record."

"I have it ready, aiji-ma."

"Dur will present it. Tati-ji, we expect you at dinner this evening. We shall discuss our strategy over brandy. We would expect that the paidhi-aiji's staff has prepared a dinner here, and that there might be sufficient for my grandson."

That was to say, stay home. Take care of the boy and his staff. Keep him contained.

They were about to do something entirely outrageous and take the boy and his guests to a venue they *knew* had security problems, and the person who most fiercely protected the boy was *driving* this insane venture, for reasons she was not going to explain right now. He understood that part clearly. And that *yes* was all he *could* say.

"Easily, aiji-ma. *And* we shall see to the parid'ja." Whatever her plans, the dowager needed to know that the creature had become part of the arrangement.

"The parid'ja," Ilisidi echoed him in a little dismay. And to her great-grandson: "Was this arranged?"

Cajeiri put on a worried face. "My servants are with me, mani, and there would be no one in my father's apartment to take care of him."

Ilisidi drew a deep breath. "Well." And cast a questioning look at Bren.

"Aiji-ma, one is certain we shall manage. Whether he will go with us . . ."

"May he, mani?" Cajeiri asked. "He has his cage, Great-grandmother! It is a very secure cage! It has rollers!"

Tatiseigi had no expression at all for the moment. Tatiseigi's desire to move the young gentleman into his vicinity had been strong enough even to accommodate young humans, at least conceptually—perhaps imagining they, like the paidhi-aiji, had acquired atevi virtues and could eat arsenic with abandon.

Boji, however, was surely another matter.

"My servants, mani, they know how to take care of him, so he is no trouble. He is *very* clean, Great-uncle!"

Tatiseigi's mouth opened. His expressionlessness

showed a struggle to warm to the idea. A heartbeat later he said, "One can agree, Sidi-ji, if you wish," and he was committed to it.

Bren almost said, in the next breath, One is certain my staff could manage . . . in the thought that the steadiness of Tatiseigi's nerves was going to be tested far enough, with Cajeiri's guests.

But the dowager had already nodded. Cajeiri had heard the one and seen the other. And that was that.

As many teacakes as he could eat, before a very good dinner, with nand' Bren's whole aishid and his own all at the table, and another dessert after dinner—that was last night; and Cajeiri enjoyed a really comfortable guest room with room for everybody in their own little cubicles.

And in the morning he could sleep late, with no tutor, no need to get up early, nand' Bren had said, and it was such a quiet household—

Except for Boji, who wanted his egg. Boji started to make a fuss, out in the sitting area.

But Eisi had an egg all ready, since last night: he was always good about that. And Cajeiri just pulled the covers over his head, snuggled into abundant pillows, and fell back to sleep on thoughts that the shuttle with his associates aboard was flying through space, getting harder and harder to turn back. Pretty soon not even his father would be able to stop it, because it would be committing itself to the atmosphere.

When he did wake, very late, at one of Boji's little shrieks, he scrambled out of bed in a sudden fear that maybe things were not going so well, and he had been out of touch for hours and hours.

He found all his aishid on the other side of the partition, playing cards in the sitting area, and his servants trying to hush Boji with another egg.

"Jeri-ji," Jegari said.

"Is there any news yet?"

"Regarding the shuttle, none that we know. But nand' Bren's staff is packing, so everything seems on schedule.

He is in his office, and Banichi-nadi says your great-grandmother and Lord Tatiseigi are in the legislative session, so everything there is what they planned."

He slowly let go a breath, relieved.

"Understand," Lucasi said, "nandi, nand' Bren's aishid has given us *some* cautions, that we should bring all our gear, and that there will be very high security everywhere."

"One is not surprised," he said. His whole life was like that.

"And you will have to watch your guests, and report them to us, if there is any question at all. Your guests will not know the rules at all, nandi. And you will have to keep them safe."

That was a scary thought. He did not want to think of having to watch everybody as if *he* were the one to tell on them. Their time in the secret corridors of the ship had been all of them hiding and playing pranks.

But they were right. They could not do that to his aishid, or to nand' Bren's, or to Great-grandmother's.

"One hears," he agreed, less happy about the situation. It was an upside down arrangement. But there were dangers. There were always dangers. He did not entirely know where they would come from, but his own grandfather was a good guess, and there was still some fighting down in the Marid.

"Will you wish breakfast, Jeri-ji?" Antaro asked. "Cook said that we should advise him when you might wish it."

"One has to dress first," he said. He was glad to change the topic. "But yes. Has everyone eaten?"

"We have not," Antaro said.

He had been inconvenient for his own staff. "I need to dress," he said to his staff in general, "as if my great-grandmother could want to see me. She really might, today."

Breakfast was extravagant, with eggs in a wonderful sauce, and Cajeiri was already enjoying the excitement of an oncoming birthday, with a good many of the rules tumbled down and overset. He was to have his guests, and Great-grandmother, and nand' Bren, and his bodyguard; and Boji, and mecheiti . . .

He was to have his associates from the ship and they were going to be so impressed. . . .

Even if he had to be careful about the rules.

They all would be a year older. They would have grown up a little, too. He was a good deal taller, in just a year. And stronger.

And smarter. He had done things they would never imagine, in their safe life inside the station, particularly: things on the station rarely changed much, and there were no enemies. They screened everybody who got up there, so there was hardly any more secure place anywhere.

He was still anxious. His mother or his father could still change their minds. But his mother was going to be happier, having a staff again. Unless she got mad at Great-grandmother and everything blew up.

Something could still go wrong in the legislature or there could be a security alert: there were a *lot* of people in the world who could cause a security alert.

But the shuttle was on its way, and once it set up on course, and once it really got moving, then it was harder and harder to change anything.

Once the shuttle started entering the atmosphere, it would all go very fast, and they would land, and then his visitors were stuck for fourteen days, or even longer. Nobody could send them back until the shuttle was ready to take them.

He was surprised to be going to Tirnamardi. The last he remembered of it, the front lawn had been a camp, with the hedges broken and a smoky smell over everything—but he was sure it was all nice now. And Great-uncle was going to let them ride. He was sure nobody born on a space station had ever seen anything like a mecheita—and he was going to get to take Boji with him, and they would be amazed by Boji, too. It was going to be wonderful.

He was surprised by his great-uncle. But Great-uncle had been very easy to please ever since Grandfather had gotten thrown out of the court.

He completely understood Great-uncle's feelings in that.

Nand' Bren was busy all day. And his aishid was gone almost all day, carrying messages, doing things nobody talked about. It was all *very* mysterious.

Boji was upset at being in a strange room, until he had eaten so many eggs his stomach was round, and then he curled up and slept.

And there was just nothing to do but play chess with Antaro with everybody else to advise both sides, which made a rowdy sort of chess game.

He had lunch with nand' Bren, who told him everything was perfectly fine, and that he was just writing letters and making phone calls all day, because of business he was going to have to leave.

After lunch, they decided to go through all the bags to make sure they had not forgotten anything they really might need at Tirnamardi, and he thought he might send for his other outdoor coat, but he decided against it, because if he even sent a message next door to his father's major domo, that could stir up questions of why he needed the coat and get his parents interested in where he was going.

Things would be busy over there: his mother would be getting new staff, including a hairdresser, and his father would have new people in, all of them from Malguri district, which was *not* what he had ever expected his father to agree to.

He did not get a call from mani to come to *her* apartment this evening. There was no word from Great-uncle, either. The only one who paid attention to him all day was nand' Bren, having lunch with him, but then nand' Bren was back in his office doing whatever he had done before. The front door opened and closed with people coming and going, and he just sat in the guest room with his aishid. Time just crawled past, hour after hour, with thoughts that things could still go wrong and they still could have an emergency that stopped everything.

He did remember a few more ship-speak sentences to teach his aishid, things useful around mecheiti, like, "Get up on the rails." He thought rails was the word even if they were wooden. And: "Don't walk behind him." And: "Don't walk in front of him." He could not remember the word for tusks.

He reviewed things useful in the house, like, "Be very quiet." And: "Stop." And: "Bow."

His associates had never dealt with mani on the ship. They might be rude, in mani's way of looking at things. Or Great-uncle's. He was worried about that.

But there was nand' Bren to keep them out of trouble and explain things. He reassured himself of that. And he resolved really, truly, not to suggest anything that could get them in trouble, because even if it was not Najida with the boat docks and all, Great-uncle's house had mecheiti.

He really, really expected that mani would take charge of him, since the shuttle had to be getting close to starting down.

Maybe she would call him to dinner.

But she did not. He ended up having supper with only his aishid and nand' Bren, who simply said, "We are still preparing things and sending letters, young gentleman, and while I understand, *please* do not attempt to discuss business at your great-uncle's table."

"One is sorry, nandi." He *knew* mani would be put out with him for asking questions before the brandy hour. And he was trying so hard to be proper.

But nand' Bren did not ask him for a brandy hour. Nand' Bren said he still had work to do at the very last moment, and would he excuse him?

So there went all the answers to all the questions he could ask.

He was sitting in the guest room, playing chess with Jegari, when a knock came at the door.

It was nand' Bren, who said, "Everything is on schedule, young gentleman. We have been in communication with the station. The weather will be fine and clear, and the shuttle landing will be at noon tomorrow. So you know. Plan on breakfast here, but lunch on the train—with your guests."

"Yes!" he cried. "Yes!"

They were coming, they were coming, they were really, truly coming.

11

It had ended up a long, long day—negotiations, letters sent out in code, letters arriving in code, and in the midst of all of it, Lord Tatiseigi's porcelains arrived by train, for exhibit in the Bujavid museum . . .

Those had to be inspected, their display approved, papers signed by the museum director, publicity arranged—it was not Bren's immediate problem, for which he was truly thankful. Lord Tatiseigi handled that quite ably, while Lord Tatiseigi's security arrangements for the trip lay forming in the able hands of the aiji-dowager's bodyguard.

That meant the hovering news services, which had focused on the vote, happened on the historic exhibition before it was officially announced, and then got wind of a rumor that the heir, expected to make news with the arrival of human guests to visit Shejidan about six days from now—was sent on holiday, evidently to celebrate his numerically significant and fortunate birthday not in the Bujavid as planned, but under the *dowager's* auspices.

The rumors rapidly ran to an assassination plot underway, hence the heir being taken elsewhere; or, most elaborate, the landing of the children from space as a dark plot involving activation of the mysterious machinery from space that still sat in various areas once Murini's strongholds.

Fueling the rumors, the same plane that had brought

staff to Shejidan from Malguri was now being outfitted for the dowager's personal use—with the configuration she used, and all the attendant changes in designation, so it was very clear that the heir was headed for Malguri with the dowager today.

The plane was real: Jago said it would take off for Malguri about the time the red train left the Bujavid station, part of a cross-continental misdirection. That jet would fly all the way to Malguri. And by the time it got to Malguri—a quiet district on the other end of the continent, where news services were much less aggressive—the dowager, Cajeiri, his guests, and, yes, even Boji, would be safely settled at Tirnamardi, where no news services were permitted access.

Rumor-mongering was a popular sport in the cafes and tea shops across the capital. No matter what people at the airport saw or didn't see, there would be persistent rumors that they were all in Malguri with a horde of humans from the station and a collection of death-machines from space, and the porcelain collection had been intended as a distraction from these movements—one point on which they were absolutely right, but not one that had originated with that purpose. Conspiracy believers were determined, and occasionally useful.

What Ajuri might believe—and do about it—depended on how convoluted Ajuri's thinking was. But they had scattered all the confusion they could.

Meanwhile, in the real world, there was a shiny red and black bus being freighted by rail up from Najida, officially scheduled to arrive at the Shejidan station this morning, for use during the official visit scheduled for a week from now. The bus would not get quite as far as Shejidan—but what did *not* appear was less likely to be reported.

The shuttle, strictly on schedule, was now traveling toward atmospheric entry under power, and the weather reports were good. In a little while it would shut down the engines and simply use inertia and gravity for what they did so well, until the crew took active control again near the very skin of the earth.

The whole arrangement was becoming a sort of bait-and-switch operation. They kicked misleading items into motion. They sowed rumors in various direction. The porcelain collection arriving was Tatiseigi's contribution to the effort. The only actual fact evident was that they were definitely on the move with the heir in *some* direction ... but then there would be some theories that everything was designed to give a false impression that the dowager and the heir had left the Bujavid, and anything anybody saw was a carefully designed appearance.

"We shall at least stretch our enemies' resources thin," Tano said, "and of all things, Lord Tatiseigi receiving these young guests is an idea most will not readily believe."

What the news services *might* note was the red car, once it moved out of the Bujavid.

That would attract attention.

And the Transportation Guild that managed the rails was far from leakproof.

The general flurry of conflicting reports, however, was likely to be livelier than the actual event. If they reported the car moving toward Tirnamardi, well, was *it* the diversion?

Or was the dowager going to Tatiseigi's ancestral enemy, their neighbor in the west, Taiben? That was Tabini's home district, the old Ragi stronghold, deep in forest and extremely difficult for any outsider to penetrate. It *was* historically the place where the aijiin in Shejidan went for safety, in times of crisis. It had existed in at least a nominal state of war, never having signed a treaty with the rest of the Padi Valley.

Likeliest spot on the continent for secret goings-on, or high security.

Of course, the thinkers among the theorists would say. The rest was a ruse. It was Taiben.

Wrong again.

Though Taiben *was* involved.

The dowager asked, and Tatiseigi agreed, not only because the dowager asked—but because the stakes were now, for him, the ultimate.

Tatiseigi had no heir.

Except Damiri, and her son, and her soon-to-be-born daughter.

The children were, through their mother, Atageini and Ajuri. And Ajuri was in extreme disfavor.

Lord Tatiseigi had absolutely no difficulties seeing the possibilities in *that* situation.

Finally make peace with the Taibeni, the *other* clan closely related to the aiji and to those children? Oh, yes. It hadn't been politic for any lord of the Atageini to do it for two hundred years, through various administrations in Shejidan, and even though the Atageini were intermittently at war with the other powerful clan in the Padi Valley.

But since the incident that had barred Ajuri from the capital, Lord Tatiseigi discovered himself willing to settle an old territorial claim, and thus the ancient feud, in *Taiben's* favor. Correspondence flowed. There was, mediated by the dowager *and* Tabini, a positive *effusion* of good will.

He began to realize that the man who had a reputation for living in the last century could do whatever it took in this one, whether that meant sitting right next to the Kadagidi during the coup and the Troubles, while maintaining his reputation of being no threat at all, standing with Ilisidi on the tribal bill—or hosting human children at a birthday party.

He definitely had a new perspective on the man ... and *knew* why Ilisidi favored him.

Supper, with Cajeiri, who was for once short of appetite, was one question after another, accompanied by what neither of them quite acknowledged: the constant coming and going in the hall, and at the front door.

Baggage was being readied.

And there was the matter of Boji. Of all conspicuous things to try to slip past the news services—

Tano was working on that one.

"One knows you very much wish Boji to go," Bren said, when they were having the brandy hour—a little soothing tea for Cajeiri, and a stiff brandy for Bren. "Please hear me on this. Getting him to the red car poses a difficulty and could attract attention. We have spoken with your servants. They have agreed to ride in baggage and take good care of him. You understand. Security."

Cajeiri had opened his mouth to argue. And shut it. "One understands, nandi."

"I think you will owe your two servants a night out in Shejidan when all this is done. They are very good young men." It was true. They were Tabini's own staff, and very conscious of their prospects in having seniority in the heir's new household.

"I shall, nandi."

"They will see that Boji rides comfortably, and they will see, too, that he stays quiet in your great-uncle's house. Understand, your great-uncle is trying very hard to make you happy, but he is not at all used to young people, and has seen very few humans in his whole life."

"One understands, nandi."

"Well, well," he said, "best you retire early. We are going to be up before dawn, and you will want to wear, one believes, fairly casual clothing, for comfort on the trip. We shall have breakfast here, in the apartment, lunch on the train, and a snack in mid-afternoon, after we have picked up your young associates."

"One is excited, nand' Bren. One is very excited."

"I know. Do try to sleep. You need to be at your best tomorrow, not short of temper, not falling asleep on the train."

"Oh, I never shall!"

"Then off to bed with you," Bren said. "And think of good things."

Cajeiri put down his teacup. And gave a very deep bow, and another at the door, as he was leaving.

It was one very happy, very excited boy, and it was not very likely that he would sleep that well tonight, and probably not that well the night after. They were kids. And they had all had a lot of adult anxieties riding on their very young shoulders.

A habitual offender with station security, a girl whose

mother had political forces nudging at her—and two about whom he had heard absolutely no complaints. One wondered how they had fared up on the station, given the politics that swirled around the visit.

Narani appeared, silent, in the doorway. "Your aishid is in conference, nandi. Will there be any other need this evening, or shall I call your valets?"

"Call them, Rani-ji." And on an afterthought: "There would not be any package arrived in all this confusion, from Mospheira."

"No," Narani said. "No, nandi. I am quite sure of it."

He sighed, thinking of the boots. But he did *not* intend to end this visit hiking cross-country through gun-fire.

Breakfast—and Cajeiri seemed a little wilted. The boy had probably not slept a wink. But with strong tea, sugared juice, and a sweet roll, spirits began to rise.

Bren just had nut-buttered toast and salt fish, figuring substance would serve better than sugar, but he took two cups of strong tea, letting staff hurry about doing those things staff did best, and most of all staying out of the way, and letting his bodyguard instruct Cajeiri's servants, and especially his bodyguard. The car would be secure, he had word—gone over and all monitoring disconnected—discretion on this trip would not be on the shoulders of a boy not yet nine. The aiji's staff would have no report, and no record, of what was said.

"When we go down to the train, young gentleman," Bren said, and got sharp attention from the other side of the table, "should we run into any difficulty, and one has the news services in mind—do not speak a word. We believe we shall evade them entirely. If there should be any other kind of trouble, do not give a second thought to your great-grandmother or anyone else. Obey your bodyguards." A thought struck him. "You have the sling-shota."

Cajeiri nodded and moved a hand to his pocket.

"One does not object to your carrying it," Bren said—he wore the detested vest, and had his gun in his own pocket. "But do not attempt to use it should there be a crisis. Do not think of your guests, either. We cannot teach them what we know, and we cannot argue. Just let your bodyguard protect you. Are we agreed, young gentleman? Do you understand? We do not think it might happen. But we can never act as if it could not. Be safe. You are important."

A very curious sobriety came over the young gentleman, who nodded very deliberately, and said, "My father needs *me* for his heir. My *sister* is a hazard."

He was surprised, even shocked at that declaration, but he simply nodded. "Well. One trusts you, young gentleman."

God, he thought, then. Where did *that* come from? He almost wanted to ask.

But not at present.

He finished his tea. Banichi had arrived in the doorway.

"We should move now, nandi."

So. It was time.

They were on their own, Ilisidi and Tatiseigi arriving on their own schedules. Tano and Algini had a lift car on hold. Bren entered the car and, with Cajeiri, stood against the back wall while it headed down and down, without a stop.

"My servants, nandi," Cajeiri said. "And will mani be there?"

"Trust your aishid," Bren said, "to have all these things worked out. It will *all* work. Do not worry."

The car headed down, and down, past residential floors, past the public floor, and down to the warehouse levels, then through a set of floors only accessible from the lift they were on—and let them out finally, in that broad cement corridor that opened out onto the train tracks.

It was huge, full of echoes. The arch above the tracks was studded with lights that did not reach the far places, the other tracks and roundhouse shunts. The space swallowed light and amplified sound. And centermost, under the lights, was the old-fashioned engine and the two cars that had taken Geigi to the spaceport.

It was three cars now, the red car and two baggage cars. They were not traveling light. The door of the red car opened and one of the dowager's young men met them, welcoming them in, while his partner, pistol in hand, stood watching.

Their collective bodyguards folded them inside, and the door whisked shut.

Ilisidi and Tatiseigi were comfortably seated at the rear of the car, on the broad bench, the dowager with her cane planted before her. Cenedi was there, and Nawari, in attendance on the dowager, and Tatiseigi's bodyguard, seated just in front of the galley, rose in respect for the young gentleman.

"We are here!" Cajeiri declared happily. "We are all here!"

"Great-grandson." The dowager gave a nod, patted the bench near her, and Cajeiri came and settled down quietly.

Bren bowed and quietly took his own seat on the end of the bench, Tatiseigi being on the other end. There was a long, general silence, a quiet so deep one could hear the occasional sounds from the station outside, the arrival of another train, the movement of baggage trolleys, the shout of a supervisor on the siding. Cajeiri fidgeted ever so slightly. He had his hands locked together as if he were absolutely determined not to let them escape to merit a reprimand.

Then came a thump from their own car, or the one next to it. Bren listened hard for any cues as to what was going on, and felt the vibrations as the next car loaded, heard the distinctive sounds as the engine fired up.

"Staff," the dowager said, "is joining us. *With* Boji."

They were operating under the most extreme security Bren had ever experienced, even in far worse times. *With* the parid'ja and its huge cage.

Doors shut, elsewhere. There was a further delay. A second, more distant thump.

And they sat.

And sat. The dowager and Tatiseigi discussed the vote count on the tribal bill, which looked good. And Cajeiri sat so very still, being so very good.

"Perhaps," Bren said, "the young gentleman might enjoy a game of chess. I think his aishid would oblige him with a challenge. There is a chess set in the galley storage."

Ilisidi waggled her fingers, a dismissal. Cajeiri got up, bowed silently, and went over to his aishid with that information.

The game set up and started, Veijico taking black.

Tatiseigi muttered, disapprovingly, "In my youth, one would have sat."

"Nandi," Bren said, "he is concerned about the flight."

"Well," Tatiseigi said, "well, so should anyone be, with such machines."

"Best young minds stay busy," Ilisidi said, not displeased, and the three of them sat quietly and talked, had one cup of sweet tea, and the chess match progressed.

Then the train, with its characteristic chuff, began to move.

The chess match paused, Cajeiri's hand, on a Fortress, hesitated in midair.

Then calmly resumed its course toward a square.

Eight, going on fortunate nine, and a mental age above that. Cajeiri, on the most intense campaign of good behavior in his whole life, set the piece down.

Cajeiri's opponent, Veijico, lifted an eyebrow, considering the move, then cast a furtive glance toward the dowager, and quietly advised the young rascal, likely, that they were indeed watched.

There were quiet remarks. Human ears, at least, could not hear them. Likely neither the dowager nor Tatiseigi could hear. Tano got up and renewed the teapot, and provided a large pot for Cajeiri and his bodyguard as the train made its slow passage along the restricted tunnel. The rest of the adult bodyguards continued in quiet conversation interspersed with Guild signs.

They cleared the hill, cleared the tunnel, gathered

speed toward the city junction, and clicked over onto the lefthand track.

Faster and faster, then, a steam-age locomotive bent again on rendezvous with a spaceship.

"Are they coming down yet, Banichi-nadi?" Cajeiri turned to ask as the train gathered speed. "Shall we see it land?"

"One fears not, young gentleman, however we will be arriving there at about the time it touches down, and we shall take the bus to meet them. You will get to see them disembark."

"One wished—" Cajeiri began to say, and then meekly said, "One is glad, Banichi-nadi."

"Security," Banichi said. "One regrets, young gentleman. But these are necessary precautions."

"Yes," Cajeiri said quietly, frowning.

Difficult for the boy, Bren thought. But one understood. They were moving as expeditiously as possible: get the youngsters under their protection, get them to the train, and get moving again, with as little exposure as possible. The shuttle landings were fairly routine. The shuttle the children were stated to be taking was not due for days. When the news did get to observers that this one had the children, and that the heir was here, any hostile action, unless extremely well-placed or very lucky, was going to have to scramble.

The whereabouts of the train was traceable—if one had agents within Transportation; but again, the exact routing for *this* train was given only at intervals necessary to shunt other traffic onto other tracks. It prioritized itself through the system on a sector by sector basis, not always at high speed, given the engine that often pulled it, but in a traveling bubble of secrecy and priority; and they would be stalling all train traffic on a very main line for at least an hour, while they performed their maneuver out to the port and back.

"The port has contact, aiji-ma, nandiin," Cenedi reported finally.

They were very near the spaceport.

And Nawari got to his feet. "Aiji-ma, nandiin, you will

find the port bus right off the platform, so it will be a very short walk. We shall enter the perimeter fence through the service gate, which will be open. We shall pick up our passengers, and their baggage, which is able to be hand-carried aboard the bus. No one should exit the bus. Aiji-ma, nandiin, as you board, please occupy the seats behind the driver. The opposing row will be reserved for our passengers, who will board as quickly as possible."

"Very good, Wari-ji," the dowager said.

The operation was on schedule, and while they had no view, Bren had an excellent idea where they were: a flat prairie with very few features except grazing herds and the occasional patch of brush.

And at a certain point they slowed, and slowed further, then took that little jog of a switchover, toward the port, everyone swaying.

"They are in process of landing, nandiin," Cenedi said. Then: "They are touching down."

Cajeiri visibly elevated off his seat, then shut his mouth and settled, locking his hands in his lap and not saying a thing.

The dowager nodded, satisfied.

Bren just breathed a sigh of relief. The train did not regain its speed. It lazily chugged around a slight curve, then took the straight for a while, and another, opposite, curve, which led to the platform.

Brakes applied. The engine sighed out a final *chuff!* And stopped.

Bren got up, as their bodyguards did. Cajeiri bounced up and offered Ilisidi his hand, as Tatiseigi used the seat arm to lever himself up.

"The bus is here, nandiin," Cenedi said. "And the shuttle has arrived."

So. From here on until the shuttle lifted again, they were in charge of a flock of youngsters on holiday. Bren moved out into the aisle, toward the door—ordinarily protocol gave the aiji-dowager precedence, but not into a security situation, and while he might technically outrank Lord Tatiseigi as an officer of the aiji's court, he didn't stand on the point—he was younger, he was stronger, he was faster, and he took the risk of finding out whether the platform was as secure as they hoped it was.

He felt Jago's hand on his arm as the door opened on a bright, sunny day, and had Banichi right in front of him and Tano and Algini at his back. Out the door, down a slightly inconvenient step—he dropped off it without a hesitation and kept up with Banichi, headed for the black, sleek bus across the wooden platform.

It was three tall steps up and inside with the driver, with Banichi and Jago and with a handful of Guild in the port service, while Tano and Algini stood outside beside the bus door, assuring a good view of the platform, just security as usual.

The dowager stepped off the train with Cajeiri and her cane to steady her, with Cenedi to offer his arm, and with Nawari and Tatiseigi's bodyguard to assist the old lord in his descent to the platform. They crossed to the bus at their own pace and boarded.

Tano and Algini came aboard, standing next to the driver—they had the heaviest armament in evidence, rifles, a little extraordinary precaution. The bus started moving, gathering speed on a gravel drive. Cajeiri sat with his hands clenched in fists, a bundle of anxiety.

Guild was in communication with Guild, talking back and forth as the bus reached a gate and a guard post. The wire gate swung open without them even needing to stop, and the bus bumped up a hard edge and onto concrete, and kept rolling.

A long white shape sat on the strip, surrounded by service trucks.

"There is the shuttle, young gentleman," Bren said quietly.

Cajeiri twisted in his seat, got up on one knee, and then reluctantly slithered back down, facing Bren, hands locked so the knuckles stood out.

"You may go stand at the front glass, Great-grandson," Ilisidi said. "But do not give the driver problems!"

"Mani!" Cajeiri exclaimed, and got up ever so

carefully and edged past her feet and Tatiseigi's. "Thank you, mani!"

"Paidhi," Ilisidi said wryly. "Go keep my great-grandson on the bus."

"Aiji-ma," Bren said, and as carefully got up and worked his way out to the aisle. Cajeiri was as close to the front windows as the dashboard let him get, as the bus pulled up near the service trucks and came to a stop.

The lift was in place, elevated up to the hatch, and the passengers were disembarking.

Two of them, Bren saw, from his vantage. Taller than children. He could see their heads as the lift started down.

They *wouldn't* promise the boy and then renege.

They wouldn't lie to all of them. *Geigi* was running this operation. He had faith in Geigi not to do something like that.

The lift settled lower and lower. He saw two men in body-armor, weapons, carrying their helmets—*ship* security. That, at least, was understandable.

And then one turned his head, looking up at the hatch, and punched the communications tab on his armor. God! That was Polano. The other must be Kaplan.

Jase Graham's bodyguards.

Those two stepped off the lift platform, and the lift went back up.

"Those are Jase-aiji's!" Cajeiri exclaimed.

"That they are. One has no idea what is going on, young gentleman. But they are, indeed: Polano-nadi and Kaplan-nadi." The lift went up again, and now more passengers were debarking. Jago turned up at Bren's side, and he said, "Kaplan and Polano, Jago-ji."

"Indeed," she said, and then the lift started down again.

With another man. Jase. *Captain* Jason Graham—fourth highest authority on the starship *Phoenix,* onetime ship-paidhi, the ship's emissary to Tabini-aiji.

"Jase-aiji!" Cajeiri said.

Then, beside Jase—three significantly shorter persons appeared as the lift lowered and the angle shifted.

Two boys. One girl. All in station-style dress and light jackets, one gray, one green, one blue, all with a single duffel, and with a few other bags about their feet.

"Gene-ji!" Cajeiri said, restraining a gesture into a small movement. "And Artur and Irene! May we open the doors, nandi? May one go out?"

"Jago will go out and bring them aboard," Bren said. "Let us not create a problem for security. They will have baggage, one is sure. Jago-ji, assist Jase."

"Indeed," Jago said, and moved past him to reach the steps and the door. It opened, and Jago and several of the dowager's young men exited onto the pavement.

Cajeiri just stood there, all but shivering, it was so hard for him to stand still.

Security in their operation, Bren thought, had just gone up several notches in firepower, if not in knowledge of the planet. Kaplan and Polano were armed to the teeth, not to mention the instrumentation on the armor. He had no idea what its capabilities were, but he knew they were considerable.

If the wearers failed to succumb to the flat expanses around them.

They were all old acquaintances, from two years on the ship together, and Jase's own visit to the world. Cenedi recognized them, no doubt he did, and so would Nawari and several others of the dowager's young men.

Protocol, meanwhile, did not leave a captain of the starship out on the concrete looking for an official face. Bren went to the steps and jumped down to the pavement, close to the shelter of the bus and beside Jago. He raised his arm in a very un-atevi wave.

Jase spotted him and waved back—came toward them, with Kaplan and Polano and his young charges . . . human kids, wide-eyed and looking around at everything.

Doing very well, however. No one had thrown up.

"Bren," Jase said—and then did the atevi courtesy and bowed. Bren bowed. The youngsters bowed, tentatively, and then looked up in surprise—one might even say—dismay.

"Hi," Cajeiri said from the bus steps. "Come in!"

The youngsters looked uncertain. Then the tallest boy, himself about shoulder-high to Bren, dark-haired, on the stocky side, waved a hand, sketched a bow and grabbed the assistance-bar to climb aboard. It was a very tall step for him. He made it, and there he and Cajeiri were, the human boy looking a few inches up at Cajeiri.

"Gene-ji," Cajeiri said happily. "Hi there!"

"You grew!" Gene said. "You're as tall as Bjorn!"

"Bjorn's not here?"

"Couldn't come. He's in school. Well, so are we, but not his kind of school. Artur, Irene—" The other two were blocking the doorway, staring up. "He's as tall as Bjorn, isn't he?"

"Get aboard," Bren said to the last two. "Everybody inside. Take the first seats on the left, facing each other. The aiji-dowager and a high-ranking lord are across the aisle. Be very polite! Bow. Low."

They didn't acknowledge the instruction. They just went scrambling up the steps. Irene, smallest, and straight from a long free fall, had to be pulled up the steps.

"Jase," Bren said, still amazed. "So good to see you! Are you running security on this trip, or what?"

"This is my vacation," Jase said. "You invited me, remember? God, it's good to see you. Sorry about the surprise. But the Council wanted to provide their own security."

"Backup is more than welcome! We're headed for Tirnamardi." Baggage was down, a lift full of it that they had not planned for, and the dowager's young men were moving to get it and load it onto the bus. "Get aboard. My security doesn't want me standing out here. Or you. Jago-ji!"

"Nandi." Jago was right by him, assisting him up, and Jase. Polano and Kaplan moved with a soft, motorized whine. Polano somewhat awkwardly managed to get a toe on the step. Then, quite amazingly, he just rose up on that one foot and took the next step. Machine-assist. Balance-assist. Kaplan did the same, and one had to get out of the way, because they took up a lot of room.

"Just stand there," Jase said, which left them no view of the shuttle and the trucks. But the rest of the baggage was coming aboard, with the dowager's young men.

Pretty damned amazing, Bren thought, and had to give a second look at Jase, to believe it.

"You're not sick," he said.

"Medicated to the max," Jase said, and patted his pocket. "'Til the brain adjusts." He spotted the dowager, and Tatiseigi, and bowed, deeply. "Nandiin. One is surprised and honored. One apologizes for the children."

In fairly good Ragi, that was. The dowager nodded, pleased. The children, having gotten toward the middle seats, were trying their best to keep quiet, but there were excited young voices, and Tatiseigi was eyeing them with unguessable thoughts about it all.

"The two in armor, nandiin," Bren said, "are Kaplan-nadi, and Polano-nadi, Jase-aiji's personal bodyguard, very responsible men, who always accompany him."

"You are very welcome, Jase-aiji," Ilisidi said, of course in Ragi. "Lord Tatiseigi, he is one of the ship-aiji now, and a very astute young man, who has come to supervise the children. One hopes Tirnamardi can accommodate another guest with minimal difficulty."

"Honored, nandi," went both directions, and Tatiseigi looked a little less stressed.

Thump! went the door, then, the last of the hand baggage manhandled down the aisle without hitting anyone, and other baggage stowed below, in the baggage compartment of the bus.

Thump! went the ferrule of Ilisidi's cane. "Let us be moving, nadiin," she said, and Jago relayed it to the driver, who put the bus in gear.

"Well, well," the dowager said cheerfully, bracing her cane against the sway of the bus as it turned, while Jase and Bren stood and held their ground. "We shall reciprocate the hospitality of the ship-aijiin, with your kind assistance, Tati-ji. You are very welcome, Jase-aiji. My great-grandson is holding forth with his young associates. Come sit with us."

"One is honored, nand' dowager," Jase said, in very

passable Ragi, and gave a second bow to Lord Tatiseigi. "We are not of close acquaintance, nandi, but you are known in the heavens."

"Indeed," Tatiseigi said—impassivity had settled over his face, but he seemed to like that information. "Tirnamardi will find room for any guest the aiji-dowager recommends. You speak very well, ship-paidhi."

"One is very flattered, nandi," Jase said with a perfect little bow, and slipped quite deftly into a seat, leaving space for Bren, next to Tatiseigi.

"A very great asset," Bren said, thinking, *Geigi*. Jase, incongruously, had a slight southwest coastal accent, and one knew the source.

"One does not suppose the children are as studious," Ilisidi said.

"No, nand' dowager," Jase said—hit exactly the right form of address for their relative ranks. Geigi's coaching in that, too, Bren was quite sure.

"How is your stomach, Jase-aiji?" Ilisidi asked.

"Much better," Jase said with a little bow, and Bren said, "They have found a medication that works."

"Excellent," Ilisidi said. The bus left the concrete and turned onto the gravel.

There were suppressed human gasps from the middle seats—children, with faces pressed to the bus windows as the scenery swung into view, trees, and grass. A quiet *shhh!*

They were under way, collected, gathered, oriented, and headed back to the train.

"Trees?" Gene asked in Ragi.

"Yes," Cajeiri said.

"You can look right at the sun," Artur said, leaning.

"Don't," Cajeiri said. "It's not good." They had never seen the sun in a sky. For them the sun was something else. A star. A place that anchored planets. A place that anchored ships. "It's a clock. 1200 hours, a little more." He inclined his hand. "0100. 0200. 0300 . . . By 0800 it's gone. It comes back around 0530."

"Neat," Gene said, and leaned forward to catch a look

as Artur sneaked another peek. "Come on, Irene. Don't be a baby."

Irene made a try, and then the bus took a turn. Irene shut her eyes.

"Just like a shuttle docking," Gene said. "Just like two ships meeting. It's all in your head."

"It's *fast*," Irene said, and Gene and Artur laughed.

"Silly. The *ship* is fast. This is just a little distance."

"There's a black and red machine."

"The train," Cajeiri said in Ragi—not knowing any ship-speak word for it. Then thought of one. "It runs on rails. Like the lifts." He made a sideways motion of his hand. "That way."

"We're going on that?" Irene asked.

"Yes," Cajeiri said. "The red one. Back there." He tried to think of words, after all his practice, and the only words he could think of for a moment were ship things. The tunnels. The places they met. Sneaking into the access doors.

"So are we going to the city?" Gene asked.

"No," he said. "Tirnamardi. Lord Tatiseigi. It's his. He's my—" He realized he didn't know ship-speak for great-uncle. "My mother's mother's brother."

"Wow. He owns a whole city?"

He shook his head, struggled again for the right word, this time for house, and was immensely frustrated. "We go to his . . . Where he lives."

"Apartment?"

"Like. But big." It came to him—they had no houses, either. There were no words for it. Even apartments for them weren't rooms in a building, but rooms off a corridor. "We say *adija*. Big. Lot of rooms. We'll be there for a few days, then we go to Shejidan, to the Bujavid, for my party."

"We've seen pictures of the Bujavid," Artur said. "It's huge."

"My father's apartment's there. That's where we'll go for my birthday. First we go to Tirnamardi. They have mecheiti there."

"It's going to be good," Gene said, and his eyes were

wide and bright. "This is so good. We *knew* it was your birthday again. We heard *about* you. We knew you were all right. But pretty scary. A lot of scary stuff."

That opened up difficult business. "Lots of trouble." He had no idea where even to start telling them about the Shadow Guild and the trouble over on the coast. Or Malguri. Or what had happened at Tirnamardi before that. "But safe now. All fine."

The bus slowed down. It was time for everybody to get out. His attention was all for his aishid for a second, for instructions, and then he realized he had forgotten to introduce them—*everyone* had a bodyguard, and bodyguards knew each other, and things passed back and forth. "Nadiin," he said in Ragi. "This is Gene-nadi. This is Artur-nadi. This is Irene-nadi. People, this is my *aishid*. This is Antaro. This is Jegari. This is Veijico. This is Lucasi. I wrote you about them."

"Pleased to meet you," Gene said.

"Nadiin," Antaro said, with a polite little nod, Guild-fashion. "We go now."

"They speak *ship*!" Irene exclaimed.

"A little, nadiin," Antaro said with a second nod, pleased, and up front, people were getting off and they would have to catch up. "We go now. Up."

"We move fast now," Cajeiri said. "Don't stop." Up front, two of mani's bodyguards had lingered, and they had opened the baggage compartment of the bus, taking out what they had put on. Antaro and Jegari led out, and he followed with his guests, Lucasi and Veijico behind them. Tano got out ahead of them, and there were Kaplan and Polano, mirror-faced helmets on, which made them look like machines—scarily so. But that was what bodyguards did—look as forbidding as possible if there was any chance of a threat. Everybody else was already getting on the train, and Tano went ahead of them as they caught up.

The steps were high, even for him, but *very* high for his guests. He made it in, and Gene, with a little jump, was right behind him. Veijico and Lucasi all but picked up Artur, setting him on the steps, and Gene hauled him up the next by the hand. Irene came next, lifted up gently by Lucasi.

"Everything's so *big*," she said, staring all around her.

"*We're* just *short*," Gene said, with his big grin. They were in the car, now, and being urged away from the door. All the bodyguards were still standing, but he caught a glimpse of mani and Great-uncle, and nand' Bren and Jase-aiji through the sea of black uniforms, settling into the seats at the rear.

One of the guards was Tano, who said, with a wave of his hand: "You and your guests may have the seats over there, with the let-down table. There will be lunch very soon."

"Thank you, Tano-nadi," he said with a little bow, and now, finally, they were going to be on their way and everything was going to work. "Is mani happy, and Uncle? Is everything all right?"

"Everything is perfectly fine, young gentleman."

He hoped it was, but some of the bodyguards were still outside. Finally Kaplan and Polano came up onto the train ahead of a few of mani's guards, and the door shut.

They were in, they were safe.

And lunch was coming.

He so wanted to introduce his guests, but it was not proper to do introductions of complete strangers to mani and Uncle in a crowded conveyance. It would have to be as if they were in two separate cars, the adults down there, and them here, at this end, and they had to be sure not to bother anybody.

"Sit here," he invited his guests. "Food. Soon."

"Food!" Gene said. "Excellent!"

Their own table, and very quickly iced bottles of fruit juice. No servants were present—they were all in the other cars ... with the baggage—so it was one of mani's guards who set down the drinks.

It was quiet, it was safe: the red car had excellent shielding—even the red velvet curtains that made it look as if there would be a window at the end of their table were for decoration only: there was no looking out. Not from this end of the car.

"We're moving!" Irene said, with a startled look, and grabbed her drink. "Oh, this is scary! How fast does it go?"

"A little," Cajeiri said. "Not like the ship."

"What's that sound?"

"Joints in the rail," Cajeiri said.

"The other sound."

"That's the train. The machine."

"Neat," Artur said. "You can hear it breathe, can't you?"

Breathe. He'd never thought of it like that, but Artur was right. It *was* neat. And they were happy. Nobody was sick or throwing up, which Bren had cautioned him could happen to them even without windows. They were eager for lunch, and the fruit drinks were fast disappearing.

But, he realized suddenly, he had to teach them things, like not eating just anything. He had told them once about nand' Bren having to be careful what he ate, but that was on the ship. He had to be sure nobody got sick now. Or dead. It could be really serious, with some dishes. And even some teas.

And he had to present them to mani and Great-uncle, once they got to Tirnamardi, in a way Great-uncle would approve. Great-uncle was so touchy. He had to make them understand where to be and how to talk to lords and servants.

And so many, many things there were Ragi words for, just Ragi words. Where did people born on a station far, far off from any world ever see a tree or a woods? There were words in the old archive, that they all knew. And there were vids. But not all of those words fit *things* and vids weren't like standing next to a tree that towered over your head and dropped leaves into your hands.

They came from a place that was all one building. Just doors and hallways and lifts and tunnels.

It was just enormous, the mass of things he had to explain. He suddenly found nothing as easy as he thought it was, and it all was going to come at them in a few hours when they got to Tirnamardi.

He swallowed a mouthful of fruit juice, and decided he should just tell them Ragi words for what they could see around them. It was, after all, the way he had learned ship-speak, when he had been in their world.

"They seem to be enjoying themselves," Banichi said, having taken a short walk down the aisle and back, as they finished lunch. "They seem to be doing very well. No motion sickness."

"One is glad," Bren said. "Thank you, Nichi-ji." He and Jase had their lunch together, a little separated from Ilisidi and Tatiseigi, and bodyguards did their own rotation, catching lunch in the little galley. Jase was doing very well, had an appetite, had no problem with the rock and sway of the train.

"Which of us is going to handle protocols?" he asked Jase. "How much have you told them?"

"That the bodyguards mean business, and that you don't touch people. Particularly people with bodyguards."

Bren laughed a little. "Children have latitude. Nobody would hurt them."

"The boy's *grown* this year."

"Eight or nine, the kids shoot up fast. Big spurt between eight and twelve. All feet and elbows in a year or so—just like a human kid. The emotions are different—there's adjustment, a little rebellious streak. Jago's warned me."

"Sounds like us."

"But girls won't be the focus. Man'chi will be. A push-pull with the parents. Rebelliousness. Quick temper."

"Sounds exactly like us, in that part," Jase said. "I was a pain. My actual parents weren't available to argue with, and I *still* argued with them—in the abstract. Wasn't fair, them being so non-communicative."

Jase's humor had a little biting edge to it. Jase was one of Taylor's Children, stored genetic material, a *special* kid, harking back to the original crew. Ship aristocracy, in a manner of speaking. A living relic. A resource.

Sometimes, Bren suspected, from what he had heard

Jase say, those who *had* raised him had forgotten he was still a human being.

"You turned out pretty well."

"Dare I say, thanks to you?" A narrow-eyed glance his way, then around the train. "Thanks to all of them. —When they decided to come back here, they decided to resurrect a few of us. Beginning a new era, I suppose. A marker. I wonder, sometimes, what they think of what they got. *Yolanda's* gone philosophical. Meditates in a dark room. She scares me."

Yolanda was another of Taylor's Children. Like Jase, but not like. Cold as a fish and as prickly, in Bren's way of thinking. "Seriously?"

"I think she's in a career crisis. She *didn't* like my promotion." Jase heaved a sigh. "Authority problems. She's always been a person who likes definitions. The planet bothered her. Translating bothered her. She's got more realities in her head than she likes and she won't go into the atevi section, won't deal with Geigi. Geigi's learned ship-speak, since she's resigned. She's dropped linguistics. She's gone over to research, records-keeping, history of the ship, that sort of thing. I think it's a cocoon. It's safe." He shrugged. "She and I don't talk."

"That's too bad." Yolanda had served as paidhi-aiji, translating directly for Tabini, during the time he, and Jase, had been away on the ship, settling the Reunion mess. She'd been there—when the coup came.

The world she'd tended had blown up. At least the atevi side of it had, and stayed in chaos for most of two years, until the ship had gotten back from its mission and Tabini had retaken Shejidan. "You think she blamed herself for what happened?"

"She wasn't you. She knew that much. It's my understanding that she made some mistakes."

The world she was trying to deal with had blown up. She'd failed, while Jase had been coopted into a captaincy, on a mission that succeeded brilliantly. So Yolanda was retreating into old records, which didn't have ticking bombs in them. Another paidhi could somewhat figure that reaction. His own predecessor had come back from the mainland completely shut down, close-jawed. A very unhappy and strange man.

"Suppose *I* could talk with her?"

"Maybe," Jase said. And again: "Maybe."

He put it on the agenda. When he found a way. Granted the world didn't explode again, because of three human kids.

"So . . . who *does* handle the protocol explanation?" he asked.

"You know the twists and turns. I'm a student. *You* do it. I'm interested in not offending the other end of this bench."

Truth—Ilisidi had found humans an unexpectedly interesting experience, and *enjoyed* her position among ship-humans. Tatiseigi was a man *atevi* rated as difficult and volatile, a proud old conservative with no good opinion of human-induced changes in the world. . . . But now the old man seemed to be undergoing a sudden and strange transformation in his attitudes—inviting the human paidhi to dinner. Having his collection televised. Inviting human *children* under his roof and accepting Jase's appearance with two armored, other-worldly bodyguards, all without a visible flicker of dismay.

Something had changed in the old man's attitude. Bren didn't know whether it was Ilisidi's doing, through persuasion, or the events of last spring, when Tatiseigi's beloved Tirnamardi had taken shellfire in Tabini's cause, and the people in villages and towns had turned out cheering Tabini's return and all of them that had helped bring him back, all the way to Shejidan. That had been an event. Tatiseigi had never been exposed to popularity.

Tatiseigi had generously lent Bren his apartment in the Bujavid during Tirnamardi's repairs—until Tabini could find an excuse to throw a last nest of interlopers out of Bren's own residence. And certainly Tatiseigi had been overjoyed to get Ilisidi back in the world—was happy beyond measure to have Cajeiri back safely—and he was delighted this year to know his niece Damiri was going to produce another baby.

A daughter that wouldn't inherit the aishidi'tat. Cajeiri would.

But there was Tirnamardi. And Tatiseigi, heirless, had become downright *reckless* in his support of the dowager's adventurism in the Marid, in Cajeiri's, regarding his shipboard associates —

One saw a glimmering of logic in it all. The old man had a sudden wealth of prospects.

"Tatiseigi seems quite happy," he said, "happy to have Ilisidi home safe, happy to have the aiji back, happy with the way things are going. The one thorn in his side got pitched out of the aiji's court with no likelihood of coming back any time soon."

"The way things are going? Seems to me you've still got some troubles rattling about the continent."

The sense of ease grew just a little less. There were things he probably needed to explain to Jase. But they could wait.

"We have some serious ones," he said. "But we've hardened the security considerably. Very considerably. Kaplan and Polano—" He shifted a glance over to the seats across the car. "I hope they get to enjoy their visit. I hope they won't need to use that gear. Actually—I hope this visit leads to others. Maybe we can arrange that fishing trip."

"I'd enjoy that," Jase said. "I'd really enjoy that. You keep the world quiet. I'll work on calming down the station."

"We'll get through this mess. Maybe the *next* birthday." A dark figure approached. Bren looked up, finding Algini in front of him. "Gini-ji?"

Algini squatted beside the bench seat. "There *is* a small security concern, Bren-ji. We have moved in some additional Taibeni assets, with the cooperation of Lord Tatiseigi's aishid. He may not be entirely pleased, but we prefer to be safe."

Damn. "Ajuri?" Bren asked. No need to translate for Jase. Jase could understand it.

Algini said: "There is a movement of Ajuri Guild forces toward their perimeter. Lord Komaji is with them.

We have not yet warned Lord Tatiseigi. We see no reason, at present, to concern him. We are working with his aishid." Tatiseigi's bodyguards were midway down the aisle, with, he saw, Banichi and Jago. "We have prepared for this eventuality, nandi. We are simply putting contingency plans into operation. Everything is prearranged, and the lord's aishid is in full agreement. They will talk to him."

Ajuri making a move toward Atageini territory put Ajuri Guild, give or take the small territories of two very small affiliated clans, right adjacent to Atageini territory.

"So our cover is not holding," he said to Algini.

"Possibly," Algini said. "Or possibly the move has relevance to Lord Tatiseigi's exhibit in Shejidan. It may be designed to get Lord Tatiseigi's attention. Lord Komaji remains technically within his associational territory and within his rights. It is possible this is wholly designed to annoy Lord Tatiseigi and embarrass him while he has public attention. But Komaji is not serving himself well by this move, if that is the case. He may have no idea that the dowager and the heir are in the path of his actions. That is one interpretation. Of course there is the chance he does know and is making a deliberate move to interfere."

"Is there danger in continuing this trip, Gini-ji? Should we reassess it?"

"In my estimate," Algini said, "the risk is much greater in going back to Shejidan, and moving assets to cover us there. We have people and equipment positioned to protect us in Tirnamardi. If we rearrange things, our positions may become evident, and it might expose Lord Komaji's move in such a way as to bring far more tension to this situation."

"I hate to nudge the Kadagidi, either."

"If they should make any gesture of hostility toward the Atageini while we are there, it would be a serious mistake on their part. They have no motive to be that foolish—granted no change in circumstances. I told you once about the Kadagidi lord's aishid. About the Guild senior."

"Haikuti." There was no forgetting that. High-level, dangerous, and possibly a holdover from Murini's regime, serving the current lord, Aseida.

"Aseida is taking his advice from Haikuti, and Haikuti cannot benefit from making a move toward Tirnamardi. With the aiji's son and grandmother at issue, Tabini-aiji would have absolute justification to act without Filing. Once they do find out the nature of Lord Tatiseigi's guests, they should worry that we are setting up exactly such a situation."

He felt a chill. Algini rarely looked anyone straight in the eyes. Algini didn't, at the moment, head down, as he kept the conversation very, very low. And Algini just didn't blurt out extraneous information. He had to ask. "Would Haikuti be *right*?"

"Say that we have already hardened the defenses at Tirnamardi," Algini said. "And are about to assume an outward posture of alert, which should warn the Kadagidi that we are *completely* serious, and that the openness of Tirnamardi to their threat is ended. More, that preparedness will not go away when we do. *We* are not attempting to provoke a situation with either clan, Bren-ji." A slight hesitation, a shift of the eyes, gesturing toward Ilisidi. "One does not, however, *know* that that statement extends to all of us."

Cenedi? More, the dowager.

Did he mean—?

Damn. The cold feeling hadn't gone away. It grew, with a fast mental sort through prior discussions of the Kadagidi, and Ajuri, and a very prime target they were going to deal with one of these days. Eliminating Murini had just been clipping the head off a poisonous weed. The roots remained—buried deeply, they believed, in the Kadagidi.

And they had, on this train, the highest-value targets in current politics, except Tabini himself.

Ilisidi was capable of a dice-roll like that. She was *entirely* capable, if the stakes were high enough.

"One understands," he said, and as Algini got up and went back to Tano, down the aisle:

"Jase, did you follow that?"

"Most of it," Jase said, and then, after a deep breath, and very quietly: "Geigi and I had a conversation."

Geigi. Whose aishid had had a *personal* briefing before he went back to space.

"What did Geigi tell you?"

"I know the Kadagidi, from my own experience. I know that relationship. I know there's some trouble in the aiji's household. I know about the grandfather. And I know there's a problem inside the Guild that's ongoing, and that it's a matter of great concern. Geigi asked me—personally—to advise the captains this is going on."

Geigi would not have done that uninstructed. There were two people who could give Geigi that kind of instruction. "What did they say about it?"

"The conclusion was that you could handle it. Go ahead with the visit. Bring my own protection. They know your bodyguards prioritize."

"I'm glad of their confidence, but—"

"In their view, there's a risk if this isn't dealt with. In their view, Tabini, and you, and the dowager, and the boy—are irreplaceable. I agree with that."

He *worked* with risks. He dealt with cold equations day in, day out, and the concept that an eight-year-old boy could be a target was a given.

But there were bits and pieces of this he began to think were missing.

"You could have postponed this and let us handle it."

"We had an invitation," Jase said. "An excuse to have a look down here. To talk, as we're doing. Tabini got caught by surprise once. Not twice, we think. But we don't intend to end up with another situation as bad as Murini in charge down here."

"You *had* an invitation. I've asked you down here. Fishing, I said. If you think it's all going to hell down here, you could have kept the kids and just sent us reinforcements!"

"We have our reasons, Bren. Internal reasons, which really don't affect the situation Algini was talking about. The kids are here because it suits our purposes. I'm here to show the Reunioners we care about those kids, enough to put one of the four captains at risk ... should there be a risk." A tilt of Jase's head. "Seriously, Bren, I'm here to assess the situation. *We* have communications methods that don't need to go through Mogari-nai. If you really need Geigi to drop one of his relay stations onto the Kadagidi's doorstep, he's prepared to do it."

And scare hell out of the general population. My God. "That's a joke."

A faint smile. "Of course it's a joke. But not the fact we're serious about your survival. If we sent a force down here—Geigi didn't have to tell me it would upset things. Upset a lot of people. Kids, however. Not so threatening. A ship-captain? Of course I have a bodyguard."

It made a sort of sense. It apparently made sense enough that even Tatiseigi hadn't been that upset.

It didn't reassure him, however, about the underlying situation.

"I don't know if you caught all of what Algini just advised me. He hints that *she* may be pulling the strings on this whole business. If that's true—she's using this the same way you are. She's positioning assets. She won't *want* to upset the boy's birthday. But she's preparing something. If it can stay quiet, we get through this and get all the kids back where they belong with no problem. If it doesn't—you understand this matter is reaching inside the Guild itself."

"I'm right with you."

The hindbrain was working, assembling pieces. *Now* he began to get a grasp of *why* Tatiseigi had so amazingly volunteered to take in a flock of human children. Tatiseigi probably didn't know exactly why he'd been asked to fling himself into the breach—Ilisidi's *last* recourse to him had entailed the whole last year repairing Tirnamardi—but he'd bet anything that the old man had gotten a flattering, urgent, and desperate appeal from Ilisidi to do it for Cajeiri, on whom Tatiseigi doted above all things.

"All right," he said. "These kids. Geigi said there were problems."

"I have a dossier on each of them."

He wasn't entirely surprised. "So."

"Basically good kids," Jase said, shot a look to the rear of the car, then said. "Irene's our problem. Not the kid. Her mother. She was very upset about Irene's association with Cajeiri. I won't say what she said, but it got to the net. Then the Reunioners figured out who Cajeiri was. That changed things. Fast. Some of the people we trust least have become good friends of this woman. When the invitation came, Irene's mother said yes with not one question about the conditions, the safety, anything. The kid was scared of the trip. Scared of the landing. Scared of her mother is my guess. *Artur's* parents asked every question they could think of. Sabin talked to them, and they were still reluctant, but the boy wanted it. This is the boy that wrote a letter every week. Of course the letters weren't getting through. But he said he was always sure Cajeiri would answer when he could."

"And Gene?"

Jase let go a slow breath. "Gene—Gene's mother's another story. Gene got swept up by security. Guess where? The atevi section. Turned out he'd been missing three days prior and his mother hadn't reported it. When the invitation came, he reported himself to admin, real scared that that detention record was going to stop him. A kid, solo, going up into admin. His mother had to sign. That's *all* she did. The other parents turned up to see their kids board. If you want my guess, Gene had four, five people for one year of his life who actually cared where he was. We reached port. The group broke up. That was it. He's waited for this. Probably more than any of them."

"Confirms my instinct," Bren said. If there was one kid of the three that—just from what he'd heard from Cajeiri—might well be the human associate Cajeiri needed, he thought it wouldn't be the compliant, pleasant Artur. Irene? She might or might not adapt. But Gene, the troublemaker, Gene, the kid who had showed them the tunnels, was the one Cajeiri always mentioned first.

And Gene was the one Bren resonated with personally. This solo leave-taking from the station felt very familiar. The scene when he'd told his own mother he was headed to the mainland for a year at a time, that his assignment had come through? Her response hadn't exactly been congratulatory.

Long while since he'd thought of that. But he certainly hadn't had the blessing of his family.

"They didn't do *anything* on the ship without Cajeiri," he said. "Now they're in a strange place. They're likeliest to take his cues. Put Cajeiri in charge of them whenever you're not there. He has his own bodyguard. And his great-grandmother is here. He minds her more than anyone."

Jase said: "We've got one more asset. Locators on the kids."

"Can they take them off?"

"Not without going barefoot."

"Good," he said. "Good!"

He felt better about the situation, hearing that. He wasn't mad at Ilisidi, or at Cenedi. She had her objectives. They were essentially atevi objectives, and for the good of the side he was on. A chance to fortify Tatiseigi, and do it by sleight of hand, so that it *looked* like the security that would attend the unprecedented grouping of herself and her grandson and a batch of foreign guests out at Tirnamardi? Of course she took it.

But her movement to that place was as clandestine as they could make it, and that security wasn't going away when they went back to the capital. It was going to stay right there, and any notions the Kadagidi had of reaching out to intimidate their neighbor or remove the dowager's most valuable ally would meet that security head on.

Sooner or later the Kadagidi were going to make that move. Sooner or later, the Kadagidi were going to realize that the sudden dearth of information from inside Tirnamardi was not a temporary condition, that the investment they'd made over centuries, getting persons of Kadagidi man'chi into positions in Atageini centers of town government, even into Tatiseigi's household—was never going to pay off. Their entire operation was being dismantled, that at Tirnamardi first. Then the others. Kadagidi Guild would realize it. They would have to watch it happen—piece by piece—and eventually they would realize at least some of the information they had already gotten was false.

That was the slow way things could evolve.

In a way, that was what had just happened to Ajuri, on a smaller scale, when Tabini had tossed out Damiri's Ajuri staff. Lord Komaji now found himself cut off, with no information, when his daughter was about to give birth, and when his grandson had started turning up on the news with Ilisidi and human children.

Komaji's move toward the Atageini made sense in that context. Komaji might well be trying to get more information, among the clans next to Atageini land—it was always a soft border, with the smaller clans dealing with one side and the other.

That the dowager, who was supposed to be headed for Malguri, was actually going toward Tirnamardi at the same time was something Komaji might *not* know.

There was a certain danger in that. Komaji had been a fool in the Bujavid. His reputation was in tatters. If, when he found out about Ilisidi and the children, he made a move down *into* Atageini land—

That was the *fast* way the situation with the Kadagidi could evolve.

But the Kadagidi would be fools to get involved with Komaji's mistake.

Total fools.

Linens arrived.

Tableware. More fruit juice. Plates with sandwiches. And eggs.

"What's this?" Irene asked.

"A pickled egg," Cajeiri said, and popped one into his mouth. "It's safe. Red eggs, don't eat. The green are all safe. Enjoy it."

Irene tried it, tasting just the end, and screwed up her

face. She put it down and carefully looked into the sandwich lying on her plate.

"Don't do that," Gene said. "If you look, you're just going to be worried about it. And you know what they said. Whatever it is, just eat it. They'll be sure it's safe for us." He had eaten his egg in two mouthfuls, washed it down with fruit juice, and took a bite of the sandwich. "Pretty good actually, together."

"I *hate* spicy things," Irene said in a thin voice.

"You're going to get real hungry in two weeks," Artur said. "Better eat it, girl. You know what the captain said."

Irene did, squeezing her eyes tight shut. She ate it like Gene, in two big bites, washed it down with sweet orangelle, which was, truthfully, not the best combination, but that was the drink she had wanted. She shivered all over. "It's *sour!*"

"Won't kill you," Gene said. "Got to do it. Or in two weeks you're going to be a lot skinnier."

"Long time 'til supper," Artur said.

"Try the teacake, Rene-ji," Cajeiri said. Everybody liked cakes.

She was upset. Irene got upset when they teased her. But after a little bite of that, her face brightened. "Oh, that's *good!*"

"Dessert," Gene said. "It'll be a good last bite."

"Come on, Reny," Artur said. *"Dare* you. You can do it. You're not going to back out *now.*"

She had another bite of sandwich.

The lunches all disappeared—in Irene's case, in large bites, quickly swallowed, washed down with the fruit drink. It was, Cajeiri thought, fairly brave of her, especially the egg, which, to be honest, he had used to dislike. He gave her his own teacake, and she looked at him.

And very reluctantly pushed it back, as his.

"I can get more," he said, which was almost always true. If they were there for dessert, there would be a supply for tea. "Do you want more?"

They did. He asked mani's guards if there were extra cakes, and indeed, they each had one more, to finish their lunch, and then black tea, which Irene also found a challenge, but she drank it.

"Ugh," she said after a big mouthful, but after a moment she took another one. And another.

He had used to bring food from mani's table to the passengers of the ship, so it was not their first sample of atevi cooking, but it was a lot more elaborate. He had been afraid what he brought would poison them, before, so he had mostly stolen sweet dried things they thought were candy.

Now they had to face slimy pickled eggs. But they liked the cakes, and they had eaten all of a whole regular meal, and nobody was sick.

That was *very* good.

After they had cleared away lunch, they sat at their table and talked and talked—about living on the station, and where they lived now, and what they had been doing for the last year—Irene and Artur had lessons, mostly, a lot of math and science. Their parents were strict about it. "We couldn't get out much," Irene said. "The station's big." She used several words he could not get, saying something about Mospheirans that sounded unhappy.

"The atevi section you can't get into," Gene said. "I tried. I just wanted to see, you know. Security is pretty tight. That was a *big* mistake."

His face wasn't happy when he talked about that. The others looked uncomfortable. Everything they said about the station sounded unhappy, but he could only get the little words, not the big ones.

He tried to think of something else in the awkward silence, something that would make them happy. Something they could talk about. Then he thought about his slingshota. He took it out of his pocket, and took out the three stones and laid them on the table.

"What's that?" Gene asked.

"One of my good things."

"That's weird," Irene said, and reached out carefully and fingered the handle very carefully. Tapped it. "Is that plastic?"

He couldn't remember their word for wood. "Tree," he said. "Tree stuff."

"You're kidding," Gene said. "Wood?" He touched it carefully. "I've never felt it."

Artur picked up one of the stones, and said a new word. Irene said it again and added: "What planets and moons are made of."

"Rock," Cajeiri said in Ragi. "That's a rock."

"Rock," Artur said. "Rock, yes. I guess it is. But I've never had my hands on one."

"You're kidding," Cajeiri said, and then he remembered they had never been outside the ship or the station. And he could not think of anywhere on the station that was rock, or stone.

"It's smooth," Artur said, then, and he rolled it around between his fingers. "Is it made?"

"Water," Cajeiri said. "Water made it smooth."

"How," Gene asked, "do you make it do that?"

That was an odd question. But then he realized he had no ship-speak word for river. Or stream. There was ocean. But no word for waves or beach. What they had talked about on the ship was the ship, usually. Occasionally stories they remembered.

He had come prepared. He had a little notebook, and a pen. He started drawing the seacoast, and the peninsula. "Najida. This. Nand' Bren's." He started describing things in Ragi, slowly, and Irene wanted paper, and borrowed the pen to write the words her way on her paper. So they started giving each other words, using the rocks and the slingshota and the juice sloshing in the cup. Waves. Beach. Rocks. Pebbles. Sand. Tides.

It was the old game, the way they had used to be, and he began to feel increasingly at ease. He showed them how the slingshota worked, and that got the attention of mani's bodyguards—but he did not fire a stone, no. He just showed them.

"That's really wicked!" Gene said, admiring it.

"Neat," Artur said.

They were impressed. And everything was perfect.

*　　*　　*

The young group back there, Jago reported, and Kaplan also observed, was entertaining themselves very happily, and being remarkably quiet about it. Bren and Jase sat and talked, and Ilisidi and Tatiseigi conversed at length, before Ilisidi invited them to sit together and do small talk regarding the ship, the persons Ilisidi dealt with— notably Captain Sabin.

"We are trying to persuade Lord Tatiseigi to pay a visit to the station," Ilisidi said lightly. "Perhaps you can prevail."

"One would realize the extreme honor of such an invitation," Tatiseigi said with a forbidding gesture. "But I would decline. Flying does not agree with me."

"There is no such sensation on the space station," Ilisidi said.

"One has no desire to be sealed into a tube and flung into the heavens. With all courtesy, nandi," Lord Tatiseigi added, with a little nod toward Jase, "toward the elegance I am told exists in the heavens. I am certain it exceeds imagination. But simply to move between Shejidan and Tirnamardi is such an untidy business. One can only imagine the difficulties of a household lifted to the station. Yet—yet I am aware both you and nand' Bren do maintain such arrangements."

"We have very capable staff, nandi. Extraordinary people."

"Ah. There is the grade," Tatiseigi said relative to the train's motion. It was slowed a bit, then gathered speed again. "That will be a quarter of an hour to our destination, nandiin. Not so rapid as your shuttle. But one is accustomed to it."

Guild around them were getting up from seats, putting away service items.

"Nandiin," Ilisidi said purposefully, then, in a tone that had nothing of banter about it. "We shall enjoy the hospitality of our esteemed Tatiseigi. We shall see nothing untoward comes near these children."

"Let me assure the ship-aiji," Tatiseigi said, "that he is welcome under my roof. We have ample room. Ample room."

"Nand' Tatiseigi." Jase gave a very courteous bow, with no hint of bemusement—though he was amazed, Bren was sure. The old man had been pleasant the entire trip. Happy in the event? Bren wondered.

The old man was going to get off the train and run into Taibeni, who were coming in, arranged by Tatiseigi's own staff. He thought a warning might be in order. He decided on it.

"There will be, one is advised, nandi, *Taibeni* at the station. An assistance. They are reliable."

A brow quirked, just a little. The iron good will stayed in place. "Our allies," he said, as if the words tasted entirely strange. "Yes. That is good to know, nand' paidhi."

12

The train pulled to a stop. The door opened. The dowager's men went out first onto the platform. The word came back, clearly, and more went out, and the baggage cars next door opened up, distant thumps.

Bren got up. Jase did, then Lord Tatiseigi, and, last, Ilisidi, as the aisle had mostly cleared and unloading was proceeding outside. The youngsters stayed where they were — courtesy of the youngest Guild present. Kaplan and Polano, who had generally tried not to block the aisle, and who had found the far side of the galley the easiest for their bulky stance, put their helmets on, as Jase slipped a communications earpiece into his ear and from that moment on was in communication with them.

"Let Cajeiri's aishid move the kids," Bren said. Maneuvering was too tight for Kaplan and Polano, and Cajeiri's aishid was getting instructions. "Bren-ji," Banichi said, his own signal, and he joined Banichi and Jago, going quickly down the aisle, in a fast sequence. Jase and his guard would be behind them. Tano and Algini were near the door. Guild moved their own baggage. Personal baggage stayed — it would get there, but not on the bus.

The open door brought a bracing waft of valley air, and daylight, a step down to the platform — baggage was piling up, and a cluster of Taibeni in brown and green were handing it out, one to another.

Bren followed Banichi's gesture, left turn, moving with dispatch; the kids all together, with their young escorts, all headed toward the vehicles waiting beside the platform, in front of a small stand of trees: the red and black bus up from Najida, and two old and well-used green and brown trucks. Taibeni colors, those, checked and secure.

The human kids stopped abruptly—frozen in place, staring . . . as three riders on mecheiti moved past the bus. Lean, towering beasts, mecheiti were built for speed, twice a human's height, with curved necks and shining brass war-caps on the short tusks that jutted from the lower jaw.

Stopping was prudent. The mecheiti had caught wind of something foreign, and the lead rider used his quirt to move his mecheita past, giving their group a wide berth. The other two followed, around the station office, out of sight.

Welcome to the Padi Valley, Bren thought, as he followed Banichi down the steps of the train station platform.

The kids were close behind, Cajeiri and Gene in the lead, then Artur. Irene was coming, holding to the wooden rail and looking anxiously in the direction the riders had come from. Veijico and Lucasi were right with her, wanting her to catch up, and she jogged a couple of steps, the kids bunching up again.

Off to the right was another group of riders. It was the trucks that were the rarity in Taiben. The lodge had them, for supply, for commerce; but the forest that was Taiben, the deep woods—mecheiti navigated those narrow trails and crossed the hunting ranges efficiently, with no need for costly and intrusive roads. It was a way of life far different than other clans—the Taibeni-Atageini war had lasted over two hundred years for one thing because the Taibeni had never cared much what their neighbors did, or thought. The Taibeni used the same train station as the Atageini. They had visitors come in, and they would get them and their baggage to the lodge deep in the woods, by the sole road.

For the rest—Taibeni sons and daughters took service in certain of the outside guilds, and there was indeed a lord of Taiben, but he rarely went to Shejidan unless a vote was close. They had had occasional disputes with the Atageini, usually around this train station—but nothing like an active war.

Bren reached the bus, where Taibeni riflemen stood—hesitated there to look back at Jase. "Best we board last," he said, and waited there while the last of their party came at their necessary pace. The train, meanwhile, continued to produce baggage that young Taibeni passed off the platform and onto the truck.

There was one large, unlikely item that came out of the baggage car. With Cajeiri's servants.

He was aware of Jegari, observing from the steps behind him. "Nandiin," Jegari said, and vanished up onto the bus. "They have it," Bren heard him say, inside. "It is coming, nandi."

A shriek rose above the platform. Boji was excited.

"A pet," Bren said to Jase, watching Tatiseigi exchanging a word with one of the older Taibeni. It was a remarkable moment, lost in the rumbling of the huge cage as it came closer to the platform edge. They were going to have to take that down the ramp and lift it in.

"They're moving fast," Jase remarked in ship-speak. "Are we worried?"

"The Taibeni want this part to go right. The dowager's involved. Tatiseigi's a new ally. And they *don't* want to linger here. Technically the rail stations are neutral ground. They want to get back into defined clan territory—which in this case is Tatiseigi's. There, what happens is Atageini responsibility."

Ilisidi and Tatiseigi were headed for the bus now.

"Your lads are going to have to do what they did at the port," Bren said. "Board last."

"No worry," Jase said.

Nawari and Casimi were with Ilisidi, help enough on the steps, and she had her cane. Tatiseigi had two of his bodyguard. Bren reached for the assisting rail, and Jago gave him a helpful shove from below. Jase came up, likely the same way; Jago and Banichi, Tano and Algini all boarded and went past them, toward the rear.

Bren sat down in the seat facing Tatiseigi; Jase sat down across from Ilisidi; and the children were in seats across the aisle. Kaplan and Polano boarded, and the driver shut the door.

"Well," Tatiseigi said. Tatiseigi was to ride a pleasantly warm bus instead of his own antique and elegant open car, but not necessarily happy about it. The kids exclaimed and recoiled from the window, as the heads of mecheiti appeared, the riders passing right beside the bus as it began to move. The kids' outcry, not the mecheiti, got a twitch from Veijico; but they were all right. Cajeiri was laughing.

"One noted Ragi colors on this conveyance," Tatiseigi said. "Indeed, *those* colors are always welcome on At-ageini land."

Bren was not about to admit it was his personal bus. No. It was going to come out. He had to say something eventually. Just—not at this moment.

Cajeiri was happily pointing at something. The children leaned to look. Bren had no idea what they were looking at. The back aisle was packed, Guild seated where they could, standing where they could find room. But not enough of them. A few of Ilisidi's young men, Bren thought, must be staying with the two trucks.

The driver took a right turn, up and over the track, and onto the road.

The packed crowd swayed. Steadied. Trees whipped past, close at hand, which had used to affect Jase. But Jase seemed perfectly steady despite the movement, the horizon problem. He even turned to have a look out the other side.

"Are you all right?" Bren asked Jase, in ship-speak. "Medication holding up?"

Jase put a hand on his forearm. "Constant dose," Jase said. And changed to Ragi. "One is faring very well, Bren-ji. One needs to settle in, now. One must get the vocabulary up."

It took only a few minutes of conversation—mutual acquaintances, the cell phone affair, the changes in the apartment and the problems getting the Farai shifted out of his residence before they could even think about reconstruction—before Jase was "settled in." Jase glitched on the occasional words, but he'd been working. And he kept a fortunate numerology on the fly; it was no small trick.

The bus reached rolling grassland, open, a relatively unlikely spot for snipers.

Thank God, Bren thought.

They had reached Atageini land, and done it without incident.

The road became a grassy track through the hunting range, and straight as an arrow. The mecheiti riders kept up with the bus quite handily, the bus taking only a moderate pace.

And there was, scarcely visible except at the very edge of the track, a peculiar condition on the road. The only vehicles that routinely took this track were Tatiseigi's magnificent open car—rarely—the estate truck, traveling either to the train station or to the town some distance to the northeast, or town trucks and vans, taking people to the train station, or bringing supplies into the estate. As roads in the Padi Valley went, it was a veritable highway—

But usually the grass stood up.

At the moment, as best Bren could observe from his vantage, the grass was quite flattened. The road was well-defined, indicating a *lot* of recent traffic. Bren glanced at Tatiseigi, wondering if the old man had noticed that, and noted how much traffic, most of it perhaps from Taiben, had gone to and from his land.

Tatiseigi, however, was busy talking to Ilisidi.

One had an idea that Guild on the bus, standing in the aisle back there, hadn't missed it. But they probably had no doubt of the cause. Trucks had been moving in equipment and supplies, setting up what Cenedi had arranged.

They took a slow curving turn.

"I see the hedge!" Cajeiri exclaimed, from his side of the aisle.

The estate hedge, indeed it was, a thick green barrier

that towered up as high as a two-story building and went on and on over the horizon, defining Tatiseigi's personal grounds. It was thorny stuff. It had grown around massive stakes, from ancient times, when mecheiti riders, cannon, and muzzle loaders had contended in district wars. Absent the cannon and modern artillery, it was *still* formidable, tough and fibrous strands with thorns the width of a man's hand, and as thick as the bus was wide—a barrier even mecheiti would not attempt.

The whole perimeter had only a formal front gate, which came visible just ahead, and a smaller, more utilitarian one on the far side of the house.

The bus slowed to a crawl, then almost immediately rolled forward as the ornate iron gates opened electronically, the riders going ahead of them.

Taibeni, moving freely into the heart of Atageini land.

"Home," Tatiseigi said, sitting with his back to the movement of those riders.

They rolled onto gravel, now. The inner road was well-kept, running beside the southern hedge, rimming a broad, rolling meadowland, a huge expanse of it. Lord Tatiseigi's grounds were famous and extensive, enclosing pasturage for his mecheiti herd and providing insulation from the world.

But something *else* showed, from Bren's view: a cluster of trucks, one with a mast and communication dishes, and a handful of tents. The mecheita riders headed off in that direction, toward what had to be a Guild field camp.

His fixed stare had gotten Tatiseigi's attention. Tatiseigi turned and took a look out the window, straight out, then further over his shoulder as the bus moved past the camp.

"There is a *camp* on my grounds!"

"There are two small camps, Tati-ji," Ilisidi said. "You know we are taking measures. They will be out of sight, quite out of the way. You will not know they are here."

"Aiji-ma," Tatiseigi said, visibly perturbed. "All this business of new men and retiring my old servants—and taking one of my storerooms—I have resigned myself to new faces; but I am beyond uneasy to be met with this *camp* at the gate. How much more is there, up at the house?"

Ilisidi held up a finger. "One little antenna on the roof. A camera or two. You will not see them from the ground."

"Aiji-ma," Tatiseigi said, and Bren decided it was a good time to study something off to the side and across the aisle.

"Is the threat that great, aiji-ma?" Tatiseigi asked.

"Tati-ji," Ilisidi said, "our conscience still troubles us, after the damage our presence inflicted this last year. You have been so staunch an ally—well, I shall say it: *brave*. You have been the bravest, the steadiest, the most trusted and the closest of our allies. I lie awake at night thinking of the danger, not so much to me—*I* have such very extensive protections constantly about me, and I have come through every attempt. But, Tati-ji, my closest associates are, by comparison, far easier targets, and the very ones my enemies will go after first, to do me harm. They know they cannot attack *me*—until they have buried my allies, my protectors, and taken away my strongest supporters. Terror is their weapon, and I know *you* do not feel it—nor do I—but let us not give them access here. These are an enemy that has no respect for such ancient premises. These are people who attack civilians and servants, and have not observed any such requirement as Filing. This enemy murders old servants, like gentle old Eidi, who died at my grandson's door, brave, loyal and holding his post. I cannot suffer such losses. I will not have such things happen here. I will not have a single *vase* shaken on a shelf in Tirnamardi, let alone these bloody-booted outlaws tramping through your halls, destroying what they are too crass ever to understand. No. I need you, Tati-ji. I shall not have your bravery putting you at risk! I will not lose you! Suffer these small changes. And stand by me."

My God, Bren thought. She had the gift.

"Aiji-ma," Tatiseigi said. "One hears. One is honored by your concern."

The bus rolled on.

Jase said, quietly, "This is all your estate, Lord Tatiseigi? It is huge. I have tried to think how long it took this hedge to grow."

Tatiseigi, still unhappy, said past a clenched jaw, "Four centuries, ship-aiji."

"It is very beautiful, this place," Jase said. "I am very grateful that you have offered your hospitality. I shall try to be a good guest."

"Honored, ship-aiji." Tatiseigi gave a nod of his head, unbending a little, though he kept looking anxiously out the window, in search of other tents, one could well imagine. "You hosted the aiji-dowager aboard your ship. One is pleased to return the gesture, in her name."

"Nandi," Jase said properly, with a little nod.

"Those two—" Tatiseigi said, resigning his search for tents with a little shift of the eyes toward the aisle, by implication Kaplan and Polano. "Is that their *indoor* uniform?"

"No, nandi," Jase said. "Not at all. They wear it now because I am traveling between safe places, but once indoors, be assured, they will be happy to put on ordinary clothes."

"Indeed," Tatiseigi said diplomatically, nodded, and looked measurably relieved.

The bus rolled on at a moderate pace on the graveled drive, and exclamations from the youngsters said they had seen something.

Bren looked ahead, between Ilisidi's seatback and Polano's white shoulder.

The last time he had seen Tirnamardi, there had been shell-holes in the masonry and broken gaps in the low, ornamental hedge of the front drive.

It sat on its low rise looking as serene as if there had never been an attack from the Kadagidi. The road curved. The grass had grown over the trampled lawn, and, on the other side of the bus, the house, a rectangular stone affair of many windows, showed neither patches nor scaffolding.

"I can see the house, nandiin-ji," Bren said, "and it is beautiful again, nandi. Absolutely beautiful."

"Well, well," Tatiseigi said, "it has been a struggle." He drew a deep breath, and courteously addressed himself to Jase. "Understand, ship-aiji, our neighbors attacked us with mortars, and even our allies made wreckage of our hedges. We sought out shrubs of exact girth and age, and we have nurtured them through last summer. We have brought stone from the exact quarries, and while the match is not perfect, it will age."

"We look forward to it," the dowager said, as the tires rolled onto the paved part of the drive, rumbling on the brickwork. On that broad curve, the bus slowly came to a halt. The doors of the great house opened, pouring out servants and Tatiseigi's security.

The bus door opened. Kaplan and Polano had to be the first off. One hoped security was warned.

"Now you must escort us, nandi," the dowager said, setting her cane before her, and Tatiseigi gallantly struggled to his feet and offered his hand.

Guild had sorted themselves out by the seating arrangement of their lords, and Cenedi and his group moved out, immensely relieving the congestion back there, and Tatiseigi's aishid after them. Cajeiri got up, and his guests did, as Bren and Jase got up.

Banichi and the rest of the aishid followed right behind them. They stepped down the far last step onto the pavings of Tatiseigi's drive, with Kaplan and Polano waiting at the left, the dowager and Tatiseigi already headed up the steps. The two trucks with the baggage were right behind them. The white dust of the gravel was still lingering in the air along the road.

The children came down next, exclaiming in amazement at everything.

"They've never seen a stone building," Jase said quietly. "Or a building, for that matter. Everything's a wonder to them. They'll want to know everything."

"It's supposed to rain tonight," Bren said. "A few showers. That should provide entertainment. So much of the world one takes for granted. We *have* to arrange that fishing trip, Jase."

"I'm going to do my damnedest," Jase said. "So many textures. So many details."

They walked up into the foyer, the hall of lilies, those beautiful porcelain bas relief tiles that were the pride of the house, and there was Tatiseigi, Cajeiri, and the dowager watching three human children standing in awe of the porcelain flowers.

"They're cold," Artur said, touching a flower petal with the merest tip of his finger. "But not really cold."

Then they all had to touch, very gently.

"Ceramic," Bren said. "Bow nicely to your host and tell him you think the flowers are beautiful."

They did exactly that, and for the old lord, clearly anxious for the welfare of his lilies, they could not have picked a better feature to compliment. He nodded benignly.

"They are very *delicious,* nandi!" Artur insisted, as if Tatiseigi had failed to hear the compliment, and Cajeiri quickly snagged his arm and Gene's and, Irene following, got them all up the steps and into the main house ahead of the adults.

"Wow!" echoed upstairs, as the youngsters got a look at the halls inside, the ornate scrollwork, the lily motif repeated, the grand hall with its gilt, the high windows, the paintings and vases.

Bren said, quietly, "One believes the boy's attempted word just now was *beautiful,* nandi. The children are absolutely in awe of the house." Indeed the old lord had just had his precedence and the dowager's violated, in his own front hall. "One sincerely apologizes."

"For my great-grandson," Ilisidi finished dourly, though Bren thought the young gentleman had been admirably quick about getting Artur upstairs before he mispronounced *beautiful* again. Ilisidi made the climb to the main floor on Lord Tatiseigi's arm, as the high hall echoed to young voices. The children were standing in the center of the hall, revolving like so many planets as they gazed all about the baroquerie and the gilt stairway and the windows.

"Lord Tatiseigi is bearing up with extraordinary patience," Bren muttered to Jase as they walked up together, his aishid walking quietly, and Jase's pair with servos whining at every step.

"Beautiful!" was the word from above. Safely in shipspeak, this time.

They reached the main floor to effect a rescue.

But, unprecedented sight, the old man stood beside Ilisidi with a smile dawning on his face, watching the children so admiring his house. She smiled, pleased as well. "Well, well," he said. "They are certainly appreciative."

Cajeiri saw them, cast a worried look at his guests, and hurried over to give a sober, harried bow. "Mani, Great-uncle! Shall we be lodged together? May I take them upstairs?"

"As the dowager permits," Lord Tatiseigi said, and nodded toward the handful of servants lined up by the stairs. "They will guide you. Do tell the servants, young gentleman, they should open the white suite for Jase-aiji and his bodyguard. —Ship-aiji, my staff will make suitable arrangements, and if there is any need, do ask my staff. —Nand' paidhi. You will have the blue suite. I am confident it is ready for you."

"Nandi," Bren said with a little bow, and to Jase—not sure Jase would have understood, since when he spoke to his own, Tatiseigi used the regional accent: "The white suite is adjacent to the blue. We'll have time to catch up before—"

About that time there was a sudden bang and a considerable clatter and sound of wheels on the marble floor downstairs.

Lord Tatiseigi looked alarmed.

A shriek echoed up from the foyer, ear-piercing and echoing.

The human kids froze in alarm. Ilisidi simply said, with a sigh, "The parid'ja, Tati-ji."

Tatiseigi drew a large breath and said, "There are no antiquities in the suite assigned to the young gentleman and his guests." He signaled and snapped his fingers for staff, who stood looking downstairs. "The young gentleman's suite, for that."

No breakables seemed an excellent idea, in Bren's opinion. He had no idea how they were to get the cage upstairs but to carry it. There were no lifts in Tirnamardi, most features of which predated the steam engine.

But they were safe. They were within walls, inside a security envelope that three clans, the paidhi's security, and ship security were not going to let be cracked. He had worried all the way. But what Cenedi had had moved in here was not just the presence of younger Guildsmen, and more of them, it was surveillance. And, he was sure, it was also armament to back it up. Nothing was going to move on the grounds without their knowing.

And count the mecheiti in that camp as a surveillance device right along with the electronics. Surveillance *and* armament: one did not want to be a stranger afoot with mecheiti on the hunt.

Uncle's house was just the way Cajeiri remembered it—only without the shells going off outside—and his birthday was absolutely certain now. Uncle had been patient, mani was not unhappy, Jase-aiji was a happy surprise for nand' Bren and for him, too, and it was what he had dreamed of, having Gene and Artur and Irene with him.

They all trooped along with the servants who guided them up the main stairs, and by the time they got up to that floor, there, making a huge racket, and silhouetted in the light of the windows at the end, came Boji's cage, and his servants, Eisi and Lieidi, and two of Uncle's, pushing it up the hall. Boji was bounding around, terrified by all the rattling and the strange place and the strange people, after the train ride and the truck, and he let out shrieks as they came, right to the middle suite on the floor, while he and his guests waited.

The servants nodded a polite respect, and rolled the

cage right through the door, into a suite with big, wonderful, sunny windows, tall as a man, and filmy white draperies that blew in the breeze from the open windows. It was a beautiful room. Nippy from the breeze, but after all the traveling, even that felt good.

"Put him near the window, nadiin," Cajeiri told the servants. Nand' Bren's servants had wired the cage door shut for the trip, and there was no way Boji could get loose. He was bouncing from one perch to another and looking very undone, panting, once the cage stopped, and staring at him with pitiful white-rimmed eyes, with his fur all messy.

"Poor Boji," he said, putting his fingers through the grillwork, so Boji could smell them and be sure it was him. "Poor Boji. I am sorry, I am sorry. —Close the window, Eisi-ji. They have spilled all his water." It was in a glass jar with a tube, and it had emptied with the bouncing about. He was *sure* Eisi and Lieidi had kept him watered and fed on the train. "Get him water. And an egg. Poor Boji." Boji was crowding close to the grillwork, up against his hand. Boji put his longest finger out and clamped it on his finger. It was very sad.

"Is he all right?" Artur asked.

"Just scared." He kept his hand where it was. Artur reached out, but Boji moved away.

"He's a *monkey,*" Irene said. "Just like in the archive."

"Sort of. He's a parid'ja. They eat eggs. They climb after eggs, for people."

"*Climb* after eggs."

"Some. Two kinds." He could not remember the word for dig. The baggage was starting to arrive, and with it, there would be eggs. He kept soothing Boji, and Lieidi came back with the water bottle filled and put that in place. Then Eisi found the right bag and came back with an egg.

"There is one egg left, nandi. He has had five, on the trip."

Five. They had stuffed him. He looked exhausted and mussed, but his little belly looked round. "Well, he may have one more. Arrange for eggs, Eisi-nadi. But, Eisi-nadi,

Lieidi-nadi, these are my guests I have told you about. This is Irene-nadi, Artur-nadi, and Gene-nadi."

"Hi," Eisi said.

"Hi!" Gene said back, looking surprised.

Cajeiri grinned. "My aishid knows more words." Antaro and Jegari were back in the bedroom, arranging things, and he thought Veijico and Lucasi had gone out a moment ago—possibly to check in with house security. That was what they were supposed to do. "They have a few words." He nodded, so that Eisi and Lieidi could get to work. "You hold the egg, Gene."

He handed the egg to Gene, then unwound the wire so he could open the door.

But the moment the door was open, Boji launched himself at him, chittering, and held on—which was going to ruin his collar lace. He calmly reached for the egg Gene was holding and held it up so Boji could see it.

Boji just reached out one arm and took it.

"You do not eat that and hold on to me," he said, and moved his arm to make Boji shift toward the cage. "Go on. Go back in your cage. You can take your egg. Good Boji."

"Does he understand?" Irene asked.

"He understands a little. He has had five eggs already. He is not that hungry. But he always wants an egg. There." He was able to transfer Boji to a perch, with his egg, and to shut and latch the door. He brushed off his sleeves and front. "He loses fur when he is scared."

"Look at him!" Artur said. Boji had opened his egg his way, tapping it with his longest finger until he could make a little hole, then widening that hole until he could use his tongue.

"Amazing!" Gene said.

The egg was empty, very quickly, and Boji, much relieved, began grooming himself, very energetically. His guests were fascinated, watching every move, but staying far enough away not to scare him. Soon Boji, very tired from all the excitement, fell asleep, and *they* fell to exploring the sitting room, and the bedroom. He showed them the bath and the accommodation, too, which were down the hall.

When they came back to the room Boji woke up and set up a moderate racket, rattling the cage and wanting out. Cajeiri went over to quiet him.

"Can we take him out of the cage?"

"Very excited. He climbs. Not a good idea."

"There's a house down there," Gene said. He had looked out the window, moving aside the filmy curtains. "Lots of rails. Look! There's one of the mecheiti."

He already had an idea what *could* be there, and he immediately came and looked out. Uncle's stables had been set on fire last year, in the fighting. And it was all rebuilt as if nothing had ever happened. That was a wonderful thing to see. "Those are Great-uncle's stables," he said in Ragi. And in ship-speak: "Mecheiti live there. If mani lets us, we can go there." Back to Ragi. "Maybe they will let us ride." And ship-speak: "Go on the mecheiti."

There were apprehensive looks. He had told them about riding up on the ship. They had thought it would be a fine thing. Now—

"They're awfully *big*," Artur said.

"I can show you. Even mani and Uncle may go. We can go all around inside the hedges. If they let us."

They were far from confident about that.

"What do you do if they don't want to do what you want?" Artur asked.

"Quirt," he said, and slapped his leg. "Doesn't hurt. They just listen."

They all looked, for some reason, at Boji.

"We try," Gene said then, in Ragi. "We do."

"We try," Artur said, not quite so confidently.

"We try," Irene said last. Irene was scared of a lot of things. She was never sure she could do things. Irene had always said her mother would not let her do this, and her mother would not let her do that. Whatever it was, her mother would not let her do it. Cajeiri remembered that, and he found he understood Irene, now, a lot more than before.

"Well, you will not fall off," he said. He became determined that Irene would get a chance to do *lots* of things her mother would *never* approve.

*   *   *

Shedding the bulletproof vest had been first on the list. Changing to a simple coat and dropping into a plump chair was second, and having Jase across from him in a quiet chance to rest and talk was something they hadn't enjoyed in a year.

Banichi and Jago, Tano and Algini all settled down to a quiet, comfortable rest right with them, standing on no ceremony. They'd all lived together. Polano and Kaplan, who didn't speak Ragi and weren't entirely informed of the political intricacies, had gladly opted for baths down the hall, and a quiet rest next door, in Jase's suite.

Supani and Koharu kept the water hot and the teapot full—there had been a very nice service waiting on the buffet. They were on duty for the first time during the trip, while Banichi and the rest had seen nothing *but* duty since well before dawn.

"I'm doing pretty well," Jase said, momentary lapse into ship-speak, when he asked. "My spine's almost quit popping, and if I can shake this headache before dinner, I'll be great."

Bren understood that. His own last shuttle flight had been as fast as they could make it, a hard burn from the station, to a fast dive and a landing on Mospheira. Jase's flight this time had been far more conservative. "You certainly were a surprise. To *all* of us. And *that's* unusual."

Jase had said the captains had sent him. And that it was for the captains' reasons—flatly that they were using the children's visit. And hadn't cleared it with Tabini *or* the dowager.

Assessing the situation on the mainland. He could well understand that.

"I have a little guess," he said, "that the situation between the Reunioners and the Mospheirans on the station is making life difficult for the ship-folk. You're outnumbered, even if you have all the power. I heard a little of this from Geigi. You and the Mospheirans and the atevi as a bloc can outvote the Reunioners on every issue. But now you've got them straining to break *away* from this station and establish a new colony out at Maudit."

Jase nodded slowly. "That's pretty accurate. It sounded good at first. Less so, considering the tone the Mospheirans have provoked out of the Reunioners. At first it seemed as if the Mospheirans hold the Reunioners personally responsible for the sins of their ancestors. But when the Reunioner leaders started calling the Mospheirans traitors—you'd believe the Mospheirs were right."

"Is Braddock at the head of this?"

Louis Baynes Braddock. That was the Reunioner stationmaster—who'd resisted all reason when it came time to abandon Reunion.

Hadn't liked relinquishing his power, not at all.

"Definitely. We could prosecute him for the things he did at Reunion. But with us voting with the Mospheirans on every issue, that action doesn't look disinterested. There's a lot of heated rhetoric. Now that the Reunioners are starting to splinter on the Maudit issue—and there *is* at least some balking on Braddock's plan—these *kids*, with a peaceful, personal connection to the aiji's son—they offer something you can't turn into a political ploy. The contact makes the Mospheirans just a little nervous. They think, I guess, that the kids' relationship will give the Reunioners some sort of special access. But they're *only* three kids—and the Mospheirans have *you* for reassurance. That's why I said it's for *our* reasons, my being here. Braddock doesn't want this mission to succeed. The moderates among the Reunioners, who have no clear leader, do. The atevi are calm about it all. The Mospheirans have had one anonymous wit say these three kids already show better sense than Braddock. That's caught on—and Braddock isn't happy. *We* are. Lord Geigi and the moderate Reunioners are watching this, not knowing quite what to hope—but hoping, all the same, that if there *were* Reunioner paidhiin—the Reunioners don't remotely understand that word, really—that their influence might win out, not just in a decade or so—but now—over Braddock's."

"Did they explain the paidhiin tend to be shot at?"

"I don't think they mentioned that part."

His aishid found quiet amusement in that. He noted it. Probably Jase did. Jase had a sip of tea and said, in Ragi, and with a nod: "I told Lord Geigi. He said he thought it was the best decision. Then he added something else. That some Reunioners may *think* they can set up a colony and run it their way. But that, in the spirit of the agreement between humans and Tabini-aiji, if we should go out to Maudit—Mospheirans, Reunioners, and atevi should have a share of it."

"You know," Bren said, "Tabini would surely appoint a lordship to oversee an atevi establishment there, if it were seriously proposed. But what Tabini *more* favors is the promised starship. The coup delayed it. He wants it. I'm sure he raised that point with Geigi. *There* is Reunioner employment."

"Braddock is not in favor."

"Poor man. He will not get all he wants."

Jase said seriously, "The Reunioners have only just become aware that the world *does* control the resources. All along they've made up reasons for why atevi came with us to Reunion. They have no understanding of just how important Tabini-aiji is to this world in general and their rescue in particular. They *missed* the last two hundred years of Mospheirans and atevi making this arrangement work, they *missed* Tabini-aiji pushing for greater tech and for making the whole space program possible. And now they have Braddock telling them everything *we* tell them is a self-serving lie."

"Ignoring the fact, as Braddock always has, that we could have alien visitors dropping by any day to *see* if we lied to them," Bren said. "The man's a fool. The last thing we need is to have him in charge of anything, let alone an entire station. He nearly got them killed once already. Have they forgotten?"

Jase shook his head. "Never underestimate the power of people to be swayed by what they want to hear. But three children, three of their own, in complete innocence, are saying something that contradicts Braddock—and no few Reunioners are following this, closely, and for the first time listening to actual information. So, yes, the

Council put pressure on the parents—promised the kids would be safe. Promised—well, at least suggested it could be advantageous. A guaranteed future for the kids."

"One is glad to hear that," he said. He declined to let Koharu make another pot. "We daren't have another round. We'll have formal dinner coming up. No question."

Algini got to his feet quietly, and Tano followed suit, the both of them excusing themselves with a little bow. It was nothing unusual.

It was a little more unusual that those two put on their sidearms and left, but security responded to a lot of signals that were simply precaution, and they equipped under whatever rules were current. They might have gotten a call about something as routine as a query from the kitchen.

Banichi and Jago, however, at apparent ease, stayed until the pot was empty, and when Jase declared he had to dress for dinner, Banichi got up and saw Jase to his room.

Jago said then, quietly, "There is, Bren-ji, still information on Ajuri movement. They are nearer, but not trending in our direction."

"Is there any interpretation?"

"It is eastward movement. This takes them more toward the road home."

"Giving up, do you think?"

"One is not certain, Bren-ji. Possibly. Or possibly not, if they decided to enter Purani territory and keep a township between us."

Those lesser clans with ties on both sides of the question—clans which typically tried to stay out of difficulties between their larger neighbors.

"We are keeping an eye on the matter," Jago said, "and we will use Taibeni Guild to advise Ajuri Guild that they are treading delicate ground. If they do not know we are here, we are not informing them."

Not sending things through Guild headquarters. He understood that.

"More of it later," Jago said. "We shall see if they

regard that, or if Komaji is bent on making a nuisance of himself."

Komaji. Damn the man.

"How is our situation?"

"We are satisfied," Jago said in a low voice. "We have removed certain suspect servants. We have confidence in Lord Tatiseigi's remaining staff, we have laid down strict rules about outside communication, and we have moved in our elements not only under canvas, out by the gates, but in positions within the house. We have set up our own equipment, that we know is clean. Lord Tatiseigi's house sits isolated within its hedges—a virtue. We control the grounds so that nothing can move unnoticed. If Ajuri comes no closer, we should be able to let the children go out and about, ride as they please, if they please, explore the immediate area of the house, and enjoy their holiday. Tabini-aiji is safe and Geigi is in the heavens. The young gentleman and his guests are under our eye and with a great deal of secure space about them."

"Despite the Kadagidi?" he asked, regarding Tatiseigi's neighbors to the east.

"We are watching them," Jago said. "We are advised that *Geigi* is watching. He has that ability. Not even a market truck has moved around the Kadagidi estate. They are being very quiet. There have been no arrivals or departures. We have temporarily detained *everyone* who has been removed from Lord Tatiseigi's estate, we swept the area of the train station, so there were no observers there. They likely know about the Taibeni making an agreement with the Atageini. They will not be happy with that. And they may be aware that Taibeni are here and about the train station—they will be wondering what that is about. They should be alarmed by the sudden silence from their spies, and they may well be conferring over there, asking themselves whether Tabini-aiji has taken a more threatening stance against them, whether the Taibeni, closely related to him, are part of this plan—but being barred from court, and forbidden to come into Shejidan, they will have to get their information from the news and from their spies in *other* places.

This area has gone dark to them. They are very probably looking to their defense and trying to get information. If that effort occupies them for a number of days, that will be enough to let the children have their holiday and go on to Shejidan. After that, we will let our detainees go, with compensation, which we shall arrange, they will be free to reveal that they have been dismissed from their posts at Tirnamardi—we have no wish to compromise their safety. But since they have worked for the Kadagidi—let the Kadagidi support them hereafter. At that point, at least, if they have not been alarmed before, the Kadagidi will realize they are dealing with a stronger and evidently permanent establishment on their border. That will not shift their man'chi in the least—but it will have warned them that Lord Tatiseigi no longer needs turn a blind eye to their trespasses."

For much of the last century, the Kadagidi had viewed themselves as the most powerful clan in the Padi Valley, and the Atageini as not quite their ally, but as under elderly leadership, clinging to the old ways, too independent to be ruled, too important to assassinate, and too lost in his own world to threaten anyone.

It *was* going to be an unhappy realization for the Kadagidi. Tatiseigi was several of those things, but lost in his own world, incapable of playing the political game?

No. Not quite.

Dinner needed almost-best clothes. Eisi and Lieidi had unpacked everyone, there were baths down the hall, and Eisi and Lieidi had steamed all the wrinkles out and helped them dress, except Irene, who, in her too-large bathrobe, disappeared into the closet to dress. They had no queues nor ribbons to fuss with—their hair was short. Their day clothing was all ship-style, very plain, blue suits, or green or brown—But Geigi had seen they each came with two good dinner coats, and shirts and trousers, proper enough to be respectful of a formal dinner. Nobody had even thought of it, but Geigi had, and the sizes were all perfect.

His guests were excited and a little embarrassed at

clothing they had never worn. There was a little laughter, and the short hair was very conspicuous, but then Artur's red hair was conspicuous on its own. They turned and admired one another, excited and nervous about it all. True, they were not quite in the latest mode, but Geigi had dodged any conflict of house colors, had everything absolutely not controversial, all beiges and browns and a shade of green and one of blue that just was not in any house. There was lace enough, and Gene said he was afraid he would get his cuffs in his food.

It really was a trick, he realized, and he had known it forever: he showed Gene the knack of turning his hand to make the lace wind up a little on his wrist, and the rest copied it.

They were very pleased with themselves. And they laughed.

But just then a little rumble sounded in the distance, a boom of thunder—and they all froze and looked toward the east.

"Thunder," he said. He had tried to tell them about weather. He remembered that. Weather was coming in, and he did hope if it rained, it would not rain a lot, and that it would clear by morning, so they would not be held indoors.

They all went to the window, to look out. But the thunder had been in the west, and the window faced east.

It was getting dark, on toward twilight.

"Come," he said in Ragi. "Come. There is a window. Likely we can see it."

He led the way out to the hall, where, at the end, there was one big window, and he led them to the foot of it, by the servants' stairs—and indeed, they could see the clouds coming in, a dark line on the horizon to the left. Lightning flashed in that distant gray mass, and after a moment, thunder sounded. "It is quite far," he said. "It will be here by full dark."

"Is there any danger?" Irene asked.

"Being outdoors, yes. If it strikes down to earth, it goes to the tallest things."

"The house?"

"The house has protections," he said.

"Those people are out there by the gate," Gene said.

"They will have a wet night. But they will know what to do. They all will be safe. Come. We can go downstairs. I shall show you from the front door if I can persuade security."

They went with him, excited, and Antaro talked with house security, and said they wanted just to look out the door, for the guests' benefit.

"They agree," Antaro said, so they all went, down all the way to the front door, and Great-uncle's major domo opened it for them, while Great-uncle's security stood by.

Just in that little time, the bank of cloud was closer, and the wind had begun to blow.

"Oh!" Irene said, as a gust came at them, and lightning obligingly flashed in the cloud.

"Neat!" Artur said.

"This is so good," Gene said, and walked out onto the porch, with the wind tumbling his hair and blowing at his coat and his lace.

They all did, and the wind blew in their faces, and the thunder rumbled.

"It smells different," Irene said.

"It smells like rain," Cajeiri said in Ragi. "You shall hear a storm your very first night!"

"It's different than the archive," Irene said, and flinched as lightning went from cloud to cloud. "They don't show us the planet."

"Who doesn't show you the planet?" Cajeiri asked.

"We're Reunioners," Artur said. "We don't get the same news as the Mospheirans. As the atevi, too, likely."

"Why not?" Cajeiri asked, while the wind blew at them, and the guards behind them.

"It's not our planet," Irene said then. "We're not supposed to know things."

He heard it. He thought about it a moment. It was not right. It could not be right.

"I never heard that," he said. "Who said that, nadi-in-ji?"

"We don't know," Irene said. "But we know Mospheirans get their news. We don't."

He had to *ask* about that. He had to ask nand' Bren,
and nand' Jase why that was. And he had to ask mani if
she knew about that.

"Well, now you have seen a thunderstorm," he said.
"And we should go in and let the major domo close the
door." He led them back inside. The door shut, and he
debated between the utilitarian lower hall, where there
were interesting things, and the gilt upstairs. "I shall show
you the main floor. You saw the upstairs foyer. But I shall
show you the breakfast room, and the sitting room."

"New words," Artur said. "Irene, get out your notebook."

"I have it," Irene said, patting her pocket. And said it
again in Ragi. "One has it, nadiin-ji."

"You have to say," Cajeiri said reluctantly, "*nand'* Cajeiri, nadiin-ji, when you are in my uncle's hearing. And
mani's."

There was a sudden silence. A little hush, and he was
embarrassed.

"It is the world," he said. And in ship-speak: "It's the
world."

"No," Gene said, "Captain Jase told us. He explained.
Nand' Cajeiri. We can't forget that. And your great-
grandmother is *nand' dowager* and Lord Tatiseigi is
nandi. And we bow."

"Nadiin-ji." He gave a little bow of his own, conscious
that, just a year ago, he had been no taller, and they had
shared things, and there were no guns and guards all
about them. It *was* different. It was very different. He
would never again be just *nadi-ji* down here, or up there.

They had tried more than once, last year, to work out
those forbidden words—man'chi, from his side, and
friend, from theirs. Love. Like. All those things he was
never supposed to say to them, and they were never supposed to say to atevi—well, they were never supposed to
talk to atevi, which was why they had met in the tunnels,
but they had found a way to talk, and they *had* talked,
and they had an association they all believed was real.

And they were back to that, with his aishid standing next to him, and with Great-uncle's guards nearby, and him having to remind them—that if they were going to continue as associates, on the world or in the heavens—he would have to be obeyed.

"Nandi," Artur said. And Irene said, after thinking about it, and with particular emphasis and a polite little dip of the head: *"Nandi."*

Thunder boomed, outside. There was silence after that. They were waiting, looking at him. *He* gave the orders.

"We shall go upstairs," he said, not sure their offering was man'chi, with no way to tell if it was friendship, no way to tell what they were trying to be, or whether he was pushing them away—but they tried. "Nadiin-ji, I shall show you the main floor, the parts you missed, and then we should be in the dining room before mani and Great-uncle."

They *were* first into the dining hall, waiting with a little light fruit juice, when Bren came in, and Jase, with just Banichi and Jago.

"Well!" nand' Bren said in ship-speak. "Nand' Cajeiri, nadiin. A very nice appearance."

"One is gratified, nandi," Cajeiri said, for his guests, who copied what he said, a faint echo.

Jase asked, "How do you like the weather? They have arranged a storm for us."

"Nandi." They all said it, and nodded in just the right degree. "Interesting, nand' paidhi," Gene said, very properly. "We went down and looked ..." He ended with something quite unintelligible. Artur choked and looked away, trying Cajeiri could tell, not to laugh, which would be rude. But Irene clarified for Gene: "Looked out from the door, nandi."

"Security approved," Cajeiri provided quickly.

"One indeed heard so, young gentleman," Bren said.

By the tapping sound echoing in the high hall outside it was clear now Great-grandmother was coming, and Great-uncle, and the bodyguards took their places, standing by, as mani's and Great-uncle's bodyguards arrived, and went to their places at opposite ends of the table. They all stood up as mani and Great-uncle came in, and servants positioned themselves to help with the seating.

"Well," mani said at the sight of them. "Such a splendidly turned out company."

"Nandiin," Gene and Artur mumbled. "Nand' dowager, nandi," Irene said, the proper form, very faintly, at the same time. They all bowed, they all sat, and to Cajeiri's relief mani and Great-uncle seemed extraordinarily pleased, though they went on to talk to nand' Bren and nand' Jase while the servants poured wine and water. Then they talked about the shipment of part of Great-uncle's collection to the museum in the Bujavid.

The first course arrived. And adult talk went on, talk about the neighbors, while Cajeiri said nothing at all, not wanting to draw his guests into *that* discussion. His guests were all quiet, very quiet.

The second course, and Great-uncle asked if the guests had noticed the storm rattling about outside.

"Yes, nandi," came a chorus of whispered answers, everybody sitting upright, eating some of everything they were offered, though once or twice with a shudder. They were being exemplary, Cajeiri thought. *He* could not eat the pâté.

The third and fourth and fifth courses came, with occasionally a question to the guests, and a little adult talk. They all kept to Yes, soup, please and not a word in excess, except that they were delighted by the fruit and cake dessert, and ate all of it.

Then Great-uncle put aside his fork and said that they might attend the brandy hour.

Cajeiri had rather planned on an escape. But he bowed and said, carefully, as everyone was getting up, "You are greatly honored, nadiin. We are offered tea with mani and Great-uncle."

They were brave. There was not a sigh, not a frown in the lot. They just got up and went to the sitting room.

And just inside the door, before they had a chance to

sit down, Great-uncle stopped, and signaled his head of security, who handed him a folded paper. "Nephew," Great-uncle said, and handed it to him. "One delights, on the approaching felicitous occasion, to present you with a gift, from your great-grandmother and myself."

Cajeiri looked at the paper, and found a name: Jeichido, daughter of the second Babsidi and Saidaro.

He knew Babsidi. Babsidi was mani's mecheita, leader of mani's herd.

"The dam was mine," Great-uncle said. "She is not a leader in my herd—you are, after all, a young rider—but she will not shame you. She is yours."

"Great-uncle!" he exclaimed.

"An earnest, Great-grandson," Great-grandmother said, "of the stable you will one day have, and a son of the first Babsidi will be yours when you have the strength and the seat."

"Shall we ride, then? Is she here?"

"We shall ride," mani said firmly. "We have the grounds under our control, we expect this storm to pass and leave us clear skies, and it has been far too long, *far* too long. If your guests will wish to ride, your great-uncle has several fat and retired mecheiti, who will go very gently."

"Yes!" he said, and bowed deeply, to mani and to Great-uncle.

"You must remember that you have guests, and not run. We shall not be other than sedate, Great-grandson."

"No, mani. We shall not. Thank you!" He was happy, happy beyond all his expectations. Nand' Bren and nand' Jase looked uneasy. But mani said it was safe, and Cenedi, right next to mani, looked perfectly content. "I shall tell my guests. Thank you!"

He took the precious paper, which, once he got back to the Bujavid, was going to go into that little box, not in his office, but in his bedroom, where he kept his most precious things ... not that anyone would ever dispute mani's and Great-uncle's gift—but that was a box full of things that made him feel good, whenever he was disheartened. He showed the paper now to his guests, and opened it, with the date of Jeichido's birth—she was ten—and the names of all her ancestors.

"Mani and Great-uncle have given me a mecheita of my own, nadiin-ji. And we shall ride tomorrow. On mecheiti. We shall go on mecheiti."

"We," Artur said. "On *mecheiti.*"

"Mani promises we shall not run. We shall be very safe. They will not go fast."

"How do you tell them that?" Artur asked, in shipspeak this time. "They're taller than the bus!"

"Not as tall as the bus," Cajeiri said, which was the truth. They only came up to the windows. He was disappointed, but he whispered back, "If you're scared—"

"No," Gene said in Ragi. "I shall go."

Artur looked doubtful, but he nodded.

That left Irene, who looked scared to death. She clenched her jaw and said, very faintly, "Yes."

"Shall we be safe out there tomorrow?" Bren asked, once he and Banichi and Jago got back to their quarters, two brandies on, and got a very, very slight hesitation.

"We have some concern," Banichi said. "But in this gift and this event, Cenedi says the dowager is particularly determined. She had planned this for after the party, in the Bujavid, and with no access to Lord Tatiseigi's stables. But the opportunity is here, and given the attractions of the visitors, and the unhappy situation in the Bujavid, which may or may not be resolved by the time we return—Cenedi's assessment: she would not be crossed in this."

It was, one understood, *Babsidi's* daughter. And a gift the dowager had waited years to give. And the perfect moment—give or take the harassment from the Ajuri side of the blanket. Ilisidi didn't make emotional decisions, or didn't—that he had ever seen. But if there was one that just might reach that degree of determination, with her—this one, involving her great-grandson and a favorite of all her years, in her lifelong passion for riding and hunting—this occasion, they had to understand, yes, approached the level of an emotional decision.

"I shall try not to break anything tomorrow," he said. "Most of all, we shall keep the youngsters safe."

The riding really was safe, as Ilisidi proposed it. Jase was dubious, worried about himself, as well as the kids—but this was not a breakneck ride through hostile territory, on a beast with a snaking neck and a disposition to use its tusks for right of way to challenge its herd leader. Nokhada, his own Nokhada, was safely pastured at Malguri, and they would be putting the youngsters on the oldest, least ambitious members of the herd, the perpetual hindmost, who would resist any order from the rein, and simply keep up with the herd, using as little energy as possible. Stay in the saddle, tie the rein to the ring, since it was virtually useless, and watch the scenery—that was what they would have.

He actually *could* ride, which put him in danger of being given one of the herd-foremost, some young mecheita with ambition, but he truly hoped not.

And when he contemplated the idea, lying in the dark and listening to the thunder above the roof, he found himself looking forward to the ride. Actually looking forward to it.

"We're going to go very slowly, nadiin-ji," Cajeiri said, as they all knelt at the sitting room window. The curtains were back and the window open just a little, so they could hear the storm and the rain, which beat down hard at the moment. "Mecheiti go in order. And I shall be riding mine—" He could hardly wait. He truly could hardly wait. He knew Antaro and Jegari were looking forward to the ride as much as he was. Lucasi and Veijico were from a mountain clan, and had not been such habitual riders, but they would manage, he was sure. "But I shall hold her back, nadiin-ji. I shall be very careful."

Lighting chained across the sky, whitening everything, the little stand of trees that ran beside the house, the stable roof, the pens. Thunder was instant. His guests jumped, and everybody laughed nervously.

"That is right over our heads," he said, laughing with them, enjoying the window, and the safety, and the storm.

"But the roof protects us," Irene said. He had established that with them.

"This is the safest place to be except the basement," he said. "And in the morning, everything will be wet, but that will not stop us, either."

"Your great-grandmother and your great-uncle are really going to ride?"

"Oh, they may ride the herd-leaders!" he said. "They are very good riders." But, he thought, mani was so frail, now, this last year. "Except they will not be riding fast at all, with new riders in the group. You shall see. We shall get you up safely—that is the hardest; and then you just stay in the saddle. There are rings and straps to hold on to." He made a ring with his hand. "Like that. *Take-holds.*" He remembered the word for the little recessed bars on the ship.

"Take-holds," Artur said. "Good!" Artur seemed a lot happier with that idea.

Irene had not said much. She had agreed, but she was scared. She always was, of new things. But she was going to try.

She was not going to get hurt. He had his mind made up on that.

He just wished he could convince Irene, who probably was not going to get a lot of sleep tonight.

She had said, when they had walked back to the room, "The table was so pretty. Everything was so pretty."

She had even eaten the pâté, and never complained, though after they had gotten back to the room, she had gone looking for the little medical kit in her baggage, saying her stomach hurt.

She had tried so hard. But Irene always had.

Now she leaned with her chin on the windowsill and watched the lightning and listened to the thunder, only flinching at the loudest thunderclaps. "It's real," she said. "Pictures aren't enough. They just aren't enough."

13

Bren dressed in his roughest clothes the next morning—his valets had packed a good outdoor coat for him, and had anticipated a country venue might require it. They had assured him through the usual servant-to-servant whispering that that would be perfectly fine for breakfast—that the guests would be in their ship-style clothing.

His aishid prepared in their own way, but their preparations were less about wardrobe than armament, in case, and in communication with the house security station. The word was, throughout the system, it was a fair morning with a light, nippy breeze, and there was nothing changed in the security stance.

Jase turned up, alone, but cheerful, in his blue station fatigues and an insulated brown coat. "Kaplan and Polano beg off. I gave them the chance. They said if anything did go amiss, they'd need rescue themselves. They said better take two more who know what they're doing."

"Not nervous, are you?"

"Not as long as I ride with the kids," Jase said. "You do as you please, friend."

"I'm perfectly content with that."

They all met downstairs, in the dining hall, the breakfast room being for intimate gatherings. Ilisidi and Tatiseigi had turned out in riding clothes, while Cajeiri wore a sturdy black twill coat, and Jase and the youngsters from the station all wore their own comfort-wear, with jackets.

It was a quick light breakfast and out and around to the mecheita pens, where a rumbling low complaint said the grooms were letting their charges know they were indeed going to work this morning. The sky was clear blue, and the air was chill—it was not quite to the stage of breath frosting, but it was close, and the mecheiti were in high spirits.

A party of their size meant saddling just about every mecheita, and while it ordinarily meant more control, with more of the herd under rein, with novice children in the group, they needed a serious rider to handle the herd leader, and whatever constellation of fractious competitors the herd's current composition afforded them. In days past it would have been Ilisidi riding foremost, with Cenedi and Nawari right beside her, hellbent for anything the terrain offered.

But that wasn't Ilisidi's choice today. Tatiseigi, who was of an unguessable age, likewise declined, and while one could have ultimate faith in the dowager's skilled hand, one worried.

Not to mention worrying about his own lately unpracticed self. And Jase.

A groom brought the herd leader out to the pen, and Tatiseigi gave the order for two grooms to take the lead, which was, in Bren's opinion, the best arrangement.

Other mecheiti came out, under saddle. Ilisidi and Tatiseigi and their bodyguards went into the pen to mount up—they had no trouble to get their mounts to extend a leg and allow an easy mount, but Ilisidi accepted a little help from Cenedi at the last. Tatiseigi managed on his own, on what Bren rather suspected was a retired herd-leader, a mecheita with a conspicuous raking scar on his rump.

And from that lofty vantage Ilisidi and Tatiseigi called Cajeiri over, and introduced him to a fine-looking ten-year-old, a rusty black, with a red tassel on the bridle ring and a ring of red enamel on each of the bright brass tusk-caps.

This was Jeichido, no question, and Cajeiri looked uncharacteristically nervous and excited—quite, quite happy, and emoting just a shade too much around a high-bred mecheita. Ilisidi gave a quiet, "Tut, tut, tut," that meant calm down, pay attention, as if she were talking to the mecheita.

The young gentleman calmed himself, took the single rein, made a spring for the mounting loop set high on the animal's shoulder, and with his left toe in the assisting fold of leather, he was up, rein and quirt in hand, the first leg over, and the second foot settling comfortably into the curve of the mecheita's nape. Jeichido fidgeted a few steps, then swung neatly about at a light tap of the quirt. Antaro and Jegari were up.

"Good luck to us," Jase muttered, then.

It was their turn. The junior grooms were kind, and afforded them the mounting block, with two grooms to steady the mecheiti, who were not likely to regard an unskilled demand for the extended leg. His aishid needed no such help, and that was six more of them safely in the saddle.

That left the children, and three quiet, older mecheiti, sleepy-looking animals—there were four younger spares and a new foal milling about the pen at loose ends, making trouble, occasioning a threatening head shake from Tatiseigi's mount and a warning from the junior grooms. But these were the oldest in the herd. They'd follow the herd leaders at whatever pace they could muster, to the ends of the earth, but they wasted none of their energy. The first stood with eyes half-shut as the grooms first lifted Artur up, and then led up a mecheita for Irene.

The herd-leader, however, had gotten wind of odd-smelling small strangers, and was circling under taps of the groom's quirt, wanting to get closer, chuffing and blowing, sloping hindquarters aquiver with impatience. He—it happened to be a male—let out a moaning rumble, a threat, a warning. They very much needed to get this lot out of the pen and moving on this cool morning.

Irene looked at the herd-leader, who had been put into another frustrated circle, and with a slip of her foot on the first step of the mounting block, she recovered her balance. Then she froze, with a look of terror on her face.

"Come on, Reny," Gene called out. "Move! You can do it!"

She came unfrozen. She settled her balance on the block, faltered her way up another step onto the top of the block, dropping the rein as she caught her balance. The groom handily caught it as it fell and gave it back, folded the same hand about the quirt and shoved her upward without any preamble. Irene grabbed the saddle back, not the mounting strap, missed the toehold, and as the mecheita took a step forward, she lost contact with the mounting block and hung there, dropping the quirt. Bren loosed his rein and shifted his quirt, deciding to ride alongside and tell Irene to go back upstairs and ask Cajeiri's servants for a cup of tea.

But she had hold of the front ring instead of the quirt, and she started hauling herself upward. The groom caught a flailing foot in his hand and lifted. Irene landed belly down, managed to drag her right leg over the saddle back and, as the groom tried to keep the old mecheita still, Irene hauled herself upright, grabbed the ring, dragged her left foot into its proper place in the curve of the neck and, panting, took the quirt a second groom put back into her hand.

"Loop around your wrist," Bren said in ship-speak. "Are you all right?"

"Yes, sir," she said. She gave her head a shake, getting the hair out of her eyes. "Yes, sir!"

Bren worried. She looked very, very small up there, and looked terrified as the old mecheita moved in response to the shifting of the rest of the herd, but she had made it.

Meanwhile Gene had tried to go up Cajeiri's way, didn't quite have the reach, but two grooms had just swept him up and put him into the saddle as if he weighed nothing at all. Gene awkwardly sorted out reins and quirt as the mecheita, let at liberty, turned and came alongside Irene's, giving it a casual butt of a tusked jaw.

"Hold on," Jase said. Gene had acted as if he had an idea what he was doing, the grooms had let the mecheita go, and there was a butt and a head flung back, the two old girls in a momentary fuss, brass tusks flashing, but there was no great fire in it. Algini rode in and settled the situation with a little flick of the quirt.

The head groom then let the leader move toward the gate, the herd-leader's rivals shouldered their way after him, and a junior groom opened that broad gate and rode it outward as it swung. The herd-leader exited, ready to stretch out and run, and the entire pen emptied out in rough order of herd rank, except the one youngster trying to keep up with its mother and scrambling with amazing shifts through the towering crowd. The impetus of the herd slowed fast—the three lead riders got them all to a sedate pace.

Bren, carried through the gate in the initial rush, looked back at the youngsters at the rear, made sure they had all made it. Cajeiri and his aishid pulled aside from the leaders, likely trying to wait for his young guests, but stopping began to entail a discussion with Jeichido. The boy was managing at least to hold his position, but only just. Jeichido was having none of it, and he began to let Jeichido move up again, but Jegari peeled off and rode back to the rear, a lad who'd grown up riding and who had no trouble violating the herd order, even on a strange mecheita.

So Jegari was going to ride with the kids.

Good, Bren thought, took a deep breath and relaxed as the mecheiti, denied a mad dash, swung into their traveling stride. They swept along beside the house and across the drive to the end of the low inner hedge. Beyond that was pasturage damp from the rains, so wide and rolling a range the limiting hedges were out of sight.

On grass, the pace stretched out and became as smooth as silk, and Bren relaxed. His aishid was with him. Jase was. The air was brisk, the sky was brilliant, and, God, it felt good to ride again, even if it was not his Nokhada—he felt a pang of longing for that troublesome but excellent beast, whom he'd not seen since he'd gone into space. He didn't know this one's name, nor did it greatly matter this morning, just that she was not an ambitious sort. Behind Tatiseigi's bodyguard was perfectly fine for him and for Jase, and Banichi and the others were on his right.

He looked back from time to time, double-checking on the youngsters with Jegari—he saw Irene laughing, riding beside Gene's mecheita with no trouble. A little into the ride, after a little argument to the side of the group, Cajeiri and Jeichido finally came to an understanding about dropping back in the order, and Cajeiri and Antaro and the older pair of his guards held back to ride with his guests for a bit. That lasted maybe a quarter of an hour. Then those three gradually drifted forward in the order. They stopped to talk to him and Jase, while Jeichido wanted to keep going, and that sparked another little exchange, which disturbed all the mecheiti around them.

"This mecheita is determined, nandiin," Cajeiri laughed. "Great-uncle said she will need work."

"She is very fine," Bren said, and Cajeiri held Jeichido steady about that long before she wanted to break forward again. He held her long enough to make the point, then waved and was off again, forward, up to his great-grandmother.

Ilisidi seemed to be enjoying herself at least as much as Cajeiri. She had walked with a cane as long as Bren had known her, but in the saddle, it always had been a different story. He had seen her, on Babsidi, take rocky hillsides that challenged her young men—worse, he had been on a mecheita who wanted to follow her. She was laughing, talking to her great-grandson, and so was Lord Tatiseigi—those who knew them only in the Bujavid would be amazed. But he was not. Open country was where Ilisidi had always been happy, far removed from the Bujavid and as removed from politics as Ilisidi ever was.

Today, everything was entirely as she had arranged it to be, Tatiseigi was happy, Tatiseigi had given the boy the earnest of the gift *she* had arranged for him—the continuance of the line of mecheiti she had ridden to national legend.

And if her great-grandson's happiness entailed three human children—he wasn't that sure she hadn't had a hand in their getting down here, too. Geigi did nothing that displeased her: if she wanted those three to come down, he'd make certain it happened.

One had to wonder, however at her *reasons* for that decision. Happiness? Possibly, but one got onto very shaky ground, assuming Ilisidi made any choice based on grandmotherly softness.

That the boy had had no atevi contacts at all who were children—that had not been her choosing. Her goal had been to keep him alive. That was first. Giving him a childhood? Not even a factor.

But when the boy went out and made his own associations among the humans, she also hadn't fought it. Ever. She was a master chess player. Had she suspected even then the possibilities in such an association?

Silly question.

What Jase had said, what Geigi had said, about the factions shaping up in the human half of that equation— did one lay any bet at all that Ilisidi hadn't heard, from Geigi, the entire business, and that Ilisidi hadn't made up her own mind that, while her great-grandson had had to come down to the world and deal with atevi and let atevi instincts shape his reactions—he should not give up his direct links to the powers in the heavens either?

When it came to atevi in the heavens, Ilisidi, who stood for the traditional—was hell-bent on being sure atevi were well-informed and in charge.

It wasn't cynicism that made him absolutely certain Ilisidi had had all the reports on the politics involved in her grandson's guests, or that she had had a hand in getting them down here. It was experience.

Their course took them far, far beyond sight of the house, but still within the hedges, in a pasturage so wide that, where one saw a hedge, it was only on one side. There was no road here, only grass. There was no disturbance in the world.

Until the lead mecheiti stopped, cold, head up, and the foremost dipped their heads and snuffed the ground.

Every mecheita in the herd jolted to a stop. Ranks closed. Bren looked back to check on the youngsters. They were all still in the saddle, their sensible mounts quiet, alert but not jostling each other.

"Track," Jago said, as Banichi talked, probably with Cenedi, short-range. "Mecheita. It was made since the rain. We advised the camp this morning—perhaps a little late—to keep their riders in camp."

One didn't want two herds encountering, not with new riders in the group. The lead mecheiti all had their heads up, nostrils working, hindquarters stretched, and one, the herd-second, actually raised up a little on her hind legs, the long neck giving her a view of all the grassland about. She came down, backing and turning under the rein and taps of the quirt.

The herd-leader gave out a moan that shocked the air. Every mecheita in the herd was head-up, alert, heads all facing toward the same point on the horizon. They had mayhem in mind, no question.

Ilisidi however, extended her quirt and swept a calm gesture as she suggested a turn. Tatiseigi ordered the head riders, and they argued their mecheiti into a sharp change of direction, back toward the estate road.

"Not trouble, is it?" Jase asked.

"No, nandi," Tano said. "There is a track going south, one of the Taibeni early this morning, one is informed, and the herd-leader has caught the scent. The aiji-dowager wants us to veer off from the camp, and not let the herd-leader believe we are letting him follow that track. He owns this range, and is very willing to prove it."

The herd-leader was arguing strongly about the direction change, fighting the rein and the taps of the quirt. The groom was struggling to control the animal, and Ilisidi, who had used to ride in competitions, was probably struggling, too, to restrain her advice to the man.

The leader, however, was unsettling the herd. Herd-second was still spoiling for a fight, looking in the forbidden direction and making that moaning threat. Bren's mecheita had gone to a looser gait, ready to jump at the least indication the leader was going, trying to move forward in the order. Jeichido was giving Cajeiri an argument, close to slipping control, and suddenly came close to the front. Ilisidi turned her mecheita about and shouldered Jeichido hard. There was a flare-up, a flash of brass tusk-caps as heads swung, but Jeichido's attack missed. Ilisidi had spun full about and come up on Jeichido's flank. Jeichido realized it and whirled around to protect herself.

Ilisidi popped the quirt right across Jeichido's nose. Jeichido shied off, haunches dropped, which could propel the mecheiti into fight or flight. Cajeiri reined hard and used his own quirt to take her away from Ilisidi.

The boy had stayed on and stopped her. Thank God. Cajeiri had a high-powered mecheita under him, and while she wouldn't break past the herd-leader, she seemed to have taken it in her head that she could move forward.

She wasn't doing that while Ilisidi was riding the mecheita in front of her.

"One apologizes, mani!" Cajeiri called back, keeping Jeichido circling to distract her.

"Best we turn back to the stables," Ilisidi called out. "They will be unsettled, now, and we have our young guests to consider. We have had exercise enough."

Tatiseigi gave the order, and the grooms reined back on a wide U, not retracing their path, but headed in the direction of the house. There was a little excess energy in the herd since the flare-up, the leader still protesting with shakes and turns of his head. It needed steady effort from the foremost riders to keep the pace slow and the direction unchallenged.

"Just as well we go back," Bren said, watching as Cajeiri reined Jeichido all the way around to go back to his guests—who had had, surely, a momentary fright.

"Indeed," Jago said, but her voice was uncharacteristically distracted, and when he glanced at her, he caught her, just for a moment, staring off toward Banichi.

Was it Taibeni, Jago-ji?" Bren asked.

"Yes," she said. "Of that we are certain. But Cenedi has ordered us back."

Caution? Bren asked himself. Communications were at a minimum. They were not sending details abroad. But the space within the hedges suddenly seemed less safe than a moment ago.

"Are you all right?" was the first thing Gene asked as Cajeiri rode close and came about. "Is your great-grandmother all right, nandi?"

"Oh, mani is *very* well!" Cajeiri was a little embarrassed to have lost control of Jeichido so that mani had had to step in, but Jeichido did not know him, and was testing whether she could get her way. He was not as good as Antaro or Jegari, even, and far from as good as mani or Great-uncle. He hoped his guests had not thought him a fool.

"What was it?" Artur asked. "What was it, nandi, on the ground?"

"A smell. One of the Taibeni, the riders from beside the bus. One had been out here in the pastures, and possibly Uncle's mecheiti have been smelling them for days, even from as far away as they are. The herd-leader caught the scent and he was ready to lead the herd over to that camp and show them this is *his* pasture."

"Would they fight, nandi?"

"The Taibeni mecheiti would probably tend to run, unless their riders turned them around. But only enemies would do that. We are quite safe. Uncle's staff told the camp we were going to be out riding this morning, and they were not supposed to be out on patrol. But evidently somebody was out early, after the rain. Are *you* all right, nadiin-ji?"

"It was scary," Artur said.

"They managed very well," Jegari said, who had been with them. "They held on and made no bad moves."

"She is a very nice mecheita," Irene said, patting the mecheita so slightly it probably never felt it. "All the others were upset, and she just stood there."

Irene's was a very old mecheita, with white hairs around her nose, but Irene was happy with her.

And no one had fallen off when the herd stopped.

"Excellent," he said. Jeichido was starting to shift about under him, wanting to move. "We are on our way back. It will be long enough riding, by the time we get there. I shall see you at the house." Jeichido swung about on her own, took a step, and he put her one full circle in the opposite direction to have it clear he was in charge. Then he took her quietly back up the line, restraining her urge to run—if she did, it would start everybody trying to run, considering they were heading toward the stables now. He had no desire to end a very good day by having Irene or Artur take a fall.

And he hoped he looked very impressive and recovered a little good opinion after the situation with mani. It might be more impressive to his guests to let Jeichido take out running. But it was, at the moment, mani and Great-uncle he wanted to impress. He rode Jeichido at a steady pace all the way to her place near the head of the column, put her exactly where he wanted her to be, and dared take a glance at mani, who just nodded, approving.

So did Great-uncle.

That was almost as good as a fast race home. He had redeemed himself. And he kept that same traveling-pace, with his bodyguards behind him and Great-uncle beside him, all the way to the house.

They crossed the drive, went down the walk beside the house. The younger grooms had the gate open, and the senior grooms rode through the gate in single file, the head groom first, on the herd-leader, and one after the other.

It was a challenge. He was determined to get Jeichido inside, exactly in her proper order, and with no breaking and rushing, and he kept his weight even and his feet still, except just a little tap, which he had begun to understand was enough with Jeichido.

Then they had to stand and keep their mecheiti from milling about, while Cenedi and Nawari slid down and helped mani get down—mani made her mecheiti drop a shoulder, and got down much more ably than he expected she could after that ride. One of the junior grooms handed her her cane as Great-uncle's senior bodyguard assisted him.

He himself, not confident he could get Jeichido to drop her shoulder, had gotten up the Taibeni way, with a jump, but that was probably not the best way to start with one of Great-uncle's stable, and it might have given Jeichido ideas she could get her way. He tapped her shoulder with the quirt, now, repeatedly, and after a little hesitation, she extended her leg, letting him swing down.

He wanted to take her into the stable himself, and work with her. But he had his guests to see to. He handed the reins to a junior groom, and thought if he could manage it he would come out to the stables later, and maybe have a little time with her.

But getting the mecheiti unburdened and into the stable had to go fairly quickly, for safety, and it was, each mecheita handed off in order, and the herd-leader led into the stable to be quieted with a little reward of grain. The leaders were all clear, following him of their own accord. All around him riders were getting down, and he went to be sure his guests knew to get clear and get out.

Nand' Bren and Banichi and Jago were with them, he saw, helping them get down; and mani and Great-uncle were safe, over by the small gate people used leaving the stableyard. He just ducked through the rails, and waited for his guests beside the gate.

Within the pens, only the grooms were moving about now. Mecheiti, still under saddle, were mostly interested in the grain waiting for them, all threat forgotten.

"Well managed," Uncle Tatiseigi said. "Well-managed, Nephew." Great-uncle and mani went on to talk to Jaseaiji and nand' Bren.

And his guests came out, last, windblown, happy and a little out of breath.

"That was good," Gene said in Ragi.

"Was it, nadiin-ji?" he asked. He hoped it was. "Rene-ji?"

"It was—" She lapsed into ship-speak. "I did it! I did it and I didn't fall off, did I?"

"Told you," Gene said.

"I want to do it again," Irene said.

"I'm sore," Artur said. "But it was good. It's so weird. You really wonder what they're thinking."

"Your great-grandmother can really ride," Gene said. "That was something! Were they going to fight?"

"Jeichido was going to move up past her," Cajeiri said in Ragi. "They try that. But mani is faster. And smarter."

"Wow," Artur said. "Jegari said they can run. I wish they ran."

Cajeiri had to laugh. "Oh, they can run, Arti-ji. They can run. We were all working to keep them just walking." They had begun, after the others, to walk back to the house. "Hot baths, now. Or we shall all hurt tomorrow." Antaro and Jegari were with him, and Lucasi and Veijico had stopped to wait for them, at the entry to the house.

"Nandi," Lucasi said somberly, and nodded to the side of the door. Cajeiri stepped aside. So did his guests. And by Lucasi's expression, whatever it was, was not good.

"Nandi," Lucasi said, "your grandfather has just been assassinated."

"Who?" he asked. Then: "Did my father do it?" He hoped not. He hoped his parents were managing to make peace while he was out of the way and not causing any trouble.

But if his father had just killed his mother's father—

"Rumor has not had time to reach us," Lucasi said. "We got this as we tapped into house base. One is not certain if Cenedi himself knows, yet. Jegari and Antaro are trying to learn details."

Mani could have arranged it, Cajeiri thought, and Cenedi would certainly know.

Nand' Bren had passed them, on his way into the house. Several of mani's young men had lingered outside, watching *them,* Cajeiri thought, or maybe also getting the news.

He did not want to be looked at. He gathered up his guests and his aishid and brought them inside, then back into the nook under the adjacent stairs, trying to figure out what happened next in the world, and how to deal with his guests.

"Is something wrong?" Gene asked, and in Ragi: "What is it, nandi?"

"My grandfather is dead." He did not want to alarm them. But they were going to find out. "Assassinated. Just now."

They looked shocked. He was shocked, too, he decided. He was not exactly sorry, because his grandfather had threatened him, and his father, and scared him so he never wanted to see him again. But he was shocked, shaken, for some reason he could not quite understand.

"That's terrible," Artur said faintly. "We're sorry."

"One regrets," Gene said in Ragi.

"What can we do?" Irene asked.

"Nothing. Nothing, nadiin-ji. He was—" He had no words for his grandfather, even in Ragi, and the more complicated things were words his guests had not learned. "He was dangerous. Bad toward me. Toward my great-grandmother. Toward my father."

His guests looked confused, a little upset, not knowing what to do or say. And he only wanted to get them into a safe place and have his staff find out things.

"We are safe here," he said. "No trouble." He led the way back to the steps, and hurried up two flights of stairs with all of them behind him.

He thought then, at the very top step: Did *Mother* do it?

"Who did it?" Bren asked of his aishid, inside the lower hallway. He had intended, when they had first gotten the word, to follow Jase upstairs to his room and see what his aishid and Jase himself could learn. But the dowager had said, shortly, with no reference to courtesy: "Nand' paidhi," and headed down the lower hall with Tatiseigi, Cenedi, and their bodyguards.

Singular, that brusque invitation had been—meaning it was a conference needing *him,* not Jase—needing his connection to the world and his particular need-to-know.

Ilisidi was, with what skill he had at reading Ilisidi, caught by surprise.

He followed with his own bodyguard, a traveling briefing, at a pace that gave them a little time, before he should be swept up and told things as Ilisidi saw them to be.

Hence the: "Who did it?"—because one real possibility was Ilisidi; but by her sudden dark shift in mood he didn't think she'd ordered it, or expected it.

"There are a range of possibilities," Banichi said. "None certain."

"Information is slower to come than we would like," Algini said. "We have notified the camps. Security is on high alert—but there is no apparent threat to Atageini territory."

The news was minutes old—had arrived on exterior Guild communications as they were riding into the stables. "When did it happen?" he asked.

"The event," Algini answered, "within the last half hour. Details are lacking as yet, but his bodyguard has reported—*they* survived. The report came from Guild Headquarters. We relayed it to the aiji, so he is aware, in case the Guild has excluded his bodyguard."

The damned restriction. The apparently petty rules question that now placed the aiji's security in the dark, while there was an assassination that had reconfigured the political landscape.

Jago said: "We just now asked Jase-aiji to notify Lord Geigi and signal we are not threatened here, Bren-ji, but to be aware."

"Has the young gentleman been informed?"

"His aishid, Lord Tatiseigi's, and yours all had the first notice from the house. He has gone upstairs with his aishid and with his guests."

Cajeiri was where he should be. His young aishid had performed as they should, right down the classic list: first, security, then their lord's duty and dignity. They had gotten word, informed their lord, and gotten him upstairs to collect himself in private and to be where they could find him.

It was not a case of a grieving grandson. Cajeiri himself had no reason at all to mourn Lord Komaji—but he was going to be upset with news bound to affect his mother, his father, and everybody connected to him. Everything had gone uncertain, until there was more information, and until someone in authority exerted that authority.

He was having a similar reaction. The world could spare a man dedicated to causing trouble—but Komaji had connections, and his death reconfigured Ajuri, and *that* meant reconfiguring the entire Northern Association.

Ilisidi hadn't ordered it. Nor Tatiseigi, if he was any judge: he doubted Tatiseigi had ever assassinated anybody. He'd swear those two had both been surprised by the news, and were headed now into conference, apparently a major reevaluation of their situation.

"Recommendations, nadiin-ji?" he asked his aishid. Ilisidi and Tatiseigi had not stopped at the security station. Neither did they.

"None at the moment," Banichi said, and they exited into the foyer of the house, and headed up the central stairs.

There were too many unknowns. That was the problem. They'd configured their security with an eye to Komaji as the likeliest problem, but one that held other, more threatening elements in tension.

Removing Komaji might improve some situations, but they might be hours away from seeing a stronger—or weaker—leader step in to replace him. Either would have repercussions. And one had no idea right now who that might be.

Damiri?

If she decided to go there, it would be effectively an act of divorcement. And it would be damned foolish, given the life expectancy of Ajuri lords over the last fifty years.

They reached the top of the stairs, where two of the dowager's young men and the junior two of Tatiseigi's stood watch outside the sitting room. They opened for him and he walked in with Banichi and Jago, Tano and Algini having elected to stay outside and talk to the other bodyguards.

There was a chair ready for him, point of a triangle with Ilisidi and Tatiseigi. He sank onto it. There was no preamble, no formality of a tea service. It had gone straight into a business discussion.

"My great-grandson has been informed," Ilisidi said. "I shall call him into private conference and we shall talk. Lest you ask, we had nothing to do with this, paidhi. Nor did our host. About my grandson, or any other, we have no information."

"We do not believe it is in any sense your grandson's action, aiji-ma," Cenedi said. "We are less sure about Damiri-daja, but we do not think it likely. We believe it *is* within Ajuri clan. That it should have happened, we find *somewhat* surprising, aiji-ma, but not greatly so — if it resulted from Komaji's actions in the capital. Many in the clan have not been satisfied with Lord Komaji's leadership. His foray southward could have lost him man'chi. In that case, a new leadership will have to establish its policies and choose its enemies. We do not even know that it was a Guild assassination, or if so, if there was a Filing."

"This is an uncommon lack of information," Tatiseigi said, and Bren took in a slow breath and kept his mouth shut on the things he knew, which, at least to his knowledge, Tatiseigi did *not* know — close links between the Kadagidi and Ajuri. The significance of Haikuti being assigned to the Kadagidi.

That hypothetical administrator sitting inside the Guild, arranging his chess pieces about the board ... would *not* want *Damiri* sitting in Komaji's place, asking questions about Ajuri's actions and Ajuri's shaky finances ... and least of all would he want her asking into Ajuri's staffing.

"The outlook for our situation here, Nedi-ji?"

A nod. "Improved, in the near term, aiji-ma. We cannot answer for the choice the clan itself may make. We are still uncertain whether Lord Komaji had any idea that Tatiseigi is here, or that you and the young gentleman and his guests are not, as generally advertised, in Malguri. Popular speculation on the assassination is more likely to center on your grandson and the consort — and a belief that the aiji has acted without Filing may raise some debate and a demand for a Guild investigation, which would come to nothing. More worrisome, the aiji's other enemies, known and unknown, may take alarm and reassess their security, fearing the aiji might have thrown aside Guild rules altogether and decided to act against them. The aiji's choice of bodyguards *is* an ongoing issue with his detractors. His most dangerous enemies care less about the principle of Guild rules than about the aiji's increasing ability to deny them information — and we *have* cut them off, we believe. In the last few days we have silenced every trickle of real information and substituted certain things that we have loosed like dye into a water source — to find out where it resurfaces. We have already seen results from that. But then — Komaji is killed, amid this silence *we* have created. The ones who killed Komaji know who killed Komaji, but certain of our enemies do *not* know, and the warier among them may no longer trust what information they do get."

Ilisidi nodded as she listened, her hand atop the cane set before her, fingers moving in a slow, even rhythm. Tatiseigi had shut down all expression. But Ilisidi — only listened.

"Well," she said. "Well-stated, Nedi-ji. We do not think, Tati-ji, that Damiri-daja has any intention of taking the lordship in Ajuri."

"One would hope not, aiji-ma!"

"And if Ajuri retreats from threatening Tirnamardi," Ilisidi said, "we are glad. Have *you* any word, Brennandi? Have you spoken to my great-grandson?"

"He has gone upstairs with his aishid, aiji-ma, and so has Jase-aiji. Jase-aiji is able to contact Lord Geigi, and will advise him, by means we do not believe our enemies can intercept, let alone interpret. My aishid will know the details." He was not about to say, in front of Tatiseigi, that Lord Geigi, of all people, could look down from the heavens and tell the condition of Tirnamardi's roof tiles. It was enough that Tatiseigi had Taibeni camped on his grounds.

"We have some concern, aiji-ma, nandiin," Cenedi said, "about the Kadagidi's reception of this news—not impossible that they had something to do with it, since a threat to Tirnamardi would call on them, as members of the Padi Valley Association, to come to Tirnamardi's aid—"

"Never mind they were the last brigands to shell my house!" Tatiseigi said, then, more quietly: "Forgive me, Cenedi-nadi, but our old enemies the Taibeni have earned more Atageini trust in recent years than our Kadagidi cousins, and we have finally written it on paper and put a seal to it. One does not believe the Kadagidi are pleased with that turn of events, and they will not trouble themselves to assist us. Now, if they thought doing away with Komaji would please the aiji and win them a way back to *court,* well, *that* I would believe, but again—they cannot simply reach out and assassinate the man! There would have to be a Filing against Komaji, and as irritating as the man had become to most of his neighbors, even his own household, we have not heard of any Filing."

"That is exactly the question, nandi," Cenedi said. "We are not surprised lately when, in this contest of wills between the Guild Council and the aiji, the *aiji's* bodyguard fails to get notifications—but when *the aiji himself* does not get advance notice of a Filing being voted on, and of the outcome of that vote? There need to be answers to this death, nandiin, if the answers do not point convincingly to a non-Guild killer."

Failure to notify a target and those living with him . . . violated the Guild's charter with the aishidi'tat.

One citizen killing another, without due process? Except in self-defense—in which case one could bring any resource one owned against the attacker—a civilian killing was simple *murder,* be it someone bypassing the Assassins' Guild, or an Assassin using his Guild-trained skills to kill without a Filing in effect.

If there *was* no Filing in Komaji's case—there might be *proof* of what had been going on inside the Guild. And, damn, it would be a risk sending anybody up there to investigate. It had happened in the territory of an Ajuri dependent. The likelihood that any Guild action would be covered and any witnesses silenced was—unfortunately—a hundred percent.

Frustrating. A crime, in every sense, and they could not make a move in that direction.

Adding to the frustration, it was entirely possible that the Kadagidi lord, right next door, who might not know who was at Tirnamardi, might well know *exactly* what had just happened up north of them. Tatiseigi's suggestion the Kadagidi might assassinate the Ajuri lord if it could get them back into Tabini's good graces—

It would not have that effect, not an assassination without that vital Filing of Intent.

Was some paper going to turn up to try to make it legal? Did they think Tabini-aiji, whose signature would *make* it legal, would quietly accept an outright false record, just because there was an advantage to his administration and his household in having Komaji out of the way? He could easily imagine Tabini signing such a document after the fact—for reasons of life, death, and the safety of the aishidi'tat. But *not* to make allies out of the Kadagidi, not even to patch a vital part of the Padi Valley back into union with its neighbors.

Initially, Tabini had isolated the Kadagidi and forbidden its lord to come to court for security reasons, because it was Murini's clan, and they were still hunting Murini and his supporters. That ruling had never meant that the Kadagidi townsmen and shopkeepers and country folk were all murderers. Tabini had actually intended to lift the ban . . .

. . . until he'd gotten a dire warning from Cenedi—Bren strongly suspected it had come from Cenedi, or possibly from Algini, who had his own accesses into the problems Murini had left behind.

That . . . was the business they were going to have to deal with in very short order, once they'd gotten Cajeiri's guests headed safely back to orbit. There was a strong possibility their problems inside the Guild, and particularly in Kadagidi clan, planned to launch another coup— eventually. If Komaji's moves had put the Shadow Guild into a crisis ... if they'd feared Tabini or Damiri, having defeated Komaji's attack, might make a move on Ajuri, might get their hands on him, ask him questions, and then find records that led to the Kadagidi's doorstep ...

That was the situation their enemies couldn't let happen.

That was the motive for Komaji's assassination. He was sure of it.

One of the chess pieces overthrown. Others were still on the board. The Kadagidi would still be worried about records Komaji might have left ... and about what the aiji knew.

Komaji had borrowed money from Damiri ... because of a financial difficulty he had gotten into. He had tried to get into Tabini's residence, as he had said, to see his grandson. He had behaved with increasing irrationality, acting like a man in a rising panic, for reasons that would not make sense unless one knew what pressure had been brought to bear on him.

Had Komaji decided to change sides and spill everything? Was that why he'd been so desperate to get into Tabini's apartment? If that was the case, once banished, he'd be in extreme danger—and ironically, the fact Tabini had cast him out would be a comfort to the Shadow Guild, an indication Komaji had not yet talked. And talking—would have been Komaji's only way to save himself. His best and only hope would be to gather his nerve, enlist the nearest person to Tabini that he could personally reach from his isolation in Ajuri—and that was his former brother-in-law, his old adversary—his daughter's uncle. Tatiseigi. Tatiseigi would have been Komaji's way to get a message to Tabini. And that Komaji hadn't reached Tatiseigi—was now Tatiseigi's protection.

He didn't say a thing about the hypothesis that had just assembled itself in his mind, predicated as it was on information he wasn't actually supposed to possess, and on pure speculation, but damned if he wouldn't discuss it with his aishid at the first opportunity.

Tatiseigi had ordered strong tea, and the servants went about pouring it, which ended discussion for a time. It took a time to empty a cup—but there was not a second cup asked for. Ilisidi set hers down with a click, Tatiseigi did, and Bren quietly put his down a third unfinished.

"We shall proceed with the holiday, nandiin," Ilisidi said. "We shall be alert. We shall trust, pending further movements in our direction, that our precautions are enough and Ajuri will have to settle its own difficulties in due time. Not today. Not tomorrow. But they *will* be settled."

That walk about the reception hall . . .

There had *not* already been some discussion of Ajuri's situation, between the dowager and Damiri—had there?

14

There was no word of what was going on in the world. Antaro said they were ordered not to use the communications unit. Lucasi and Veijico had gone downstairs a while ago to try to find out what they could from house security. They had told Eisi to keep the door locked. It had been a while, and still they had not come back.

Cajeiri could see his guests were worried, though he tried to assure them they were safe here and that he was perfectly fine—Antaro and Jegari still had their sidearms, that they had worn on the ride, and any danger was far, far off to the north.

Footsteps approached the door. Antaro and Jegari got up. Cajeiri thought it might be Lucasi and Veijico, but it sounded wrong. A knock came, and someone tried the door.

Then Jase-aiji identified himself and his bodyguard, and *that* was all right. Eisi glanced back for permission, and Cajeiri nodded. Eisi unlocked the door and let them in.

"We know nothing useful," Jase-aiji said, first off. "Except that nand' Bren is downstairs with your great-grandmother, young gentleman, and Lord Tatiseigi, and one expects they are finding out all the details." Then, in ship-speak: "The young lord's grandfather is dead, his mother's father, a lord in the north of the continent. Understand, the grandfather has been a threat. He had been told not to come back to Shejidan. Ever. But he was the lord of a northern clan, head of a major association. Someone killed him, and we need to know who did it, and why, and whether it was a personal feud or something to do with the government. Don't expect the young lord to be upset about it. It was not a close relationship. Beyond that, just accept that this is one of those instances where our way of thinking and the atevi way of thinking are very different, and just carry on as if nothing had happened."

"We're not going to have to leave, are we?" Irene asked.

Cajeiri wondered that, too ... not that they could leave the planet, but he did not want to leave Tirnamardi, and Jeichido, and all, and above all he did *not* want to have another war break out. It was his birthday in just a few days, and he did not want a war and he was furious at his grandfather, who had done his best to be inconvenient just one more time.

He was scared that it might turn out it was his mother who had done it, and that would make his father mad, and when they went back to the Bujavid for his birthday festivity, it was all going to come out right in front of his guests.

He was furious, but he did not think he ought to try to explain that to his guests. It all went back too far.

He could hardly stand it. He walked over to stand by the window, which made him not have to listen to Jase-aiji telling his guests everything was fine. A little breeze stirred the curtains, bringing a little welcome cold into the room—they had come in overheated and warm from exercise, and they had not even gotten a chance for their baths.

Antaro and Jegari came over near him, instinctive move—which helped a bit.

Jase-aiji was wrong that he was not upset. He *was* upset. He was very worried that all of this was going to upset his guests and make it so they would never, ever want to come down here again.

He was *damned mad*. That was what nand' Bren would say.

"Young gentleman," Jase-aiji said.

He took a deep breath, put on his best face, as mani would tell him to do, and was quite calm when he turned around.

"Nandi?"

"We shall be down the hall," Jase-aiji said. "If you need us."

"Thank you," he said. Thank you was in order. Jase-aiji had certainly taken the trouble to look in on them. "We shall be fine."

Jase-aiji and his guard left. Eisi shut and locked the door . . . which made the room feel less like a fortress than a prison.

"We *are* sorry," Artur said in Ragi.

"I am fine," he said. "Thank you, nadiin-ji." He wanted a distraction. He went over to Boji's cage. Boji had not trusted strange people in the room. He was rocking back and forth, clinging to the perch, and looking upset too.

He took Boji's harness and leash from the little hook at the corner, and opened up the door to put it on. Boji started to get right onto his arm, then balked and wanted to smell his hand and his sleeve—of course: Boji smelled the mecheita, and licked his hand, finding it curious, and a little upsetting.

He had the harness. He slipped it over Boji's head and under his chest and very quickly did the little buckle that secured it, keeping the leash in his last two fingers as he did. Boji fidgeted, Boji bounced around and chittered at him, bounced from him to the cage top.

Boji was an excellent distraction. His guests came over to see Boji, and he called for an egg and let Irene feed it to him.

Boji liked that. He even sat on Irene's shoulder, and she gave an anxious laugh and flinched as Boji grabbed her loose hair.

They were rescuing Irene from Boji's grip when a knock came at the door.

This time it was nand' Bren and his aishid, and they came in.

"Nandi, nadiin," nand' Bren said. "You had the news about your grandfather, nandi."

"He was assassinated, nandi. That was what we heard." Boji had climbed onto his shoulder, and he held the leash with enough slack to let Boji bound over to his cage top, where Boji liked to sit at times. "Was it in Ajuri?"

"In a tributary clan's territory. We still do not know the reason, or the person who ordered it — perhaps some quarrel inside Ajuri. We see no reason to be concerned at present. This could change, but your great-grandmother sees no reason to change the security level here or to make any alterations in plans."

He let go a breath, much, much happier at that news. It was a little odd to think that Grandfather was no longer in the world at all — but evidently his mother had *not* Filed on her father, and he could not imagine that his father had done it — he was, for a few days, still only infelicitous eight, but he knew enough of the politics to know that *two* actions against his grandfather in a very short number of days was inelegant, and his father had just taken one extreme action in throwing him and all the Ajuri staff out of the Bujavid.

No, his father wouldn't have done it, not without extreme provocation, and if that were the case, nand' Bren would tell him.

So there would be a new lord of Ajuri. He hoped it was not going to be his mother.

But that was all too complicated to talk about in front of his guests.

"Is my mother still with my father?" he asked. That was what he wanted to know, and that would tell him everything.

Likely nand' Bren knew exactly what he was asking, and Bren answered quite cheerfully: "Yes, young gentleman, and they both are safe."

The way he said it, and the way he added that second part was a relief. He hoped it was the truth.

But nand' Bren was particularly bad at lying, and rarely tried to. And nand' Bren had come from talking to mani and Great-uncle, so he knew the latest, and nand' Bren's bodyguard was usually very well-informed.

He thought then, If Mother did not do this, Great-grandmother could have. Moving us all out here and moving all these bodyguards in, getting Great-uncle to deal with the Taibeni . . .

Boji grabbed the tail end of his queue ribbon, which Boji sometimes untied, a trick he knew got immediate attention.

"Stop that!" He was immediately at disadvantage, and Boji, sitting on the cage, had him caught.

Nand' Bren, amused, reached out to intervene. "Is he going to bite me, young gentleman?"

"He does not, often." He was annoyed and amused at once, and he could not, even by twisting his body, get at Boji's hand. Nand' Bren's reach, however, frightened Boji, who let go and bounded across the cage top, rattling it all the way.

"Boji! Behave." He still had the end of the leash, which had a clip, and secured the leash onto the sturdy metal fretwork of the cage. "Stay there, and hush, Boji."

Boji, who regarded no authority, chittered at him.

His ribbon was probably a sad thing, since the ride, and now Boji's attentions.

"Are we to be let out now, nandi?" he asked. "We have not gotten our baths."

"By all means. We have the bath at our end, you have this one, and one is certain your guests will by no means be insulted if Eisi guides them to the servant baths on this floor and the next above. Everyone will feel better. And if we are not all too sore to walk tomorrow, we shall take another ride."

He brightened entirely. "One hopes so, nand' Bren! One really hopes so."

"There should be a light late lunch, served to the room. Staff is getting to work. Enjoy your guests. There will be music tonight: I understand your great-uncle has arranged it. And there should be nothing to trouble you.

Your great-grandmother is determined that nothing will spoil your time here."

"One is grateful," he said, and Bren bowed and headed for the door, stopping to have a word with Eisi and Lieidi, probably about the baths, and Banichi and Jago had been talking to Antaro and Jegari, probably about security.

But they were all right. He felt a great deal better, after what nand' Bren had said. Great-grandmother was *determined* that he should have his birthday, no matter what. Nobody had ever quite put him at the top of priorities, not even his father and mother. He was quite struck by the notion of having someone like mani protecting what *he* wanted and bent on having that happen.

Boji had come back to the cage edge. He absently stroked Boji's head and scratched his cheek, which got a happy clicking sound out of Boji, who had quite settled down.

"Eisi-ji," he said, "Ledi-ji, we shall all need baths, did nand' Bren explain about that? We shall be happy to use the servant baths if we may. A maid to attend Irene-nadi. And then we shall meet back here and have lunch." He saw his guests much more cheerful. "We are promised we are all quite safe, and there is no trouble at all."

Baths were a very good place for a quiet discussion, and Bren and Jase sat and soaked in the communal bath.

Banichi was in attendance, at the moment—guarding the door and assuring their privacy even from trusted staff, so that discussion was not a problem.

A few more details had come in. Komaji had been moving south, toward Atageini territory. The Taibeni had moved to within striking distance, while staying within Taibeni territory, and not made any secret of it. That threatened Komaji. Komaji had begun to move, not toward, but away from that encounter.

And, as he was getting into a small bus, one of four vehicles, the bus and three trucks, involved in the movement, he had been struck down by one very accurate shot. No one else had been hit. No one had seen the shooter.

It could have been Taibeni. There was no reason for the Taibeni lord *not* to have done it, no consequence but a continuation of a two-hundred-year-old feud if he *declared* he had done it, and the Taibeni had no desire at all to make peace with Ajuri clan.

But the Taibeni lord had hastily informed both Shejidan and the units assigned here at Tirnamardi that Taibeni had *not* done it, and that he believed the style of the assassination, a shot from a small woods, was deliberately arranged to make it appear they had.

Bren personally laid his bets on the Taibeni telling the truth, particularly as it would look very bad to make such a move right now, while they had members of their clan sitting encamped on Tatiseigi's grounds. If they were going to do it, it would have been better politics to wait until the aiji's son was not also sitting in Tatiseigi's house. The messiness of that move—no. Even the Taibeni's several enemies would not believe it.

That still left a lengthy list of those who *would* have done it, quite cheerfully.

"Lady Damiri," Bren said out of that thought, "is pretty well out of the question. *Her* bodyguard was dismissed. They *could* still be suspect, operating on her behalf, possibly on orders given before their dismissal, but we actually suspect they were reporting to Komaji. Her current staff is the dowager's." That was no guarantee, he thought. "She has been upset, but she would not *act* for emotional reasons, not on that scale. I think we can eliminate any of Tabini's house, our host—"

"The dowager herself?" Jase asked quietly. "That has to be asked."

"Perfectly possible," Bren said, "except there's no reason for *her* to deny it. And not without a proper Filing."

"If it's an in-clan action, policy says I'm not officially interested." Deep breath. "Humanly speaking—I'm entirely damned curious. How many Ajuri lords is that, just in the last decade?"

"Going on four," Bren said. "The succession in Ajuri is a problem. Has *been* a problem for generations. You can see why Tabini doesn't want Damiri under that roof, and he damned sure doesn't want his son taking the lordship. That's Komaji's whole branch. His half brother died, likely with help, without an heir, so it's the end of that entire line, except for a handful of females who lack the disposition and backing to rule. It *has* to go to a completely new branch now. There are two, and it may be a noisy transition."

Far, far too noisy, Komaji. From his highly dubious ascension, to his equally dubious ending. He had started out doing very well for Ajuri clan—a little too ambitious, perhaps, and then far *too* ambitious, culminating in that final, jealousy-driven assault on Tabini's apartments, damaging to the clan's interests, possibly for years to come.

If there were records left in Ajuri—he'd bet those were already ashes.

"Politics," Jase said. "But you think we're safe."

"Physically safe." Bren said. "Nothing's crossing the hedge. Nothing's passing the gate. And down here, your problems generally come in two dimensions, not three. We're all right. Or at least—all right enough."

"Two dimensions." Jase shook his head. "But with far more cover."

Lunch was mid-afternoon, very late, after their baths, and served in the suite rather than down in the dining rooms, but it was good, and they could sit in their casual clothes and be comfortable—even if they were all a little sore in places it was not polite to mention.

They talked about the morning, the ride. And Lucasi and Veijico, who had come back in time for baths and lunch, told what they had heard downstairs. Cajeiri translated the important parts, and then—

Then he told them story after story about Grandfather, including the night Grandfather had tried to get into the apartment when he was there with just a reduced staff and the servants. He told about his father banning his grandfather from the Bujavid, which really meant he had to stay out of the city, too.

Gene said, after a little silence, "If you act like that on the station, you get arrested, and they cancel all your cards and keys, and there you are, until they figure out how dangerous you are." Gene added, with a downward glance, "I lost all my cards for sixty days, this year. But I was *right*."

"I let Gene use mine," Artur said.

"I got him into places," Irene said. "And Bjorn did."

They would have done that. Cajeiri entirely approved. And Gene told him why he had gotten in trouble—he was trying to get into the atevi section of the station where humans were not supposed to be—like the mainland and Mospheira.

And Gene told what it was like to get arrested on the station, if one did not have a person like mani to straighten things out, or a father to call on, just one's own cleverness, and the cleverness of one's associates. He made it funny, even if he had been worried at the time. For a while, listening to their adventures on the station, it was like being back on the ship.

His guests wanted to hear, too, about the escapes he had had, and how it was, when he had flown back with mani and nand' Bren and they had had to do all sorts of things, like riding on a train with fish, to get here to Tirnamardi without being shot or caught. He had written about it in the letters, but he had been very careful what he wrote, then, especially careful about naming names; and now they wanted to hear it all, through two rounds of tea and cakes.

They had gotten down to the shells falling on the lawn at Tirnamardi, and the stables being wrecked, and young Dur landing his plane, and—

A black streak bounded for the top of a chair.

That could not happen. Boji had his harness on. His leash was clipped to the cage.

Boji took another bound, toward the cage, and Cajeiri leaped up. "Close the window!" he yelled at Lieidi, who was closer, and ran to do it himself.

They all moved, knocking chairs aside, and Boji panicked. Boji dived straight for the open window, dodged Lieidi's hands, and was out the window.

"Gods less fortunate!" Cajeiri leaned out over the sill, as far as he could, and heard his bodyguard, who had been caught by surprise, object to that effort, warning him not to try to reach too far.

Boji was down on a line of stonework trim, just out of reach. Cajeiri stretched further, felt hands on his coat, not pulling him back, but being sure he stayed in the window. "Boji," he said quietly, reasonably, holding out his hand. "Boji, come back. Do you want an egg?"

Boji looked at him round-eyed and frightened, then ducked down and skittered right down the sheer wall below, using his clever little fingers to find the joints in the masonry.

"Go out, nadi," he heard Lucasi say to someone, "try to get him from below."

"Boji," Cajeiri called, holding out his hand. "Boji, the game is over. Come back."

Boji stopped, down by the next tier of windows, and looked up at him.

"Get me an egg," Cajeiri said, upside down, and with the blood rushing to his face and his hands.

"Egg," he heard Veijico say, as the door of the suite opened and shut, and he could hear his guests' voices, offering to help.

He could see the harness and leash on Boji, or about a hand's length of the leash, and a ragged end where Boji had chewed it through. He lay across the windowsill as far as he dared.

"Egg, Boji! Egg!"

"Nandi." That was Lieidi's voice, and he did not leave the window or make any sudden move that might frighten Boji. He just held out one hand backward, and when an egg arrived in it, he slowly brought it down and offered the egg clearly to Boji's view.

Boji had climbed down another little bit. The movement had gotten him to look up, and Boji did see the egg: the fixed stare of his golden eyes said he had.

"Come on," Cajeiri said. "Come on, Boji, Boji, Boji."

Boji was definitely interested. Cajeiri held the egg to make it completely visible.

"Boji? Time for your egg!"

Boji started climbing up the wall, one large stone and the other, his thin little arms holding him as strong little hands found a hold on the stones.

"Hold my legs!" Cajeiri said, and more than one person grabbed his legs and held on. He leaned a bit more, and Boji climbed after the egg.

Boji reached up to snatch the egg, Cajeiri positioned his other hand to grab the harness, and just then someone came running around the corner of the house below.

Boji looked down, screeched, bristled up, and took off diagonally, far, far across the wall, headed for another open window, not in their suite. He reached that window, clung just outside it.

Gods. Cajeiri counted windows, divided, trying to figure how many rooms that was and what suite Boji had gotten to.

Great-uncle's.

"Boji! Come back! Egg, Boji!"

Boji disappeared into the window.

Cajeiri began pushing at the sill and trying to get back inside, intending to run to Great-uncle's suite, knock on the door, and avert disaster ... but just then Boji came flying out the same window and came scrambling back toward him across the stonework, chittering and screeching. He was almost to the window, then veered off in renewed panic, diagonally downward, while the person below—Jegari—waited there to try to get him.

"Take the egg!" Cajeiri yelled down, and dropped it. Boji had descended almost to Jegari. Then that egg went by and Jegari caught it with a sudden move. Boji suddenly screeched, leaped away from the wall, clean over Jegari's head, and took out across the lawn toward the stable fence.

"Damn!" Cajeiri cried, and began struggling to get back in, at which several people pulled him in and set him upright. "He went into Great-uncle's suite and came out! Now he has gone down into the stables! Come help me!"

"Nandi," Veijico protested.

"He will not regard you," he said, and saw Eidi hurrying to get his outdoor coat from the closet. "Never mind the coat, nadi!" He ran for the door, and his guests and his bodyguard ran after him. "Bring more eggs!" he cried, and went out the door, followed by whoever could keep up with him.

Guards in the hall were in short supply today, mostly at the other end, and Great-uncle's doors were standing open—possibly *because* of Boji—but the guards were looking in the wrong direction. He dived down the servant stairs, down and down, with his bodyguards and guests pounding down the steps behind him. He caught the wall to make a tight turn where the stairs gave out, and headed for the little side hall and the stable side entry, where there were two guards.

"Do not stop us, nadiin!" he cried, waving at them to open the door. "Boji has run for the stables! Open!"

They did, looking confused and dismayed at the outbound rush.

He ran out—they had collected a trail of Uncle's guards from the lower hall and the door, following them, and he heard Lucasi say, in Guild directness, "The young gentleman's parid'ja escaped into the stables, his aishid pursuing. Quiet! Do not alarm it!"

This, while they were still running. Three mecheiti who were out in the pen had their heads up to see what was going on, rumbling and threatening—and there was Boji, walking the railing, near the stable itself.

"Boji!" Cajeiri said. But Boji was having none of it. He made a flying leap for the stable wall and swarmed right up it onto the roof.

He started to go closer.

"Nandi!" Lucasi exclaimed, putting out a hand to prevent him. He stopped.

But so had Veijico stopped, and every Guildsman, all at once.

But not because of the mecheiti. The Guild were suddenly listening to something only they could hear.

"Alarm," Lucasi said. "Into the house, everyone. Now!"

Cajeiri's heart leapt to double-time. It was trouble. Danger. General alarm.

"Run," Cajeiri said to his guests, waving them back toward the house. It was his job to translate for them, to get them safely back inside. His bodyguard was doing what they had to do, and as more of his uncle's guard came around the front of the house, weapons in hand— they ran up to the back door.

It was shut. Locked. Cajeiri pounded his fist on it, shouting, "Nadiin!"

Immediately it opened, in the hands of one of Greatuncle's older house guards, who let them back into the safe dim light of the lower foyer.

They could stop there and catch their breath.

Boji had escaped, and he had no idea how far Boji would run. But there was something far, far more scary going on. The halls echoed with people running. Guards were moving into position, checking what they were assigned to check.

And others were out there near the stables, looking for someone.

"What happened?" Gene asked, bent over and panting. "What's going on?"

"One has no idea," Cajeiri said.

"Stable side door is secure, nandiin," Banichi said, standing listening to what Guild could hear, and Bren and Jase could not. "The first alarm is accounted for. The parid'ja seems to have gotten loose. Jegari made an authorized exit in pursuit. The young gentleman and his guests exited, authorized. He is now inside with his guests, and safe. The parid'ja is still on the loose."

"Could that have set the alarm off?" Bren asked, but just then Algini and Tano, who had gone outside, let Kaplan in.

"Sir!" Kaplan said to Jase.

"We've got a motion alarm," Jase said to Kaplan. "North end of the house. The kids are downstairs, the little animal escaped its cage, and we've got some confusion going on out by the stable—but surveillance has picked up a more significant movement about twenty meters out. It appeared, then disappeared into the house perimeter—into range, then gone like a ghost."

"Something came out of the house shadow," Jago said in Ragi, "then went back *in*. The parid'ja is too small to trigger an alarm, nandiin-ji. This was an unauthorized exit, and someone came back *in*."

"And is *in* the house," Bren said.

Banichi said. "The young gentleman and his guests have been escorted upstairs."

"Condition yellow," Jase said to Kaplan. "Go advise Polano. Stay on this floor. Keep in touch."

"Yes, sir." Kaplan saluted and left.

"Taibeni are saddling up," Banichi said, "but they will not come within range of the house stables. One doubts they will find anything. A malfunction—a blowing scrap lofted on the wind, to the roof . . . it might be either. But we had a great deal going on at once just now, and Komaji's assassination is still unattributed. We cannot dismiss this."

"Yes," Bren said, asking himself what in all reason *but* an exit from the building could have caused that alarm.

Evidently whoever it was hadn't kept going, but had come back inside again. A servant who'd accidentally caused an alarm should be contacting house security immediately and explaining the problem.

All the youngsters were apparently accounted for. *They* had gone out the other door, come back in when the alarm went off.

"This isn't good," he said to Jase. "We have a serious worry, here. I don't want the kids spotting that little creature and creating a problem."

"I'll go find them. Make sure they understand."

"Do," he said, relieved to have someone covering that angle.

The people the dowager's staff had sent to Tatiseigi weren't novices in any sense, and Cenedi had furloughed every servant and guard whose records gave any doubt. None of the ones still on duty were the sort to forget the alarms and sensors they'd installed and blunder into them. Even the youngsters had gone properly past a checkpoint and come back the same way. How did one *avoid* a checkpoint?

Banichi spoke to someone in verbal code.

And Algini and Tano came in from the hall.

"There seems no present danger," Algini said. "Nor any reason at the moment to raise the level of alert. But we have asked Lord Tatiseigi to order all persons assigned to an area to stay in that area, and not to have staff moving about until we resolve this matter."

That seemed a very good idea, in Bren's estimation. "Is there any word from the capital," Bren asked, "or should one be asking that question?"

"There is no alarm from the Bujavid," Banichi said. "We have Taibeni moving on foot to the site of the disturbance, to locate any visible clue, and in case there is another such movement."

Jago had been listening to something, sitting silent at the side of the room. "Word is now officially passing," she said, standing up, "that the assassination this morning was carried out in a Guild manner. There has still been no public notice of a Filing."

Without a public Filing.

No way was that legal, under any ordinary circumstances. A within-clan assassination could be kept quiet—but it still had to go through Guild Council to show cause and it required substantial support within the clan.

"Gini-ji," Banichi said quietly, and Algini looked Banichi's direction a moment. Then Algini nodded.

"Bren-ji," Banichi said. "Algini will tell you something which the dowager knows—but Lord Tatiseigi does not. This has been affecting our decisions and our advice. This is the information we sent Lord Geigi. We are not, at this point, briefing Jase-aiji. This regards the inner workings of the Guild, and *how* the coup that set Murini in power was organized, how the organization persisted past Murini, and why Tabini-aiji barred Ajuri from Shejidan. The aiji also is informed. Whether he has informed the aiji-consort is at his discretion. We have urged him not to."

Answers. God.

If they had figured all *that* out—on the one hand it was possible they had found what they had been trying to find for most of the last year; and on the other it was possible what they had been trying to find had located *them,* and this whole rearrangement of key individuals and their security was under threat.

Algini rarely gave anyone a straight and level look. He did now, arms folded, voice quiet: "We have known much of this since the affair on the coast, Bren-ji. Information we sifted out of the Marid confirmed what we increasingly suspected: that Murini was no more than a figurehead. Convenient, capable of some management, yes, but he was at all times only nominally in charge. He appeared. He gave orders. But there were individuals who pressed a more organized agenda on him. That agenda involved isolating the aishidi'tat from the station—which they accomplished, as you know, by grounding all but one shuttle. Once isolated, they intended to put a completely new power structure in place in the Bujavid, and, once the aishidi'tat was secure under their rule, to restore contact with Mospheira and the station. Geigi would be removed in some fashion, with the specific goal of putting the atevi side of the station—and its capabilities—under their control."

Bren pressed his lips on a burning question and Algini said: "Ask, Bren-ji."

"*Is* the station compromised? *Have* they agents up there?"

"No."

Bren took a slow, deep breath, greatly relieved. Without firsthand knowledge of the station, any hope of threatening it as outsiders was sheer fantasy. Atevi in general simply had no idea what Geigi could do from his post in the heavens.

"Needless to say, this goal was kept very quiet. Murini's *public* stance was *against* the new technology, which touched on conservative aims, and led certain individuals to accept Murini as backing traditionalist views. Tatiseigi was safe, despite the Atageini feud with the Kadagidi, because the last thing the powers in charge wanted was to antagonize the Conservative Party by assassinating an elderly man and a head of the conservatives. Tatiseigi at no time supported Murini. He remained an uneasy neighbor of Murini's clan, even a defiant one. But he remained, as they thought, harmless and useful."

And hadn't *that* assessment backfired, once Tabini returned?

"As to the means by which the coup was organized, Bren-ji, and this leads to information the Guild does not discuss, regarding its internal workings—there are Guild offices traditionally reserved for members from the smallest clans. For centuries, this has been the case, so as not to allow an overwhelming power to gather in the hands of the greater ones."

That was not something humans had ever known.

"The Office of Assignments," Algini said, "is such a post. It is a clerical office, with what would seem a minor bit of power. It does two things. One: it keeps records of missions and Guild membership. And two: it makes recommendations for assignment based on skills, specialization, clan—there are in fact a number of factors involved in designing a team for a mission, or a lasting assignment."

Algini relaxed a degree and leaned against the buffet edge.

"Historically, and this is taught to every child, the same document that organized the aishidi'tat centuries ago also reorganized the guilds—at least in the center and north of the continent—insisting that the Office of Assignments of all Guild personnel should attempt to find out-clan units to assign within the clans, rather than permitting the clans to admit only their own. Theoretically, this would place the whole structure of the Guild under the man'chi of the aiji in Shejidan. The theory

worked to make the guilds far more effective, to spread
information, to stabilize regional associations, to unify
the aishidi'tat in a way impossible as long as clan man'chi
and kinships overpowered man'chi to one's guild. Without that—the whole continent would not have flourished
as it has. The East and the Marid declined to accept the
out-clan rule, and these regions have remained locked in
regional feuds, exactly as it was before the aishidi'tat, to
their economic and social detriment. The aiji-dowager
has made some inroads into the tradition in the East—
one need not say—and the new legislation is bringing
change to the Marid."

A pause. A deep breath.

"Historically, then—the out-clan provision has
worked. And—for much of the history of the aishidi'tat,
the Office of Assignments of the Assassins' Guild has
done its part well. It has kept its records, formed teams,
and sent its recommendations to other offices to be
stamped and approved by the Guild Council. There are
so many of these assignments across the continent . . . it
is routine. The stamp is automatic. One cannot remember there ever being a debate on them. Most often the
local authority accepts, at its end, and the assignment is
recorded. Understand, the Office of Assignments is a little place, smaller than this room, except its records-room.
It is *not* computerized. The current Director of the Office
of Assignments has been running that office for forty-
two years. He has his own system, and he has resisted
any technological change. He refuses to wear a locator,
he will not accept a communications unit. The wits have
it that he would have resisted electric light, except it had
been installed the day before he took the office. It was
not quite that long ago, but modernity does not set foot
there. His name is Shishogi. And he is Ajuri."

God. His administrator with the chessboard. A fusty
little old man in a clerical office. A little old man who
happened to be Ajuri.

"One had begun to suspect," Bren said, "that this
might involve some individual with an agenda."

Algini nodded. "On the surface, it seems a little

power, but placed in the hands of a person with an agenda, it is a *considerable* power—to know all the history of a team, and their man'chi, and to make assignments the Council traditionally approves without a second glance, before it gets down to its daily business."

A system grown up over time. A man sitting in that office for four decades, moving Guild personnel here and there by a process that had no check and was a matter entirely of personal judgment. . . .

It was a terrifying amount of power, in the hands of someone who saw how to use it.

"How can the Guild have been so careless?" Algini asked, rhetorical question. "Senior members have known him for years. He is quiet. Efficient. The wits find him amusing. He has become an institution. His assistants—he makes *those* assignments, too—do things exactly as he likes them done. A minor officeholder may also do a few favors for his own clan, and one would not call it improper. Careful selection of Guild members, to support a lord of Ajuri—or Damiri-daja—who could question it?"

Oh, my *God*.

"This is terrifying, Gini-ji."

"Less so, now that we know where to look. —Damiri-daja may or may not know the situation. It is within Tabini-aiji's discretion to tell her. —We have been, for the last while, reviewing our own associations within our Guild, personally informing those we know are reliable, and trying *not* to make a mistake in that process that would alert Shishogi-nadi that we are targeting him."

"Do you think he set up the mechanism that supported Murini?"

"Very likely."

"And the last two assassinations within Ajuri . . . were they at his direction?"

"Difficult to say—this man is exceedingly deft—but we suspect so, yes. Shishogi had, in the prior lord of Ajuri, a man who would support Murini. When Murini fell, and the Ajuri lord decided to change sides and take advantage of his kinship to Damiri-daja, we suspect Shishogi feared the man would tell Tabini-aiji everything once Tabini's return to power was certain. That lord died quite unexpectedly. Komaji immediately stepped in, then began to behave peculiarly. He attached himself as closely as he could to the aiji's household, did not spend much time in Ajuri, was trying to find a residence in Shejidan."

"Possibly he understood his situation. Possibly he did *not* participate in the prior lord's assassination."

"It is entirely possible. Komaji may have known from the start that he had information that could, if he dared use it, place him in Tabini-aiji's favor—if he was absolutely sure Tabini was going to survive in office. Unfortunately for him, Damiri-daja had staff that were not only a threat to Tabini-aiji—they were watching Komaji. We suspect he was trying to gather the courage to make a definitive move toward Tabini-aiji. And when the Marid mess broke wide open, and the aiji seemed apt to make an agreement with Machigi that might bring the aiji-dowager more prominence—Komaji decided it was the time. Possibly he feared the aiji-dowager's closeness to Tatiseigi. He was *not* invited to the signing of the agreement with Machigi precisely because Tatiseigi *was*—and it was the aiji-dowager's choice. This upset him—possibly because he saw his opportunity to break free of Shishogi was rapidly dwindling, and he feared he was under Shishogi's eye. He went upstairs to the aiji's apartment. He was refused admittance. And at this refusal, in high panic and absolute conviction Tatiseigi and the dowager meant to separate him from the aiji and from his grandson, he broke down in the hallway. His nerve failed him, he no longer trusted his own bodyguards, and when the aiji, beyond banning him from court, sent Damiri-daja's bodyguards back to Ajuri along with him, Komaji had nowhere to go *but* Ajuri. Once there, he remained non-communicative, secretive, and ate only the plainest food, prepared by one staff member. Then he made his last move, toward Atageini lands, with a handful of Ajuri's guards, *not* his own bodyguard. —Did anyone of that company survive, Ja-go-ji?"

"They are, all of them, dead, short of Atageini land."

Algini nodded slightly, acknowledging that. "Not surprising."

"Where was he going?" Bren asked. "What was he trying to do? Do we know?"

"We surmise that in the failure of all other options," Banichi said, "he may have been seeking refuge here, in the house of his old enemy Tatiseigi, whose staff might get a message to the aiji-dowager, to his daughter, or to Tabini-aiji himself, offering what he had to trade. Likely he hoped that one of them would sweep him up and keep him alive in exchange for the information he had. He was not a brilliant tactician."

One could almost find pity for the man. Almost.

"Nadiin-ji. How long has this ... dissidence in the Guild been around? Did this Shishogi organize it?"

No one answered for a moment. Then Algini said:

"That is a very good question, Bren-ji. How long—and with what purpose? It began, we think, in opposition to the Treaty of the Landing."

"Two hundred *years* ago?"

"We think it was, at first," Banichi said, "an organization within the newly formed Guild, a handful who were opposed to the surrender of land to humans. Originally they may have hoped to lay hands on stores of human weapons and simply to wipe every human off the Earth. There were such groups in various places, and there was that sort of talk abroad. It did not happen, of course. No one found any such resource. Then, as we all know, the paidhiin were instituted. They were set up to be gatekeepers, to provide peaceful technology, not weapons. It is, perhaps, poetic, that you, of all officers of the court, have been such a personal inconvenience to the modern organization, Bren-ji. The paidhiin were, from the first human to hold the office, the primary damper on such conspiracies."

"One rather fears that I have become their greatest hope," Bren said, feeling a leaden weight about his heart, "and a great *convenience* to them—in bringing atevi into space and putting the shuttles exclusively under atevi control . . . if their aim truly was to take the station."

"No," Jago said.

"In the station program, Bren-ji," Algini said, "you have linked atevi with humans, economically, politically—even socially. You *are* their worst enemy. *You* brought reality home to Shishogi, we firmly believe it. You negotiated the means to put humans and atevi into association, which his philosophy called impossible. *You* negotiated the agreement that put Geigi in control of weapons they are only just beginning to appreciate. The Shadow Guild planned, naively, to get into the atevi section, convince atevi living up there to wipe out all humans, overcome the armament of the station and the ship, and seize control of the world, using the station. This is, demonstrably, not going to happen. It would not have happened, even had Murini succeeded in getting teams onto the station. Shishogi knows, now, that amid all the technology the humans have given us, their most powerful weapons remain under the control of one *incorruptible* ateva, in the person of Lord Geigi. They could not succeed. Not on the station. Down here . . . Down here is another matter." Algini glanced in Banichi's direction. "I have asked myself, Nichi-ji, whether we could have seen it coming, and I do not think we could. Shishogi found changes proliferating and the world changing faster than he could adapt. He found himself in danger of irrelevancy. But there was also unease, in ordinary people both wanting and opposing the space program, at a time when there was considerable doubt as to human intentions—especially given the interim paidhi."

Yolanda Mercheson. A disaster, who had *not* been able to convert her linguistic study into an understanding of atevi. She had tried. But she had not gotten past her own distrust of Mospheirans, let alone atevi.

Jase, meanwhile, had been with the ship.

God. Twenty/twenty hindsight . . .

"Tabini-aiji's popularity was slipping. Lords were maneuvering to get a share of the new industry, even as public doubts arose regarding whether humans on earth or in the heavens had any intention of keeping their agreements. The conservatives and the traditionalists were gathering momentum in the aishidi'tat. And when a crisis came in the heavens, and it seemed humans might have lied to us, every pressure on the aijinate was redoubled. Tabini-aiji escaped assassination, but his bodyguards were dead, his staff was dead, Taiben had suffered losses and the Atageini were too weak to help. His attempt to reach the Guild met a second attempt on his life, and within hours it was announced Tabini-aiji was dead, that the majority of the shuttles had been grounded to protect the aishidi'tat from invasion from orbit—"

And Yolanda Mercheson had run for her life. He had heard the account before, but from a very different perspective.

"Within an hour of the announcement of Tabini's death, six of the conservatives *and* the traditionalists declared man'chi to Murini," Algini said. It was a set of facts they all knew. But Tano and Algini had seen it all play out.

Banichi and Jago had been with him, the dowager, Cajeiri—and Jase—on the starship, headed out to try to deal with the Reunion situation.

"We do not see now," Algini said, "that this situation will repeat itself. We have not changed our recommendation to the aiji and we have removed the one vulnerability we think gave the aiji's enemies access to his schedule and his apartment."

"It is the aiji's belief, Bren-ji," Tano said quietly, "that Damiri-daja's staff, knowingly or unknowingly, supplied information to the conspirators. Tabini-aiji's staff died. Certain of Damiri-daja's escaped."

"And returning with Komaji," Banichi said, "came Damiri's aunt, her cousin, and her childhood nurse. The nurse, oldest in the consort's service, stayed on when the others went back to Ajuri. When we recovered the records from the situation on the coast, and began to peel back the layers of the Shadow Guild, when we began to realize that Murini was more figurehead than aiji, and when Komaji had behaved as he had, we bypassed the aiji's guard to advise Tabini-aiji to discharge the consort's staff and bodyguard immediately. We wanted them detained. Unfortunately—and we have not had a clear answer about the confusion in the order, they were simply dismissed."

Damn.

"At the moment," Algini said, "we have asked Tabini-aiji to observe a restricted schedule, do business by phone and courier, and that he and Damiri-daja stay entirely within the guard we have provided. The aiji has confidence in the consort's man'chi. She was with him through his exile, her bodyguards were all assigned to her service—by the process you now understand—on their return from exile, and they were all Ajuri folk, as a particular favor to her. Afterward, the night of the reception for Lord Geigi, she told the aiji-dowager that she was close to renouncing her connections with Ajuri."

That walk about the reception all. And a private tea the next morning.

"She has also, under strong advisement from her husband, accepted staff from the aiji-dowager."

Advisement from *Tabini*.

"Assignments had a very close call with Komaji," Algini went on. "He could take the dismissal as the aiji's displeasure with his wife. He knows that Komaji did not get to the Atageini. He may believe he has averted that threat. We do not believe Shishogi would make an attempt on Tabini-aiji at this point. His organization has been disrupted. We did, however, separate the heir from the household to compartmentalize our problems. We had a choice: to go to Malguri, which would better protect the heir, the aiji-dowager, Tatiseigi, *and* these young guests—but which would have us remote, reliant on transcontinental communications which are extremely risky, and put us in a position where assets such as Tirnamardi could be peeled away from us or damaged, which we cannot allow. We decided to strengthen Tirnamardi, and at that point, we had to put our own plan into motion and be sure we could keep Tirnamardi safe.

We decided to involve Lord Geigi, and see if he could assist with equipment which we are—one apologizes, nandi—not supposed to have. Not weapons, but communications methods independent of our Guild, and protective equipment."

Apologize? He could only be thankful for his aishid's foresight. Profoundly thankful.

"We did not expect nand' Jase and his guards to arrive with the equipment," Algini added, "but we accept the assistance. We do not expect a move against us yet. We think our opposition has made one necessary move, in stopping Lord Komaji. They are surely looking us over and finding out that Tirnamardi is no longer an easy mark. They are surely finding out that the Taibeni and the Atageini have made an alliance beyond a signature on a piece of paper. They are surely aware that the situation immediately surrounding the aiji has changed. They might naturally expect, given the foreign visitors, that there *will* be precautions taken and personnel shifted about, and of course we gave out that we are all at Malguri. How soon they penetrate that story will tell us something about their sources and their capabilities. We are unashamedly using the presence of our young guests to make those changes. And we *hope* our adversaries will believe that everything we are doing is just a temporary change and that things will go back to their former vulnerability, once the shuttle returns these children to space."

After the official birthday celebration. Back in the Bujavid . . . with all the danger it might entail, including exposure to *other* Guild, who would have been put in place by Assignments.

"At that time," Algini said, "there will be the option to send Cajeiri to the station with them. Temporarily. Possibly the aiji-dowager as well. At that point—we will go after Haikuti, and we will go after Shishogi. There will be no Filing. We will otherwise observe the law. If *you* wish to go up to the station with the aiji-dowager and the young gentleman, Bren-ji, it will be safer, and we will be free to do what we must do."

He took in a breath, instantly sure. "No. No, I *will not* leave you, nadiin-ji. Where I have influence, where I have any authority, I shall use it in whatever manner you need, and if *I* am present in any situation, you are protecting *me*. What you do then—is legal."

Banichi said, quietly, warmly, "We are not surprised, Bren-ji. We only ask you keep your head down. Literally."

God. So it *was* coming.

One *hoped* Tabini was right to trust Damiri. The coming operation, their lives, the security of the whole atevi world relied on that one emotional judgment.

But couldn't he say, lacking the hardwiring to feel atevi emotions, and going solely on his human senses, that he trusted the four people who were telling him this?

When push came to shove, he bet *everything* on them. And had no doubts.

They'd just had, perhaps, a trial of Tatiseigi's new security arrangement, this morning.

From *inside,* as it looked to be.

They'd chosen to be separate from the Bujavid—but to have as short a distance as possible to the spaceport; now he knew why *that* was; and as short a distance as possible between them and the capital—and Guild Headquarters. *He'd* been anticipating trouble from Komaji.

Scratch that, as of this morning.

"The Kadagidi," he said. Murini's clan. Tatiseigi's next-door neighbors. "This bodyguard of Lord Aseida's. Haikuti. Is *he* the force we're imminently worried about?"

"Yes," Banichi said, from across the room. "He is a *significant* problem."

Algini said, just a flick of the eyes toward Banichi, "Very significant. —Lord Tatiseigi, Bren-ji, has been a somewhat special case in the matter of out-clan assignments. He supports the rule. Officially. But he is very inclined to prefer Atageini Guild be assigned here to him—and he has occasionally, on personal privilege, put pressure on the Office of Assignments. Assignments never complained, you may be sure. Shishogi inserted a few Atageini with kinship to the Kadagidi—and beyond that, assigned some Atageini personnel who, frankly speaking, were not the caliber that a man in Tatiseigi's position should have gotten. Conversely, where there has been *extraordinary* promise in an Atageini candidate who might have come in and identified these people, that person has been shifted to other service, and made unavailable to Tatiseigi's house."

And in just such a way, one at a time . . . or in this case in twos and fours . . . the balance of power throughout the aishidi'tat had been shifted—for forty-two years. Forty-two years of lethal man'chi being slipped into key positions. It wouldn't even take special training or instructions, nothing that could be traced directly to some individual. A time bomb with a purely instinct-driven trigger, right out of the machimi plays. Instincts that would, at some key instant, jump the wrong way. Silent. Nearly untraceable. Shadow Guild, indeed.

Algini continued: "Tatiseigi's clan has bled talent into the system and consistently gotten back less. Rusani and his team, the senior bodyguards—are not much younger than Tatiseigi. They are too old to keep up with training in the way of younger men; and ironically, when we approached them, with Lord Tatiseigi's permission, they were convinced the general quality of Guild training has sadly declined over the years. We cannot at this point tell them the truth of the situation, but we told them the aiji-dowager herself would send them help. Tabini himself told Lord Tatiseigi that he must accept, for the safety of the aiji-dowager and the heir. That is the situation. We have a few remaining of the old staff. And now we have to ask if we have somehow *missed* one. If we have, that individual may be desperate to try to get word to his control. And we are equally determined he should not get that word out, either who is here, or how we are configured. Alternatively, *we* may have a source of information we can lay hands on."

"If he uses communications equipment, we will be on him in an instant," Tano said. "Otherwise, he will have to make a run for it. And getting across the grounds and through the hedges is no small difficulty. He is trapped. Whoever he is."

"Kadagidi would be the logical direction," Bren murmured.

"We are watching all directions," Jago said, "by every means."

They would find this—hopefully last—infiltrator, he had every confidence. With luck, they'd take him alive and have a chance to extract information. And then, or at least very soon thereafter, they were going to try to fix what was broken.

Forty-two years of problems in the Guild.

That dated from before *his* predecessor, Wilson, had been paidhi-aiji. It dated from the time of Tabini's *grandfather.*

From before there was anyone living on the space station. From before there *had been* significant human technology in atevi hands, and from before there was any real flow of communication between Mospheira and the mainland. An old movement, an *old* resistance to human influence . . . had shifted course radically—with this wild notion of moving into the space station.

Not technophobes, however. The old man sitting in that office had declined computers, which would have opened up his records, a locator bracelet, which would have told other Guild where he was.

But he was seeking control of the highest powered technology available.

While Murini had put himself forward as *opposing* human influence, *opposing* the changes in atevi society, *opposing* the factories and the space program, to get Conservative Party support—until his assassination and intimidation tactics had crossed a line and people realized this was *not* the government they wanted.

Not a repudiation of the space program and human influence. A takeover . . . *using* that technology.

And the one way, *the one way* they could have inserted *their* people into the station was to get Geigi off it. Off it and, preferably, out of the picture completely.

No *wonder* the Shadow Guild had been setting up a trap for Lord Geigi, *hoping* he'd find reason to visit his estate at Kajiminda. They'd hijacked Machigi's original plot to get his hands on Geigi's estate. They'd taken over the operation and come scarily close to succeeding in delivering a major blow to Tabini's year-old second administration.

Until they'd crossed the aiji-dowager.

Geigi had come down from the heavens, however—

And then of all things the Shadow Guild had taken to the field and decided to throw mortars at Najida.

"A question," he said. "Nadiin-ji. *Why* did the Shadow Guild take it to the field? Why did they blow the cover off?"

"That," Algini said, "is an interesting question. And a sad situation. The ones most exposed fled south and to the coast when Murini fell. They began recruitment of Marid Guild, whose man'chi was to the region, with a lie: they told these people that the out-clan rule was going to be imposed by northern Guild, who would isolate them and impose northern lords over the Marid. The lie was *too* potent. The Marid recruits slipped control, they took to the field, and they were not coordinated. The action now has evolved to words and reasoned argument, where possible—and the skirmishes that do take place now *are* with those we have no reluctance to take down. Cenedi has had experience in the East. He asked Machigi for names from the Taisigin Marid, called respected persons out of retirement, and set them in positions in the Marid where their influence can be useful. The opposition is feeling more threatened by these influential seniors than by weapons, and local Guild is becoming aware that Murini's people are, principally, outsiders to the Marid. The remnant of our enemy is resorting once again to *Murini's* tactics of intimidation and threats, and they continue to spread the rumors, primarily in the more rural areas, that the out-clan rule is coming and the aiji means to take over the Marid—which is still a rallying cry for the misled. It is a district by district struggle, in a region where the Messengers' Guild does not operate, where there is no television, and radio is often short range and delivering disinformation. We have taken to distributing radios, and broadcasting our own message."

Communication. A world perspective. Messengers' Guild. Scholars' Guild. Get those throughout the Marid and misinformation and truth could at least fight on a level field.

"Ironically, in the past, Assignments has not had the ability to deal with the Marid as well as it has in the north, but that situation is changing. The local Guild has taken a beating they are being told was the fault of their leaders. Machigi—is regarded with great suspicion in the northern Marid."

One very much hoped that the next word would not be that Machigi himself was one of their problems.

"Whatever Machigi has been," Banichi said, "he probably still is—but right now his best chance of survival is as a lord in Tabini-aiji's man'chi, and by assuring *everybody* goes over to the out-clan rule. Assignments, we are quite sure, is already lining up candidates to be installed the moment the aiji and Machigi agree on that move."

"If Shishogi were removed," Bren said, "would that settle it?"

A look flew between Banichi and Algini, Jago and Banichi. Tano just looked worried.

"It would not," Bren concluded.

"We have a choice of targets," Algini said, "but there are several what you call *loose ends* we must deal with *before* we can move—before we *should*, prudently, move—on Shishogi himself. And we are not sure—" Again the glance toward Banichi. "—who actually has the man'chi within that structure. We are of several opinions."

"But it is between Haikuti, and Shishogi?"

A quick dip of the chin. "Haikuti has not the evident seniority or the authority Shishogi has," Algini said. "He is a tactician. He was running Murini from his position as his cousin's bodyguard. Cenedi believes his letting Murini do as much bloodletting as he wished was cold-blooded policy—and that once the enemies had been eliminated, Murini would die, and Aseida would step in with clean hands and a new policy the aishidi'tat would be glad to accept."

"Haikuti let Murini go as far as he did," Banichi said, "because he was likely selecting Murini's targets. He is a tactician who does not mind bloodshed, so long as it is not his own. Shishogi has no field experience. He is, perhaps, the philosopher of the Shadow Guild, but he is a numbers man that arranges teams. He analyzes people. He is the one we need to get. He is the architect. Haikuti— No. He is what someone will use. He is not the *intellectual* master of this organization."

There was a small silence. "I *agree* with you," Algini said.

Tano said, "Nandi. Nadiin-ji. The aiji-dowager has just ordered Cenedi to a conference with the young gentleman. She has asked Jase-aiji to remain with the guests. This will be a briefing, similar to the one we have just held."

While they had an intrusion alarm still unaccounted for—the highest level of Guild present had decided briefing him, and now the heir, had priority. Presumably what Cajeiri learned would include names. And warnings.

So that, whatever happened, in any confusion that might break here, the young gentleman would have some idea who his allies were—and who his enemies were.

One, Haikuti, was right over the hill.

Another—depending on what the dowager decided— might be Damiri.

God. He hoped—*hoped* the boy didn't have to hear that.

Cajeiri was not happy with the situation, with Boji loose outside, and hostile strangers somewhere about— strangers desperate enough to try the borders of Great-uncle's estate.

Perhaps they had no idea Great-uncle had come

home. But there had been a lot of noise and dust at the train station, and along the road. It was hard not to be noticed, if there had been anybody paying attention.

If they were prowling around because they knew who Great-uncle's guests were, they were stupid, and bad things could happen, and if people started shooting he was going to be really mad.

But he could not be scowling and making his guests worried. They had had the alarm. They had been escorted upstairs. Then they had Jase-aiji with them—Jase-aiji was sitting in a chair, commiserating with them about Boji escaping, being pleasant otherwise, and casual. But Kaplan and Polano had come in not too long after, and sat over across the room, wearing sidearms, which of course his own bodyguard did, too—but it was just not that usual with the ship-folk. He knew it. His aishid didn't. But his guests had certainly given their presence an uneasy look.

Now Antaro and Jegari had come in from the hall—Lucasi and Veijico were already with them, over near the window, keeping a watch there; and straightway Antaro went over to Jase and Jegari came to him.

"Your great-grandmother's bodyguard's word, nandi. She wishes you to go to the sitting room."

Him. Only him. In Ragi it was perfectly clear.

"Why?" he asked. "Is my father all right?"

"As far as we know," Jegari said, "everyone is safe." He added, "One of the house staff says she saw Boji, nandi, right when I was outside. I could not see him, but she says he was up on the haystacks. And there is water in the mecheiti troughs. There is every good chance he will stay where he is. We cannot go out there during the security alert. But we may be able to lure him down if he gets hungry."

"If a mecheita does not step on him," Cajeiri said, rising to his feet. "Nadiin-ji," he began, then decided on ship-speak. "Mani wants me," he said to his guests. "I have to go. Back real soon."

"Nandi," Gene said and got up and gave a proper little bow, much more than he really was obliged to do, but the others did, too, and Jase nodded.

Jegari was with him. Antaro joined him. Lucasi and Veijico looked at him and he thought if there was anything mani had to tell him it could well be about Grandfather, and that was Guild business. It would be a good idea for his entire aishid to go. He gave a nod to them, they fell in and they were not the only ones out in the hall. Nand' Bren and his aishid were headed down the stairs, and his aishid, Antaro and Jegari foremost, headed downstairs right after them.

Not a question of going down to mani's suite, down the hall, then, but downstairs, onto the main floor. He quickened his pace, and arrived at the door of the sitting room not far behind nand' Bren and *his* bodyguard. It was Banichi and Jago who took up guard outside, and Tano and Algini who went inside with nand' Bren, which was unusual in itself.

It made him think fast about his own aishid: Jegari and Antaro were seniormost in his household, and they knew the Padi Valley up and down; but Veijico and Lucasi were senior in Guild rank, and he reversed the usual order of his bodyguard, too, said, "Taro-ji, Gari-ji, take the door," straightened his coat, and went in with Lucasi and Veijico.

Mani was there, no question. So was Great-uncle. And nand' Bren. And he was the last piece, he decided. He paid a quiet bow to mani and to Uncle, and a lesser one to nand' Bren, and picked the chair beside him.

There was tea. So it was not an outright emergency and nobody else was dead. He took a cup that the servant offered him, and they all sat and sipped tea awhile, until he was not breathing hard, and his heart had settled. And he was being included with the adults. That was something. Things were serious, but they called him to tell him what was going on. He was a few days short of felicitous nine, and he was being taken seriously, more than ever in his life.

So he put on his best manners, and drank at the rate

everybody else did, and when mani set her cup down, he set his down, finished or not; and everybody else did.

Then Great-uncle said something very unusual. He said, "Only bodyguards may remain. Clear the room, nadiin-ji."

The servants left, all of them.

"Paidhi," Great-grandmother said, "for convenience of language and accuracy, we leave Jase-aiji to wait for your briefing. You may relay to him the nature and content of what we say—be somewhat sparing of detail internal to the Guild. You have been briefed already by your aishid."

Nand' Bren said, "Yes, aiji-ma."

"Well," Great-grandmother said, "Great-grandson."

"Mani." If he were littler he would have stood up at that tone. He was nearly nine, and twitched, but he stayed seated, and only gave a polite nod.

"You know that your grandfather was one reason for the security surrounding your birthday celebration. You know that since this morning he is no longer at issue."

"Yes, mani."

"You also know that your great-uncle, while he has reached agreement with his neighbors to the west, has not been at peace with his neighbors to the east."

"The Kadagidi, mani. My father banned Lord Aseida. He is Murini's cousin."

"There is another man of that clan," mani said, "who is more worrisome than the lord of the Kadagidi. Lord Aseida's chief bodyguard, Haikuti. Pay attention, and I shall tell you a little story about this Haikuti."

"Mani."

"He was born Kadagidi, he trained in the Guild. He and his team reentered Kadagidi service some five years before the Troubles—Aseida's bodyguard, which had been with him from his youth, had been removed."

That was a scary thought. Bodyguards did not get removed.

"They were reassigned to a Dojisigi house. We would like to know more about their current whereabouts. Murini was in the Dojisigin Marid—more than once—prior to his attack on your father. Aseida stayed at home. He was a student. He and several others of the Kadagidi youth were frequently in the Kadagidi township, frequently drunk, frequently a difficulty for the town Council, and an ongoing expense for his father, who died under questionable circumstances."

That meant—possibly he was assassinated.

"Kadagidi of various houses have been a nuisance for years, quarreling with your great-uncle over land—several times with your father over complaints from their neighbors. They have five townships, seventeen villages, and they dispute the possession of a hunting range with the Atageini. They have overhunted. They have founded one village without license, and attempted to attach it to the disputed range. They have a sizeable vote in the hasdrawad and they have weight in the tashrid when they are not banned from court, which has happened three times in my own memory. They have connections in the Dojisigin Marid, and of course—they are Murini's clan. Exactly. They are one of the five original signers of the association of the aishidi'tat, and a permanent ban would be politically difficult—not to mention a disenfranchisement of a large number of farmers and tradesmen who have committed no fault but to be born to a clan whose ruling house has multiplied in numbers and declined in all social usefulness." Mani's voice was clipped and angry. "Which adequately describes that nest. Murini had some intelligence. He made contacts in the Marid—made a marriage with Dojisigi clan, another nest of trouble—which formed an alliance that greatly worried his neighbors and any other person of sense. All this while, Aseida and his fellows were living their useless lives, showing no enterprise in the things they should have been doing. Staff saved them. Things were done, efficiently and well—give or take a little dispute with your great-uncle."

Great-uncle looked angry just thinking about it.

"Murini came in. Things changed—one would have said, for the better, if one were a town official needing action. The staff grew larger. Aseida and his useless associates no longer came to the township. Security tightened. Murini, back and forth between the Padi Valley and the Marid, was planning the coup. When your father was overthrown by conspiracy, and nearly killed, Murini left the Kadagidi estate and established himself in Shejidan—never surrendering his lordship over the Kadagidi, but not devoting much attention to it, either. When we drove Murini and his lot out—the ruling house of the Kadagidi clan was nearly wiped out. But not all. This obscure man, this useless man, Aseida, turned up in the Kadagidi lordship, writing numerous apologies to your father for the actions of his cousin. Your father is not deceived about his quality, and has not forgiven the clan."

"Nor have I," Great-uncle said.

"Yet," Great-grandmother said, "Aseida is lord. And Kadagidi is rebuilding. It is not Aseida who is so industrious. It is his bodyguard and his staff."

"Haikuti," Cajeiri said.

"He was never part of the coup. He was never attached to Murini. Yet—things run exactly as they did when Murini was alive. The same rules. The same policies. One might say the Kadagidi were merely doing what worked well—but we suspect that the difference in Murini's administering Kadagidi lands and his behavior in Shejidan is this man. And you would say that he is doing no harm, governing Kadagidi from behind Aseida's shoulder. But we have a little more information of this man's connections now, and this is the *last* man your father should admit to court."

He thought he followed that. He was not sure. But under the circumstances, only one thing really mattered: "Shadow Guild?"

"Definitely," mani said. "Definitely."

Cenedi, standing to the side, said: "There was a strategist behind the coup, and we do not believe that that strategist was Murini, or even one of Murini's bodyguard. We are now watching the contacts between Kadagidi and the outside, by means that we do not think the

Kadagidi have. Your grandfather's assassination provoked an interesting flow this morning."

"*Kadagidi* did it?" That was a lot better than learning his mother had done it. But it was not good news about Uncle's neighbors.

"Possibly." Cenedi walked forward a step. "Nand' paidhi."

"Nadi?" nand' Bren said.

"You were briefed, nandi, concerning the Ajuri officer in the Guild."

"Yes," nand' Bren said, and Cajeiri took in his breath, resolved not to interrupt. One learned nothing by stopping people. But he *had* to know—

"Cenedi-nadi. Who?"

"There is an old man, Ajuri, your very remote elder cousin, a high officer in the Guild," Cenedi said, "who may have wanted your grandfather silenced—regarding the relationship of Ajuri clan to the Shadow Guild. You are not to discuss this, on your great-grandmother's order, young gentleman. This is what you urgently need to know—and your aishid needs to know; but none of your guests. This man, Shishogi, *or* Haikuti, who would not want Shishogi exposed, sent the assassins."

"This knowledge is worth *lives,*" mani said. "Believe it, Great-grandson."

"Shishogi-nadi has held his office," Cenedi said, "for forty-two years. He has worked in secret—placing his people in various houses. We believe that some of these were on your mother's staff, young gentleman."

His heart beat hard. He knew these people. He had passed them in the hall. He had slept with them outside his door.

"Does my father know?"

"Yes," mani said.

He never expected to be told the whole truth—he never was—but it seemed likely he was hearing it now.

The air in the room seemed heavy. His heart was beating unbearably.

"Understand this, Great-grandson. This man, this

Ajuri, is the stone on the bottom of the stream. He is a constant, and events flow around him. You do not see what makes the turbulence, but once you study the patterns, you can begin to see that there is a certain rock that makes it flow that way. That is how we have detected him. His agents, we suspect, have deliberately kept certain quarrels going—your great-uncle and I have discussed that matter."

Great-uncle cleared his throat. "We have completely revised our security."

"The alarm," he said. "Did you catch anyone, Great-uncle?"

"Not yet," mani said. "But we are looking. Quietly. Meanwhile I rely on you to stay indoors, devise clever entertainments for your guests, and think. Think about your safety, do *not* be in a window once it gets dark, and take care your guests do not. You are in *less* danger than you would be anywhere else in the world, but *only* if you obey instructions and do not take chances."

"Boji got away out the window," he said. "I am very sorry, mani. We had no idea there was any problem and I wanted to find him. We came right back."

"Ha." Mani seemed even amused. "Your little Boji had doors opened, people running out to the stable—possibly it startled someone into a mistake. Perhaps we must thank Boji. We shall keep him in mind, if we have anyone out searching. We shall catch him for you if we can."

"He likes eggs, mani."

"I am sure he does. Go back to your guests, Great-grandson. Keep them contained. And do *not* venture out to catch Boji tonight. We are on a completely different set of priorities than we have admitted to the world. This is no time for a mistake. Do you understand?"

"Yes, mani," he managed to say.

He got up. He made his bows. He left with a racing heart and an upset stomach, thinking: *So Mother did not do it.*

But what did my grandfather have to do with the Shadow Guild?

*   *   *

There was a lengthy pause after the young gentleman had left. Bren waited, sensing it was not a general dismissal.

"In our opinion," Ilisidi said, "we doubt Lord Komaji suffered a moral change that brought him to his end. It seems likely that he *was* attempting to escape his situation. Considering the man, we suspect his strange behavior in the Bujavid was complete panic. He was carrying far too much knowledge. My grandson and his wife—and, more importantly, her bodyguards—were not in the apartment at the time he attempted to get in. I think he wanted to talk to Cajeiri, to enlist *him* to reach my grandson, with the hope of meeting my grandson with Cajeiri to stand in front of him—as he exposed Damiri-daja's staff and everything else he knew. He was in a truly desperate situation—he had excellent reason not to trust his own bodyguards. Being rebuffed at the door—he slipped into total, unreasoning panic. He blamed us for creating it. He sought a public place as the place least likely his own bodyguards would choose to kill him—and quite, quite broke down. The poor man had no knowledge how to survive without a staff—he probably had no idea how to walk out the door, down the hill, and buy a train ticket."

"Who carries money?" Tatiseigi asked. It was true. Lords didn't. Staff did.

Ilisidi gave a short, ironic laugh. "I have found," she said, "that a piece of jewelry serves." The smile vanished. "Damiri-daja had no wish to see him again. Nor to commit herself to Ajuri."

"She *has* an uncle."

"That she does, Tati-ji."

"You do not think, aiji-ma," Tatiseigi said, "that she in any wise has contact with this old man, this Shishogi."

"No," Ilisidi said, and moved her cane to lean on it, as she would when she had something more to say, of a serious nature. "She said herself that she had refused to visit Ajuri, that they would have been happy to have her daughter born there, and she would not consider it. That not please Komaji in the least. She pleaded her condition. And the distance. She did not want to fly. Excuses. But, Tati-ji, she carries very unhappy memories—no few unhappy memories. She is sensitive on the matter. Born here. Sent there. Back here. A long sequence of going there and here, all with the single question—whether she should ever have been born."

"One never implied such a thing!" Tatiseigi said.

"She heard it somewhere: 'The child of an unlucky alliance.' Only she knows what remark, from whatever source, instilled that impression in her. I had it straight from her. This I have from my grandson: her father showing up in my grandson's return—his having the lordship of Ajuri and courting her with such devotion— waked man'chi in her that quite upset her, and worried her. And with that man'chi still unsettled, came the incident that sent her father from court and removed her staff. She was quite, quite shaken. It took *courage* for her to wear the Atageini colors that evening, Tati-ji. Great courage. But it was her choice. I told her that evening that I appreciated the situation she was in. That I *knew* it took courage. That I understood her hesitation at acknowledging man'chi to either clan. I recalled my marriage as an Easterner, coming to reside in a Ragi household. I told her when she was my age, she might find value in the position of outsider, and mother of the heir—but, I said, that power had to come from staff with good connections, and allies on whom one could call without doubt. She had made one step in that direction on her own. I offered another. I pointed out that she might gain you, Tati-ji, and me, and various others who are her son's most important allies. That in him is the source of power for *her* one day to stand where I do, doing as I do. *That* is what I said to her. She was not pleased to hear all of it. But her subsequent choices have, indeed, been better choices. She is sitting in my grandson's residence with Malguri and Taibeni security, and she is still alive. She is much too intelligent to go to Ajuri. One may only imagine how eager this Shishogi would be to have her open Ajuri records to my grandson's inspection."

One could only imagine, Bren thought.

"She is," Tatiseigi said, "a part of *this* household. As is the young gentleman. No one will ever again utter any word to the contrary. Never under this roof!"

"A good resolve," Ilisidi said, and called for more tea. "We shall think on these things. We shall let Guild solve the problems." Which had a more ominous ring than usual. "And we shall enjoy the evening, shall we not, Tati-ji?"

"We shall by no means alter plans within this house," Tatiseigi said. "Perhaps we shall find this new-fangled *thing* on my roof has simply had a malfunction. We shall enjoy our dinner, though I fear we have had to cancel the choir. And if the Guild insists this fancy equipment *cannot* fail, well, we cannot ride. We shall entertain the children with a tour of the premises tomorrow. I shall show them my collections."

The collections were famous—though Bren had never seen them. And one could not imagine the old lord entertaining a flock of children all day with case after case of tea services.

"The other collections, Tati-ji," Ilisidi said. "The taxidermy should interest strangers to the world. They will not have seen those creatures."

Taxidermy. *He* was curious himself, what might be there. Great houses threw nothing away.

Tatiseigi nodded, and gave a rare little laugh. "We should send them in by lamplight. That is how I remember them, from my youth. Fangs and claws appearing out of the darkness. We promise it for tomorrow, since the basement knows neither day nor night, rain nor sun. We would wish them to sleep tonight." He accepted a teacup, after which only small conversation was mannerly. "And just as well we shall not be riding tomorrow. Likeliest we shall all be limping about. I know I shall."

"It is ridiculous that we should ache," Ilisidi said. "We have gotten soft, Tati-ji. And we resent every ache.

Paidhi-ji, be glad of your youth, and know what you have ahead."

"One regrets to say, aiji-ma, that one does feel it."

Ilisidi's expression lightened. She liked to be flattered, if the flattery was subtle. So did Tatiseigi.

Tea continued, and the house remained quiet, except the servants hurrying about their preparations—and except, one was certain, the unheard transactions of the Guild, those in communication with the Taibeni units, and those in communication with others about the grounds, where it was not tea service and light conversation. The best the lords involved could do in that matter was to stay out of the way. The answer to the alarm was not being obvious.

"We shall rest before dinner," Ilisidi said, after a single cup. "Perhaps have a nap."

With that, their little conference adjourned, and they got up, bowed, and gathered up their separate guards.

Banichi and Jago joined them outside.

"The Taibeni have found sign, but they dare not bring the mecheiti in close to Tatiseigi's herd," Banichi said quietly. "One of Tatiseigi's grooms is bringing the herd-leader over to see what he picks up and where it came from. There is however, a very faint trace of old sign, from before the rain. The direction of approach was from the Kadagidi perimeter."

"One is not that surprised. Is there any guess how old?"

"Difficult," Jago said. "They think possibly *before* the new equipment went in. Four days ago."

"One of the Taibeni," Banichi said, "has made a search of the stables, to see if he could locate the young gentleman's parid'ja, or anything else, but if it is there, it is hiding."

"A good thought, at least," Bren said, and as they started up the stairs: "We are given leave to brief Jase on our situation, not the details inside the Guild."

That, by the fact of language, was his to do.

"He is back in his quarters," Tano said, and added: "And Cajeiri and his guests are sitting in theirs and talking. We have been given a lower level of alert. That could change at any moment."

And that ... was the least surprising news of the entire day.

"Understand," he said to Jase, "that we are in a relatively safe position. There's no danger to this house at the moment, and we are very sure of the people around us. What has changed today is a security alert, and traces of a Kadagidi intrusion here some days ago. And the fact that Cajeiri's grandfather apparently reached the end of a relative's patience—not a family quarrel. Guild politics; and connected to this lot that arranged the coup, and that we've been trying to track down for the last year. Apparently Cajeiri's grandfather talked too much about another member of that clan. The short version of it all is—there's this old man in the Guild who's sat there for forty years, Ajuri clan. He's used a minor post to stack the deck in various clans, putting less able Guild into certain positions, shunting some to other duties— weakening his enemies, strengthening his allies, and possibly inserting spies here and there. We believe that's how the coup was organized, and how the trouble has kept coming back. We've got our eye on him. We're going to take care of him. We *don't* want to do it until the boy's had his party and the guests are home safe. Politics, again. We can't let this fellow dictate what we dare and daren't do. More immediate to the alarm situation, and what has us just a little worried, we've also had our eye on one other man, who's running security over to the east, in Kadagidi clan's manor house. And I swear to you, we hadn't planned to have an assassination in Ajuri clan happen while we had the kids here."

"You say we're safe here."

What did he say? That Cenedi was, hand over fist, setting up for conflict within the Guild, that the dowager had ignored Assignments and Guild procedure, and fortified both Tabini-aiji and Cajeiri—separately—*preparing* for enemy attack?

If the old man in Assignments didn't get a clue that it

was check and damned near mate, he wasn't as smart as they thought he was.

"We think we're safe because we've taken measures to *be* safe, but if all hell breaks loose, we think it's still going to be reasonably quiet hell this time, and we *think* we can take care of it."

Jase thought about that a moment, then said, "Well, we. told the parents that assassination goes on down here, that it's specific, and it doesn't take out bystanders. And we didn't dwell on the point that, when it happens, the whole political picture can shift."

"Exactly. Understand that aiming at the kids would be way outside civilized rules. Shooting Cajeiri—maybe. Me or our host, again—permissible. But don't rely on civilized rules with this enemy. Public opinion hasn't stopped them. They *want* the public terrified."

Jase nodded. "Understood."

"One opinion they do fear—is Lord Geigi. They now know they'd be small burned spots if Geigi lands one of his machines in their district. That word has gotten around, and nobody wants another of those machines to wake up. *Everything* in their eyes is politics—and they think the one he did turn on was purely a demonstration of what he can do."

"Not far wrong on that score," Jase said. "I have the picture."

"These are a type you and I know. From your first visit. If you want my opinion—it's the same lot. Deep connections. But we're getting close to the heart of their operation. I am, frankly, very glad you're here."

"What are friends for? I'll explain the situation to the kids, without scaring them. They haven't caught that noisy little creature, have they?"

"They haven't. They probably won't. They're arboreal. They go for the deep woods. And there's a small woods between us and the Kadagidi, and a very big one, well, you saw the area around the train station. Taiben, forest from one end to the other, very friendly territory for that little creature. I'm afraid he's lost his pet."

"Too bad," Jase said. "Interesting little creature. But if

we can have our holiday without a shooting war—ideally without the kids or their parents ever noticing there's been a problem during their visit, well, except the grandfather—I won't explain it to them. Briefing Geigi and the captains, yes."

"Definitely," Bren said.

There was supper, an uncommonly very fine supper. The cook was doing his best, given the young gentleman's grandfather dying, his disappointment at being restricted from *his* birthday gift, and his having lost his parid'ja into the bargain. Do him credit, the boy had been bearing up with a determination that Bren feared even to compliment, for fear the boy would dissolve on the spot. He was bearing up on a sheer charge of nervous energy—that downhill rush that could spin into disaster if one began to notice anything but the obstacles. Dodge, dodge, and dodge. Keep going. Smile. Keep his guests from upset. Bren knew that state of mind. Knew the effort it took the boy to laugh when the others did.

Did the guests pick it up? Bren had a slight suspicion they did—and *they* had had warnings up and down the line to avoid any emotional upset with atevi. They were surrounded by strangeness, they were fed unfamiliar things, and there were signs all around them that there might be dangers, that their atevi hosts were trying to keep it from them, and that Cajeiri's grandfather was not only dead, not of natural causes, but nobody was acting in the least sorry about it. He had no complete knowledge of what Jase had told them when he talked to them, but they were getting a quick lesson on what upset atevi looked like, and they were doing their best to eat what was put in front of them and get it down their throats no matter what it tasted like.

"Nadi," Bren said to one of the servants, the one bearing the bitter-spiced eggs, and ladling two onto his plate, "the human children will find this too strong for them and will be embarrassed. Kindly pass by them."

"Nandi," the servant said, going on his way, and Bren managed one egg, with a healthy dose of sweet relish.

There was nothing but pleasant talk. Cajeiri and Jase translated for the guests their elders' assurances the weather would stay fair, assurances that Cajeiri's mecheita would be stabled here quite happily and would always be available for him—and Tatiseigi's personal regrets for the inconvenience of the change in schedule.

The attempt to have the herd-leader locate their problem had not gone well—or given them any reassurance it had been a stray leaf or an electrical malfunction. Someone had strewn a massive amount of deterrent in the area. The mecheita had gotten a nose full of it, shied off, and they had just had to let him run it out—which had taken him much too close to the Taibeni camp at the eastern end of the estate. If he had not had his sense of smell disrupted, and if the wind had been blowing in the other direction, they would have had a serious problem. They had warned the Taibeni—but riders had also gone out from Tatiseigi's stable and found him in time to get him calmed down. They were back in the stable, the grooms had treated the poor fellow with vapors and an abundance of water, and Tatiseigi was both irate, and now convinced it was a Kadagidi spy, equipped with the noxious weed, and somewhere on his premises.

The children had seen some of the goings-on from their window. They had sent Veijico down to find out what was going on. House security had informed Veijico. Veijico had doubtless told her team, and told Cajeiri what was going on. Whether Cajeiri had then told the real story to his guests—one was not sure. But they had their door locked and that young aishid was doing everything by the book . . . a very good thing, in Bren's opinion.

Tatiseigi signaled a desire for attention, and declared that there would be a treat tomorrow in place of the canceled ride. A tour of the basement collections.

It was, after a long and trying day, a complete puzzlement to the youngsters—Cajeiri and the human children looked equally as if they had missed a translation.

Tatiseigi said, "You shall see, you shall see," and was amused.

"You will enjoy it, Great-grandson," Ilisidi said, preserving the mystery, and young spirits visibly lifted. A mystery. A treat. And Tatiseigi, God save them, was going to take the youngsters in charge.

Dessert arrived. Between a mystery and an abundance of sugar, the human youngsters' spirits rose. The guests were happy ... and Cajeiri had a second helping of cake.

15

The bitter-spiced eggs had been a mistake. Cajeiri decided he never wanted another one.

He was exhausted. But he had had enough sugar his nerves were wound tight. Everyone was in that state: Lie-idi and Eisi had had their supper in the room, and Antaro and Jegari were down in the dining room, having theirs, along with Banichi and Jago and Cenedi and Nawari and Tatiseigi's senior bodyguard, Rusani, and the rest.

There was every chance they were going to find out *something* of what was going on. He had heard about the powder, and the herd-leader nearly running up on the Taibeni camp. That was nasty—and it was mean, and it was a very good thing nobody had been outside that camp right then. There had been two searchers out in the little woods, and at least they could climb a tree, but that was just scary, what could have happened.

And some of the Taibeni were Antaro's and Jegari's cousins. They were not pleased with the trick, either.

"If my cousins lay hands on that fellow," Jegari had said, "they will give him a dose of his black powder."

He and his aishid agreed.

"It is certain," Veijico told them then, "that there is someone here up to no good. And it seems that person is *still* here. He tried to get out, then realized he had set off the alarm, and went back into his hole."

"Maybe," Jegari said in a hushed voice, "he is in the basement."

That was the scariest thing anyone had said yet. Great-uncle was going to take them on a tour of his basement, for a surprise. But if some Kadagidi assassin was hiding down there in the dark—

"Maybe you should tell them to search the basement, nadiin-ji," Cajeiri said.

"One is sure they *are* searching it," Lucasi said. "But we will mention it."

Meanwhile, Cajeiri thought, he just had to take deep breaths and think of things to do so his guests had a good time and did not get bored. And he hoped the basement was better than it sounded. Mani had thought so.

Meanwhile—meanwhile, of all things, Artur had come up with a pocket full of rocks, and provided his own entertainment, laying his treasures out for everybody to see.

"Where did you find those?" Cajeiri asked. On a day when they were all pent in with a security alert, he *knew* where his guests had been, and surprises were not a good thing, today.

"The stables. Where we walked."

Artur had been hindmost, going out the door, and Cajeiri recalled indeed, it was a gravel walk—a lot of places had gravel, or flagstones. And Tirnamardi had gravel all along by the stables.

There was a sandstone, a quartz, and a basalt one— "That one I got at the train station," Artur said. "This one in the front of the house." That was the pink quartz.

"You can almost see through it," Irene said, admiring it against the light. "Those are so great!"

Artur had been collecting them all along. None of his guests were used to walking on rocks, or dirt. And trust Artur to do something unusual.

So now that Artur tallied up his collection, all very small ones, he used what he had learned from his tutor to tell everybody what they were, and how they had formed, and even where they came from. They were river-rounded. And it was very likely they had been under a glacier once.

Everybody was impressed with what he knew. And he

did not have his big map, but he drew one for them in Irene's notebook, a map of the Padi Valley, and he showed them where they were, and the river where probably the rocks had come from—he had never been there, himself, but he knew about it.

And the idea that water and wind could smooth them into eggs, and how mountains formed and wore away, and how volcanoes happened, down near the Marid, and down in the islands in the Great Southern Ocean—all of that was wonderful to them. They knew about magnetic fields, and about dustball asteroids, and interesting things up in space. They said Maudit had volcanoes, a lot of them, but not much water.

"If we have to live there," Irene said, "we'll really live in another space station, in orbit, but it won't be very nice as the station here is. Nothing will be." Irene frowned and rested her chin on her hand. "I don't want to live on Maudit Station. I don't." She wiped her eyes. "I'm not supposed to get upset. Sorry."

He did not want Irene to live on Maudit Station either. Not any of them. And he did not want to think about anything else sad or upsetting today, he truly did not. He was very glad Irene was getting the better of her upset. *Everybody* had gone quiet.

"Right," Irene said in a moment, and picked up the smoothest of Artur's collection. "It's like a little world, isn't it? In space, rocks can't smooth out and be round until they're huge. And here's this little round rock that spent hundreds of years in running water, and it's just lying there on the ground this morning for Artur to find it. That's something."

"I can bring this back with me," Artur said, then explained. "No animals, no biologicals, like seeds or anything. Everything has to be processed. They're not going to argue about rocks. But there's so much, like almost everything we touch. Everywhere I look—there's things that are just—random. Shaped however they want to be."

"Most things," Cajeiri said. He remembered, how everything about the ship was made by machines, smooth, shiny, or plastic. He thought of his own room, where he had gathered living plants, and pictures and weaving, and carvings of animals on every chair and table ... he knew what Artur meant by random. It was a good word. He had been on the ship two years and found himself wanting windows, wanting the open sky and the smell of plants and curves on everything his eyes touched. And he had told his associates how the world was and promised them they would see it. They had fourteen days. That was all they had, until — until — he had no idea. He had not mentioned his *next* birthday yet, and they were talking about being sent to Maudit, which none of them wanted to happen.

And now some stupid Kadagidi had gotten into the house and Boji was gone ...

He was not going to give up on Boji. And the guards were going to catch that Kadagidi who had pulled that nasty trick with the black powder.

And he knew beyond any doubt that his guests were enjoying everything they saw. Even pebbles on the ground were treasures to them. They had pills to take because the sky would make them sick — but Gene said he hadn't needed them today; and Irene said she wanted not to need them, and then Artur said the same thing — Artur said looking toward the horizon was like looking down the core-corridor: scary, because the place could look like the edge of the world one moment and a pit, the next.

But he had seen the core-corridor on the ship. He had been there, in a suit too big for him, and floated in air. He had looked right down it, which was the scariest place he had ever been.

And maybe, for them, having dared each other to look down the core, where gravity just didn't exist, it had made them ready to look at the sky.

They were all brave. He knew that. Irene had been scared of the mecheiti, but now she said she wanted to ride again, even if she was limping tonight — poor Irene was the skinniest of them, all bones and pale skin, and she looked even skinnier when she was wearing her stretchy clothes. The saddle and Irene's bones had been very close together this morning.

But she tried. Artur collected the rocks that pleased him—and Gene—

Gene looked at everything, and he said he had really wanted to bring something to take pictures of everything, but security said no. So he just looked at things. Really looked at them. If Gene was standing still, not doing anything for a moment, he was looking—at the sky, at the edge of the meadow, at the mecheita he was riding. Like sketching things, only doing it all in his head.

Cajeiri had never had a camera. He had no idea how one worked. And he did not think mani or Great-uncle would approve: it was a lot like television.

But there were books with pictures. He thought he should give Gene one.

And there was Gene again, with Artur's sandstone in his fingers, just looking at it, and thinking.

They had so very little time, so very little, and his grandfather had managed to get in the way of them having it. And there was this relative of his, another great-uncle, Shishogi, or something like that, who had been a problem for years and years.

And who even knew what went on in this Shishogi's brain, or what he was even after, except he could be involved with the Shadow Guild.

Had Grandfather known about that, and not warned them?

That night when Grandfather had tried to get into their apartment and get to *him*—that was still scary.

And now they had this Shishogi person trying to kill everybody, and a troublesome Kadagidi over the hill who was up to no good. Was anybody really surprised? Kadagidi had always been trouble.

He had no idea why they were. But he became interested in finding out.

They talked about all sorts of things, he and his guests, in the sitting room of his suite, with its tall, wonderful windows. The sun being down, they had to keep the curtains drawn and stay away from the windows—but they had comfortable chairs they could pull up in a circle, and there they could sit and talk the way they had used to do in the echoing service tunnels of the ship. In the ship's tunnels, they had shivered in the cold and had to find nooks where it was safe to sit, where nobody would find them and where none of the machinery would run over them.

Now they had this comfortable room with the windows and soft furniture, and Eisi and Lieidi to serve them tea and teacakes, as many as they could eat—not many, after the supper they had had; and his aishid had the rest. Lucasi and Veijico understood some of what he and his guests were saying—but Antaro and Jegari were a lot better at it, having studied ship-speak longer.

Antaro and Jegari were a little close-mouthed, however, not saying what they might have heard during their own supper, with all the high-up Guild. Cajeiri fairly burned to ask—but if it was really, really important, they would have called him aside and told him, he was very sure.

His guests talked about what the space station was like now—a place he had never really gotten to see that much of. It was the ship he really knew. And he heard that the ship, *Phoenix* was docked at a distance from the station, and only working crew could go out there.

That did not include Reunioners who had only been passengers.

Another pot of tea, a trip to the accommodation, one by one, under escort, and they were out of teacakes— Cajeiri talked about the west coast, and Najida, and where nand' Bren lived, and Lord Geigi's house; and how he had gotten lost in a storm in a rowboat. His guests were impressed.

By the end of that story, however, they all were flagging. Artur's eyes were closing. And despite the beds his staff had made ready for them, Cajeiri thought he would happily just fall asleep in the chair, and they all could just sit there together, all night, talking whenever they waked up and felt like it.

"Nandi," Eisi said quietly, at his side, "will you like to come to bed, now?"

He had had his eyes shut. For a moment he had been seeing the fields, feeling the mecheita moving under him.

Artur had fallen asleep, and Irene and Gene were trying not to nod off.

There was a weird sound from outside, far off: mecheita, he thought. And then he heard a mecheita grunt, and another moan, and then three or four.

Mecheiti did that when they were disturbed. It could be vermin in the stable.

Then there was a horrid screech that woke up Artur and had Gene and Irene wide-eyed.

"Boji!" Cajeiri cried, leaping to his feet, with every intent of going to the window to open the drapes.

But then a rifle shot echoed off the walls.

"Lights," Veijico said sharply—she was already on her feet. All his aishid was, and he was. The rest of them stood up just as Lieidi, close to the door, threw the light switch.

The room went dark, all but a light in the bodyguards' bedroom.

"What's going on?" Irene asked in a whisper. "What's that sound?"

"Mecheiti," he said. Down in the stables, the mecheiti were telling everybody to keep out.

Their last light went out, except for the tiny seam of light under the main door—Eisi had gone into the bedroom and gotten that one. By that last seam of light, he saw Jegari putting on his jacket—and Gene bumped into a chair arm—humans did not see well in the dark, he knew that. "Everybody stand still," he whispered. "Listen."

He was trying to hear anything coming from his bodyguard's communications unit, faint as it might be. Outside, another faint seam of light at the edges of the drapes: someone had just thrown on the outside lights. The mecheiti continued threatening and moaning about something.

He heard a faint scratching, then, right at the window.

Guild, was his first thought, even up here.

But then there was that tap-tap-tap of a bony, long finger, on the window glass—the way Boji opened eggs.

"That's *Boji*!" he whispered. "Open the drape, nadi-in-ji! Please! He wants in!"

Antaro was nearest. She very carefully pulled back the drape, and there in the gap, against the glow of flood-lights below, was a little spindly-armed silhouette, look-ing in, hands spread on the glass.

"Let him in," Cajeiri said. "Let him in! Let him *in,* Taro-ji!"

"Gari," Antaro said to her brother, and Jegari worked his way to the other side of the window. They let the drape fall a moment, as the two of them, each on a side, loosed the latches and carefully eased the window up a little.

"Boji!" Cajeiri said softly, and made that clicking sound he used to imitate Boji's own. "Egg, Boji! Eisi-ji, quickly, *find him an egg, Eisi-ji!*"

The commotion down in the mecheita pen was clearer with the window open. There were voices outside. Lucasi and Veijico were talking on Guild communications, tell-ing whoever they were talking to that Boji had just come up the wall.

"I have the egg, nandi," Eisi said.

"Let me have it. Quickly!" Cajeiri took it, and held it in his hand—Boji's kind could surely see it even in the dark. He obeyed Antaro's furious signal and kept back against the wall as he reached the window. She shoved him down, low, and he held it on the windowsill, deter-mined not to let Boji snatch it and run.

Boji's head appeared, under the curtain, in the barely adequate opening Antaro and Jegari had created.

Then more of him eased in under the window. Every-one in the room stayed very still.

"Come, come, come, Boji. *Egg.*" He kept it just out of reach. "Take the egg."

All of Boji came in.

"Now!" Antaro said aloud, and down went the win-dow, smoothly, from both sides.

The window slamming down panicked Boji. He jumped for a chair in the dark and jumped again, one place after another, and lost himself in the recesses of the high ceiling, where no light reached.

"Lock the window," Veijico said quietly. "Get the young gentleman back from it, nadiin."

She had just said it and he had gotten up, about to back away, when a shot went off, *not* near the mecheita pen. North of that, his ears told him. On the grounds outside, but under Great-uncle's and mani's windows.

"Mani!" Cajeiri said. "Nadiin! Mani's rooms!"

"They are safe," Lucasi said. "The grooms are closing the herd into the stables. Taibeni riders are coming in. They will be searching that little wood near the garage and all up and down. They may try that powder again. The riders are aware of it."

Damn, Cajeiri thought. They were all standing in the dark, he still had a stupid egg in his hand, and now his aishid was shifting about, putting protective jackets on, and strapping on their sidearms. He set the egg down on the table nearest, intending to explain to his guests as much as he knew, when of a sudden something dropped like a missile and left again.

And the egg was gone.

"Any word?" Bren asked—he and Jase were in the dark, literally. The two of them had been in late conference in Bren's suite when the alert had come down. Banichi and Jago had grabbed up jackets and pistols and headed out to liaison with Cenedi at the first alarm. Tano and Algini had stayed—armed, in the dark, with the door locked, and talking to someone. Jase had advised Kaplan and Polano, next door, to arm and expect news as it came in.

"We are receiving word," Tano said calmly, "that fire came from one of the house guards. A sensor picked up someone near the stable. The young gentleman, meanwhile, reports the parid'ja came back to the window and they let him in."

Guild reports were not sloppy. The report said *someone,* not *movement,* or *an animal.* Some*one* had been at the stables, and if Cajeiri's pet had had anything to do with what followed—it had probably run for a high spot when some*one* had come close to its hiding-spot.

"We have a problem," he said in ship-speak, for Jase's benefit. "Near the stables. Our problem didn't get out on foot. He might have decided to risk taking the herd-leader. Meanwhile Cajeiri's little pet made it back to his window and they let it in." He was not happy about the youngsters near a window at the moment.

"You think he'd survive to get a saddle on that fellow?" Jase asked, and simultaneously someone knocked on the door. A human voice said, "Captain?"

"Kaplan and Polano," Bren said to Tano, who was nearest the door. "Let them in, nadi."

A quick unlock let Jase's bodyguard into the room from the lighted hall—and both of them arrived in tees and knit pants, Polano with his rifle, Kaplan with a pistol.

The door shut quickly, leaving them back in the dark.

"We're all right," Jase told his guards. "Tano and Algini are with us. The house seems secure but we've had an intruder out by the mecheiti."

"There's nothing we can do at the moment," Bren said. Two ship's security officers trying to assist would only add to the problem—especially with Taibeni riders coming in. "We just sit in the dark and let the Guild figure this one out."

"Cenedi sent Nawari down the hall to see to the children," Algini said. "The young gentleman's aishid reports they opened the window very slightly to retrieve the parid'ja, not having their lights on at that point. They say no one was exposed."

Cenedi was going to have an extensive word to say to the young gentleman's aishid, Bren thought. They were all young. Cajeiri was hard to tell no. Thank God they hadn't had a shot fired through that window.

"The second shot was from a member of Lord Tatiseigi's Guild, who fired from an assigned position to try to stop two fugitives along the back of the house. Lord Tatiseigi's man did not pursue. This was his order—not to leave his post for any reason."

Two fugitives.

Algini was silent a moment. "Taibeni are coming up, part of them through the woods. The western camp has riders out now to sweep the perimeters."

One would not want to be in the fugitives' situation. Tatiseigi's herd was locked in, stout doors and heavy bars assuring that herd was not going to break loose and take after the Taibeni, who were going to be fanning out along the hedges, through the woods, and looking for a scent trail—

Once the mecheiti found it—it was going to be an ugly business out there. The fugitives couldn't run fast enough—no one could. They could try the powder, they could try shooting from ambush, and they might bring riders and mecheiti down—but not all of them, not before the riders would run them down and the mecheiti would take them apart. They'd saddled fast—the Taibeni might or might not have the war-caps on those tusks, but with or without, they were lethal. He didn't want to see the result. But it was a near certainty he would have to. They needed to know whose these men were.

He sat down, feeling his way by the table edge. In the house, everything was quiet.

"Unfortunate," he said. "The Taibeni aren't going to go half-measures. The Taibeni value their animals—and control in a hunting herd is on a thin thread, as it is. If they try that powder trick again—we may not have anyone to question." He heaved a sigh. "I'm *sorry* about this."

"Seems to us your security is handling the problem."

"I'm very glad they are."

"Any bets it's the Kadagidi?"

"We have no few choices." Tano turned the lights back on. "Are we clear, Tano-ji?"

"Not yet," Tano said. "But this floor is clear."

It was late. It had been late before the trouble began. But there was no chance they were going to go to bed until they had answers. And Supani had stood up, standing at the side, but back on duty, the room having guests. "Tea?" Bren asked Jase. "It seems we're going to be a while at this."

"There's a chill," Jase said. "Not sure whether it's the night or the events."

"Tea," Bren said, "all around." Supani nodded and set about it, Koharu moving to help him, while Tano and Algini talked to someone who presumably was in touch with those outside.

"It's not the way the Kadagidi normally go about things," he said to Jase, "up close like this. Usually it's sniping from a distance. Political maneuvering. However, they've been pretty well confined to their own borders this entire year. The people can come and go, but Aseida's been bottled up—not his bodyguard, but Aseida himself. If he's picked this time to make a nuisance of himself to Tatiseigi, it's a bad time."

"Not part two of the grandfather's assassination."

"I don't rule anything out—from either side of that matter. If it's a probe—they already suspect their answer. And finding that out's fairly inevitable. We only figured the Malguri story to last a few days, as is— possibly not past a Kadagidi spy on the road here. There's a reason the Taibeni met us at the train station. They were sweeping the area before we got there, and they've been watching the road between Kadagidi and here. The Kadagidi have their own train station, two of them, one in the township, one closer to the Kadagidi estate. It's not as if they need to be using the road past Tatiseigi's estate. As far as I know—it's not been an issue."

Koharu poured tea for them, as Supani was doing the same for Kaplan and Polano. Bren took a sip.

"The Taibeni have located them, nandiin," Algini said. "The signal is *located but not taken.*"

Damn. A complication?

"What do you think is going on, Gini-ji?"

"One rather suspects," Algini said, "that our problems are up a tree."

They could have the lights on now, Nawari said as he arrived, and kindly turned them on.

Cajeiri was relieved that the alert seemed to be winding

down, and he drew easier breaths with Nawari in the room to look things over. He *trusted* his own aishid, that they could take care of things if they happened, but he by no means wanted things to happen tonight, with gunshots going off. He had heard that sound all too often in his life, and one could not trust being absolutely safe even on the second floor.

And his guests were impressed and seemed reassured, now that the light was on. Nawari walked around with his rifle in hand—Nawari was lean and particularly good-looking and very professional-looking in his glance over things.

"Good you had the lights out," Nawari said.

Antaro said firmly, "The moment the alert came, Nawari-nadi."

Nawari looked at the window latch, took a look outside, moving the filmy curtain with his hand, and looked satisfied.

Then he looked at him. "One understands you recovered the parid'ja, nandi."

Cajeiri took a careful breath: Nawari would *not* chastise him or his aishid in front of his guests, no.

But he could not let his aishid be pulled aside for a reprimand, either. "Nawari-nadi, I ordered it. We heard the mecheiti. And then we heard Boji scratching at the window. We had turned the lights out."

"We put the lights out immediately when we heard a disturbance," Veijico said, which was right. "Records will note we notified security simultaneously."

"Then Boji tapped the window," Cajeiri said. "He makes this sound. My aishid was very careful. They opened the drape from the sides, we had the lights out, and we did not open the window but a crack. I had an egg, and Boji came in on his own."

Nawari looked at Antaro and Jegari.

"The tap is distinctive, nadi," Antaro said, "and we at no time presented a target."

"Bear in mind that the window-glass would not stop an intruder, nadiin. —Our allies have deployed riders from both camps, tracking two targets. Do not look out the windows, even after the all-clear."

"Great-uncle's herd—" Cajeiri said, thinking instantly of Jeichido out there.

"Shut in," Nawari said. "Safe and shut into their stable. Our allies are dealing with the matter. There may be unpleasantness. Your guests, young gentleman, should not be confronted with the view."

He understood, then—he absolutely understood. "Yes, Nawari-nadi," he said.

"You seem to be in good order here. Are you anxious about being by yourselves tonight, young gentleman? There will be guards in the hall all night."

"We are perfectly fine," he was quick to say. "Only no house servant should open our door."

"That word is already out, for all the house." Nawari headed for the door, and Cajeiri cast a fast look about the tops of the curtains and hangings.

"Please," he said as Nawari laid his hand on the latch, "please be very careful with the door, Nawari-nadi. Boji is hiding somewhere in the suite, and one does not wish him loose in Great-uncle's house."

"One will be very careful," Nawari said solemnly, and was exactly that, in leaving them alone in the room.

The Taibeni had the mecheiti hunting the intruders.

At least they were not in Great-uncle's basement.

He *hoped* there were no more of them.

He faced his guests, who had not, he thought, gotten all of that past Nawari's Malguri accent.

And he did not want to tell them all of it, about the mecheiti, or he would never get them back near the stables.

"Everything is good," he said. "All safe." He glanced at his aishid, very sorry that he had gotten them in trouble. "Nadiin-ji, one regrets—"

Antaro gave a little oblique nod, as if to say, yes, there would be a problem, but his aishid would deal with that for him, too.

"We have Boji back," she said.

"Wherever he is," Lucasi said.

But they all sat down to talk it over, late as it was, with his aishid nominally still on duty, still armed, leaning rather than sitting.

And in a little while Boji put his head out from the top of a drape.

"Egg," Cajeiri said, and Lieidi, nearby and with his eye on Boji, calmly reached into his pocket and produced one. "His egg, nandi."

"We are strongly suspecting," Tano said, still listening to the communications flow, and still with no word what the situation was out on the grounds, "that this infiltration was prior to the sensors going up. It would take a very expert sort to get in here now. I know only four who could attempt it and three of them are under this roof."

"The fourth?" Bren asked. Jase was doing a short-hand translation for Kaplan and Polano. Algini was checking Banichi's black box, doing something.

"Far too wise to take off across that meadow with the mecheiti let loose. We believe they were inside, decided to try to get out. At the moment, we are more worried about anyone who may be left inside."

"Somebody our housecleaning missed?" Bren asked.

"Possibly, nandiin-ji. We have kept staff frozen in place for hours for individual interviews. We have begun to release certain staff, one area at a time, as their personal quarters are searched and cleared. Lord Tatiseigi's security is proceeding now with a roll call, all staff to report for individual recognition and clearance, and it has been slow. We are not accepting a supervisor's word without an interview and an examination of identification—we are doing this as delicately as possible, considering we are treading over Atageini prerogatives. We have conducted interviews. We have asked about unlocked doors, pilferage, or unusual behavior, about persons late, or otherwise out of routine. We have had chiefs of staff cross-compare the schedules and duty reports. We are now going over those records ourselves. We have checked the furloughed servants: five groundskeepers who were put on holiday before our visit—three mechanics sent on furlough the day before our arrival. They are registered at the hotel in the township. We have sixteen questionable individuals lodged in a house, under guard, which represents every individual who might know anything about our activity and security arrangements here. We have not had any deliveries, no one coming or going."

"We are not satisfied with the garage," Algini said sharply. "It abuts the area where we had the first alarm. We are rechecking."

"The three mechanics," Tano said, "normally have quarters in the loft above the service area. We started processing that area this afternoon. The vehicles, the loft, the fueling station, the service pit ... the searchers say most access doors are painted shut and undisturbed— they opened the plumbing access, and checked for signs of entry, but found none. The place is evidently a dense clutter of tools, pipe, chain, all sorts of things. Four of Cenedi's men spent two hours going over the place—but we also have had the basements to go through, and the staff checks. The team in charge locked the garage and put a guard on it, then went to check plumbing accesses that branch off from that one."

"We are not satisfied," Algini repeated. "We have been through the basements—we are assured the basements have no access at all except through the door in the main hall, and Lord Tatiseigi confirms that is the case, but we have been surprised before by some detail that dates to the last century. The garage holds two dead vehicles besides the current, besides, we are told, every tool and spare part ever needed on this estate, besides plumbing and electrical parts, hose, chain, and parts for an earthmover not in the garage: there are accesses, plates welded shut, painted shut, accesses built over with shelves—the moment we had the second alarm, we unlocked that door and started another search. Banichi and Jago, with Rusani's men and the original four, are rechecking the place right now. We have cleared the entire house to our reasonable satisfaction. Not the garage.

And we are having to proceed with caution, nandi, in the event of some sort of trap."

He had never seen the garage—there was a drive, a cobbled spur off the wide sweep of the drive at the front door, but it was offset somehow from the frontage, not apparent from the approach, and its east wall, also inset, was screened in shrubbery, vines, and an arbor—which he did think of when he thought about the nearness of the garage to their trouble spot of the afternoon. There was the shrubbery, the arbor—and a very long stone's throw removed from that, the little woods started, with its little path for walks on summer days. That woods was what he had been looking at when they had the first alarm. The garage, behind its camouflage, he did not even recall as a stone wall. The two upper floors rose above what looked like just part of the landscaping. A place out of mind. Never visited. Lord Tatiseigi himself had probably never ventured into it—just stepped into his car at the front door. Get rid of the old tools? They had met Lord Tatiseigi's notions that old was perfectly good, that getting rid of what one had paid good money for was just unthinkable . . . the mechanics had had help in that accumulation.

Maybe, he thought uneasily, they should just call the mechanics back from the township and have *them* go through the place. They probably knew what belonged there, and didn't.

Damn, he didn't like it.

"What's the story?" Jase asked him. "I missed some of that."

"The mechanics' quarters. It's apparently a cluttered mess and it's right near where they had the first alarm. They've searched it once. They're increasingly sure that's where we need to look, and Banichi and Jago are in there now."

Banichi and Jago were good, but Tano and Algini were the demolitions experts. He'd feel better if it were Algini in there doing the bomb search. If it was Kadagidi mischief, even an assassination attempt, it was one thing. But if it was Shadow Guild—

Scratch that thought. What he knew now said that the Kadagidi *were* the Shadow Guild, or as good as, and that group didn't stick at civilian casualties, explosives, wires, damage to historic premises—anything to take their targets by surprise and anything to create fear and panic. They couldn't claim they hadn't hedged Guild regulations themselves: Tano and Algini had taken out two rooms right here in this house, eliminating one of Murini's mainstays.

He hoped to God the Shadow Guild hadn't returned the favor.

What did it take to get a load of explosives into Lord Tatiseigi's estate, between packing off the resident mechanics to the township and the dowager's men doing a massive security installation?

Before their security revision—it could come in as a load of foodstuffs.

He sat and sweated, listening to what he could overhear from Tano and Algini—not wanting to say or do anything to distract anybody, and wishing they would hear from the Taibeni. He *hoped* they had gotten information out of the intruders. He hoped they were in shape to talk, and that, even if they weren't forthcoming with information, they could find out what they were. That alone—

Then again—the routine homecoming for Lord Tatiseigi would have involved the touring car and the truck.

If they had not used the bus, Bren thought with a slight chill, if they had come in at the train station and called to be met by the estate truck and that huge open car, as Tatiseigi always traveled—and if drivers who were not the regular Atageini drivers showed up—

Tatiseigi would have taken alarm at once. But he might not have had time to do more than realize that fact.

God.

He did *not* interfere in a Guild operation. He had sworn it to himself in the Najida affair; and already violated it. His mind kept racing, actually *hoping* that that was the case, and that it did not involve explosives. But he kept his mouth shut. His team had to investigate what bore investigating, and find out, not guess.

Algini took a deep breath, reacting to something he'd heard. Then: "The Taibeni have them, nandiin-ji," Algini said. "Two of them. Guild. The Taibeni are bringing them back."

Have them. Not *killed* them.

"The report is they climbed a tree, and surrendered, though there was a lengthy negotiation," Algini said. A pause. Then: "They have asked to speak to *you*, Bren-ji."

16

So what did one wear to an after-midnight meeting with men who had attempted one's life?

A bulletproof vest was the first choice.

Banichi and Jago were on their way—they had broken off the search and sealed the garage. Ilisidi and Lord Tatiseigi also intended to have a look at these intruders: but as Jase put it, four humans downstairs was probably too many, and he had no desire to be a distraction. He and Kaplan and Polano were headed down to the house security station where he could get a report and translate the situation for his two guards without getting in the way.

Bren changed coats for a better one ... with the weight of his small pistol in the pocket. Tano and Algini waited at the door for him—and now he narrowed his focus to just them. From now on they entered a kind of choreography in which, indeed, it was just him and his guard going down there, to meet up with Banichi and Jago. From here on, it was his aishid in charge: he had to be completely aware of their signals, position himself exactly where they wanted him to be, and believe that he could concentrate on his job only when he *was* where they wanted him.

If anything went wrong down there, or if they weren't liking the situation, he'd pick it up in his peripheral vision—by mind reading, he sometimes thought, awareness of them so keen he could feel their reactions right up his backbone. Right reactions for an atevi world. He settled into that, uncommunicative, as they headed for the stairs—Cenedi had asked the paidhi-aiji's bodyguard to see these prisoners, find out what they had intended, before they let them anywhere near Ilisidi and Tatiseigi, and find out *why* they had asked to see the paidhi-aiji.

But they were not meeting them alone. Cenedi had lent them twenty of his own.

Twenty. And two of them. Intimidation: just as his best coat was meant to put two fugitives, just pulled from a tree, at a disadvantage.

Banichi and Jago were waiting for them, down in the foyer, along with that number of the dowager's guard—so many black uniforms the light in the foyer seemed dimmed and the echoes were dead, overwhelmed in the slight shift of very tall bodies. Bren stepped onto the floor, his aishid moving around him, making space for one pale, shoulder-high human in a towering, black-skinned company. No one spoke. After only a moment of their waiting silence they could hear the sounds of mecheiti in the distance, coming from the north end of the house.

Mecheiti arrived on the drive at a slow pace, walking, with the rhythmic sound of harness and the scrape of blunt claws on the cobbles.

That stopped. There were voices, footsteps ascending. Banichi exchanged a word with someone on com, gave a quiet signal to the men in charge of the doors. The whole foyer whispered with the shift of bodies, the movement of weapons.

One door opened; the other was pinned fast, and the night wind came in, a breath of chill. The porch light showed a number of Taibeni, in their green and brown, the only district where the Assassins' Guild did not go in black. In their midst, came two windblown strangers in Guild black—not restrained, but surely disarmed. They came in, and their eyes made a fast search of the reception—a little surprised, perhaps, at so many weapons.

Then they saw Bren, and Bren saw instant focus—awareness, emotion of some sort. Nerves twitched, his aishid was already on high alert, and he heard one simultaneous rattle of weapons around the foyer.

One of the prisoners dropped to one knee. The other did, like some scene out of a machimi play—and Bren just stood there, jolted into an improbable frame of reference.

"Nand' paidhi," one said to him, showing both hands empty, "do *not* put it out to the Guild that we are still alive. Hear us out."

"Nadiin-ji," Bren said—not to them, but to his own aishid. He had no idea what had and had not gone out to the Guild system.

"We have reported nothing as yet," Algini muttered, at Bren's shoulder, and Bren stood there, aware of his aishid, of the protection around him. And the intent in front of him didn't read as a threat—but as strange an approach as he had ever seen. Nobody *knelt*. Not even to Tabini.

"My name is Momichi," the first man said in a hoarse and thready voice. "My partner is Homuri. The ones who gave us our orders take theirs from a man named Pajeini."

"We know that name," Banichi said, and there was nothing of warmth about it. "Is he still in the Dojisigin Marid?"

"Yes. Probably he is. Nand' paidhi, they have our whole village hostage. If a report goes out, if they learn we failed—and talked—they will kill everyone, without exception. You spoke for the Taisigi. Speak for us. For our village. For Reijisan. The aiji dowager can move Guild on orders Shejidan cannot track. If anyone can help us—she can. If you could persuade her—"

"What *was* your mission?" Jago asked sharply, and with a nod to Bren, but likely no shift of her eyes off the two on their knees: "Forgive me, nandi, but there is a great deal of information missing in this business. They come here by stealth, lie in wait, inconvenience the aiji-dowager, all to ask your help? We believe the paidhi-aiji would like to hear your reasoning!"

"Our target was not the paidhi. Nor the aiji dowager. Lord Tatiseigi was our objective."

"Why?" Bren asked.

"We do not know, nand' paidhi. We can guess . . ."

"Who helped you?" Algini interrupted him, wanting specifics, facts and names. "What *was* your route?"

"From our village by boat," Momichi said, "to Lusini on the Senji coast, to the railhead at Kopurna . . ." He looked at Algini, as if judging if that was the answer Algini wanted. And kept going. "To the station at Brosin Ana . . ."

Brosin Ana was the last stop in the Senjin district. It was the old rail line, a route up from the Marid, through the mountains, and the territory of several small associations, finally joining the new line north and east of the capital. Trains from Senji had carried commerce and contraband for two hundred years.

And that line ended in the Kadagidi township, where Marid commerce had always come in, an old, often problematic association that had not been happy, one suspected, to see Tabini back in power, certainly not happy to see the southern Marid talk about its own rail link.

His doing, that talk about a new line—a realization in two heartbeats of stretched time. That the northern Marid wasn't happy with *him*—he perfectly well understood.

"To the Kadagidi township," Momichi said. "We were met, given specific instructions for our mission, and we walked in."

"Walked in," Algini said. "From the Kadagidi township."

A hesitation. But geography made it obvious. "From the Kadagidi estate, nadi."

"When?"

That was the question, Bren thought. *How?* ran right beside it.

"Five days ago. We were directed simply to get into the garage, substitute ourselves for the garage staff—and wait until Lord Tatiseigi arrived at the train station and called for his car."

"Give us the detail," Algini said. "How were you to accomplish this?"

"It was all laid out. We were to come onto the grounds

by the back gate, keep well to the north hedge until we had passed the stables. We were to find an iron plate under the vines, in the corner near the arbor, and that would get us to the water system—we should work behind the pump housing, and follow the pipe to an access."

"Which access?" Banichi asked. "Where?"

"Beside the hot water tank."

"Go on," Banichi said.

"We were to deal with the staff," Momichi said. "We did *not* want to kill any of the staff. We were prepared to keep the garage crew drugged and confined. But when we got in—there was no one there. So we thought—they are on leave; they will come back when their lord advises them he is coming. We just need to wait. Our information said the garage staff used its own kitchen, rarely mixed with the rest of the staff—that it was very likely no one would come to the garage at all, except the garage staff when they came back. That was the plan. But there was no one there. We never used the lights. We never used the stove. We just waited." Momichi drew breath. "Then two days on, the house began to stir. And grew busy, as if there was something going on. We caught some voices, and we began to realize there was a great deal of construction going on in the house and on the roof. We went out through the trap, onto the garage roof, that night, and we saw a patrol, Taibeni, on mecheiti, on the front grounds; we saw a glow against the hedges, lights moving. We had no idea what to think—whether Taibeni had occupied the Atageini lord's estate, or whether *they* were preparing an ambush— We stayed very quiet. We thought, if they kill Lord Tatiseigi, the garage staff may not come back. But everything had changed. We decided to stay to find out what was going on—but then we began to realize it was more than Taibeni, that there were other Guild about. And nothing made sense. We thought—we might take the car, claim we were on some errand, and drive out the gate— granted the Taibeni would not know the regular staff. But we decided we might still accomplish what we were sent to do; and even if we failed at that—if we could find out what was going on at Tirnamardi, we might be able to trade that information to the rebels.

"Then we realized Lord Tatiseigi had come home without calling for his car—that the aiji-dowager was in the house. That was the point at which we decided we were in something so far beyond our understanding—it could bring the whole north and East down on the Marid. We thought—we even thought of simply calling on the house phone and reporting ourselves. But we thought—the rebels would get the news. So we opened the same access and tried to leave. Going straight forward, we immediately set off an alarm on the premises. We had used up our only defense against the mecheiti—to keep them from finding the access. We decided to make a second try, but we knew we would never make it on foot if another alarm sounded and the mecheiti were let loose. We thought of taking the car—but doubted we could ram the gate. We thought then—if not afoot—then we might use the mecheiti native to the grounds. If we could bridle two of the leaders while they were settled for the night, we could loose the herd, ride for the east gate, and hope the mecheiti would create enough confusion with the Taibeni riders for us to get through the gate. Well, it was a fool-hardy idea." Momichi sighed and shook his head. "We no more than opened the door when some night creature bolted across the rails setting up a racket, the mecheiti all rose up in a panic—and a shot went off. At that point—we ran. We just ran."

Boji, Bren thought. *Boji.* Of all damnable things.

"We expected," Momichi said, "the Atageini would immediately loose the herd on us. We headed for the trees. We made it a distance into the woods, and since we had not had the Atageini herd behind us—we were expecting the Taibeni riders. They cut us off. We climbed for it. We had our rifles. They had theirs. We shouted back and forth a while. We exchanged views—they were upset about the black powder. We granted their point. And we knew the danger should the report about us get out to the south—we told them about that. They said that we could present our case to the aiji-dowager and Lord Tatiseigi, and you, but that they had no sympathy. So we said—if we could talk to you, nandi, we would surrender. And we did."

If there was bad luck to be had, Bren thought, these two had found it at every turn—bad luck their security had arranged, true. But bad luck that had come full about. These two had come back alive.

And, damn, the expressions looked sincere. They were exhausted, they had spent days in a situation progressively going to hell, and their story made sense, step by miserable next step, so that he was almost inclined to believe them. They'd had rifles. They'd had a chance to use them. They *said* they'd come for one target, only one—strictly regulation, give or take the lack of a Filing. They had not harmed anybody on staff. At the end, they hadn't shot it out with the Taibeni or aimed at the mecheiti—which had probably persuaded the Taibeni to stand back and talk them down.

He *hoped* his aishid could figure them out: he looked at Algini, and at Jago, who gave no offender any grace.

"You posed us quite a difficulty," Algini said to the pair in an easier tone. "You are *not* village-level."

"No, nadi." No hesitation in that answer. A little return of spirit.

"Where assigned?"

"We served in Amarja, nadi," Momichi said. "In the citadel."

"In whose man'chi?" Algini asked.

"In the aiji's," came the curt answer. "But not *this* aiji."

This lord of Dojisigi clan, and aiji of a quarter of the Marid at the moment, was a fifteen-year-old spoiled brat of a girl, who had once expected to marry Geigi's nephew. She was twice lucky—first that the nephew had been packed off to the East, and second, that she was alive, and thus far getting her own way, where it regarded personal comforts and the illusion that she was in charge of the district.

But was young Tiajo likely to remain in office another

year? Bets inside and outside the Marid ran counter to that. She was lord only because she was next in line, though under house arrest. She might have been a convenient rallying-point for the remnant of the Shadow Guild, but evidently even *they* had found her more liability than asset.

"Does your partner have a voice?" Banichi asked.

"Nadi," Homuri said. "Yes."

"*Why* were you in your village?"

"We were dismissed from the citadel," Homuri said, "when the Shejidani Guild took over. We were told, all of us, to go separately back to our home districts, our own villages, and maintain order. We went to Reijisan. We both came from there. Our partners went another direction. To Meitja."

"And with your skills, you could not protect this village?"

"Nadi," Homuri said, "we could not. They took our weapons."

"Who took them?"

"The Shejidani Guild. They confiscated all our weapons, all our equipment. When they sent us out, we went afoot, with *nothing*, nadi, from the point the truck dropped us, a day's walk from our village. We had no communications, no weapons, no equipment, not even a canteen or a folding knife."

"In the night," Momichi said, "when the rebels drove this truck into the center of the village—we were called out. They said in the hearing of the whole village that it was full of explosives, and that if we did not come meet with them, they would set it off. So we did. They gave us their proposition, that we undertake an easy, limited mission, one man, and when they had news Lord Tatiseigi was dead—they would leave the village and we would never see them again."

"Did you believe that?" Algini asked.

A hesitation. "No," Momichi said. "But we still have to believe it."

That, Bren thought, had the sound of a man who had actually made that decision.

"Where is your man'chi?" Bren asked them outright.

"To our village, now, nandi," Momichi said.

"And to which Guild?" Algini asked shortly.

That brought silence, a careful consideration, and for the first time, Bren thought, they were going to hedge on the answer.

"Not to the rebels, nadi," Momichi said.

There had to be an attachment, Bren thought. Man'chi had to go somewhere, it always *was* somewhere, or there were dire psychological consequences.

"Where?" Bren asked again, and drew their attention back. "If you want my help—start with the truth."

"We are Amarja Guild. We are *not* these new people. We are *not* these people who take hostages and threaten villages. We are not the Shejidani Guild, dispersing us, confiscating our equipment, and leaving the countryside open to our enemies."

"You followed the *old* rules," Algini said.

"We are Guild, the same as you, nadi. This was a mission we were given—and we would do it honorably. We would observe the mission limits. Honorably. We have no personal grudge against Lord Tatiseigi, but if he died, it would throw everything in the north into chaos, and the Shejidani Guild holding Amarja might even be pulled back. We thought that might be their plan. But if that happened, *we* might come back, too: we had had our assignments, under the old lord—if the rebel northerners set Tiajo free, we might take up guard in the citadel again. But they lied to us about the mission. Or they had no idea what was going on up there. We found ourselves in deeper and deeper trouble, and a situation the meaning of which we did not know, except that it involved the aiji-dowager and the heir and humans—which could bring down the powers in the heavens into it all. So we decided to abort the mission and get out."

"Where were you going?" Tano asked.

"As far as we could. Home, if we could get there. Out of that place, in the open air, if that was all we could get. We had no hope of reaching the aiji-dowager. We feared we were set up to bring war down on the Marid. The

Taibeni ran us down. But when they said the paidhi-aiji was here—nandi, you *spoke* for the Marid. So we agreed to surrender, if we could talk to you. We ask—we ask you go to the aiji-dowager and tell her what is happening in the Marid."

"Go on," Bren said.

"We ask you, nandi, first report our deep apology to Lord Tatiseigi, and to the aiji-dowager, and tell her—tell her in the first place, we did not do this willingly, we know there was no Filing, and we are guilty of that. But, nandi, we need protection. The Shejidani Guild is in Amarja, safe and secure; but those of us out in the villages, nandi, we are down to hunting rifles we borrow from our neighbors, and if a truck full of explosives drives into a village center, even if we *had* our communications units—what chance the Shejidani Guild would come running on *our* word, and what chance the village could escape reprisals? This is doing her associations no good either. We ask you to ask the aiji-dowager to do something—to tell *someone* with associations in the Marid that the Dojisigi countryside is in trouble, and that we and our Guild are helpless to do anything."

Silence followed that.

Bren looked at Algini, at Banichi, at Tano and Jago.

Claims. But no proof—except the presence of a very good Dojisigi unit and detail on a mission they had apparently aborted—with no collateral damage.

Finessed, as the traditional Guild said. An operation carried out within the law—give or take the critical matter of a Filing.

The dowager, intervene? The dowager's action in the Marid had shifted over to diplomatic and legislative efforts, to advance Machigi, *not* the Dojisigi's favorite Marid lord, to take power over the whole Marid. Tabini had agreed to that solution, not because anybody considered Machigi the perfect answer, but because the alternative was another round of assassinations and wars that would let the Shadow Guild rebuild in the south.

Precisely what was starting to happen in the Dojisigin Marid—*with* a Guild force sitting in the Dojisigin capital.

"Cenedi has just heard all this," Banichi said quietly. One was far from surprised Cenedi had been listening in. "He wants to talk to them."

"Nadiin," Bren said to the two, aloud. "Get up. I shall present your case upstairs. *You* will be talking to the dowager's Guild senior. One urges you be very forthcoming with him—including your situation in the Marid. He will hear you. He will inform the dowager. I make no promises. But I shall see she knows."

"Nandi." The Dojisigi got to their feet. They bowed, as deeply as Guild ever bowed, bowed courteously to his aishid, too, and Banichi directed the two into the keeping of Cenedi's men.

Bren set his hand on the banister and started up the stairs. But he stopped on the bottom step, and asked, "Am I a fool, nadiin-ji?"

"They are a high-ranking unit," Banichi said. "The Dojisigi lord was very deeply betrayed by the Shadow Guild; and killed by our forces. A conflicted man'chi? We have no way to know. The order to dismiss the local Guild from the citadel and confiscate equipment makes sense. But the occupying Guild has no force adequate to handle all that territory. We have to ask—does Dojisigi Guild already in outlying districts still have their equipment, or what happened to that? And if they ordered these units out of the capital—knowing the Shadow Guild was still operating out there—why did they not return their equipment? A confused clerk? A misfiled order? Or did that clerk come through Assignments? But *if* that happened, and *if* the situation in Dojisigi is unraveling, there is nothing quiet we can do right now. We are going to question these two in greater depth. And advise the dowager. We can at least do that. What they may or may not know, Bren-ji—*she* has accesses as well as associations in the Marid. Whether she will use them—she will decide that."

A signal had passed. Cenedi was just exiting the door of the sitting room where the dowager and Lord Tatiseigi waited, and Banichi and Algini left with him—not the usual partnering. Bren went inside with Jago and Tano, past two of the dowager's young men and two of Tatiseigi's at the doors.

The presence he hadn't expected was Jase—who had arrived in the sitting room solo, and sat there, sipping tea and, atevi-fashion, *not* discussing the business at hand.

Bren walked in quietly, gave a little bow to the dowager, and to Tatiseigi.

"Well, nand' paidhi?" the dowager asked, setting aside her teacup.

"Their names are Momichi and Homuri," he said. "They are Dojisigi, of the village of Reijisan."

"Dojisigi!" Tatiseigi said.

"They asked me, aiji-ma, nandiin, to speak for them, I promised, and I shall—but they are still being questioned downstairs, and everything is still in flux. They say they served the former aiji in Amarja, in the citadel. When the northern Guild took over—all the citadel guards were disarmed, then sent out to maintain order in their own villages and districts. This is their report."

"Disarmed and then given duty," Ilisidi said.

"That is their report, aiji-ma. The order to go to their native villages split them from their partners. And one night the Shadow Guild drove a truck with an explosive device into the center of the village, threatening to kill everyone in the village if these two would not undertake a mission—against you, nand' Tatiseigi. They had no orders regarding the aiji-dowager."

"What is this world coming to?" Tatiseigi asked. "To destroy a village!"

"These two men say they undertook the mission, understanding it was limited. They went by the old train, from Senji to Kadagidi township, and from that house received specific plans to get into Tirnamardi, to take up position in the garage, and substitute for your drivers when you arrived home. They succeeded in reaching the garage, your staff being furloughed. Thus far everything was going smoothly. But then the Taibeni appeared, and Malguri Guild, setting up alarm systems—though they had no idea what was going on outside, only that more clans were involved than the Atageini, and they began to think things were not as they were told. When you suddenly appeared in the house with the aiji-dowager and the rest of us, they realized their entire plan had gone astray. They maintain they are traditional Guild, that they emphatically are not Shadow Guild. They apologize to you, nand' dowager, and to you, nandi. They believe they were lied to, that the objective was to bring war down on the Marid, and they wanted only to abort the mission and get out. They tried and met an alarm. They tried again, this time with the notion of using the mecheiti, and that failed. They finally surrendered to the Taibeni, with no shot fired. They ask their capture be kept secret, for fear the Shadow Guild will carry out their threat. Second, that you, aiji-ma, use your resources, and your associations in the Marid, to stop the Shadow Guild. They ask you help their village."

"The destruction of a village," Ilisidi said, flexing her fingers on her cane, "and by such a means—would create fear, in a district where northerners are deeply distrusted. The Dojisigi are ruled by a fool, occupied by northern Guild, and then the local Guild was stripped of weapons before being sent to the countryside. Is that the story, nand' paidhi?"

"One expects Cenedi-nadi will extract more information, aiji-ma, but yes. That is as I understand it."

"Unfortunately we cannot phone the Guild in Amarja and *ask* them the truth of the situation. *Stupidity* in that guild does not survive training. This has the appearance of enemy action. Let us wait, then, and hear what Cenedi recommends to us. May we hope for your forbearance in this situation, Tati-ji, if they are proven to tell the truth?"

"Aiji-ma," Tatiseigi said, and gave a nod. "At your asking, without question. One is absolutely appalled."

"Well, well, we shall know nothing until Cenedi has a report for us, with more detail." She flexed her shoulders. "We are tempted to go back to bed at this point, and let Cenedi sort this out."

Of all decisions, one had hardly expected that one.

But the dowager was *not* dismissing the matter. She had the salient parts of the Dojisigi statement. What Cenedi, Banichi, and Algini together could sift out of close questions to those two was going to be names, knowledge, contacts, and the fine details that might prove or disprove the situation as they gave it. *Cenedi* had kept his finger on the situation in the south. The dowager had direct contacts down there through the Marid trade mission. Lord Machigi of the Taisigin Marid knew the northern Marid; and the dowager had direct links into the Guild units that protected Machigi. It was not impossible she had links into units in Dojisigi and Senji, and every *other* district of the Marid.

Sources. Indeed the dowager had them.

"We are well after midnight," Tatiseigi said, "and with those two in hand, we have reason to expect the rest of the night to be quiet."

"Brandy," the dowager said decisively, and Tatiseigi asked for his servants.

"I advise," Bren said to Jase privately, at Bren's door, upstairs, and with Tano and Jago right by them, "that you and your staff go to bed and sleep hard. I'll wake you if there's reason. That's a definite *sleep hard.*"

It was ship-speak. It meant—don't depend on a long sleep. He hadn't had a chance to explain the details. Jase hadn't had time to tell him what he'd heard between the dowager and Cenedi or the dowager and Tatiseigi, in the sitting room.

But Cenedi had been tapped into the com flow, hearing everything they had heard from the Dojisigi downstairs. It was more than possible that Jase already knew a good deal of it, and knew why the urging to get to bed now.

"Just wake me if you need me," Jase said, and headed for his suite.

Bren watched him open the door and go into his suite, then went into his own with Jago and Tano. Supani and Koharu were waiting inside, and he immediately began to shed the coat and the vest into his valets' hands. "Is there any outcome?" he asked Jago and Tano.

"Not yet," Jago said.

"We are operating mostly dark," Tano added, "to give the impression we are continuing a search on the grounds. Patrols are still out."

"Then I *am* going to get what sleep is convenient. Do as you need to, nadiin-ji."

"Yes," Jago said, which was all-inclusive. She was listening to something, watching that language of blips and beeps and flashes on the locator that told her where her partner was and whether things were going smoothly.

He took himself straight to bed. Tano, Jago, and his valets continued in the sitting room.

The dowager's reaction hadn't been disinterested. He knew that look, that half-lidded consideration of a matter. Banichi had said there was nothing they could do in the south without touching off the whole business in the north—but—God. He wished there were an alternative.

The Shadow Guild plot against a leading conservative was useful—when the dust settled and they had to prove the case to any doubters.

That the Kadagidi had provided local transport, aid, and comfort to the Dojisigi—and likely detailed house plans and even the deterrent powder and the specific route to take into Tirnamardi—right down to that concealed access—*that* was something. The Kadagidi had gotten caught before, but they were slippery, always able to claim some provocation.

Actions against Tirnamardi out of the blue, however, when there had been *no* active exchange of hostilities since Tabini retook the capital, and while the Kadagidi were already under a ban that barred them from court *and* any *legal* access to the Guilds' functions—that was going to be hard to deny. The Transportation Guild was forbidden to convey them. The Messengers' Guild could not allow them phone service: they were allowed only messages to and from Tabini's office. The Treasurers' Guild had frozen their assets, only allowing routine expenses.

Yet they had been the receiving end for two Assassins dispatched by a Shadow Guild operation out of a Dojisigi village, to Senji and then, via the old freight line to, likely, a waiting car in the Kadagidi township—

How would a residence and a lord under a Messengers' Guild ban even *get* a phone call from two Dojisigi bent on mayhem over in Atageini territory?

Damned certain Lord Tatiseigi should go to great lengths to preserve these two men's account. They had never gotten the Kadagidi so dead to rights . . . with no Filing and, this time, Guild who had been coerced, and a Shadow Guild communications network operating between the Kadagidi and their old associates in the Marid.

Banichi had said it—there was nothing they could do from here that did not risk breaking the entire problem wide open, north *and* south.

But it could be coming. *They* were all in position, like that move in chess, lord-to-fortress.

He stuffed his pillow under his head and deliberately thought not about the Dojisigi village or the Kadagidi over the hill, but about the Najida estate repair budget, complicated enough and dull enough to blunt any imagination.

That worked . . .

. . . too well. He came awake with the feeling he had slept much too long, and that someone had either come in or gone out. He rolled out of bed, located his robe and the light switch, and went out into the suite's little sitting room to find it still dark outside the window. Banichi and Jago were sharing tea and a plate of sweet rolls.

"What time is it, nadiin-ji?" he asked in some chagrin.

"Just before dawn," Jago said. "Things are relatively quiet. The aiji-dowager is awake, and Lord Tatiseigi is waking."

"The Dojisigi?" he asked.

"The Dojisigi have provided very interesting information, Bren-ji," Banichi said, and added with a quirk of the brow: "The dowager sent units to look at Reijisan. They reported two hours ago."

He had been about to propose he should go dress. "What did they find?"

"Two units we have wanted to find," Banichi said, "one of which is no longer at issue. Our Dojisigi immediately named a name. Pajeini, Chief of the Shadow Guild in the Marid—*personally* involved in the threat to them, and, they suspect, similar dealings with the other half of this aishid. He is not yet in our hands, but the second-in-command is. The dowager dispatched units very close to Reijisan, found things as described, and they took out the senior unit with very little fuss."

Bren sank into the third chair. "Is the village safe?"

"There were explosives. They are removed. We have not heard all the details," Banichi said. "This is Cenedi's network, prearranged signals to several teams in Dojisigi, prearranged responses, by a physical means Cenedi does not discuss even with us. Cenedi has directed the other half of that unit be located. We want to know where *they* are. Our pair tells us the freedom they were given on this mission was very worrisome to them, since they *could* have gotten off that train at any point, and they *could* have walked up to Lord Tatiseigi's staff and reported themselves and their situation—but they so strongly believed failure would kill their relatives in Reijisan, they did not take the risk. That has been the character of the Shadow Guild from the start—to instill the belief they know everything, that reprisals inevitably come of crossing them, that they are threaded throughout the Shejidani Guild, and that they *will* target civilians. Our two believe it can happen, even yet, and we cannot assure them otherwise until *we* are absolutely sure, ourselves."

"So they essentially told the truth," Bren said.

"They were, they say, one of three teams protecting the former lord. And Pajeini knows them—*wanted* them, and, they think, the intent was to create a crisis in the north to draw forces from the south. We do not *want* to undertake operations with the young gentleman's guests present, but—" Banichi said, "we know where Pajeini is, we have a good idea where Haikuti is, and we know where Shishogi is, a rare thing, in itself. The dowager is inclined to move."

It was what he had feared, last night. It was everything he had sworn to Tabini would not happen—risk to Cajeiri, a potential for their young guests to be involved in a Guild action. Not to mention the risk to Ilisidi herself.

But *that* would exist, no matter what. Ilisidi was not going to fortify herself in Malguri and wait for an outcome. Far less did he believe she would go up to the space station . . . possibly that she would not want to send Cajeiri there—for political reasons. The heir of the aishidi'tat had been absent from one crisis. Even at his age—there was a problem in having him in human keeping during a second one. He saw that. But—

Damn.

"We have perhaps an hour before we get any other call," Jago said. "Perhaps less. Will you share breakfast, Bren-ji?"

"Where are Tano and Algini this morning, nadiin-ji?"

"They are catching a little more sleep. They should be with us very soon now."

"A cup of tea. Part of a roll, perhaps."

Jago got up, got a cup and poured for him. The hot liquid helped the external chill. But not the one inside. His bare feet were freezing.

"There are actions under way," Banichi said. "We have sent a warning to the commander in Amarja. We cannot be specific about it in this circumstance, but the dowager's forces at Reijisan have now gotten their own sources of information on the Shadow Guild's operation, and they will inform command. The matter of sending out locals unequipped—that requires a more delicate inquiry than we can make directly at this point—but the one to blame is likely one individual whose principle threat is in records, not weapons. We are not sending out couriers, badly as we need to pass word. We are not, at the moment, making any stir on the road or near the train station. The Kadagidi, meanwhile, have landed in a very uncomfortable position. One of the great advantages of Filing Intent, beyond, of course, operating within the law—is that the target is limited, everyone is advised, and there is *far* less chance of the sort of mistake the Kadagidi have made. Their intelligence does not seem to have penetrated Tatiseigi's security, and consequently they have launched their operation in the presence of the aiji-dowager, the heir, and foreign guests. Is the aiji-dowager to let an Unfiled move in her vicinity pass without comment? No. Their illegal action has run head-on into the dowager's intentions, while they are already under a ban. And that, one thinks, is exactly what the dowager is assessing. She could challenge them in court over this, and Tabini-aiji could remove Aseida from the lordship. But that would take time. The Shadow Guild connections would quietly rearrange themselves and we would still have them operating, not much inconvenienced: Haikuti would survive. Aseida might not."

"She should go after them," Jago said in a low voice. "We *have* the route the Dojisigi were to use. There is a hole in the hedge, Bren-ji, carefully concealed, and a door to the Kadagidi kitchens arranged to stay open. A trap, very possibly, but there are also reasons the Kadagidi would like to have a report from this pair. There is even a reason Haikuti would want to talk to them and that Pajeini would want these two back in the south. They *would* be an asset not lightly to be thrown away. And by then—they would be outlawed in the north, perfectly suited to take Pajeini's other orders, possibly against Lord Machigi."

"Are we ready for an operation? Did you get *any* sleep last night, nadiin-ji?"

"By turns," Banichi said, and shrugged. "Do not worry about *us,* Bren-ji. We manage. Unfortunately, Cenedi chooses the teams to go. For *this* one—he will not risk us."

"Do we *know* yet who on *their* side is directing operations?"

"To a certain extent," Banichi said, "this far up the chain of command, it may make less difference. Assignments makes the strategic decisions, but he is very old and has never taken the field. Haikuti is the tactician.

They both give orders. Shishogi believes he is firmly in charge. Haikuti is disposed to believe he has the authority if he chooses to use it, and that Shishogi will be forced to take care of the details. That is my own interpretation. Haikuti is the reckless one, the engine that drives things. If there is another coup in the making, at present, it will come from him."

Something had changed. Something more had gotten into the equation last night. Banichi spoke as if he had some window into Assignments that he had not had a few days ago. And he looked unhappy with the situation.

"This is a chancy business," he said. "To go into that house—"

"If the Kadagidi are paying any attention," Banichi said, "and it is certain they are—they will have noted the furor last night. They may wonder was it the execution of the mission—or did it go astray? And if their spies have already gotten close enough to get a distant view of children out on the grounds, though we have tried to prevent that—they may now know it is not Tatiseigi alone in residence, and any question of *where* the dowager has taken the young gentleman and his guests is answered. The Dojisigi did not communicate with the Kadagidi once they were here and realized they had a problem with the mission. We have the means to be sure of that. But the news of what has happened this morning in the Dojisigin Marid will travel. Once it reaches Assignments, and the Kadagidi, one is relatively confident the Kadagidi—and possibly Assignments as well—will start taking protective measures. Assassinations, attacks from the field, political accusations—any means by which they might throw us off balance and destabilize the aishidi'tat. One does not like to think of explosives targeting villages anywhere, north or south, but such things may be used in the north, just as easily, attacks aimed at our allies. These people are outnumbered. The majority of the south is now against them. If the light shines on them too directly—*fear* is the only weapon they have that we do not. The dowager's view is that we have, in these few hours, a very narrow window in which to act or decline acting—and we concur. *We* should take action, in this venture into Kadagidi territory, but Cenedi will not permit it. The dowager will send Nawari, and two of her high-level units."

Into a likely trap. If it were his own aishid going—he would be beside himself. That it was Nawari, genial, competent Nawari, closest to Cenedi himself—Cenedi was likely no less worried, but he had sent his best. His closest associate, the closest thing to going in, himself—with high, high risk in the operation.

"There is," Bren said, "another way into the Kadagidi house."

They looked at him, both. And he recalled he had sworn to himself *not* to interfere with his bodyguard.

"You are *not* to contemplate it," Jago said. "No, Bren-ji."

"If access and Lord Aseida's attention is what you want, nadiin-ji, *I* can get it. We have the bus. We do not need to walk *into* that house, but I certainly can call on their lord. Socially. Noisily. Lord Tatiseigi has a grievous complaint against Lord Aseida, the dowager has one, Jase has one, and I am perfectly willing to deliver it in person. If we can pose a distraction while, say, Nawari and his men take a careful look at the other access . . ."

Banichi said, "The risk would still be extraordinary."

"The bus has armor."

"In some areas," Jago said.

"There is also Jase's bodyguard. He is the other paidhi. *Another* offended guest with his own complaint against Lord Aseida, and his bodyguard is formidable— and proof against our bullets. Kaplan and Polano cannot sit down in that armor, not in the bus seats. They have to stand where they stood on the way in. If the Kadagidi take alarm at that, and take a shot at the bus, even their armor-piercing rounds are not going to get through that armor. And *after* that—after an attack on us, we have the right to use any force we please. So, for that matter, does Jase, his ship, and Lord Geigi."

There was a moment of silence.

"There are rather heavier weapons in their hands

than armor-piercing rounds, Bren-ji," Jago said. "And we may well meet them."

"Is that more danger to us than a Shadow Guild campaign, violating every rule—while *we* have to obey the law? I am not happy with the notion of explosives being brought to villages, and I am not willing to see people of the dowager's man'chi and mine take every precaution to observe a law these people freely disregard in their attacks. The Kadagidi have a history of raising claims about *their* rights. But we have them on failure to File, we have them in the two Dojisigi, who can give the lie to any claim of innocence Kadagidi clan wants to make. If they fire first, with them already under a ban, Tabini-aiji has justification to remove Aseida as lord, with any force it takes. The Shadow Guild has been constantly shifting targets, in this region and that, striking and departing, doing damage as they please. But Kadagidi is a fixed asset. We have them pinned down. And I do not intend to see *any* of our people observing Guild rules while the other side breaks them. We have the dowager to protect, and these foreign guests to protect. Jase-aiji has every right to use the defenses *he* has, and those run all the way to the station."

There was a moment of silence, two guarded, worried looks. Then Banichi said: "And what will you answer if they accept a conference and Lord Aseida invites you and Jase inside?"

"I should then ask my aishid what I should answer, and I doubt you would advise that, in a household under the aiji's ban."

"They may simply bar the door," Jago said.

"Frightening them is surely worth something. And meanwhile we have them pinned down, we can interdict anyone who comes *out* of that house, and Lord Geigi *can* drop something on their land, with a great deal of precision."

"Bren-ji," Banichi said, "your resolution never to advise your bodyguard is in serious breach."

"Then advise me. I shall certainly hear advice. But I cannot lose you. And the dowager cannot lose Nawari.

You—and Cenedi's team—*you* have more importance than I do, when it comes to a fight inside the Guild. You know the names and histories of these people. You have accesses nobody else does. You are *not* expendable and I am, comparatively, in this part of the fight. If it requires a readjustment in your man'chi—make it. We cannot risk you, and I do not countenance Cenedi risking Nawari, either. He is *doing* this because he needs you, and he is staying meticulously within the law—but I do not agree he should. We should go in there prepared to deal damage, and Jase and I should make the approach, because our status gives *you* the right to take them on without a Filing on our side, if they compound their offense with one bullet headed our direction. If there is any legal question—any political question that follows this—then that is *my* expertise, nadiin-ji, and I will defend this decision. I would look forward to dealing with *any* counterclaim this old man in the Guild or his allies can make."

There was a long silence. "We shall have to talk to Cenedi," Banichi said, "and advise Tano and Algini. Not to mention the dowager herself. Speed in this is advisable. We do not know *when* news from the south may reach Guild Headquarters. —Jago."

"Yes," Jago said, got up, and headed for the door.

Banichi also left. *They* had things to arrange. Cenedi to consult.

He, meanwhile, had to talk to Jase—urgently.

"We have a problem," was how he started the explanation, while Jase, roused from sleep, sat amid his bedclothes. Kaplan and Polano had opened the door, and stood in the little sitting-room, in their shorts.

He explained it. Jase raked a hand through his hair; then said: "We're in. Can we get a pot of that strong tea in here?"

"Deal," he said. "I've got a spare vest. Choice of colors, brown or green, and bulletproof. I'll send it with the tea."

"I'm not particular." Jase raised his voice. "Kaplan. Polano. Full kit, hear it?"

"Aye, captain," the answer came back, and Bren headed back through the sitting room, to get back next door and send Supani and Koharu in with the requisite items. Tea for three. One vest, proof against most bullets. He and Jase were about the same size.

The dowager could still countermand the operation, but while he was dispatching Supani and Koharu, Tano and Algini came in to gather up needed gear, and it was clear that that wasn't happening.

"The aiji-dowager," Algini said, "has sent for the bus."

"We do not know the capabilities of Jase-aiji's guard," Tano added. "We understand they are considerable."

"They are," he said. He put on the green vest: he had sent the brown brocade over to Jase. He had on a reasonably good shirt, his good beige coat, and Koharu handed him his pistol and two spare clips. He tucked those into his coat pockets.

Banichi came back. "The bus is well on its way. The dowager has waked Lord Tatiseigi, who is not yet coherent, and she has instructed Cenedi to tell me to tell you to stay behind your bodyguard."

"One earnestly promises it," he said. It somewhat troubled him that Banichi seemed cheerful—in a dark and businesslike way. Banichi and Jago both had looked worn and tired less than an hour ago, when they had explained to him that they had been outranked on the mission. Now they were full speed ahead—and he had to ask himself whether he had put temptation in their path.

But he was *right,* damn it all. Putting Nawari in there to try to draw a response was the best of a bad job. Nawari was a perfectly legitimate target. They *could* not risk the dowager going over there—though she wasn't a legitimate target. And Cenedi was going by the book, against a Guild problem that wouldn't.

He was far from as cheerful as his aishid in the prospect—it wasn't in his makeup. But he'd been through hell down in the Marid, and he *wasn't* Guild, with a traditional bent. He'd begun his career with a far simpler book, a dictionary of permitted words—and he'd watched that dictionary explode into full contact, up on the station.

He'd watched it work. There. Down here ... he'd watched the world change, and he understood atevi for whom it had changed too fast. His job—his *job,* as Mospheira had originally defined it—was to keep the peace and recommend the rate at which star-faring technology would be safe in atevi hands.

In that sense, he'd failed miserably. But *events* had proceeded too fast, there'd been no time to temper the impact, and now ...

A descent into the dark ages that had preceded the organization of the aishidi'tat would put a *hell* of a lot of inappropriate technology into inappropriate use. Hell if he was going to watch that happen.

And the instant he'd seen Jase, with a captain's personal defenses, descending from the shuttle with the children—he'd had a little chill thought that Lord Geigi had sent him. Lord Geigi had gotten that briefing on his way to orbit. Geigi knew the situation inside the Guild. Knew exactly *how* it had to be stopped.

Geigi might have recommended the children come ahead. And he might have given the facts of the situation to the other captains, who were hell-bent on seeing the children's mission work out, not in some ideal situation, but involved in the world as it was.

Jase had come down with just his bodyguard. The ship-paidhi.

With his bodyguard. From the starship.

Geigi, he suspected, had sat back at his desk, scarily satisfied.

17

The bus trundled onto the drive at the very edge of dawn, a slight blush to the sky above the hedges. It had a secret, sinister look, its red and black both muted by the dim light, except where the front door light cast its own artificial brilliance.

Black, too, the uniforms of the Guild who quietly boarded, stowing some pieces of heavier armament Bren hoped did not come into play. The rest, and the electronics, were hand-carried briskly toward the rear. It was war they were preparing.

Bren waited at the foot of the steps. His aishid was in conference with Cenedi and Nawari, beside the open door of the bus. Jase was on his way.

So was Jase's bodyguard—in armor that trod heavily on the stone steps as they came out of the house, servo-motors humming and whining constantly. Jase came down the steps of Tirnamardi, and Kaplan and Polano followed, weapons attached to their shoulders, not swinging free, but held there, part of the armor itself. They were taller, wider than human—taller and wider, even, than most atevi, and gleaming, unnatural white. They carried their helmets, and their human faces looked strangely small for the rest of them.

"That should make an impression," Bren said, as Jase joined him—Jase in his own blue uniform, with, one surmised, that borrowed vest beneath it.

"Projectiles will ricochet off the armor," Jase said. "Your people need to know that."

Jase had a com device on his ear, and behind it.

"I'll remind them," Bren said. "Is that two-way communications?"

"With my own, not with yours," Jase said, as they went toward the bus. Bren stopped to relay the information to Banichi, then climbed up the bus steps and went to his usual seat.

"Sit with me," Bren said to Jase. Banichi and Jago were coming aboard, and took seats across the aisle. Tano and Algini went further back in the bus, where the dowager's men had gathered in the aisle by the galley.

Last of all, Kaplan and Polano came aboard, rocking the bus somewhat and occupying the space between the driver and the door—an armored wall.

One of the dowager's young men held the driver's seat. He shut the door and put the bus gently into motion on the curving drive.

Dawn was coming fast. There was almost color in the stone of the house as it passed, in the straggle of woods that ran down the side of the house.

The situation, with Kaplan and Polano blocking out the view in front, and the hedge scrolling leisurely past the side windows, assumed a surreal feeling—a journey like others this bus had made in its brief service; but different. Far more desperate. Before, they had gone in with some hope of negotiation. Now, admittedly, they were not going in any hope of it.

It was a northern house they meant to visit—and all the accumulation of antiquities, associational ties, and politics that went with it—and this one, troublesome as it had been, was one of the core clans of the aishidi'tat. Political fallout was inevitable.

He had indirectly consulted with Ilisidi and Tatiseigi. But those two still had deniability. Tabini's hands were nowhere near the situation. Ilisidi and Tatiseigi were having breakfast. Geigi was in the heavens. Had they met with the paidhiin to spark this retaliation? Absolutely not.

In the list of things one had planned to do to manage a boy's birthday in some degree of peace and security— deliberately staging an incident between the two oldest houses in the Padi Valley had not remotely been on the horizon.

But here they were.

And if *he* had been in this kind of situation before, on this bus, and knew its resources—Jase hadn't, and didn't.

"Snipers are at issue," he said to Jase. "Keep your head down if—and when—shots start flying. We have armoring below the windows: the front windows are bulletproof. The tires will hold up against most things. The roof is reinforced. If you have to duck, get as low as you can below the windows and don't put your head up."

The kids were, one hoped, sleeping off their late night . . .

As the bus gathered speed toward the gates that would let them out to the road.

There had been the most amazing sight in the hall: Kaplan-nadi and Polano-nadi in their armor, heading toward the stairs, making that weird racket as they walked. The thumping tread had waked Boji and Boji had waked all of them, and Antaro had looked out the door and told them what it was. So Cajeiri and Gene had gotten there just in time to see Jase-aiji's bodyguards go down from the landing and out of sight.

"Stuff is still going on," Gene had told Artur and Irene, who had arrived too late to see anything. "The captain's guard is out in armor and everything."

"What *is* going on?" Cajeiri asked his aishid, who were all up and dressed. Boji was rattling his cage and setting up a fuss, shrieking and protesting.

Antaro had gone out to find out from the guards in the hall what had gone on, and why Jase-aiji's guards were in armor.

"They caught the intruders last night, nandi," Antaro came back to report, after far too long. "We were told the emergency was over—that we should all go to bed. They maintain the emergency is still over. They have no idea why the ship-folk are in armor."

"Everyone," he said. "Clothes. Taro-ji, call and find out what is going on."

"We cannot, nandi," Lucasi said. "We are getting a short-range red. That means no communication at all. Shall I go downstairs to find out?"

"Go," Cajeiri said. Eisi was up and dressed. Lieidi was nowhere in sight yet. "We need our clothes, Eisi-ji," he said. "Quickly. Never mind baths. We may have to go down to breakfast to learn anything. Luca-ji, find out, while you are down there, if there *is* formal breakfast."

The bus was not proceeding at any breakneck speed—far from it. And there was no space in the aisle at the rear—the dowager's young men had sat down on the floor back there, rifles and gear with them, ready, and out of view of any observers.

"Nawari's units have already moved," Banichi leaned close to say. "We are pacing them on a timetable. That is why we are not up to speed."

"Yes," he said, acknowledging that, and relayed it in ship-speak to be sure Jase understood. "Nawari's group is afoot. We are keeping pace with their movement. We'll get there just before them—we know this distance, absolutely. Now we just go over and wish the Kadagidi good morning and see how mannerly they are. Unfortunately—I don't think we'll get a good answer."

He watched the countryside roll past the windows. They'd made the turn onto the main local market road, such as it was, a long low track in a land of scrub and weeds. The road, parallel to the railroad tracks, connected the Kadagidi and the Atageini, and the desolate, unmown condition of the road said worlds about relations between the two clans. The only legitimate traffic between Kadagidi and Atageini territory all year had likely been railway maintenance vehicles.

Before that—before that, for two years, as Murini ruled the aishidi'tat, likely there had been very frequent patrols down this route, Kadagidi keeping an eye on the Atageini, in Murini's name.

Change of fortunes, decidedly.

*   *   *

Breakfast was downstairs, and they were told to come down at their leisure. Great-grandmother and Great-uncle were already in the little dining room—Cajeiri knew that immediately by Casimi, one of mani's secondary guards, being outside the door, along with Great-uncle's senior bodyguard. And there was no room for four more in that room.

Casimi, however had seen them, and signaled them, so Cajeiri came and brought his little group—his guests, and his bodyguard—with him.

"One expected you might sleep late, young gentleman," Casimi said.

"Jase-aiji's guards were in the hall in armor. And where is nand' Bren, nadi?" Nand' Bren's guard was nowhere in evidence in the hall, nor was Jase's, and things seemed more and more out of the routine.

"Jase-aiji and nand' Bren have gone to call on Lord Tatiseigi's neighbors," Casimi said.

"Kadagidi!"

"Exactly so, young gentleman. One requests you please do not alarm your guests. Your breakfasts this morning will be in the formal dining room. One is also requested to inform you that Lord Tatiseigi has planned a tour through his collections this morning after breakfast, at your convenience."

Please do not alarm your guests.

And nand' Bren and Jase-aiji had gone over to talk to the Kadagidi, after what had happened last night. That was about the most dangerous thing he could think of.

"What *happened* last night, nadi? We know about the intruders. We understand you caught them. Were they Kadagidi?"

"Dojisigi, nandi, but they had come here with the help of the Kadagidi."

"Assassins' Guild?" He was already sure of it. "After Great-grandmother?"

"Their target was your great-uncle, young gentleman. They claim to have had no idea your great-uncle would arrive with guests. They have apologized and stated they wish to change sides. So do not trouble yourself about that business, young gentleman: they are under this roof, but under watch. Be sure they are under watch. One understands you were able to recover the parid'ja last night."

"Yes, nadi. He came back to the window when all that happened. But—"

"Kindly be very careful to observe house security today. We are strong enough to repel any problem— granted our young guests stay inside and with you. For your Great-grandmother's sake—please be sure of their whereabouts at all times today."

Casimi and his partners were such sticks.

"Yes, nadi," Cajeiri said with a polite nod.

"Hear me, young gentleman: should you lose track of anyone, do not try to find the missing persons. Notify us and let us deal with the matter. We had two Marid Assassins living in the house garage when we arrived, and while we do not believe there are any other surprises in the house—consider any untoward occurrence a matter for us to know, immediately. Please assure me you understand this."

In the *garage*. They had imagined intruders living in the basement . . . where Great-uncle was proposing to send them today, to tour the collections.

Casimi was a stick, and Casimi probably had never forgiven him for the tricks he had played on him, getting away right past Casimi's nose: Casimi probably thought he was a thorough brat, too; maybe even that he could be a fool.

Which was unfair. He had been *months* younger.

"Please do not share much of this with your guests, young gentleman. They should have a happy visit. And touring the collections will put you in a very safe part of the house today."

"One thought we were worried about Assassins in the basement, nadi."

"The basement has been searched very thoroughly, young gentleman. So has every room and closet in the house."

What about the garage? he wanted to ask pointedly—

but it being Casimi, who already had a bad opinion of him, he decided just to do as he was told.

"The formal dining room," he said. "Thank you, nadi, nadiin."

So there was nothing for it but to do as Casimi told them to do. He gave a second little bow, said, "Please tell my great-grandmother and uncle that we are very glad they are safe, nadi," and to his guests:

"Breakfast is in the big room. We can say more there."

Not that long a drive—and they were still in no great hurry about it—it was a leisurely cruise down the road. The sun was up, now, gilding the tops of dry weeds and the branches of leafing scrub. On any ordinary day, at this hour, he'd be having toast and tea and going over his mail. Right now his heart kept its own time, dreading the encounter and wishing they'd get there faster.

The bus nosed gently downward, the slope of the other side of the hill, and ran at just a little greater speed, breaking down weeds and small brush.

"Polano says there's a structure on a hill, on the horizon," Jase said quietly. Jase's bodyguards had an unobstructed view out the windshield. They didn't.

"That would be," Bren said, "the Kadagidi manor house. Asien'dalun."

He wished he could see the place. He urgently wished he could see what was going on, or whether there was any sign of trouble. But not seeing ahead of them was part of their protection—and he wasn't about to get up and take a look.

Once they reached the estate, Guild protocols *should* swing into operation, but there was no guarantee they wouldn't be met by mortar fire.

Lord Aseida, at this hour, would be having breakfast, or answering his mail, and the lord might continue at that, while his security asked, officially, using Guild short-range communications, who was arriving. When they did arrive, the house would open the door and the major d' would come out, with his assistant, wanting to know officially and formally, for the civilian staff, who was arriving ... this was a matter of form, the form having been devised long before radio.

The major d' would ask, they would answer, restating their business.

Considering the circumstances, they would likely be asked to leave—a formal request.

They weren't going to. That message would be conveyed to Lord Aseida, who would, at that point, have two choices: send his major d' out to talk to the offended neighbors, in which case things would proceed eventually to a civilized talk between neighbors—or—Lord Aseida would send out his bodyguard to talk to the neighbors' bodyguards.

The temperature would go up at that point.

But they had no contact yet. In point of fact, he expected none. And the bus would keep rolling as they skipped steps in the protocols ... and as Nawari and his team did their best not to trip any alarms or traps, from the hole in the hedge to the side door of the house itself—necessarily a careful business; and if they did have to stop for a problem—that complicated things, considerably.

Haikuti, *if* he was on the premises, and if he was admitting to *being* on the premises, would warn the bus to stop and to go back—while he'd be positioning defenses. Or possibly he'd let the bus come in, and position *offenses*. Whether or not the Kadagidi had already picked up movement to its northwest would dictate how and when the local bodyguard would react. A protest against an overland intrusion would certainly be in order—plus a threat to call Guild Headquarters and get the matter on official record, which the Kadagidi could make—and they didn't dare.

"At this point," Bren said to Jase, "it becomes a complicated dance. They'll protest; we'll say it's a social visit. They may notice our people coming up overland. Then we see whether Lord Aseida comes out to talk. He *should* demand to talk to me—which is his job—but we don't think it likely he's actually speaking for himself, or that he has any power at all over his guard."

"Haikuti."

"Exactly. Aseida's either so smart he's run everything all along, even through Murini's administration—or he's nothing. By all I know of Haikuti, he'd have no man'chi. Not to a living soul."

"Aiji-like, in other words."

"A member of the Assassins' Guild can't be a lord of any kind—legally. You can be in the Physicians' Guild and happen to be lord of a province and serve in the legislature—there is actually one such. But the compact that organized the aishidi'tat drew a very careful line to keep the one guild that enforces the law entirely out of the job of making it."

"Has it worked?"

"Yes. Until now. But we suspect Haikuti fairly well took power under Murini's administration—and Shishogi had to move him there. How far under Shishogi's control he is now—is a question. If anything should happen to me, I should say, tell the captains to protect Tabini, the dowager, Cajeiri, and Lord Tatiseigi. Four people. Get them up to the station if there's no other choice. *They* have the people's mandate. But one bullet can send all plans to hell."

"God, Bren. I sincerely take what you're saying. But just keep your head down, will you?"

"I intend to. But a little risk, unfortunately, goes with the job."

"So what's going on?" Gene asked in ship-speak, once the servants were out of the dining room. "Where's Lord Bren? What happened last night?"

It was upsetting to be questioned during breakfast. Great-grandmother would never approve of such behavior. But they were all at one table, Cajeiri, his bodyguards, his guests, and the mood was not at all festive.

"Nand' Bren went to the Kadagidi," he said, also in ship-speak. "Next door. Lord Bren and Captain Jase, too. With Captain Jase's guard. To talk."

It didn't help the frowns, and just then a servant came in with another plate of spiced eggs and toast. "We are going to walk around the basement." Cajeiri tried to change the subject entirely during the service. "Great-uncle's collections are famous."

"I wish we could go riding again," Irene said. "If they caught those people—"

"Not that easy," Cajeiri said. "We're safe in the house. But still under alert."

"For *more* people?"

"Not sure," Cajeiri said. If they kept it to ship-speak, at least the servants would not realize they were being improper. "Don't worry. All fine. But we don't go outside."

"Tomorrow?" Irene asked. And unhappily: "Ever?"

"Maybe," he said, wishing he knew the answer.

Conversation limped along. He knew ship-speak for things on the ship, but he struggled for words about things on Earth. And he had no words to explain the Kadagidi.

"Luca-ji," he said quietly to Lucasi, who was good at talking to senior Guild, "see what else you can find out. You can do it after breakfast."

"Yes," Lucasi said, swallowed two bites of toast and got up from the table, leaving a whole piece of toast and an egg on his plate.

So his bodyguard was as desperate to understand the situation as he was.

The bus slowed to a stop. Bren took a look out the window, as much as he could see, which was scrub trees and pasturage, and a low fieldstone wall.

"We've come to a gate," Jase said, having the report from Kaplan and Polano, who had the vantage up there.

"Whether they'll open it will say something," Bren said.

"We can take it down," Jase said. "That's no problem—if you need it."

"We'll see," Bren said, and looked up as Banichi arrived beside his seat.

"When we get to the Kadagidi house, Bren-ji," Banichi said, bypassing the question of modality, "we will bring the bus as far as the front porch, at an angle where sniping from the roof is not easy.

"Jase-nandi,—one understands the armor is good against armor-piercing rounds?"

Jase looked at Bren, wanting translation.

Bren gave it.

"Yes," Jase said in Ragi, and nodded. "No problem, Banichi-nadi." And in ship-speak: "Rules of engagement, Bren."

Bren translated the question.

"Fire only if fired upon," Banichi said. "Avoid servants and civilians."

Bren translated that, too.

"This is the plan," Banichi said to Jase, leaning on Bren's seat-back. "We would ask Kaplan and Polano to go out the instant we stop, and take position to screen us from fire as we exit the bus."

"Exit the bus," Bren said, interrupting his translation. "Banichi-ji—"

"If the situation calls for it, Bren-ji, we all four will escort you out. *Only* if the situation calls for it. And, much as your aishid covets the honor of defending you, stay behind Jase's bodyguards and do not go beyond one step from the bus. Your greatest danger is a sniper in the upper floors. Pay attention to that. We shall. The house will be on the right side of the bus and we will pull up close to the door to inconvenience targeting from those floors. A grenade remains a possibility. We can do nothing about that—except interest them in finding out what we have to say, and be aware whether those upstairs windows are open or shut."

"Understood."

"And, Bren-ji, you will *not* accept an invitation to tea in this house."

"I promise that," he said with a startled laugh. But it did nothing for his nerves.

"The gate is opening," Jase said in Ragi.

Banichi straightened. "So. We shall see."

The bus started to move. The road between the gate and the Kadagidi front door was not as long a drive as that from Tatiseigi's gate to the house. It was a gravel road, by the sound under the tires, and the bus gathered more speed than it had used thus far, not all-out, but not losing any time, either.

"They're going to let the bus all the way up to the house?" Jase asked. "What if *we're* loaded with explosives?"

Bren shook his head. "We're the good guys, remember. Guild regulations. A historic site, and civilians. We're supposed to finesse the situation all the way. And of course *they're* supposed to talk to us, on their side, lord to lord. If they refuse to talk to us, we have an automatic complaint—for what it's worth."

"This is that 'little risk' you were talking about. Going out there."

"Banichi's thinking this through. He has a reason. The dowager's men, back there, may get off, too; and if they do, keep the aisle clear. And if things do go to hell, just get down below the windows and let the driver follow his orders, one of which is to get you out of here."

"God, you're insane on this planet."

"It's an eminently reasonable system—when you're not dealing with scoundrels."

"The hell." Jase levered himself to his feet and went up to Kaplan and Polano, delivering low, quick instructions of his own. Bren couldn't hear exactly what he said, above the noise of the bus, but Kaplan and Polano nodded solemnly more than once. Jase clapped each on the shoulder and returned to his seat, while Kaplan and Polano started putting their mirror-faced helmets on— their smallest movements accompanied by a whining sound that rose above the roar of the bus on the gravel.

"They understand," Jase said. "Those helmets have sensors. They can see *behind* the wall. Three-sixty and overhead. They'll know where we are and once they've mapped that, they'll spot any other movement. I warned them about grenades. And snipers."

"Is there going to be any complaint from the captains on this?" Bren asked. "Say I asked it. Urgently, I asked it."

"Understood. And understand that they're here to handle whatever my presence or those kids' presence might provoke. *I'd* say this is partly due to my presence. For the record."

The bus had begun the curve that would lead it right in front of the house. Bren caught a scant glimpse of the stone facade, past Jase's men, a blockish, formal Padi Valley style manor, in situation and aspect not unlike Tirnamardi.

A fortress, in the day of cavalry attacks and short-range cannon, with windows only on the high upper floors.

"The paidhi-aiji and the ship-aiji have come to call on Lord Aseida," Bren heard Banichi say, talking on Guild communications while the bus rolled. The calm tones had a surreal quality, as if it were old territory, a scene revisited again and again. "They are guests of your next-door neighbor the Atageini lord, and they have been personally inconvenienced by actions confessed to have originated from these grounds. These are matters far above the Guild, nadi, and regarding your lord's status within the aishidi'tat. Advise your lord of it."

Time to pay the rent on the estate at Najida. He'd said it. Lordships came with responsibilities.

And one *didn't* give tactical orders to one's bodyguard.

The bus gathered speed, took a gentle curve, and then ran into shadow, the Kadagidi house looming between them and the cloudless sunrise. A hedge passed the window, then a windowless expanse of pale stonework, ancient limestone, and vines, passing more and more slowly as the bus braked.

Full stop. Immediately the driver opened the door. "Go," Jase said in ship-speak, and Kaplan and Polano immediately took the steps, jumped from the last one and landed on their feet as if the armor weighed nothing—gyros, Bren thought distractedly. Beyond the windshield, now that they could see, and about a bus length ahead, were low, rounded steps, a single open door, and black-uniformed Kadagidi Guild arriving outside to meet them with rifles in hand.

But the Kadagidi reaction stopped on those steps. *What* the Guildsmen saw facing them beside that bus door, the world had never seen. That was certain. Kaplan and Polano had taken up position, mirror-faced, tall, and bulky, atevi-scale and then some.

"Bren-ji, come," Banichi said, from beside Bren's seat.

He didn't stop to analyze. He flung himself up and went behind Banichi and Jago as they passed, with Tano and Algini bringing up the rear. Jase himself might be visible to those on the steps, through the front window—but the rest of their company stayed out of sight, crouched among the rear seats . . . he had seen that as he got up.

Banichi and Jago alighted on the gravel drive. Bren grabbed the assisting rail and landed beside them, followed by Tano and Algini, all behind the white wall that was Kaplan and Polano.

Banichi, rifle in the crook of his arm, stepped out from cover alone.

"Are those alive?" the senior confronting them called out from the porch steps.

"These are the ship-aiji's personal bodyguard," Banichi answered. "And the ship-aiji is present on the bus. Be warned. These two ship-folk understand very little Ragi. Make no move that they might misinterpret. The paidhi-aiji and the ship-aiji have come to talk to your lord, and request he come outdoors for the meeting."

"Our lord will protest this trespass!"

"Your lord will be free to do that at his pleasure," Banichi retorted. "But advise him that the paidhi-aiji is here on behalf of Tabini-aiji, speaking for his minor son and for the aiji-dowager, the ship-aiji, and his son's foreign guests, minor children, all of whom were disturbed last night by Guild Assassins who have named your estate as their route into Lord Tatiseigi's house."

Banichi had them. Legally. There was a decided pause on the other side, a consultation.

"We will relay the matter to our lord," the Kadagidi said. "Wait."

A man left, through the door to the inside of the

house. That left the unit on the steps facing them, but without direct threat, rifles down, and there seemed some remote chance of getting Lord Aseida out here on the steps—in which case there would be some use for the paidhi-aiji, and some chance, if Haikuti was not here, to argue the Kadagidi lord into an act of common sense—*if* there was a chance Lord Aseida wanted to get out of the predicament he was in.

Cast himself and his clan on the aiji's mercy—if there was any way he dared walk away from the guards on the steps and board the bus. If they could detach Aseida from his bodyguards and get him under the dowager's protection, they *might* have a source of information, a sure bet in any legislative hearing, *and* they could stabilize the Kadagidi for—at least a few years, so long as the fear lasted. That was what they could do if Aseida would walk out here and tell his guards to go back inside.

Beyond that remote chance—if Aseida refused the request to talk, the paidhi-aiji still had a job to do: take charge, and keep the company on the porch distracted and arguing, while Nawari probed the house defenses and found out whether the Kadagidi intended the Dojisigi to survive their return to the Kadagidi house—or not.

He was overshadowed on every hand, too short, behind Kaplan and Polano, in their white, faceless suits, to get a good look at the company on the porch. His bodyguard loomed head and shoulders above him.

They waited.

Another Guild unit came out that door and brusquely joined the first—a unit which could *be* Aseida's personal bodyguard. The senior of that group exuded a force of presence and, God! an *anger* foreign to the Guild, a hard-faced man, absolute and furious as he had ever seen any man—except Tabini.

Aiji, was what the nerves said.

Haikuti. He had never seen so much as a photo of the man—but he had no doubt.

"Banichi!" that man shouted, swinging his rifle upward.

Banichi moved. In a time-stretched instant, Haikuti went backward, Banichi spun and went down, bullets hit the bus, and a buffeting shock went through the ground. Grenade, Bren thought, finding himself falling. It had all gone wrong. Banichi was on the ground right in front of him, moving, but dazedly.

Bren lurched forward, grabbed Banichi's jacket, and pulled with everything he had, dragging Banichi back toward cover, aware that Jago and Tano and Algini had gone past him.

In the next moment the dowager's men poured out of the bus past him, dodging him and Banichi as they charged past Kaplan and Polano. Gunfire went off inside the building. And Banichi moved, got a hand on the bus step and started to get up, while Bren was sitting on the ground.

Other pale hands arrived to help haul Banichi up. Jase had come to help, and was giving orders to Kaplan and Polano to stand fast. Banichi got a knee under him.

"Stay down, stay down," Bren said, with a hand on Banichi's arm.

Banichi took a breath, got one hand on the communications earpiece that had fallen from his ear and put it back, listened, on one knee, and said something in code, the three of them sheltered behind Jase's steadfast bodyguard.

"Get aboard the bus," Banichi said. There was a hole blown in Banichi's jacket, exposing the bulletproof fabric, and blood.

"*You* get aboard," Bren said. "You were *hit,* Banichi."

"He," Banichi said, looking toward the stone steps of the porch. Bren looked, past armor-cased legs. The stonework was shattered and black-uniformed bodies lay every which way.

"*He* went down," Bren said, looking back at Banichi. "You hit him. They fired. Jase's guard fired, and if anything else came from our direction it was ricochets." If Banichi had to ask the sequence of events, he had been hit hard, and he did *not* want Banichi to get up and go staggering into the house.

"If it got him," Banichi said, "good." He did gain his feet, grabbed Bren's hand and hauled him up as if he weighed nothing. Then he leaned back against the bus to check the bracelet and listen to communications. "Nawari's group is arriving," Banichi said. "Jase. Allies to the west. Tell Kaplan and Polano."

Bren repeated that in ship-speak, to be sure—east and west were not concepts Kaplan and Polano knew operationally, and Jase relayed it in ship-speak and coordinates.

"They understand," Jase said. "They've adjusted their autofire to that fact."

Gunfire broke out somewhere beyond the house. He heard servos whine as Kaplan and Polano simultaneously reoriented.

"Ours," Banichi said instantly.

Jase said, "Hold fire, hold fire. Rules of engagement still hold. Fire only if fired on."

"Stay here," Banichi said. "Get on the bus, Bren-ji, Jase-nandi. *Now.*"

They had become a distraction. Banichi was linking the operations together, Nawari's group coming in overland, the ones that were behind the house, and *in* the house.

"Get aboard," Bren said to Jase. "Keep Kaplan and Polano where they are—Guild can tell each other apart. We can't. And they can't."

The bus was still running. The driver still had the door open. Jase grabbed the assisting rail and climbed the steps, and Bren followed close behind him, hoping Banichi would stay where he was, behind Kaplan and Polano, and direct matters from there, but by the time Bren had gotten to the first seats and turned around, Banichi had crossed open ground to the side of the house, and along the way, had gathered up his rifle.

Bren put his hand in his pocket, felt the gun in place. He planted a knee in the seat and looked outward. Banichi was on the steps, taking a closer look at one of the fallen.

"That was the one you were after?" Jase asked. "The one Banichi got?"

"If we're lucky," Bren said.

Banichi! that one had said and fired.

So had Banichi.

They'd known each other by sight, at least. But that anger . . . that instant reaction . . .

How, when they had known each other, he had no idea. But he had that impression.

He watched Banichi go into the house.

"Nandiin," the driver said, "there is still resistance in the house. One believes they may be attempting to destroy information. We are moving to prevent it."

"One hears, nadi," he said. The driver was Guild—linked into communications and willing to tell them what was going on. That was unprecedented. Banichi's arrangement, he thought . . . with the hope of keeping him in his seat.

The windshield was starred with a bullet scar. Simultaneous as it had been—the other side had fired first. He'd swear to it. Damned right he'd swear to it. Kaplan and Polano had fired when fired on.

The renegades had *not* followed Guild rules, had *not* called for a standstill and consultation with Guild authority.

They had done everything by the book—and the Shadow Guild hadn't, damn them. The carnage on the porch, terrible as it had been, was thanks to that. There was no *need* for so many to be dead. It wasn't the way the Guild had operated, before the Shadow Guild had tried to take the rules back to the dark ages, the clan wars, the days of cavalry, pikes, and wholesale bloodshed. Atevi had climbed out of *that* age the hard way, before humans had ever arrived in the heavens. It was *their* common sense, the Assassins' Guild was their solution, and the Shadow Guild was doing their damnedest to unravel it.

Suddenly Kaplan and Polano reoriented, machinelike and simultaneous, toward the windows above. Bren ducked down to see what they were looking at, could not spot it.

"A man in an upstairs window," Jase said, with a better view. "Waving and shouting."

That would not be Guild. And they *must* not harm

civilians. The bus door was shut, cutting off sounds from outside. Bren shoved himself out of his seat, Jase right with him, and ordered the door open, trusting to Kaplan and Polano for protection.

He got to the bottom step and looked up. The man was dressed as a servant, and seeing him, waved furiously, shouting down, "My lord requests respect for the premises! My lord requests assistance!"

"A house servant," Bren said for Jase: the Padi Valley accent was thick. "Speaking for Lord Aseida." He called up to the man: "Can you come down, nadi? Come to the front entry. You will be safe! We—"

A shot hit the folded bus door. Kaplan and Polano fired, robot-quick, before Bren could react and recoil. He had felt his hair move; he had felt a sting in his cheek; and then thunder blew past him. He blinked, and saw the window at the building corner—missing, along with the masonry around it.

The window from which the servant had called to them was undamaged. But empty.

Sensors. A sniper in a window up there in the corner room. He stared for a few heartbeats. Jase was hauling him back by the arm. He moved in compliance, backed up the steps, still looking up in disbelief.

"Nadi," he said to the driver. "Advise those inside. Sniper strike, building corner, top floor. Jase's guard just took them out."

"Nandi," the driver said calmly, and relayed that information.

Bren said: "Lord Aseida's possible location is also the third floor, third window, next to the missing one." His cheek stung. He touched it, bringing away bloody fingertips. Not a real wound. There might be a splinter of some sort. He was disgusted with himself. "My fault, standing there. Sorry, Jase."

"Your local problems don't miss an opportunity," Jase said. "Sit down. Let me look at that."

He sat. Jase looked, probed it, shook his head. "Not too bad."

"Missed my head," he said, and sucked in a deep

breath, mad at himself, and now he second-guessed his sending information into the house. He *hoped* his information wouldn't draw his people into some sort of trap. About Lord Aseida's rescue, he didn't at the moment give a damn. "My bodyguard's going to say a few words about my going out there."

"Nandiin," the driver said. "They acknowledge. They say keep inside."

"Assure them we are aboard," he said, with an idea *who* had said keep inside.

There were medical kits aboard, a small one in the overhead storage, a larger one in the forward baggage compartment. He got up and got a small bandage to stop the cut from bleeding; but they were, he thought, unhappily apt to need the larger one before all was done, and he was not going out there.

Things grew quieter. He became aware he was no longer hearing gunfire through the insulation of the bus.

"They have located the lord and his servants, nandiin," the driver said.

"Good," he said. Then the driver said:

"Lord Aseida requests to speak with the paidhi-aiji. They will be bringing him down."

He was not, at the moment, enthusiastic about dealing with Aseida. His cheek was throbbing and he was developing a headache—those were the sum of *his* stupidity-induced injuries; and he could certainly do his job past that discomfort, but all of a sudden he felt entirely rattled. It seemed a crushing responsibility, to get the necessary dealings right, to react, knowing the record would be gone over and gone over by political enemies. His people had risked their necks to get the renegades identified and removed—everything had worked. They'd gotten their chance, and they'd made the most of it. *He* couldn't give the opposition a loophole in his own sphere of responsibility . . .

Most of all he couldn't give Assignments' allies in high places in the Guild any excuse to charge a misdeed to Tabini's account, and the station's. Aseida was not, counting the damage to his house, going to be an asset.

He *was* rattled, he thought, by that trifling hit. He drew deep breaths, steadying down, getting control back.

The exchange of gunfire was over. He wanted to know his people were all right, and that the dowager's were, that first. Lord Aseida, already under ban, was not in charge of events now. No. Only the aiji could unseat Aseida, and *he* had the excuse Tabini needed.

"Whatever Aseida is," he said to Jase, "he's representative of a major clan, a lot of people, a lot of connections, historic and otherwise. He's a patch-together sort of lord—the clan's lost one after the other—but he's what they've got, all they've got. Banned from court. They couldn't let him into the Bujavid, for security reasons. Most of all, they couldn't let his bodyguard in. He's alive. And we're going to keep him that way. His own allies probably won't like that."

"They are bringing out the casualties first, nandiin," the driver said.

He got up to look out the bullet-starred windshield. Jase stood behind him. He saw, one after the other, three of the dowager's men helped down the shattered steps by comrades, all ambulatory. Thank God.

He asked the driver the question he dreaded to ask, "Have we lost anyone, nadi?"

"No, nandi," the driver said. "We have not. All are accounted for. Six injured, none critically."

He drew a deep breath and let it go slowly. He saw Banichi, conspicuous by his stature, walking under his own power, but with his right hand tucked inside his open jacket. He saw Jago, walking beside Banichi. And, escorted by two of the dowager's men, a young man in blue brocade came out the door, hesitating at the broken steps and the dreadful sight there, and trailed by two agitated servants.

Aseida.

Time to risk his head a second time, going out there in the courtesy due the Kadagidi lord? He didn't think so. The mess was Aseida's and he didn't owe it courtesy.

He stood where he was. He waited until the driver

opened the door, and he was there to meet Banichi and Jago as they came up the steps.

He didn't embarrass Banichi with inquiries, and Banichi delivered his report in two sentences: "We have the house secure. The lord requests to speak with you."

"Shall I go down?" Bren asked.

Banichi frowned at him, perhaps noticing the new bandage on his cheek. "Lord Aseida can come aboard," Banichi said, "under the circumstances. He is requesting Atageini assistance to secure the premises."

Things had shifted immensely in the last hour. The Kadagidi-Atageini feud had gone on, intermittent with periods of alliance, for centuries.

Now the Atageini were being invited in—preferable to the Taibeni, likely.

Bren shot a look toward Jago, who had smudges of pale ash on her chin and cheek, and a bleeding scrape on her hand. He was overwhelmingly glad to see her and Banichi both in one piece. "Tano and Algini, nadi-in-ji?"

"They are supervising the document recovery," Jago said. "The servants attempted to destroy records. We stopped that."

Records were involved. That was *very* good news.

The servants being at the business of destroying them, while the front porch was exploding—was peculiar, and spoke volumes about the character of the Kadagidi servants.

And the Kadagidi lord was standing at the bus door, with his two valets, waiting for his permission. "Come up, nandi," he said, "without your servants." He saw the frown and gave back one of his own. "Your servants may stay with the premises, under the watch of the guard we set here. You, on the other hand, may come aboard and make whatever request for protection you wish, and I shall relay it to your neighbor Lord Tatiseigi, to the aiji-dowager, and ultimately to the aiji in Shejidan. Be aware, since one does not believe your bodyguard adequately reported to you, that a ship-aiji is with us. It is *his* bodyguard outside.

Your bodyguard, sadly, fired on them. So did someone from your upper windows."

Aseida turned and looked up. His mouth opened. He turned back with an angry expression.

"These are historic premises!"

"Fire came, in a ship-aiji's presence, at a ship-aiji's bodyguard, from *your* historic premises, nandi. And one strongly suggests that you give no more such orders!"

"I did not order it!" Aseida protested. "I gave no such order!"

Bren backed up a step, in invitation. "Then you would be wise to come aboard, nandi, and explain to Jase-aiji just who *did* order it."

18

They were all down in the basement of Uncle's house, which might have been an interesting place to visit, except the circumstances reminded Cajeiri all too vividly of the basement at Najida, where they had had to go because of the attack on the house.

Only this time mani had chosen to stay upstairs with Cenedi and Casimi. Cajeiri was sure that was because Cenedi was in contact with Banichi and nand' Bren and possibly Nawari. Very serious things were going on that his guests were not supposed to know about, and since he was the only one who could talk to them—*he* was obliged to act as if everything was perfectly ordinary.

Nothing in fact was ordinary. Great-uncle, who had never in his life approved of humans, had come down himself to guide not just children, but *human* children on a tour through his clan's most precious things. And they had security with them, of course, two of Great-uncle's, and all of his own aishid—which meant, of course, that he could *not* have them upstairs trying to find out things.

Great-uncle had begun by pointing out the beautiful porcelains, and talked at length about glazes in terms Cajeiri struggled to translate at all—though his guests were all very polite about it and nodded in proper places, seeming impressed by the porcelains, and the pictures, and the fact people had painted them a long time ago.

And once, when Irene's eyes grew wide and damp and she whispered *How beautiful,* in very careful Ragi,

Great-uncle did a very strange thing and actually opened a case and took out a cup and let her hold it for a moment before putting it back behind glass.

They came to another door, and Great-uncle, his face very blank, ordered lamps brought and the lights turned off, and for a moment Cajeiri forgot all about nand' Bren and the Kadagidi, as the great double door opened, and huge eyes glimmered in the flickering light. Claws reached. Fangs glistened. Irene gave a great squeal, and pressed up against Gene, who laughed and put his arm her and swore, quite loudly, that he would protect her.

More than that, Great-uncle . . . smiled.

That . . . was scarier than the taxidermied creatures.

But Great-uncle did not insist the tour continue in the dark for which Cajeiri was glad. It had been a surprise, and his guests had enjoyed it, but somehow ambush in the dark seemed just a little too real this morning.

So he was glad when Great-uncle ordered the main lights turned back on and proceeded to show them the ferocious taxidermied beasts in his father's father's collection, creatures Cajeiri had only seen in drawings. His guests were excited and amazed and so was he. There was a legless reptile as big as a man, all coiled up and threatening, almost as good as a dinosaur. There was ornate old armor that was real, not made for machimi. There were swords and spears that probably had killed people, which was a sobering thought.

There were lots and lots of really interesting things to see, aisles and aisles as crowded as the warehouses under the Bujavid, and he found himself going for whole periods of time without thinking about the people they had caught in the garage, and how they had been afraid there might be Assassins in the basement.

Besides, they had their bodyguards. And from here on they had the lights on, bright as day, where they were, though it was scary to look off through doorways into sections where they had been, that were dark now, or sections where they had not yet been, which were a little more ominous.

They came to dull spots: there were, in one nook, rows

of plain brown pottery that looked like nothing at all—until Great-uncle said it was the first pottery ever made in the Padi Valley—which, Great-uncle said, showed that the Atageini ancestors had come from the south coast a long, long time ago, thousands of years ago, in fact. Uncle said the Scholars could tell all sorts of relationships because of the way the pots were made and the patterns on them, because the ancient peoples had particular ways of doing things, even particular ways to make a pot.

Cajeiri had not known that, himself, and for a moment he forgot about the trouble outside, in a flight of imagination about his own Atageini ancestry being from the coast where Lord Geigi and nand' Bren had their estates. It was almost like being related.

Artur got right up close, not enough to touch, but staring at the details, and he asked questions about the differences he saw, which Cajeiri translated, and Uncle was quite pleased to talk about those differences ... though Uncle had an amazing good sense about getting them back to collections of fierce fish, with amazing teeth.

But in the intervals, the grim thoughts came back: there was real danger coming near the house, which was *never* supposed to happen in historic premises like Tirnamardi, with so many ancient, precious, *fragile* things. Cajeiri knew, he was sure, why they were being kept down here—he had been through shelling. And he very much hoped mani was in some sort of a safe place, too, and especially he hoped that they were going to hear something from nand' Bren soon—

He hoped that there would not, *not,* he hoped, be gunfire, or grenades or people sneaking up on the house to do mischief.

And that there were not accesses down here in the basement that could have ambush waiting in one of the rooms.

They went on to a different part of the basement, where lights went on, and there were cabinets and cabinets of record books. It was records going back hundreds of years, Great-uncle said, showing them books bound in leather so old it was flaking, and Irene said she wished she knew enough Ragi to read them.

Had they been scanned into a computer, she asked, in case something should happen to them?

He didn't translate that part. He didn't think Great-uncle would like that idea, not this morning. "I shall ask him that later," he told Irene.

Beyond that place, in another room, a dimly lit display case held a skeleton of a person that Great-uncle said was thousands and thousands of years old. They had dug him up on the grounds, when they had built the house, and the broken pots around him were what he had been buried with.

That was a scary place. That was a real dead person. Cajeiri did not want to linger there.

"Can you tell anything," he whispered to Lucasi, while his guests crowded close to the case. "Is there anything going on the house network?"

"They have us cut off completely, nandi," Lucasi said. "We cannot pick up anything at all, not even routine things."

There were two Guild Assassins locked up somewhere in the house, maybe down here in the basement, right near them.

And he could not forget the sight of Kaplan and Polano suited up and looking like nothing the Earth had ever seen. It was a sight from the ship—walking down the stairs of Great-uncle's house. And it was all crazy.

Nand' Bren was going to try to talk to the Kadagidi and get an accounting for those two Assassins, apparently, and maybe warn them they were in trouble.

Nand' Bren had gone right in and talked to Lord Machigi, in the Taisigin Marid, and gotten an agreement with him, which nobody would ever think could happen. So if *anybody* could talk to the Kadagidi, nand' Bren might.

But the way they were keeping everything secret, putting them down in the basement, and not letting his guard know anything, he was getting more and more anxious about what the Kadagidi were doing.

He *hoped* he had not invited his guests down for all of them to get in the middle of a war.

On his *last* birthday they had started a war.

They had had the whole Najida business just weeks ago.

And here it was his birthday and they were going to start another war.

It just was not *fair,* was the childish thought that surfaced; but there was so much more at issue than *fairness,* now. He wanted everyone safe. He wanted the world not to have selfishness, and stupidity. And it was bound to have. But he wanted not to have it in places where it could do so much damage.

He heard footsteps in the room behind them, which was no longer dark. The head of Great-uncle's bodyguard had come downstairs. He overtook them and called Uncle aside to talk to him, while they were in the room with the skeleton in the case. They waited, all of them, while Great-uncle talked, and now none of his guests were looking at the display. They were all looking at Uncle and three of his bodyguards, now.

And given all that had gone on in the house last night and this morning, they would be really stupid if they did not figure out there was something wrong.

Gene moved over close to him. "What's going on?" Gene whispered in ship-speak. "What's happening?"

He could not lie directly. "Trouble," he said quietly. "Nand' Bren and Jase-aiji went next door. Bad people. The Kadagidi."

"Something to do with last night?" Artur asked, at Gene's shoulder. Irene just looked worried.

"Next door—" He did not have the right words in ship-speak. "Trouble with the Kadagidi. A long time."

The bodyguard went back down the hall. Great-uncle turned to them and said, "My staff may continue the tour this afternoon, young gentleman, if you wish. There is some little more to see. Some business has come up, and I must go upstairs. Nephew, please have your bodyguard escort you back to the stairs at your leisure. You may bring your guests up to the breakfast room and enjoy refreshments."

"Great-uncle." The bow was automatic, while his brain was racing. What was it? Was everything all right now? They were being let out of the cellar and offered lunch alone, with no grown-ups.

But was the trouble over?

Great-uncle and his bodyguard went ahead of them through the basement, headed up the stairs, and left them with just his bodyguard for guides.

"What did he say?" Gene whispered urgently. "Jeri, what just happened?"

"I don't know," he said. "I don't know. Lunch, is all. If it were bad I think they'd want us to stay downstairs." He *hoped* his bodyguard remembered the way out.

But they did. They went back through the rooms fairly quickly, the lights going on and off as they passed through, not too far behind Great-uncle. They went upstairs and out the door, to a little alcove in the main hall. Great-uncle and his guard were still ahead of them, on *their* way toward the sitting room, where one would easily bet Great-grandmother was.

The breakfast room was a little distance away from that.

"Is that an all-clear?" Jegari asked suddenly. He was looking at his bracelet, the same sort that most Guild wore.

"Yes," Veijico said, looking at her bracelet. "Nandi, we are receiving again."

Kadagidi fortunes had certainly sunk today. That was clear in the bedraggled, soot-stained person of the Kadagidi lord, who had to negotiate with intruders on his clan's territory, in a bus sitting on his land.

"We do not surrender," Aseida had said first, frayed and rattled as he was, once he stood aboard. "We appeal to the paidhiin to prevent damage to our estate. We are innocent of all offense!"

Ship-paidhi. Jase was that.

Innocent, however, had been an interesting claim.

So was Aseida's insistence on addressing Jase by his lesser, onworld title.

Let him, Bren had thought, showing him to the first of the seats, arranged as the first rows were, in facing pairs, with a let-down table.

Let him spill whatever he wants of his thinking, his views, his presumptions.

He hadn't let down that table. He wanted full view of Aseida's hands. He had Jase sitting beside him. Kaplan and Polano had come aboard, and, unable to sit in the armor, they had taken their places again beside the driver, in front of the damaged windshield.

"We were betrayed," Lord Aseida had said for openers. "We were *forced* by Murini-aiji's bodyguard. We *never* wanted the man'chi of that aishid. They *attached* to me when I was a child, and I had no choice in the matter."

The account went on and on, somewhat incoherently, if interestingly.

It did follow one scenario they had surmised—that there had been an unusually strong Guild presence in the house before and *during* Murini's sojourn in the Dojisigin Marid; that the bodyguard that had escorted the usurper into exile and died with him had *not* been Haikuti's team, no, they had stayed constantly in the house, and, well, perhaps, Aseida thought, possibly had contact with others about the region, but they always had that.

Definitely Haikuti and that aishid had not gone down to the Marid with Murini, before the coup, nor had they conspicuously stood beside him in his ascent to power, though they had been physically with him during some of his administration.

But they had been Aseida's aishid for years. How assigned? Clearly by Shishogi, who had held his office through more decades than that.

The records that had accumulated in the house during Murini's tenure possibly still existed, among those they had confiscated within the Kadagidi estate.

But now they had, indeed, very interesting things pouring out: a Kadagidi lord, the very person involved, claiming that Haikuti had taken over the household, that Haikuti had effectively run the clan by threat and intimidation, possibly using Murini as a puppet—and that he, Aseida, was innocent as the spring rains.

The paidhi's job, however, was a good deal easier than Aseida's, who had to explain what the situation *had* been, a lot of it unlovely, and precisely *how* he was innocent.

"Do not accuse us," Aseida said hotly, at one point. "We had no way to respond to you. It was you who elected to come onto Kadagidi land, with these men dressed as machines, it was you who called out my guard and blew a hole in an ancient house. Who is my neighbor to send *humans and machines* to attack us, on the charges that we *aided* an attack on Tirnamardi? You have fired without judgment and damaged historic premises! You have shattered treasures older than your presence on this Earth! You had no right to come here and fire on us!"

"We were fired upon," Bren said with careful patience.

"That is *your* word, paidhi, after you have killed all the witnesses! One side's word is no proof before the law!"

"Is he saying we fired first?" Jase asked.

"That's what he's saying. He's saying we can't prove it legally, because we have no witness from his side surviving."

Jase shook his head. "He's wrong. The armor's been recording everything. Audio. Video. Three-sixty-degrees and overhead, ever since they put the systems live, which was the moment we drove through that gate. *Our* regs say when we have weapons go live—we record it until they shut down."

Bren drew in a deep breath. Smiled deliberately at Aseida. "Jase-aiji notes that we have it recorded who fired first. Video, nandi. Video and audio. Just like television. You can slow it down and know *exactly* what happened first."

Aseida's face changed.

"And since we're citing the *law,* nandi, let me remind you that when you attack, a person's response may be at *his* level. *I* am the lord of Najida and Lord of the Heavens. Jase is a ship-aiji. Your bodyguards fired on this bus.

Twice. If Jase-aiji had responded with *everything* he has, the damage, I assure you, would have been far more than a corner of your building and its front steps. As for my other office, as paidhi-aiji, let me remind you I do not merely represent the offended parties in last night's events: I represent *Tabini-aiji,* who would observe, were he here, that you have placed yourself at considerable disadvantage in any dealings with your neighbors and indeed, with *him.* You have attacked the aiji-dowager. You have attacked the aiji's son, a minor child. You have attacked his guests, minor children, and citizens under Jase-aiji's protection. You have attacked your neighbor Lord Tatiseigi."

"Not I! I had nothing to do with it! It was Haikuti! Haikuti did as he pleased! There was no way I could have prevented him!"

"You claim you were under duress?"

"Constantly."

"Yet," he said, "yet, lacking a corroborating witness, nandi, it is impossible to prove that you ever desired to go against these persons. Certainly at some point you made a very bad bargain with them, perhaps, indeed, to keep yourself alive and comfortable—"

"To keep my staff alive, nandi, and to preserve our house!"

"Yet do we know your staff themselves are pure, and will not turn on you? My aishid found them trying to destroy records in the security office, which, whatever the crisis, is rarely the job of *domestic* staff."

A silence ensued.

"Tell me," Bren said softly, "nandi. How confident would you be at this point, in committing yourself and your house to your current staff, after their certain suspicion that you have unburdened yourself to us aboard this bus? One would suspect, by the behavior of those servants, that they are not altogether innocent, either. I would rather expect that, *if* this matter is argued in court, there will certainly be some among them to testify—as your surviving witnesses—but who knows what they may say? That *you* compelled *them?*"

Aseida was not at the moment master of his expressions. His eyes twitched when he considered his possible answers.

"Suppose that we installed you back in your house this hour and left the servants to resume their duties. Would you have any personal apprehension?"

Far from master of his expressions.

Bren asked: "Are you more afraid of those within Haikuti's instruction—or of reprisals from those who were *not* under his influence?"

"There *are* none outside his influence, paidhi."

"Not a one, nandi?"

"No. No. There is not."

"Then you have rather an unhappy situation, nandi, were I to send you back to your house at this hour—because I would certainly discourage your traveling south, say, to the Marid at this point. Startling things have happened there, early this morning. And one does not suppose you would care to lodge in one of your own townships—lacking your bodyguards. In fact yours is a sad case, Lord Aseida. Have *all* Kadagidi been happy with Haikuti's direction?"

Aseida started to answer, and faltered, perhaps becoming aware how he was being led.

"Are there none you would trust," Bren asked, "on *either* side of Haikuti's influence?"

"The ones who would support me would have no chance against Haikuti's people."

"That is probably true," Bren said. He and Jase were no longer interviewing Aseida alone. Tano and Algini had come aboard, Algini seated and Tano standing, on the other side of the aisle. "So yours is an unfortunate situation, nandi. What would you wish to do now?"

"I appeal to Lord Tatiseigi," Aseida said, as if the words were stuck in his throat. "He is honest. He is my neighbor. The Padi Valley is not like other places."

"Without staff, without bodyguard, and without alliances, nandi, you are in a very desperate situation. But you do recognize that."

The chin stiffened, brows drew down. Aseida finally

located his backbone. "The Padi Valley is different, I say, paidhi-aiji. We have traditions. We are the old blood. We stick together."

"I shall certainly convey your request to him, nandi. You wish, then, to apply to Lord Tatiseigi's hospitality."

"I so wish," Aseida said, jaw clenching hard. "*He* will understand."

"Undoubtedly," Bren said, very tempted to cast a look at Algini to see how *he* had read the man; but he refrained.

They had given first aid to the injured while he conducted his interview with Aseida, both their own, from the two parties, and also to a Kadagidi servant who had suffered a broken arm in the upstairs hall. They had given two servants permission to take that man on to the hospital in the township, by Lord Aseida's van. They had packed boxes of interesting documents into the baggage compartment, and they were putting the estate under Guild seal, meaning it and its historic treasures would be strictly guarded until there was some judgment about the clan leadership—a temporary duty for Nawari and the party that had come in overland—they would, Algini said, have relief coming in from the Taibeni on Lord Tatiseigi's estate truck. "Time to get underway," he said to Jase. "Get this situation back to safer ground ... get in contact with Tabini and get *his* seal on the house as well, under the circumstances, where we *don't* have a video record." He changed to Ragi. "Kindly take charge, Gini-ji."

He wanted to be back in Atageini territory, with the documents they had recovered. He wanted to get the Kadagidi lord off his hands and under the dowager's authority.

He wanted to know the dowager and Cajeiri were as safe as they could make them.

And most of all he wanted to know how Banichi was faring. Banichi had gone back to the bus's galley, he had said, for a cold drink, a painkiller, and a rest in the rearmost seats. The aisle, given most of the dowager's men were staying to assist Nawari, was all but vacant between them. He walked back toward Banichi and Jago, and was reassured to see that Banichi finally had the ruined jacket off and a proper bandage on the arm. "Lord Aseida is appealing to Lord Tatiseigi for protection. He says he can trust no one of his people. How are you faring, Nichi-ji?"

"Bruises," Banichi said grimly. "Nothing broken, no deep wound. Nothing to worry about."

He shot a look at Jago, who sent one back, confirming Bren's instincts—that it was something more than the physical injury that had put such a grim expression on Banichi's face.

"You cannot possibly doubt," he said quietly, "that you are in the right, Nichi-ji."

Banichi gave him a surprised, wide-open look. "One in no wise doubts that, Bren-ji."

"One wishes you to be sure of it," he said.

More than acquaintances, that man and Banichi. Every instinct he had said so.

A man whose skill Banichi had rated very highly.

With a team probably of the same caliber, and a second team that had been first out of the house.

No one had survived what Jase's bodyguard had thrown at that porch. But he knew Banichi's return fire had been a killing shot. He had seen it hit. It was branded in his memory—before the world had exploded.

Before two renegade Guild units whose opinion it was that humans were not a good influence . . . had been blown to hell by human weapons.

Confirm for Banichi that his shot *had* in fact taken Haikuti out before the world blew up?

Not without knowing exactly what that relationship had been.

The bus, with a damaged windshield and a bullet marring its door, pulled up to the front of Lord Tatiseigi's house, stopped, and opened the door with a soft pneumatic sigh.

Bren gathered himself up as Jase and Aseida did. Banichi and Jago came forward to escort Lord Aseida off the bus. They all got down, followed by Tano and Algini, preceded by Kaplan and Polano.

Servants opened both doors atop the tall steps. Lord Tatiseigi came out onto the porch, forewarned at the very last moment and frowning like thunder ... not an entirely comfortable welcome for the Kadagidi lord as he stepped onto the cobbled driveway.

"I request lodging," Aseida said, "nandi, if you will be so gracious."

"Gracious, is it?" Tatiseigi shot back, looking down from the top step. "After the events of last night?"

"Asien'dalun has suffered utter calamity in the conflict of one faction of the Guild against another. *We* have in no wise—"

"We are not a faction," Banichi's low voice cut in. "Make no such claims against the legitimate Guild, Kadagidi lord. You have supported renegades against the Assassins' Guild, you have supported outlaws, those protecting you fired first, and any damage done is the result of your own choices."

Aseida stood there stammering slightly, confused and angry and, if he was sane, deeply afraid at this point. He made a small gesture toward Lord Tatiseigi. "We appeal to the Atageini. These Guild renegades forced themselves on us. They threatened our lives. They *forced* their way in even before Murini's time, they stayed on against our will, and we have no doubt they will attempt to kill us to prevent us telling what we saw. If these are indeed legitimate Guild—and I believe they are, nandi!" He shot a nervous glance aside at Banichi, and back to Tatiseigi. "Have consideration, nandi! Extend your protection to a neighbor of the Padi Valley!"

"I have guests," Tatiseigi said coldly, "guests who have nothing to do with your bad choices and the problems of Kadagidi clan, nandi. Foreign *children* as well as a ship-aiji who are guests under my roof have been threatened and alarmed by acts of outright lawlessness, the paidhi-aiji, another guest, is inconvenienced, and, we see, even *injured* while protesting the situation on your estate! The heir to the aishidi'tat, my relative, is affronted by your actions and embarrassed by the threat to his personal guests! And the aiji-dowager, my guest, who I assure you has no patience with this situation, is irate beyond measure!"

"If Kadagidi goes down, you will lose the most ancient member of your own association, nandi! We strengthen each other! We are the first of associations, powerful in council—"

"One begs to remind you, your previous treason has disgraced the association and barred you from court! All you can contribute is the stain of your fingers on any action the Padi Valley Association might take!"

"Unfair, nandi!"

"Unfair? Your situation is consequent of a chain of decisions stretching back to your predecessors and culminating in your kinsman Murini the traitor—whose murderous administration of the aishidi'tat alienated all your neighbors and offended the peace of the heavens and the earth alike! You have the effrontery to seek shelter in my house ... when I would be within my rights to lock you in the deepest cellar Tirnamardi affords and feed you on grain and bitter herbs until I have you before the association itself!" Tatiseigi drew a deep breath. "But unlike your allies, who fire on civilians and attack children and servants, *I* regard the laws of the aishidi'tat. I shall appeal my grievances against you directly to the aiji in Shejidan, if his grandmother does not File on you first. And should trouble come to my doorstep on your account, I shall hold you further responsible! Give him over to my bodyguard, nandiin. If he wants protection, *we* shall take charge of him!"

Tatiseigi's temper was well-known, and this time directed at the truly deserving. Tatiseigi snapped his fingers, and his two senior bodyguards took charge of the man and bundled him right back onto the bus.

"Well!" Tatiseigi said in satisfaction, and to the servants standing by. "The bus will need immediate cleaning, nadiin. The dowager has need of it. But, Jase-aiji, nand' Bren, we are dismayed. Are these *all* that have survived with you?"

"One rejoices to report no losses on our side at all, nandi," Bren said. "The renegades were not so favored. *None* survived in that house, except the servants." It was as politely as he could put the terrible business on the front porch, and at the back of the building as well, by what he had since heard. "The dowager's men and some of your own guard and allies will secure the place until more reinforcements can arrive, and I understand we shall send for them."

"You shall have whatever you need, as quickly as we can provide it. Come in, come in." Tatiseigi started up the steps, and they walked with him, bodyguards and all. "Is Asien'dalun truly missing a section of its walls?"

"A large window and part of a corner, nandi."

Ilisidi wanted the bus, he was thinking. For what did she want it? Where in hell was she going?

"They deserve it for my lilies," Tatiseigi said. "An extraordinary day, nand' paidhi! I shall support the Kadagidi and speak for the clan in court when it comes to that. But this scoundrel has gotten everything his predecessors have deserved, heaped up in his bed and set alight." The old man looked back from the top step and waved at the servants, who had opened the baggage compartment. "Do not offload anything from the bus, nadiin-ji. Leave it all aboard!" To Bren he said, as they passed the doors and entered the lower foyer. "The dowager has called a train. Her men at Asien'dalun are to be relieved soon, you say."

"Within the hour, one hopes." Called a train. Leave the baggage on the bus. "Where are we to *go,* nandi?"

"To Shejidan, nand' paidhi. If reinforcements indeed are on the way to Asien'dalun, we shall pick up her men in my estate truck with the baggage, and we shall all rendezvous at the station. The servants are packing. Baggage will be coming down very soon. The children are all downstairs with staff, again touring the collections."

"Has something changed, nandi?"

Tatiseigi hesitated, took account of who was near them—which was, at the moment, only their aishidi, and Jase. "On the contrary, we are taking action, nand' paidhi.

We are not calling the aiji's train. We have diverted a local far closer. The Guild is currently arranging a problem on the rails."

Meaning *Cenedi*, through his contacts, had arranged a problem on the rails, a move to isolate the local line and keep a bubble of vacant track available. He began to get the picture.

"The young gentleman," Lord Tatiseigi said, "has not been informed of the action at Asien'dalun, nor will be until the last moment. We are telling none of the servants. We shall take all our detainees with us. We shall not put that burden on my staff, nor leave anything to draw an attack here. Go up to the main floor, nandiin. Take refreshment. There is tea in the breakfast room, and my staff will give you something stronger should you wish it."

Tatiseigi waved his hand in invitation and was off, up the stairs at his best pace, with his aishid around him.

God. Back to the capital?

At Ilisidi's direction?

He was exhausted. Drained. Mentally. He had looked to have a quiet hour to debrief with his aishid—which he had not been able to do, sharing a bus with Lord Aseida—then he had intended to see that Banichi had his injury looked at by the dowager's physician, and then to take some critical notes—before he sat down with Tatiseigi and the dowager to find out what they knew. He had had his agenda all mapped, and thought it quite enough for a day.

Clearly not.

And Jase, standing near him, was looking a little distressed. He probably had gotten only half of Tatiseigi's information.

"Jase. We're heading for the train station. We're being shunted straight to the Bujavid. The dowager's ordering us all back to the capital immediately. I *hate* to ask your guard to stay in armor, but we're going to be going back on the bus and making a run cross-country, and I'm a little anxious." Another switch of languages, for his aishid. "Nadiin-ji, check in as you need to, find out what we have to do. Banichi-ji, please see nand' Siegi about that shoulder. I shall be safe here with Jase-ji."

"Algini," Banichi said, just that. Banichi and Jago headed down the side hall, which could involve the security station. They were not leaving him alone, no, not even with Kaplan and Polano sticking close to Jase. Tano and Algini stayed right with him.

"Imminent attack here?" Jase asked.

"We're the ones attacking," he said, with fair confidence that was exactly the case. "Jase, I *apologize* for this. It was not at all the plan. I'm sure it wasn't the *dowager's* plan until those two turned up in the garage—but pieces are falling one after the other and we're having to do something, before the other side reorganizes, I suspect. We can settle it. I swear to you—I personally swear it—no harm is going to come to you or those kids. Or if you think so—we can get you to the spaceport, and *that* place is a fortress. You could wait—"

"There's a reason the Council sent me down here," Jase said. "They *want* this venture with the young gentleman to succeed, if it *can* succeed. For various reasons, they want to know *now* if it can—or not; but no question they know things are unsettled. I hope to hell *I'm* not what touched off this situation. And I hope what we did back there didn't make it worse."

"You're not. And you didn't. Listen. Basic atevi law—if you attack a person, that person is entitled to respond with his full force and all his resources. That's exactly what you did. It's what we're doing now, going to Shejidan. If we let this slide—now that we know where the problem is—we'd not be supporting our people. And in the dowager's case—*our people* includes the aiji and the aishidi'tat. You don't attack her, even by accident, and expect to get a free pass. That's why she's moving. That's why she has to move. And she's sure of her target. One man in a Guild office. And probably a very, very tough target to reach. It's serious. But so is she. Absolutely serious."

"I get your point." Jase drew in a deep breath. "Hell of a birthday party you put on, friend."

"Isn't it? But, Jase, remember, too, it's not a human war. This is about boundaries. This is all about boundaries. The opposition misjudged everything. Go down there and explain to the kids, would you? Reassure them. I think they'd like it to come from you, calmly, before we put them back on the bus."

Jase nodded. "Good," he said, and left, up the stairs, Kaplan and Polano staying with him.

Bren heaved a sigh and rubbed his cheek. Which hurt when he touched it. He hoped his own little medical kit hadn't already gone into the general baggage. He wanted an aspirin.

And he looked at Tano and Algini, who were smudged with dust and who'd done the moving and fighting, and gotten the records out. "Well done, nadiin-ji. Very well done today."

"Nandi."

"At least we'll get to sit down, on the bus."

Nods.

"How bad is Banichi's wound?"

"Considering," Tano said, "not bad. It was close."

"He *knew* that man," Bren said, trying for information.

Algini nodded—not forthcoming, no.

"I am at a loss," he said, and pressed the matter. "Something is wrong, nadiin-ji. He is clearly upset. And *I* cannot interpret the cause."

Algini looked at the floor, then up, arms folded. "Haikuti was his first partner, Bren-ji."

"God."

"This was in training, understand, Bren-ji. Haikuti left him, in the field, in a very bad situation. Two others of the team died. Banichi hunted him down, they fought, associates separated them, and that partnership ended."

One could only imagine.

"One had no idea," Tano said.

"Before your time," Algini said. "Banichi and I were in training together. Banichi and Haikuti came to blows over that matter, Bren-ji, against Guild rules, and in secret. Associates on Banichi's side intervened to get them apart and no record was made of the incident. But from that time there was hostility. They avoided assignment together, thereafter, but Haikuti's influence reached high places. Banichi did not get favorable assignments. Banichi found, but could not prove, that Haikuti had favored his clan with information that should not have left the Guild. He reported it, as he should have." A group of servants passed, carrying down baggage, and Algini was silent for a time.

Then said, once the servant had reached the downstairs. "Matters came very close to Council action. Then Banichi was swept up into the aiji's service, by the aiji's order, not Assignments, and *removed* from that conflict. That did not please Haikuti at all. Almost immediately after that, he was assigned into Kadagidi."

"Haikuti's clan, Gini-ji. *Was* it Kadagidi?"

A hesitation. "Ajuri," Algini said. "He is our target's nephew. Favored, at every turn. Haikuti and Banichi have had occasional encounters since. And Banichi was the person Haikuti least wanted to find on his doorstep this morning. There are many, many within the Guild who will be very glad to be rid of Haikuti and particularly glad to know who did it."

Favored, at every turn. Close to the top. And evidently taking his orders from one man in Assignments, during Murini's rise, during the coup, during the last year.

Bren nodded slowly. "I very *well* understand, then. Take care of Banichi, nadiin-ji. Keep him safe."

"Bren-ji," Algini said, "we are entirely in agreement."

19

There was permission for one brief trip out to the stables ... with the bus sitting in the front drive. And Guild all about Cajeiri and his guests. They had to go out and come back quickly. Bad things had happened over at the Kadagidi estate. And the Taibeni were on high alert.

But they had pulled back from the stable area, so the grooms could let the mecheiti out into the pen. The doors opened, and they came out in a rush—the herd-leader, and two others, then the rest, pushing at the door-posts, as if they all could widen the door by shoving. Brass tusk-caps shone in the noon sun. Mecheiti snorted and blew and pawed the ground, maybe smelling the Taibeni mecheiti, or just because they had been pent up too long. The herd-leader had taken a noseful of black powder, but he was fine now: he had asked, and Great-uncle had said so—they had had the herd-leader breathing vapors, and he had coughed for a few hours, and his eyes had run, but he had come through very well.

One understood the Dojisigi had done very properly not to intend to shoot at the mecheiti. Cajeiri would not have forgiven them if they had done that. But they had behaved very well, Great-uncle had said, all things considered. The only mischief they had done was to eat up all the food in the mechanics' refrigerator, out in the garage.

It was not quite all the mischief. They had messed up

his plans. But there were far more serious things going on than his birthday. He had to look at it that way. He was almost fortunate nine.

He climbed up on the rail, a little reckless, but he was in his traveling clothes, a little plainer, and his guests tried, but it was not easy for them. Lucasi and Jegari simply took Gene and Artur and lifted them up, so they could stand on the rail, and Antaro lifted Irene up, saying, "Jump down if one shows any interest in you, nadi."

"Jeichido!" Cajeiri called out, seeing her, and made the sound riders made. "Chi-chi-chi, Jeichido!"

Jeichido actually looked his way, turned her entire body, and looked at the odd gathering on the fence. Several mecheiti had, nostrils working.

But it was Jeichido who took a step in their direction, then wandered halfway to the fence.

Jeichido was not Boji, who would go *anywhere* for an egg, and offering a treat to anybody but the herd-leader would start a fight. He just set Jeichido in his memory, and called out, "I shall be back, as soon as I can! We all will, if mani can get everything settled again! And then you will have your pasture back!"

"Do they really understand?" Gene asked.

"Not a bit," he said, feeling better for having said it. "But she knows her name. And she has seen me twice now. And I *will* be back. I have to! I can't fit her into my father's apartment."

They laughed at that. He thought his great-grandmother's bodyguards were probably getting impatient to have them off the back grounds, but it was his choice, whether to go back through the house, or to take the little walk in the sun, down the garden walk to the driveway, where he could see the rear of the red and black bus.

The truck was going to come and get Boji and his cage to the train, and Eisi and Lieidi would go with the truck and the baggage, and make sure they had a cover over Boji's cage, and that he had a nice egg for the trip.

And there would be a van from the township to take the Kadagidi lord and the two Dojisigi and several of mani's bodyguards to the train station.

They would go on the bus with mani, and Great-uncle, and nand' Bren, and all their bodyguards and all their staff.

And the train would take them all to the Bujavid train station. They would go upstairs—and at that point he had absolutely no idea where his guests were going to be. Nand' Jase and his bodyguards would probably be with nand' Bren. He understood everybody was trying to make arrangements.

He really hoped his mother would be in a good mood.

They reached the bus. And Artur picked up a stone that caught his eye.

Gene said, "This place is amazing. I can't wait to see the Bujavid."

"It's so beautiful," Irene said. She stopped at the edge of the cobbles and turned and looked all about her. Two entire turns. "It's so beautiful, Jeri-ji. Is there any chance we can come back here before we leave?"

"One wishes so," Cajeiri said. "One very much wishes so.".

CJ Cherryh

The Foreigner Novels

"Serious space opera at its very best by one of the leading
SF writers in the field today." —*Publishers Weekly*

"Her world building, aliens, and suspense rank among
the strongest in the whole SF field. May those
strengths be sustained indefinitely, or at least
until the end of *Foreigner*." —*Booklist*

To Order Call: 1-800-788-6262

www.dawbooks.com

CJ Cherryh
Complete Classic Novels in Omnibus Editions

To Order Call: 1-800-788-6262
www.dawbooks.com

DAW 9

Tanya Huff

The *Confederation* Novels

"As a heroine, Kerr shines. She is cut from the same mold
as Ellen Ripley of the Aliens films. Like her heroine,
Huff delivers the goods." —*SF Weekly*

A CONFEDERATION OF VALOR
Omnibus Edition
(*Valor's Choice, The Better Part of Valor*)
978-0-7564-0399-7

THE HEART OF VALOR
978-0-7564-0481-9

VALOR'S TRIAL
978-0-7564-0557-1

THE TRUTH OF VALOR
978-0-7564-0684-4

To Order Call: 1-800-788-6262
www.dawbooks.com

DAW 73

RM Meluch
The Tour of the Merrimack

"This is grand old-fashioned space opera, so toss your disbelief out the nearest airlock and dive in."
— *Publishers Weekly* (starred review)

THE MYRIAD	978-0-7564-0320-1
WOLF STAR	978-0-7564-0383-6
THE SAGITTARIUS COMMAND	978-0-7564-0490-1
STRENGTH AND HONOR	978-0-7564-0578-6
THE NINTH CIRCLE	978-0-7564-0764-3

*Now available
in brand new two-in-one omnibus editions!*

Tour of the Merrimack: Volume One
(The Myriad & Wolf Star)
978-0-7564-0954-8

Tour of the Merrimack: Volume Two
(The Sagittarius Command & Strength and Honor)
978-0-7564-0955-5

To Order Call: 1-800-788-6262
www.dawbooks.com

DAW 48

S. Andrew Swann

The Apotheosis Trilogy

It's been nearly two hundred years since the collapse of the Confederacy, the last government to claim humanity's colonies. So when signals come in revealing lost human colonies that could shift the power balance, the race is on between the Caliphate ships and a small team of scientists and mercenaries. But what awaits them all is a threat far beyond the scope of any human government.

PROPHETS
978-0-7564-0541-0

HERETICS
978-0-7564-0613-4

MESSIAH
978-0-7564-0657-8

To Order Call: 1-800-788-6262
www.dawbooks.com

DAW 161

00561 2055

DARKOVER®

Marion Zimmer Bradley's Classic Series

Now Collected in New Omnibus Editions!

Heritage and Exile   978-0-7564-0065-1
  The Heritage of Hastur & Sharra's Exile

The Ages of Chaos   978-0-7564-0072-9
  Stormqueen! & Hawkmistress!

Saga of the Renunciates   978-0-7564-0092-9
  The Shattered Chain, Thendara House
  & City of Sorcery

The Forbidden Circle   978-0-7564-0094-1
  The Spell Sword & The Forbidden Tower

A World Divided   978-0-7564-0167-2
  The Bloody Sun, The Winds of Darkover
  & Star of Danger

Darkover: First Contact   978-0-7564-0224-2
  Darkover Landfall & Two to Conquer

To Save a World   978-0-7564-0250-1
  The World Wreckers & The Planet Savers

To Order Call: 1-800-788-6262
www.dawbooks.com

DAW 6